ABOUT THE

Brought up in Lincolnshire, Judith Thomson studied Art in Leicester before moving to Sussex, where she still lives. She is passionate about the seventeenth century and has gained much of her inspiration from visits to Paris and Versailles. In her spare time she enjoys painting, scuba diving and boating. She is the author of four other Philip Devalle novels, 'Designs of a Gentleman: The Early Years', 'High Heatherton', 'The Orange Autumn' and 'The Distant Hills'.

Follow her on:-
Judiththomsonsite.wordpress.com
Judiththomsonblog.wordpress.com
and on Twitter @JudithThomson14

DESIGNS OF A GENTLEMAN

The Darker Years

Judith Thomson

Matador
9 Priory Business Park,
Wistow Road, Kibworth Beauchamp,
Leicestershire. LE8 0RX
Tel: (+44) 116 279 2299
Fax: (+44) 116 279 2277
Email: books@troubador.co.uk
Web: www.troubador.co.uk/matador

ISBN 978 1789016 581

British Library Cataloguing in Publication Data.
A catalogue record for this book is available from the British Library.

Printed and bound by CPI Group (UK) Ltd, Croydon, CR0 4YY
Typeset in 11pt Bembo by Troubador Publishing Ltd, Leicester, UK

Matador is an imprint of Troubador Publishing Ltd

.

ONE

Lord Shaftesbury was out of town when Philip Devalle first arrived in London. The Earl was visiting The Chase, his property in Dorset, but directly he returned he sent for him.

"What brings you back to England?" he asked.

"I wanted to visit Buckingham and Monmouth." Philip had no intention of letting him know that he was curious about the proposition that Shaftesbury's physician, Dr. Locke had mentioned to him when they had met in Paris. He guessed that Shaftesbury would raise the subject soon enough, and he was right.

"What are your feelings for the Duke of Monmouth?" Shaftesbury asked.

"I am very fond of him, I always have been."

"How fond? Would you be prepared to risk your life for him?"

"Certainly. I pledged that years ago."

"Did you now?" Shaftesbury eyed him shrewdly. "And why would you do that?"

"Because he asked it of me. Monmouth is a sentimental sort of person."

"Yes, he is, but you are not that sort of person, I would say. What is it that you want from life, my Lord? Wealth? Power?"

"Purpose," Philip corrected him. "That is what I need at present, although, since my father teeters on the brink of this world and the next, then money would be a desirable commodity as well!"

"And have you any notion as to how you will support yourself if he dies?" Shaftesbury said.

Philip shrugged. "I suppose I shall rejoin the French army and aid them in their glorious conquest of Flanders. Or I may seek out a rich wife!"

"I hardly see you dependent on a woman," Shaftesbury said, smiling. "As for your first course, Englishmen taking up arms for France are now considered with disapproval. I have persuaded Parliament to request that all English forces in France be disbanded, since they are employed in fighting the Dutch, who are supposed to be our allies. I have a better proposition for you - work for me."

"In what capacity? To obtain information for you, as I did before?"

"No. I have a job which ought to suit you better. You need a master, Philip Devalle, a master other than your own whim."

"A master?" Philip raised an eyebrow at that. "I was not born to serve, you or anyone, my Lord Shaftesbury. To do an occasional favour for a person is somewhat different from binding oneself with any promise of obedience."

"Did you not obey the French Generals, Condé and Turenne, when they gave you orders?"

"That is altogether different."

"You are a proud young man," Shaftesbury said, "but have you thought of the difficulties of returning to army life? It is one thing to go to war a gentleman of means, quite another to exist solely upon army pay. Pledge yourself to me and, if you prove satisfactory, I will make you an allowance sufficient to cover your most extravagant needs."

"I don't believe, my Lord, that you can have the least idea of how extravagant my needs can be," Philip began, but Shaftesbury interrupted him by throwing down a sheaf of papers.

"These are the amounts by which you have run yourself into debt since you arrived back in England only two weeks ago.

During that time, you have dined out every night in Chatelain's or Pontack's, lost at least eight hundred pounds at cards and run up the most extensive accounts with tradesmen, your tailor most of all, accounts which you cannot have the remotest hope of paying, since it is expected that your father will die any day and leave you penniless."

Philip looked at him in surprise. He wondered how Shaftesbury could possibly know so much about his debts, considering the Earl hadn't even been in London whilst he was incurring them!

"How did you discover all that?"

"I made it my business to discover it. What do you think, that Buckingham will help you out? He's sunk what little he has left of his vast fortune into making mirrors, another piece of tomfoolery which he imagines will give him credibility as a businessman, and now, I hear, he spends his days in trying to write a play! A spell in debtor's prison will do little for your reputation, or your prospects of ensnaring some rich heiress. I think you need me, just as I need you."

"Would you clear my debts?" Philip knew the Earl was rich, for he owned a large estate in Carolina and a sugar plantation in Barbados, but Philip could not imagine why he might be worth so much to a man who hardly knew him.

"I shall not pay them all at once," Shaftesbury warned, "but they will each be paid in full, in return for one or two small services at the start."

"Such as?"

"Such as acting as a courier for confidential messages between Locke and myself. I can't imagine that would be too onerous for you, since all you will be required to do is to take frequent trips back to Paris."

"And what would I have to do to earn the rest?"

"Whatever I asked you to do," Shaftesbury said simply.

"But to what end?"

"Can't you guess? To place your friend, Monmouth, on the throne in the Duke of York's place."

"Monmouth ruling England?" Philip shook his head at the dreadful notion. "He's not fit for such a task."

"I never said that he would rule, merely that he would sit upon the throne," Shaftesbury corrected him.

"A puppet king with you as his controller?"

"I do not need your answer yet," Shaftesbury said, ignoring the question. "Consider what I have said and I advise you to consider it most privately," he stressed. "Even your beloved Buckingham does not know the full extent of my ambition, although I shall confide in him before too long. Politically inept though he is, his name will add weight to the Cause."

"The Cause?"

"The Protestant Cause. York is a Catholic, Monmouth a good Protestant. What loyal Englishman would prefer the King's Papist brother to the King's Protestant son?"

"The King's *bastard* Protestant son," Philip reminded him.

"What if I were able to give the world proof that Monmouth's mother, Lucy Walter, was married to King Charles at the time of Monmouth's conception?"

"How?"

Shaftesbury tapped the side of his nose in a knowing sort of way. "By unearthing a certain mysterious Black Box, filled with documents. What would you say then?"

"I would say that you were an extremely clever and devious deceiver," Philip said decidedly. "Not even Monmouth claims he is legitimate."

"Not yet he doesn't." Shaftesbury's eyes met his. "One of your duties, should you accept my offer, will be to convince him of it!"

It took Philip less than a week to make his decision. His father died during that week and the family solicitor travelled from Sussex to inform Philip of that which he already expected; the estate of High Heatherton and the entire Devalle fortune had been left to the new Earl of Southwick, Henry, who had granted his younger brother the princely sum of twenty pounds a year.

Shaftesbury smiled when Philip told him the news. "Which debt do you want discharged first then?" he asked, thumbing through the sheaf of accounts again.

"My tailor's bill," Philip said unhesitatingly.

"Very well. Your debt to your tailor, Monsieur Robertin, shall be discharged this very day, and tomorrow you will take the ferry to Gravesend and then the coach to Dover."

"A coach? I would be quicker riding post."

"I know that but you must take a portmanteau with you, in order that you may slip this inside and bring it back again," the Earl explained, handing him a small wooden box. "Whilst you are in Paris I want you to be seen in the company of Monsieur and all your other friends at Court. Be as conspicuous as you please, then none will suspect your motives, but do not tarry there too long. I want you back here, with whatever Locke gives you, before the month is out."

"A courier?" Morgan, sniffed disdainfully, as he packed the wooden box amongst his master's clothes. "Seems hardly fit employment for a gentleman."

"True, yet it would appear I am no ordinary courier, not if I am to be paid so much for one trip, for I happen to know that Robertin's bill was over a hundred and fifty pounds. "What do you suppose I shall be carrying back in that box?"

"Something best left where it is, I'd guess," the Welshman muttered.

What, in fact, Philip carried back from France was a sealed letter as well as the box, which was now locked and so heavy that he had to leave some of his own things behind so as not to excite suspicion.

When he and Morgan disembarked from the packet at Dover and confronted the Customs Officials Philip realised that, if he was going to make the trip regularly, he would need to establish a rapport with them and, more particularly, with the sharp-eyed representatives from Dover Castle, who stood with them. They were always on the look-out for likely guests to detain and Philip suspected that a search of his portmanteau might prove troublesome!

"Did you enjoy your visit to France, Lord Devalle?" asked one of the Customs men, recognising him.

"Indeed I did, officer," Philip told him pleasantly. "There is a certain lady at the Court who made my trip most enjoyable!"

The officer grinned broadly. "You're sure you did not smuggle her back with you in here?" he joked, indicating Philip's portmanteau.

Philip winked at him. "I fear the lady's husband might have something to say about that!"

They were back at Dover within a few weeks and at regular intervals after that. During each visit to France he saw a great deal of Monsieur, played cards with the Comte de Grammont and attended upon King Louis. On each trip back, he brought with him a sealed letter and the box, although he noticed that this was heavier on some occasions than on others. His luggage was never searched.

Shaftesbury always took the box and the letter without the slightest comment and never opened either in Philip's presence but the next day Philip would be summoned to select an account for payment. In addition, there would be a little money, but never quite enough and he was finding it difficult to maintain his house in Paris. It was filled with so many memories that he could not bear to sell it but, if he requested more money, the Earl's reply would always be the same - he would receive all he had been promised when the time was right.

It was an infuriating answer, for he gave no indication of when that was likely to be, and no more mention was made of the grand scheme with which he had first fired Philip's interest.

Philip spent his abundant free time in England drinking and gambling and growing increasingly discontented with his lot. Even Monmouth had employment these days for, as Master of the Horse, it was his duty to charter hackney coaches to transport royal servants to the royal residences, and he always made a great play of being busy at it.

Philip visited Nell Gwynne as often as he could, for she was still his loyal and sympathetic friend, but he did not tell her the real truth behind his frequent visits to France, not because he thought she would betray him but because he did not wish to burden her with secrets she must keep from the King.

He sometimes saw Barbara as well, a sadder and wiser Barbara. John Churchill, having taken all the money she would give him, had deserted her for Sarah Jennings. Philip felt a little sorry for her and, although he had no desire to become her lover once more, they did make friends again. Barbara was now the Duchess of Cleveland and involved, as ever, in all the intrigues of the Court, and Philip listened to everything she told him.

Some of it confirmed his suspicions.

"I think I have discovered what is in the box, Morgan," he told the Welshman after one of their trips.

It had rained continually for the past two days and the mail coach on which they had been travelling had stuck fast in the mud, so that all the passengers had needed to help heave it free. On top of that they had suffered almost a day's delay at Gravesend, where the harbour was blocked with trading vessels awaiting customs checks, and Philip was feeling more than a little disenchanted with his employment, and his employer, by the time they finally got back to Wallingford House, where he was residing as Buckingham's guest.

"Well? Aren't you even curious?" he asked Morgan irritably. "I shall tell you anyway. It is bribe money from King Louis, and I suspect the letter that accompanies it confirms the amount."

"Why should the King of France bribe Shaftesbury?" Morgan said. "Surely the Earl fights against the French."

"The Earl also fights against Lord Danby, who Louis blames for England's peace with Holland, so Danby bribes the Parliament to support King Charles, Charles takes money from King Louis to uphold the cause of France and Louis subsidises Shaftesbury's fight against Danby. In addition, we have the Spanish and Dutch Ambassadors offering bribes to whoever will accept them! This is a twisted and corrupt age in which we live, my friend."

"Seems to me it is politics which are corrupt and you are better off back in the army." Morgan shook the water out of his master's dripping cloak as vigorously as Philip guessed he would like to have shaken Lord Shaftesbury!

"Believe me with Winter fast approaching I find the prospect of these journeys less and less appealing," Philip assured him. "I have been thinking of returning to live in France, but I have in mind to take advantage of the situation before I have an end to it. Unfortunately, for the moment, I can't see how."

Exhausted though he was, Philip could not permit himself to rest, for Shaftesbury demanded the delivery of his property the instant Philip returned to London. He was about to down a resuscitative measure of brandy before leaving when a visitor arrived.

"He seems a common, rascally fellow to me," Morgan said, "although he claims to be a colonel. He says that he is here to repay some money you once loaned him."

Philip stopped in the act of raising the brandy glass to his lips. "Not Colonel Scott?"

"That was the name he gave, but I little thought you truly knew him, for he appears to be a tricky sort of person."

"You're right, he is," Philip agreed. "Tricky, dishonest and thoroughly unprincipled. Exactly the fellow I need!"

"My Lord Devalle," Scott cried as he entered, pulling off his hat and sweeping the ground with its plumes. "It is indeed a privilege to be received by such an esteemed person as yourself."

"And why should I not receive a man who owns himself to be in debt to me?" Philip said smiling, for it amused him to see the pretty behaviour of a gentleman from one he knew to be a rogue and, he guessed, a very lowborn rogue at that, for all the handsome clothes he was now wearing.

"It is for the very reason of repaying the debt that I am here, my Lord. I tried to find you in Paris but I heard you had ridden off to war with Condé."

"You have my money?" Philip said in surprise, for he had not expected that.

"Well, not exactly, but I am here to offer you the opportunity to make a great deal more than your fifty guineas."

"Which means, no doubt, that having got yourself once more into difficulties you wonder whether you will find me good-natured enough to be your saviour again," Philip said.

"No, no, you have me wrong, for I have twenty guineas in my pocket which, with your help, I could turn to fifty times that amount, and I would split half my gain with you. What do you say?"

"How is this wonderful fortune to be made?"

"With this." Scott pulled aside his coat and produced a pistol from his belt.

Philip regarded him calmly, though he sensed that Morgan's hand was ready upon the hilt of his knife. Philip downed his brandy and poured another for himself and one for Scott. "Are you going to shoot me or are you proposing that we both turn highwaymen?"

Scott grinned and tossed the weapon to him. "Take it in your hands, my Lord. Feel how well it sits there, is it not finely balanced?"

"It's a pretty enough piece," Philip allowed, for it was, "but there is only one way to judge a firearm and that is to test it at a target."

"Ah! Now there's the difficulty."

"It won't fire straight?" Philip guessed.

Scott coughed. "I have had some trouble with the earlier models but I do believe I have improved upon the design now. What I am asking is simply that you, a well-known soldier, should let it be seen that you carry this weapon at all times."

"A weapon that cannot hit a target?"

"None save us and Hill, my iron founder, need know that."

"What about your previous customers, those who purchased your 'earlier models'?" Philip asked. "Might their testimony not prove damaging to the pistol's reputation?"

"Not at all. They are both dead," Scott said cheerfully. "The problem was that the barrels exploded when fired, but I think I have controlled that fault now."

Philip quickly passed the pistol back. "I think we shall have to consider another way of making us both some money. How good a forger are you, Scott?"

"The best. There's not a document I cannot copy to perfection," Scott boasted.

Philip looked over to Morgan who, guessing what was passing through his master's mind, slowly shook his head.

"Trust me," Philip urged him. "Show Scott the seal upon the letter."

Morgan reluctantly handed it over.

"Can you copy this too?"

"I could make duplicate of that seal so exact that not even its owner would suspect it," Scott assured him.

"And it goes without saying that your associate, the iron founder, could fashion a key to fit this lock?" Philip said, pointing to the box upon the table.

Scott signified by gesture that he could.

"Then I think I have a proposition for you, Scott. One you will find very advantageous. Make me a copy of this seal and a key for this lock. I'll contact you in a few weeks. Where are you lodging?"

"At Hill's foundry in Houndsditch, my Lord," Scott told him, fishing from his pocket a ball of soft wax, which he pressed professionally into the lock, "but I can be found most days in Newman's Coffee House, or dining with the widow of Sir Harry Vane, a most accommodating lady who says the very sight of me feeds her soul!"

"I can imagine! Copy the seal next," Philip said, "and quickly, please, for I must deliver these within the hour."

"Might I be so curious as to enquire to whom you must deliver them?" Scott said when he had sketched the seal and pocketed the silver pen which Philip had loaned him to do it.

"I'll tell you when we next meet." Although Philip rather liked Scott he would be a fool, he knew, to trust him at this stage. Far better to wait until Scott was committed too deeply to betray him without also betraying himself!

Nearly a month went by before they returned from the next trip and Philip had need of Scott. Morgan finally located him not at any of the places he had named but imbibing in the 'Dog and Dripping Pan.'

When they arrived back Philip was pacing the floor impatiently.

"What took so long? I must make the delivery soon."

"I had a little trouble seeking out the Colonel," Morgan said sourly. "I must have searched a score of taverns in the area before I found him."

"You had better not be drunk," Philip warned Scott. "You'll need a steady hand for this night's work. Have you the seal?"

Scott produced a small box from his pocket and took out of it a seal bearing what appeared to be the exact same markings as Locke's device.

Philip laid a sheet of paper in front of them and melted a stick of sealing wax on one of the candles that burned upon the table. Then he pressed on the seal. He studied the pattern closely with the original before passing them to Morgan, who did likewise.

"I can find no fault with it," Morgan admitted.

Scott scrutinised it too. "What did I tell you?" he said triumphantly. "I am the best."

"Now the key." The lock turned smoothly and Philip opened the lid of the box, and then looked at the faces of the other two. The box was filled with coins.

Morgan carefully broke the seal on John Locke's letter and read it. "There are two hundred and forty pistoles in there."

Scott whistled appreciatively. "How many are you going to take?"

"Sixty," Philip decided, "of which twenty are yours if you can make a copy of the letter, changing only the amount." He passed Scott ink and paper. "You can use the silver pen you stole from me the last time you were here!"

Scott looked sheepish. "I fear I no longer have that, for I grew a little short of funds."

Philip threw him another pen, a plain quill this time, and Scott set to work. The document he produced was a perfect copy in every way, even to the flourish of Locke's signature.

When both Philip and Morgan had checked the words, Scott folded the paper in exactly the same way as the original and Philip sealed it with Scott's seal. He next counted out sixty pistoles and locked the box again.

"Might I know now to who these are to be delivered?" Scott asked when he had pocketed his gains, which amounted to over four hundred pounds.

"Certainly. The Earl of Shaftesbury."

Scott blanched visibly. "Shaftesbury? Are you mad? If he discovers what we've done he'll kill us."

"I very much doubt it. You, in any case, are safe, since he will never learn your identity from me," Philip reassured him.

"But what about you? Be on your guard, my Lord," Scott advised him.

Philip shrugged. "What can he do? The very nature of this money would make any recovery through the proper channels difficult. Don't worry about me, Scott. With luck he will never discover us."

"And if he does you'll both need all your luck," Morgan warned, for not even the generous gift of two of the coins could make him approve the venture.

"Don't mind Morgan," Philip said to Scott. "He always was a cheery little soul!"

Shaftesbury received the letter and the box with no more than a cursory glance but the following night, when Philip was summoned to his house in Aldersgate Street, it was evident that all was not well, an impression verified directly Shaftesbury spoke.

"I shall be direct with you, my Lord; you are a liar, a cheat and an ingrate."

"That is somewhat direct," Philip said uneasily. "Might I know what I have done?"

"You already know. You opened up the package that was entrusted to you, removed a portion of the money you were carrying and forged a document so perfectly in Locke's own hand, and bearing his seal, that I might never have discovered it but for one thing; before every trip you make Locke sends me, by ordinary mail packet, a letter which contains, in code, the amount of money you will be carrying."

Philip knew the game was up for certain now. "So you never did trust me?"

"Of course not. Why should I?"

"I can pay you back the money if you like," Philip said resignedly.

"I am not concerned with that so much as why you took it. Have I not kept my word and paid your debts as fast as you incurred them?"

"Yes, you have," Philip admitted, "but I still needed money, a larger sum than you would give me."

"Why?"

"I have a house in Paris. I am very loath to part with it and I have expenses there which must be met, as well as servants who I ought to pay. I did not think your generosity would extend to paying my debts incurred across the Channel. That is why I took it."

"With whose assistance?" Shaftesbury said. "You could not have forged the letter yourself."

"I have nothing more to say, my Lord," Philip said firmly. "I have offered to return your money and that should be an end to it."

Shaftesbury nodded. "I would have expected that from someone of your kind. You may keep the money, Philip Devalle, unjustly gotten though it was, but you tried to cheat me and you will suffer for that."

He clapped his hands and from the anteroom appeared three men, the biggest of which Philip recognised as he who had once dealt with him so harshly outside the theatre in Drury Lane.

Philip looked from him to Shaftesbury. "Again? Have you ordered him to kill me this time?"

"You are a peer of the realm, Lord Devalle, the brother of an earl and a hero to the French. Such a man's life cannot be lightly taken but you are going to be punished, and in a way that you will understand."

The three men moved on him simultaneously. He felled the first with a well-aimed kick in the groin, then spun around and punched the second one hard upon the jaw.

In the big fellow Philip had met his match, however. A blow in the stomach with the full force of one of those giant fists rendered him helpless for an instant, long enough for his jacket to be forcibly removed and for him to be tied firmly to an oak sconce.

As Shaftesbury's brawny servant tore the shirt from his back Philip realised what was coming, even before the Earl produced a thin, barbed willow twig. "You will beat him, Parkes," he told the man, "until I order you to stop or until he begs for quarter."

"You bastard!" Philip hissed, as the first stroke stung him, cutting the thin skin on his back, still scarred from the beatings his brother, Henry, had given him when he was a child. "I don't deserve this."

"Maybe not, but I believe it is the only form of discipline that you will ever respect."

By the third stroke Philip needed to bite hard upon his lip to keep from crying out. He had learned long ago to bear pain in silence. Again and again the willow came down upon him, and he felt the blood trickling down his back as each stroke cut a fresh strip of his tender skin. Through it all he stared ahead, neither flinching nor exclaiming, until faintness overcame him and Shaftesbury intervened.

"Cut him loose," Philip heard him tell Parkes, though his voice seemed far away. "I never expected him to take that much. Get him back to Buckingham's and make sure the Duke does not see him in this state or he will kill you, and probably me too."

Philip did not remember too much about the journey home.

Morgan bathed his cuts with oil and bandaged them as best he could, vowing dark and bloody vengeance on Parkes and Shaftesbury both.

Phillip did, eventually, manage to find respite from his pain in sleep, but it was not too many hours before he was awakened by voices outside his door. One belonged to Monmouth and Philip groaned, for he did not feel up to dealing with him now.

Morgan was unable to prevent the Duke from entering.

He was soon at Philip's side, clutching his hand and making no attempt to hide the tears that started down his cheeks.

"My dear, dear friend. When you vowed all those years ago that you would die for me I little thought you would be called upon to suffer so much for my sake."

Philip said nothing for a moment as he allowed Monmouth to help him into a sitting position. He was confused, but not so stupefied by pain or sleep that he did not realise there was every advantage in letting him talk first!

Shaftesbury told me everything," Monmouth continued, "how my uncle had you set upon because he's heard it rumoured that you know the whereabouts of the Black Box."

Black Box! That, at least, sounded familiar and Philip searched his mind to think where he had heard of it before. "The proof of your legitimacy," he recalled.

"Oh, Philip, I would sooner be considered a bastard by the whole world than to have you harmed the least bit for my sake," Monmouth assured him. "Do you know its whereabouts, by the by?"

"Can we talk about it later?" Philip pleaded. "I'm feeling somewhat fragile at the moment."

"Yes, of course. How inconsiderate of me, but you understand what it would mean? Why, if I was declared legitimate then Shaftesbury says that I, and not York, would succeed my father to the throne. Just think of that!"

Philip had thought of it, many times and with dismay. Despite the military honours heaped upon him and high appointments that he held, Monmouth still seemed like an earnest child to Philip, and he always would.

"You shall be the general of my forces," Monmouth promised him. "Rest now, I shall return when Shaftesbury has gone."

"Shaftesbury is here?" Philip leapt from his bed, moaning as the sudden movement opened up some of the cuts upon his back. "Of all the confounded impudence!"

Monmouth looked puzzled. "But it was him who brought me here. He is most concerned for you, although he insisted I should see you first."

"I'll bet he did!" Seething, Philip struggled into his dressing gown, refusing Monmouth's aid. "Very well, I'll see him for your sake."

"I'll send him in then. He is conversing with the Duke of Buckingham, who is also angry with my uncle. I tell you, this has stirred more feeling than you know."

"Oh, I imagine I could guess!" Philip retorted.

Despite his resolution to receive Shaftesbury on his feet, Philip found it difficult, especially since Buckingham rushed in first and embraced him.

After a torrent of barely distinguishable, passionate words, Buckingham dashed off, afire with indignation and plans of retribution for the Duke of York.

Left alone with Shaftesbury, Philip grasped a table for support. "What did you do? Print it on handbills and circulate it in the Coffee Houses?"

Shaftesbury smiled at that. "I have always found that word of mouth is infinitely more effective. Not only can the originator never be properly proven but the story gains a little in each retelling until it reaches quite fantastic heights. By the time this day is out you will be hailed as a Protestant martyr!"

"I can't recall that was ever one of my ambitions," Philip said crossly.

He was managing to stand but his hands were trembling where they gripped the table.

"Sit down," Shaftesbury suggested, for he was observing him closely. "I can talk to you just as well from your bed."

"To begin with I have no desire to talk to you at all but, if I must, then I prefer to do it standing."

Shaftesbury sighed. "Shall you ever learn to obey me, Philip? Don't be such a fool. Sit down. I want your full attention and I won't have that whilst you are fighting the pain of the swellings on your back."

"Swellings *you* put there, not York," Philip snapped back, obeying all the same for he had begun to feel dizzy. To pass out before the one who had caused his suffering would, he felt, be the final indignity.

"That's better," Shaftesbury said approvingly, seating himself on the bed beside him. "You see you can do it if you try. You don't think, surely, that I enjoyed watching you being flogged? It was a punishment, a necessary punishment, but it is over now and, from what Buckingham once told me, it was no worse than you have suffered at the hands of a member of your own family."

"A madman," Philip reminded him.

"But I am not a madman, Philip, never think that. I see in you qualities of greatness which are being obscured by petty weaknesses. If properly disciplined you will go far. With your abilities and my help your power would be limitless."

The Earl spoke softly now. He was practised in the art of winning men and his words could goad one moment and cajole the next, but Philip was not so easily won.

"As to power, I am to have my share of that, it seems. Monmouth tells me I'm to be a general, after this Black Box, which I apparently know so much about, has helped to place him on the throne!"

"Well, wouldn't you like to be a general?"

"You speak as though it all were possible."

"It is," Shaftesbury said simply. "The Queen is still barren and seems likely to remain so now. The people fear to have a Catholic king, and they will fear it a damn sight more by the time I have finished blackening the name of York and those who support him. Who, then, will succeed Charles?"

"The Orangeman," Philip guessed, "much as it galls me to say it, having fought him for two years." William of Orange was already making overtures to wed York's daughter, the Princess

Mary. "If the people won't take York perhaps they will take his daughter and her Protestant husband."

"Or perhaps they will take King Charles' legitimate son by his marriage to Lucy Walter."

"The legal proof of which is in the mysterious Black Box?" Philip finished for him. "You are indeed a madman if you hope to produce evidence that will stand up to close inspection."

Shaftesbury shrugged. "Documents can be falsified, signatures impersonated, devices copied – as you yourself have proved," he said pointedly. "In any case I doubt I shall ever actually have to unearth the Black Box. It is sufficient that folk suspect it to exist."

"So all you have to do now is to win support for Monmouth and turn the people against the Duke of York That should be easy enough," Philip said cynically.

Shaftesbury did not look put out. "Yes, it should, but needless to say it is a delicate and dangerous matter. It is one that must be handled by a man of courage, someone close enough to Monmouth to be able to persuade him to whatever I resolve, someone I can absolutely trust. That is why I am offering you the opportunity to work for me again."

"And are you saying that you trust me?" Philip said, after a short pause to digest the Earl's words. "I am the liar, cheat and ingrate, remember?"

"I remember, but I think I can trust you now. You are fortunate," Shaftesbury told him, "for I am rarely known to give a second chance."

"That's all very well, but what induces you to think that I would ever work for you again?"

"Your circumstances have not changed, so far as I am aware, except that you have now acquired a notable enemy. The Duke of York will not take kindly to your accusing him of something that he did not do. You need me now more than you needed me before."

Philip was speechless as he considered the absurdity of his situation. Shaftesbury had ordered him flogged, Shaftesbury had circulated the rumour that the beating had been York's doing and now Shaftesbury was offering him protection from the Duke's wrath!

"You seem to have manoeuvred me into a difficult position," he said slowly, "and I see no way to extricate myself without falling victim to York's revenge and losing the friendship of Monmouth."

"You can't, so swear allegiance to me and have done with it," Shaftesbury advised, reaching into his pocket and taking out a key, which he put upon the bed. "This is for you. It is the key to an apartment I purchased for you this morning."

Philip made no reply, suspecting he was the victim of Shaftesbury's wayward humour.

"I see you don't believe me. Well I guess it's little to be wondered at, for I was somewhat rough with you last night," the Earl admitted, "but I am quite in earnest. It is in King Street, close to your friend, Monmouth, and an elegant enough address, I would have thought, for any gentleman of fashion. You may furnish it exactly to your taste and I will settle the accounts. I will also engage a decent servant for you."

Philip picked up the key and turned it over in his hands. "Thank you, but I already have a servant."

"But he is a coarse and ugly fellow. God knows where you ever acquired him."

"I didn't. He acquired me, and I would never part with him," Philip said firmly.

"Have it your own way. Are there any others you employ?"

"Two blackamoor coachmen, who I have loaned to Buckingham for the time being, and I also have a housekeeper and gardener in Paris," Philip finished evenly.

Shaftesbury looked amazed at this audacity. "You think I shall staff your Paris house as well? Close the blasted place down."

"No."

Their eyes locked, but Philip was determined not to give way on this point, for he realised now that Shaftesbury must need him every bit as much as he needed the Earl.

"Very well, I'll not fight you over such an issue," Shaftesbury decided, "but I think you take advantage of me. Are we agreed now upon the terms of our alliance? You will be my agent. You will recruit to Monmouth's Cause those most likely to advance it and, by employing whatever means and resources are necessary, you will ensure the success of my designs and the ruination of the Duke of York."

Philip nodded. "I think I can do that."

"I have no doubt of it. In return you will ultimately have a position of the highest authority and the wherewithal to purchase an estate more magnificent than High Heatherton. For the present you must be content with the property I have bought for you, an allowance which I am sure you will find adequate and my name to obtain sufficient credit with the tradesmen of this city to satisfy even your lavish tastes!"

Philip knew it was a more than generous offer. He did not relish being totally dependent on the scheming little Earl and yet, in spite of everything, he could not help but feel some admiration for him. He had never met a man so confident of his own abilities and, because Shaftesbury believed so wholeheartedly in himself, it was easy for others to believe in him too.

"Well, shall you support the Duke of Monmouth's cause or not?" Shaftesbury said impatiently.

"I will support *your* cause, in the name of Monmouth, my Lord."

"And are you truly for me this time, Philip Devalle?"

"I will fulfil my part of our arrangement," Philip pledged, "but there is one other thing I would ask of you."

"What is it now?"

"I'd like a carriage and two trace horses."

"Only two?" the Earl said sarcastically. "Buckingham draws with six!"

"Two will suffice."

"Very well," Shaftesbury agreed in a heavy tone. "But nothing too elaborate, mind."

Philip smiled. "Indeed not. It would never do to have it said that I am ostentatious!"

TWO

A shining black carriage with a gilded domed roof and the initials 'P.D.' entwined on its doors drove down Fleet Street, where its progress was noticed by all it passed. It was pulled by a perfectly matched pair of jet-black horses, and driven by Jonathon and Ned, wearing smart black and gold uniforms.

Philip looked out with mild interest at the construction work which had begun on the new cathedral, designed by Christopher Wren to take the place of the previous St. Paul's, which had been destroyed in the fire. He thought about his old school, which had once stood beside it, and about his fellow pupils, who he had detested. Just for a fanciful moment he wished that they and Doctor Harman, his tutor, could see him now! The childish whim soon passed. Philip was not one to indulge in flights of fancy and, besides, he had a job of work to do.

The carriage drew into Talbot Court and stopped outside Newman's Coffee House. All heads turned as Philip entered the building, all, that is, save one. In a corner, sitting by himself and looking melancholy, was the gentleman that Philip sought.

"What ails Colonel Scott?" he asked the proprietor.

"Oh, his usual trouble, my Lord. His creditors and the law are chasing him and he knows not which will catch up with him first!"

Philip crossed quietly over to where Scott sat and watched him for a second, amused at the sight of such a picture of despair.

"Problems, Scott?"

Scott glanced up, his dismal expression changing immediately to one of delight. "Philip Devalle! I never thought to see your handsome face again."

"And why not, pray?" Philip sat down, carefully arranging the folds of his new pink brocade coat. "Did you imagine I would be fleeing from the Duke of York's wrath?"

"I never did believe the tale they put about concerning that. I figured it was Shaftesbury got you. Did you tell him of my part in the swindle?" Scott said worriedly.

"What do you think? I may be many things, Scott, but I am still a man of honour," Philip said.

"I'm grateful that you are." Scott looked Philip up and down quite enviously. "From your appearance I take it you are well enough now?"

"Never better," Philip assured him, "and rarely more prosperous. What of yourself?"

"Alas, I have been nowhere near as fortunate. Directly it is known that I have money then wenches and my creditors descend on me."

"You paid your creditors?" Philip said disbelievingly. "Is this the Colonel Scott I thought I knew?"

"Well most of it did go upon the wenches," Scott confessed, "and I am no nearer to paying you back your fifty guineas. Money just slips through my hands, I fear."

"So it appears! You never did tell me, by the way, what you did with my fifty guineas."

"Oh, I took your advice and went to Holland," Scott told him brightly. "I am bound to say that De Witt welcomed me with open arms. I settled for a while in Bergen-op-Zoom supplying him with maps of England, very inaccurate maps if I say so myself, and supplying the Dutch with hope. They were so grateful that I was given the command of a regiment, with access to regimental funds!"

"Which I suppose you stole?" Philip guessed.

"I'm afraid I did, for matters were getting a little difficult for me. There were some tradesmen I had cheated and the trifling matter of a forged deed, which I won't go into now, and then on top of it all I'd taken a wife, which was a foolish thing to do, as I should know, for I already have one in Long Island. Anyway, to be brief, I decided I was better out of the whole thing and the regimental funds gave me the means to flee to Flanders. I believe they hanged my effigy at The Hague," Scott ended proudly.

"I'm not surprised! You're lucky that is all they hanged. Will I regret it if I ask you how you fared in Flanders?"

"I robbed a convent there," Scott said. "I could have paid you back if I had managed to catch up with you then."

"With money you stole from nuns?" Philip shuddered at the thought. "Fortunately, I have not come here today to chase you for my money, but to offer you the opportunity to make some more and to advance yourself with Shaftesbury and the members of the Green Ribbon Club."

The Green Ribbon club was the stronghold of the Country Party, Shaftesbury's formidable Opposition force, and Philip now wore a piece of green ribbon tucked into his hat band, the sign of a member.

"It was certainly my lucky day when I first met you, my Lord," Scott said with feeling. "What do you want me to do this time?"

Philip glanced around. He was still the object of most people's attention. "I think we'd better talk inside my carriage."

"This is yours?" Scott said admiringly as he sank into the black velvet upholstery of the gilded carriage.

"This and a magnificent apartment, not to mention an allowance of inordinate generosity," Philip told him, "all by courtesy of Shaftesbury."

"After you cheated him? He must be in love with you!"

Philip laughed. "Hardly! It's not my body he has bought but my soul, and I will now attempt to buy yours. How well are you acquainted with the criminal fraternity of this city?"

"Pretty well," Scott admitted. "What is it that you want? A theft? A murder?"

"A riot."

Scott raised a bushy black eyebrow. "I suppose you know what you are doing."

"Certainly. I am beginning my onslaught on the Protestant consciences of the citizens of London."

"Are you telling me you're acting upon religious principles?"

"Don't be absurd! I want 'No Popery' banners in the streets and I want rumours spread that the King desires to mobilise a standing army and that there are Irish cut-throats ready to turn upon any who oppose the Duke of York. Whilst we are at it I will have effigies of the Duke burned. That will suffice, I think, for a beginning. Can you manage it?"

"Most certainly, but where will it lead?"

"It will lead you to money, which I believe is the object dearest to your heart, it will lead Shaftesbury to power and my poor friend, Monmouth, maybe to the English throne."

"And what of you, my Lord? Where will it lead you?"

Philip gave him a wry look. "To hell, I shouldn't wonder!"

A fortnight later he stood with Scott viewing the chaos in Lime Street.

"Rowdy enough for you?" Scott asked him, indicating the screaming, surging, banner-waving mob before them.

"Yes, we have done rather well, I think. The 'Mobile Vulgus' is a powerful thing when roused!"

Actually, the demonstration had exceeded Philip's wildest dreams. Bonfires blazed at the corner of every street from Fenchurch Street to Corn Hill and the Duke of York's name was shouted in hatred by the crowds, whipped to a frenzy by Philip's own men, carefully placed in key positions. Philip looked up as a large shape materialised silently upon the other side of him.

"Who the devil is that?" Scott whispered.

"That, my friend, is Parkes," Philip told him. "He is the Earl's henchman. So far I have received from him four broken ribs and a bleeding back!"

"But what is he doing here?"

Before Philip could answer, Parkes groaned and dropped to the ground, a knife embedded in his back.

"We shall never know now."

Scott swallowed. "Was that meant for you?"

Philip recognised the handle of the knife and shook his head. "No. That was meant for Parkes." He put his boot upon Parke's back and drew out the bloodied blade and then wiped it on the dead man's coat before pocketing the weapon.

"Why did you do that?" Scott asked, looking disgusted.

"I want to return it to Morgan. It is the very least that I can do."

"Jesus! We were standing right next to the man. Does Morgan ever miss?"

Philip smiled. "I hope not, if he is going to avenge himself that way on all who have hurt me! Come, the bonfires have been lit, the effigies are burning, the windows of Papists all over London will be stoned by morning. Our work is done."

As they turned to go, however, they saw a coach caught up in the crush and heard a cry go up.

"A Yorkist! A Yorkist!"

In the coach sat Samuel Pepys, who was now the Secretary of the Admiralty.

Philip recognised him as his coachmen attempted to force a way through the milling crowds. "Well, well, I do believe it is the pompous Mr. Pepys!" he said to Scott.

"Samuel Pepys? Is he a Papist?"

"I don't believe he is, but Shaftesbury stirred up some trouble for him last year, nothing that could be proven but enough to cast suspicion on him. Now he goes about with an air of self-righteousness."

"He has no cause to be self-righteous," Scott said scathingly. "I've heard that when he was paymaster for the garrison at Tangiers one tenth of everything went straight into his own pocket! Talking of swindlers, I had best make myself scarce. If you recall I once relieved his cousin, the late Earl of Sandwich, of a sum of money, and it may be that Pepys knows my face."

"I wonder sometimes whether you will prove to be an asset or a hindrance to me," Philip muttered as Scott dived for cover. "Well, Mr. Pepys, a pleasant evening is it not?"

Pepys's coach had drawn level with him and the Secretary of the Admiralty peered out, his face red with fury and his slightly protruding eyes appearing as though they would pop right from his head. "Lord Devalle! What are you doing here?"

Philip immediately adopted the affected manners that Pepys would have expected of him. "Oh, I merely take the air, you know. Indeed, is this not better than a play?"

"I fail to understand, my Lord, how you can find this unseemly demonstration in the least amusing," Pepys said angrily.

"But surely, Mr. Pepys, it is only Papists who need to fear this crowd. You are not a Papist, are you?" Philip was thoroughly enjoying Pepys' discomfiture.

"You are welcome to accompany me home to Derby House this minute, my Lord, and if you find a single crucifix or altar then I will resign my office and my Parliamentary seat," Pepys said, tight-lipped. He was the elected Member for Castle Rising. "That is if you can first discover a way to move my vehicle through this rabble."

Philip only laughed as he leapt up a flight of steps to a nearby house, from where he could be seen by his men. "Let Mr. Pepys through," he commanded them.

Immediately the crowds parted and the coach moved on.

As Pepys looked out, Philip touched his hat with the silver-headed cane he had taken to carrying. "Your servant, Mr. Pepys, and my compliments to the King!"

Pepys did not go straight home to Derby House but called first at Whitehall, where King Charles listened gravely to the news of the riot.

"Lord Devalle appeared to me to be somehow in control of the situation," Pepys said.

"It would not surprise me. He has lately come under the influence of the Earl of Shaftesbury," Charles said grimly, "and it is a combination which I frankly do not relish. It was not by accident that Lord Devalle was there this evening, you may be sure of it."

After he had dispatched the officers of the guard with orders to disperse the mob and douse the fires, Charles sought the company of Louise de Quéroualle. The Brêton girl who had once accompanied his late sister on a visit from France was now the Duchess of Portsmouth, and his mistress.

Although he passed some of his most pleasant hours with Nell Gwynne, it was Louise who Charles loved best. With her he could relax and he need have no secrets, for her political affiliations were his own.

"You cannot afford to have this kind of trouble now," she warned him, for Charles had, only that month, pledged to aid the Catholic Cause in England and had signed a fresh private treaty with France, a treaty in which both kings had agreed to conclude no alliance with any country without first obtaining the other's consent. "Louis will expect you to quell any anti-Catholic demonstrations."

Charles could see problems with that. "To do so would turn my people against me. It is already rumoured that my brother had Philip Devalle flogged because he hinted at the whereabouts of documents to prove Monmouth's legitimacy."

"Is it true?"

"That Monmouth is legitimate? No, I never married any woman but the Queen. As to the flogging, that was real enough. Monmouth has seen the scars, but whether or not it was by

James' order I cannot determine. He has denied it, of course, but I am not sure whether to believe him."

Since James had ignored his advice and openly declared himself to be a Catholic and then taken a Catholic wife, Charles had reckoned him capable of anything.

"What *are* you going to do then? You have to act, and without delay."

Charles agreed. "Yes, before Philip can become the people's hero. I fear that with his good looks and his reputation on the battlefield he is far too well-suited to the role. Perhaps you could visit him and persuade him to work for France instead. He seems to think more highly of my cousin, Louis, than he does of me."

"Why don't you just have him killed?" Louise said matter-of-factly.

"What, and have him called a Protestant martyr, not to mention risking Louis' wrath and Shaftesbury's revenge? Let us rather offer him money, for I know he is impoverished."

"Supposing he still refuses?"

"Then use your charm upon him, Fubbs." That was Charles' pet name for her. "It will be for my sake, after all, although he must never know that I have sent you."

Louise pulled a face. "It will be a distasteful task."

"Most women seem to find him irresistible! "Charles was under no illusions concerning his own looks. He had never considered himself particularly handsome and now that he had almost lost his own hair and was forced to wear a wig he knew that he was even less so.

Louise kissed the deep lines that age and bitter experience had furrowed on his brow. "Lord Devalle holds no fascination for me," she assured him. "I despise him utterly."

"I'm glad to hear it," Charles said, "but let us hope he does not realise how you feel about him."

～

Philip knew exactly how Louise felt about him, and he was extremely surprised to receive a visit from her the day after the riot.

"Your Grace." He took the hand she offered him and kissed it dutifully. "To what do I owe this unaccustomed and most unexpected honour?"

"I needed to see you privately." She looked about her. "Are we quite alone?"

"I have only the servant who admitted you." Mystified, Philip closed the door. "Now, what is this all about?"

"It's about France, my Lord, a country you have served well in the past, so well, in fact, that you have caused King Louis to hope that you will do so again."

"Did King Louis send you to me?"

"Is he mistaken in judging you to be a person who holds him in high esteem?" Louise said.

"In extremely high esteem," he assured her, aware that she had not exactly answered his question!

"It has come to my notice that you have lately been associating with the Earl of Shaftesbury. It is even possible that his generosity is responsible for all this." Louise indicated their surroundings.

The room in which they stood was furnished with elegant walnut pieces, all inlaid with silver. Leather carpets covered the floor and two huge, silver-framed mirrors made the room appear even larger than it was. The air, too, was pleasant, for along one wall stood open caskets of fragrant spices, an idea Philip had picked up in Holland.

"What of it?" he asked.

"I merely wish you to consider whether your talents may not be wiser employed in working *for* Catholic interests, not against them."

Philip studied her. Louise was a pretty woman, even if she was too baby-faced and plump for his taste, but, like a doll, she had no animation in her features so that it was hard to tell exactly what was passing through her scheming little mind. "Explain yourself, your Grace."

"King Louis already thinks highly of you and it is in his power to reward you far more generously than Shaftesbury ever could."

"I dare say, but I don't believe he instructed you to tell me this," Philip told her frankly.

"King Louis has instructed me to serve my country in the best way I can," Louise said. "If you were to, say, inform me of the matters discussed at the meetings of the Green Ribbon Club then you, too, would be serving France. I suggest you think about it."

"I don't need to think about it," Philip said. "You can have my answer now, for it will be the same tomorrow, next week or next month. Whilst I served King Louis to the best of my abilities upon the battlefield I would never serve him in any way that was detrimental to England."

"But your mother was French, was she not?"

"And a Protestant," Philip reminded her. "I would not help to put a Catholic on the throne of England, for to do so would bring nothing but unrest and tribulation to her people."

"You make your motives sound extremely noble," Louise said sneeringly. "Is not the truth of it that you hope, through Shaftesbury, to gain advantage for yourself? The world knows you are penniless and people without money can't afford to have principles. Since you are evidently seeking nothing but your own advancement should it matter who you serve, so long as they can give you what you want?"

Philip smiled at her sudden change of tone. He had no doubt that Charles had sent her with instructions to be persuasive, but Louise had evidently forgotten that!

"We need you, Lord Devalle," she began again, in a sugary voice. "And we will bid as high for you as Shaftesbury."

"No matter how much you are prepared to offer me I will

not help you and King Charles to crush the Opposition Party," Philip said firmly.

"There is another reward you could enjoy, one which Shaftesbury cannot offer you," Louise said softly. "Myself."

Philip had certainly not expected that. "I don't quite understand," he said, although he feared he did.

"I would have thought my meaning was clear enough. After all it will not be the first time you have seduced a mistress of the King. What do you say now?"

"I am lost for words," he said truthfully, looking down at the hand she had rested on his sleeve. "I am also filled with esteem for a person who loves her country so much that she would contemplate giving herself to a man she finds detestable."

Louise started to protest but Philip put his finger to her lips. "Don't trouble to deny it. I know women well enough. It does not matter for, to be quite candid, sweetheart, I desire you as little as you do me."

Louise's eyes opened wide and the colour rushed up to her cheeks as she snatched her hand away. "Are you declining my offer, you ungrateful pig?"

"Whilst I am incredibly flattered that you think me so important to your schemes, I fear you will just have to go back to your royal lover and tell him you have failed to win me over," Philip said. "As for your 'offer', I would rather forget that."

Louise faced him angrily. "There are some things a lady cannot forget, particularly a lady of my rank and breeding."

Philip shrugged. "I care nothing for either your rank or your breeding, Lady Portsmouth. If you behave like a harlot you must expect to be treated as a harlot."

The cold light of hatred burned in the eyes that only a moment before had gazed at him so seductively. "You will regret this day, my Lord," she warned him. "You have made an enemy, one who will not rest until she is avenged for your insult."

❧

"You totally mishandled it," Shaftesbury said when Philip related the incident to him.

Philip sighed. He was growing accustomed to the Earl's constant criticism but he really could not see how he could be faulted this time. "What would you rather, that I had informed her of your plans, taken the King's money and Lady Portsmouth's body?"

"Don't be so ridiculous! It would have been sufficient for you to bed the Duchess. You would have had a hold upon her then and, with luck, you might even have made her fall in love with you."

"That evil jade? I have no wish for her to be in love with me. Besides, she dislikes me," Philip pointed out.

"I would have thought a man with your experience with women could have won her round if there was some advantage in it."

"She may be a whore but I am not," Philip told him.

"You are exactly what I tell you to be, if you want to live off my money, and you will do exactly what I tell you to do," Shaftesbury insisted.

Philip's eyes flashed. "Not that. I have sacrificed a good deal of my pride to work for you, but I still have my self-respect and I shall not discard that, not for you or Monmouth. I'll see you and your precious cause in hell first."

Shaftesbury glared at him for a second then, unexpectedly, he laughed. "Of course. You are quite right."

"I am?" Philip asked in surprise.

"Yes, Philip, you are right. I ought to thank you for your loyalty and not berate you for incompetence."

"Don't trouble. I've grown used to being addressed in the tone one usually reserves for a servant," Philip said huffily.

"Do I ruffle your feathers, eh, my pretty peacock?" Shaftesbury said, smiling. "I'm really rather pleased with you. I know not how you managed it, nor do I desire to know, but there was insurrection in the city last night. By the way, Parkes was killed in Lime Street." The Earl looked at him closely. "I had instructed him to be your bodyguard."

"That is a pity," Philip answered calmly, "but, in truth, you have no need to protect me with a bodyguard."

"So it appears. No matter, you have done well. In fact, you have done so well that I have a gift for you." Shaftesbury opened a drawer in his bureau. "It came to my attention that before coming to work for me you were forced, as payment of a gambling debt, to part with something of considerable sentimental value."

Philip looked with amazement at the article in the Earl's hand. It was a silver and sapphire bracelet, the one he had once bought as a gift for Jules Gaspard. The sight of it brought back bittersweet memories of the poet who had been such a good friend to him and whose death has been such a devasting blow. "How the devil did you get that? Lord Rochester refused to part with it, even though I offered him twice what it was worth."

"I offered him considerably more than that! Here, take it, it is yours again and I earnestly advise you next time to cease your play before you are forced to part with your jewellery, or that belonging to a person who was evidently very dear to you."

Philip slipped the bracelet onto his own wrist. "My Lord, I am most grateful for your generosity."

"You're not. It pains you greatly to be beholden to me for the return of something so precious to you," Shaftesbury guessed, "and I can see why. You have not learned yet to be either grateful or obedient to me, but I hope you will one day. Now I have to speak to you upon a matter of extreme importance. King Charles has announced today that Parliament will reconvene upon the fifteenth."

"Is he in need of money?" Philip was surprised, for Shaftesbury had long suspected that Charles was receiving money from King Louis whilst the Parliament was not sitting.

"I expect he wishes to act the part of peacemaker between

France and Holland," Shaftesbury said. "William desires to wed the Princess Mary, which will suit Charles very well, for with feelings running high against the Papists it would be a most politic move to encourage the Orangeman. He needs the Parliament now to vote him funds, for he can scarcely remain in the pay of Holland's greatest enemy."

"Will it suit you to have Parliament reconvened?"

"It would suit me better to have another Parliament elected," Shaftesbury admitted. "I intend to remind the King and the country that, under an ancient Act of Edward 111, a Parliament which has been prorogued for over a year is legally dissolved, therefore I intend to declare this Parliament illegal. Buckingham has promised to support me in this and so have Lord Salisbury and Lord Wharton."

"The King won't stand for it," Philip predicted.

"That is a chance I am prepared to take, but you should know the risks. He may decide to clap the four of us in prison for a while. If he does then you will be left with no protector. Charles may even decide to seize you too, in view of your refusal to accept his offer."

Philip weighed that up in his mind. It did seem likely, particularly after Portsmouth's threat. "What should I do?"

"Go to France and wait until I contact you, that would be the best," Shaftesbury reckoned. "You can reside in that damned property of yours again and make use of the servants whose wages I have been paying for so long! And you are not to forget that you owe your loyalty to me now."

"Meaning?"

"Meaning that no matter how attractive any offer the King of France might make to entice you back into his service you are to refuse. Is that understood?"

"It is, my Lord. I have no wish to work for anyone but you."

"Why?" The Earl regarded him cynically. "Is it because you

would lose your fine carriage and your fashionable home, or is it, perhaps, that you have begun to believe in Monmouth's Cause?"

"I have begun to believe in something," Philip was forced to admit, "but it is not Monmouth's Cause. I may not have learned obedience or gratitude, my Lord, but I have learned respect for a clever and ambitious man. It is you I believe in."

Shaftesbury looked pleased at that. "Thank you," he said, offering his hand, which Philip took. "I suggest you leave for France immediately. I am intending to travel down to Dorset, whilst I am still at liberty to do so. There is a person who I must see, for I don't know how long it will be before I see her again."

"Your mistress?" Philip guessed, smiling.

Shaftesbury nodded. "She is the daughter of my neighbour in Wimborne St. Giles. It is my intention to bring her to London in due course but, in the meantime, I must ensure that her father does not wed her off to some country parson, for I expect that would be the limit of his ambition for her."

"And how do you propose to do that?" Philip was amused at the romantic prospect of the Earl enduring a coach trip of at least three days in the bitter Winter weather in order to wrest his country sweetheart from the clutches of the local clergy!

"With money, of course," Shaftesbury said simply. "I loaned Theresa's father a considerable sum and I am sure that if I agreed to wipe the debt and find a tame husband for her at Court he would be reasonable."

Philip shook his head in wonderment. "Is there nothing you cannot buy?"

"Very little, I have found," Shaftesbury said, "and I am bound to say, Philip Devalle, I am very pleased that I managed to buy you!"

THREE

❧

Seeing the gardens of Versailles with King Louis was a very different business from seeing them with Monsieur, Philip found. The King of France enjoyed walking, and he was not at all concerned that the fresh air might ruin his complexion! He also enjoyed his gardens. They were taking shape most beautifully thanks to the skills of his garden designer, Le Nôtre, and his favourite painter, Le Brun, who, having enhanced the inside of the chateau, was now turning his talents to designs for fountains and statues.

"I really think I should write a guide to the gardens, do you not agree?" Louis asked Philip as they stood before the fountain of the Pyramid.

Philip, who knew it was not really a question, did agree.

"This fountain, I feel, should be viewed from a raised position," Louis decided, "near the chateau so that one can see the Pond of Neptune, which I plan to build behind the Fountain of the Dragon."

Philip obliging looked in the direction of the Dragon, which gave out such a fierce jet of water it seemed to reach nearly to the sky. "How do you do that, your Majesty?"

"My machine at Marly pumps the water from the Seine," Louis told him proudly. "There are two more new fountains that you have not seen. They represent Autumn and Winter, to complete the four Ponds of the Seasons. They are only on the other side of this lawn, if you would care to see them." Louis pointed to the piece of grass known as the Tapis Vert, or Green Carpet.

"I should be delighted," Philip lied, but Louis laughed.

"You may fool my brother but you cannot fool me, Philip. You have no love of gardens, have you?"

"Not really," Philip admitted. "We had extensive gardens at my home when I was a child, your Majesty, although I never paid them too much mind."

"What kind of gardens?" Louis wanted to know.

It was a long while since Philip had given any thought to High Heatherton. "My grandfather had them laid out on formal lines," he recalled. "Not a tree or flowerbed out of place, an exercise in perfect symmetry. He must have had a love of order, which was strange for one with the disorderly mind of a madman!"

"Why do you suppose a love of symmetry to be the prerogative of the sane?" Louis said. "After all a garden is no more than an arrangement of masses, light and space. Descartes claims that they are the primary qualities of life, not mere experiences of the senses, and that in geometry we can clearly see proportion, symmetry and the agreement of the whole with its parts."

Philip stared at him blankly. Louis had spoken on too high a level for him. "I know nothing of geometry, your Majesty and I thought a garden was merely a place to grow flowers."

Louis smiled. "I forget, Philip, that you are a soldier, not a mathematician."

"And an unlearned soldier at that," Philip admitted.

Louis himself had been poorly educated, although his desire to learn had encouraged him to study when he had the opportunity. "You have done well without such knowledge but I can't help but wonder what a person like you might have achieved with the benefit of a better education."

"Would learning have helped me gain more favour in your Majesty's eyes?" Philip said.

"Of course not. I value you for the talents you have and what you are," Louis assured him.

"Then I have no need of education, since my dearest wish is to be valued by the greatest king in all the world," Philip said smoothly.

Louis smiled. "You have no need of lessons in charm, that's evident. In that respect, at least, your education is complete. But do you not desire to be valued by King Charles as well? I wonder he can bear to let so decorative an ornament leave his Court."

Philip bowed his head, acknowledging the compliment. "Thank you, your Majesty, but I don't believe King Charles especially values me."

"Is that why you are here? Come now, be truthful with me."

Philip had too much respect for Louis to be less than honest with him about his reasons for returning. "I fled from England to avoid arrest," he admitted.

Louis' eyes searched his. "What have you done?"

"Nothing, save ally myself to the Earl of Shaftesbury."

"Truly?"

Louis' eyes were hard to meet without averting one's own gaze, but Philip steadfastly returned his look.

"Yes, truly. Does your Majesty believe that I would come seeking sanctuary if I had committed some crime, particularly a crime against my own king, your cousin?"

Louis appeared to be considering that for a moment, and then he nodded decisively. "I am certain you would. You have friends here, powerful friends like Monsieur, who would protect you whatever you did. I doubt you have anyone to protect you in England now, for I expect the Duke of Buckingham will be mixed up in this as well."

"I hear that he is already in the Tower, your Majesty." News had reached Philip that Buckingham had supported Shaftesbury's motion to declare the Parliament to be illegal, and they had both been imprisoned for it, as Shaftesbury had feared they might be.

"And has he done no more than you, ally himself with the Earl of Shaftesbury?"

"He has done a little more than that," Philip admitted.

"Buckingham is a fool to go against King Charles, and so are you," Louis said. He did not speak again for a few minutes, for they were walking past the Pond of Spring, where the goddess Flora sat surrounded by garlands of painted flowers. The noise from the fountain made conversation difficult for the softly spoken Louis. "Go back into my army," he advised, when they had passed by. "Even if I do make this peace with Holland that my cousin Charles so desires, there will be other wars to fight."

Philip brought out an enamelled snuff box on which was painted a portrait of Louis himself, a neat piece of flattery of the kind that never went unnoticed by the King of France. He inhaled the snuff delicately, without sneezing, and then returned the box to his waistcoat pocket.

Louis watched him all the while. "Well, aren't you going to answer me?" he asked impatiently.

"I fear the answer I give will not endear me to your Majesty," Philip said uneasily, for the last thing he wanted to do was to alienate King Louis, especially now that he needed to take refuge in his country. "I regret that I cannot return to your army at present, for I am honour bound elsewhere."

"By that you mean Shaftesbury has bought you," Louis guessed.

They lapsed into silence again, for they were passing another fountain, this time the Pond of Summer, where Ceres lay on golden sheaves of corn.

"I trust this will not cost me your Majesty's most gracious favour," Philip said.

"You are still welcome to reside in France for as long as you like. As for my favour, you will always have that, so long as you never turn your hand against me. You have proved yourself a loyal servant to France and I hope you will one day serve her again."

Philip was relieved to hear those words. He knew that Louis

never believed in releasing those he valued from their obligations to him but it was still good to know exactly where he stood. "That would be my dearest wish, also, your Majesty."

"Good. You are a solder, first and foremost, Philip. You have too much brain to waste your life in idleness at Court and too little to be a politician. A man should do what he does best, and what you do best is to lead men on campaigns."

Monsieur would have disagreed with that. It was obvious that he was delighted to have Philip back in Paris. He was as fussy and demanding as ever, and insisted on Philip accompanying him everywhere. Philip had to be present when Monsieur rose in the morning, when he ate, rode in his carriage or attended a play. Even in the middle of the night he might be summoned to the Palais Royale, for if Monsieur could not sleep it would be Philip he sent for to talk or play at cards.

Every night before retiring, no matter how late the hour, Philip had to take a promenade with him around the grounds. The walk was never far, for Monsieur had a healthy dislike of night air, but his physicians had convinced him that a little exercise after his evening meal was beneficial to his weight, which had increased again. It also gave him the opportunity to be quite alone with Philip for a while, and to tell him of all the trifling problems which had beset him during the day.

Philip always listened patiently, or appeared to listen, which was just as good, but one evening his soldier's instincts warned him that something was amiss. He glanced around, searching for what he could not see.

"You're not paying attention to me, are you?" Monsieur complained.

"No, but keep talking, there is someone watching us."

Monsieur froze. "Where?"

"Behind that column," Philip whispered, finding at last what he had sought. "Don't let him know we have seen him."

"What are you going to do?"

Philip said nothing but watched the figure in the shadows until he saw moonlight glint upon the barrel of a pistol.

Without more ado he gave Monsieur a mighty shove which knocked him to the ground. At the same instant a shot rang out.

The bullet grazed Philip's arm but he barely noticed as he set off in hot pursuit of the assailant.

Monsieur was now shrieking loud enough to bring out the palace guards but Philip caught up with the would-be assassin before he reached the courtyard. By the time the guards appeared, he had his sword drawn and the frightened fellow pressed against one of the pillars supporting a balcony above.

He waved the blade menacingly before his captive's face. "Who told you to kill the Duc d'Orleans?"

"I will say nothing."

"Indeed you will." Philip slashed his sword across the man's cheek, drawing blood. "Upon whose orders are you here?"

"No-one sent me."

"Liar!"

"No!" the man screamed as Philip cut his cheek again. "Wait! I will tell you."

A pistol fired from a first-floor balcony above the courtyard and Philip's prisoner fell to the ground. He was dead.

Philip looked up to see a figure he did not recognise standing on the balcony, a smoking pistol in his hand. "Why the devil did you do that?" he cried in a fury.

"I feared for Monsieur's safety if the creature escaped, my Lord."

Philip cursed, kicking viciously at the inert body lying at his feet. "Who was that man on the balcony?" he demanded of the guards.

"That was Dubois," one told him. "He works for the French Ambassador in London."

Philip frowned, for he had never seen Dubois before. "Does he? Well I shall have words with him. Thanks to that bloody fool we shall never know this man's master."

He returned to Monsieur, who had been helped to his feet but was still shaking.

"Is it over?" he asked, putting his arms around Philip.

"Yes, all over," Philip reassured him. "He is dead, whoever he was. I apologise for the rough way I treated you, Monsieur."

"No, no, you were wonderful." Monsieur buried his face in Philip's shoulder. "You are a brave, brave man. You saved my life."

"Oh, hardly that. Your guards were all around you." Philip gently disengaged himself, for it did not do to allow Monsieur to become too affectionate. "Who would want to kill you?"

"How should I know? Every man has enemies." Monsieur fanned himself with his handkerchief. "You're hurt," he noticed. "There is blood upon your sleeve. Take me inside before I faint."

But Philip did not move. As he watched the body being carted away he had a sudden, sobering thought.

"Perhaps, Monsieur, you have no need to be upset. It may be that the bullet was not meant for you but for me."

"For you?" Monsieur recovered remarkably. "Who would desire your death?"

"I have enemies in England now. Perhaps they have decided I should not return."

"Well that's a relief," Monsieur said joyfully.

"I'm glad you think so!"

Monsieur collapsed on him once more, this time helpless with laughter at his own tactlessness. "I only meant we have no need to worry. No-one ever catches you unawares, my dear, you're far too clever."

"Am I? This time I believe I have been rather stupid. What was Dubois doing here anyway?"

Monsieur shrugged. "I don't know. Lately he is often in Paris upon my brother's business."

"I'll warrant he is not upon your brother's business this night," Philip said grimly, "but it could be," he added to himself, "that he is on the business of Louise de Quéroualle."

It was very late before Monsieur would let Philip leave him and by the morning Dubois was long gone.

Louis' cousin, known as the Grande Mademoiselle, was said to hold the most agreeable salon in Paris. Agreeable, that is, to the intellectual set, but much less so to Philip, who had nonetheless been expected to attend. Since the days of his holding his own salon he had become accepted by literary society but, in truth, the writers, philosophers and wits all bored him, for he had only ever courted them for Jules' sake.

Violins played at the Luxembourg, the Grande Mademoiselle's palace, and guests could dance and talk without restraint. However, Philip preferred of late to play at cards rather than dance, and gambling was the one thing his hostess did not allow, for she had seen her father lose his money too many times.

Monsieur had not attended with him on this occasion, primarily because his wife, Madame, was going to be present. Monsieur viewed his forceful German wife with horror. After the birth of his daughter, two years before, he considered he had fulfilled his marital obligations and now he associated with her as little as possible. Philip always tried to keep out of her way too, for Madame detested all of her husband's close friends. She was also a strong supporter of the Prince of Orange, with whom she had played as a child, and she had a very slight opinion of any who had fought to take his country. Philip, since he qualified for her disapproval on both counts, had more than once received a portion of her loud abuse!

Even so, her ebullient presence would not have been enough to drive him from the Luxembourg before he wished to go but, when he saw that both Elizabeth de Grammont and Barbara were there as well, Philip decided to beat a hasty retreat.

45

Barbara had lately taken up residence in Paris, but she had grown lewder and more vicious as she competed with women younger than herself, and Philip avoided her whenever he could. Elizabeth, the mischievous friend of his early days at Court, had become quite insupportable. She had turned to religion as a solace for her husband's neglect and now, with all the fervour of the newly converted, she lectured him constantly upon his bad ways.

"Leaving so soon, Philip?"

Philip turned around to see Marie, once Mademoiselle de Bellecourt, but now wed to the Chevalier Benoit. Despite Louis' suggestion that he take a French bride and Monsieur urging him to pursue Marie, Philip's heart had never been in it and their relationship had never progressed beyond an occasional passionate encounter. He had run into her several times since his return to Paris and, although they had not exchanged many words, she had always cast reproachful looks in his direction.

He bowed to her. "I think it would be best, Marie. This evening I have already encountered Madame, who despises me, the Duchess of Cleveland, who tries to publicly seduce me and the Comtesse de Grammont, who aspires to save my soul! I don't believe I am now up to facing you, who hates me."

Marie smiled at him. "Why do you say so, Philip? You were not an easy person to forget but you are dreadfully easy to forgive. It can hardly be counted your fault if I failed to make you care for me."

Philip was surprised. The last thing he had expected from Marie was humility. "It certainly wasn't your fault," he said gently. "You are a pretty girl and as amiable a companion as a man could want, but I was simply not ready for marriage."

"Also, you would have preferred to choose your own bride and not have one chosen for you by Monsieur," she guessed, dabbing her eyes.

"That too," he admitted, "but please don't cry. Are you not now wed to another, so that it is I who am the loser by it all?"

He had hoped to comfort her and make a quick escape, but it was apparent that Marie was not about to be comforted.

"Oh Philip, I am so unhappy with him. I only married him to save my face."

Philip glanced around. Marie's outburst had not gone unnoticed, although the company was too discreet to watch them openly.

"Not here, sweetheart," he warned her. "Do you want the whole Court to know your business?"

"I don't care who knows that I am still in love with you," she sniffed. "My life is in ruins because of you and all you care about is your damned reputation."

"Stop it, Marie. You are not in love with me, you never were." He took her arm and hastened her through the door. "If you are not happy with Benoit then that is your misfortune, for you married him of your own choosing."

"What else could I do? You made a laughing stock of me. There were not too many men prepared to take a woman who had been rejected by a Hero of France."

"I must confess I never once considered your position," Philip said, "but, to be fair, I had not proposed to you."

"Nevertheless, all Paris thought we would be wed. Monsieur told everyone."

That much was true and Philip could find it in himself to feel a little sorry for her. The carriage placed at his disposal by Monsieur waited for him outside and he decided that at least he ought to offer to drive her to her house, but once inside it she flung herself into his arms and sobbed hysterically.

"Take me home before I quite disgrace myself," she begged when he had managed to calm her down.

Philip willingly complied with that request, for he was growing weary of Marie's tears, but he was not to escape her so easily.

"Stay with me awhile," she pleaded when they arrived and he had helped her down. "My husband is at Versailles with the King. He'll not be back before tomorrow afternoon."

"I hardly think that would be wise," Philip began, but fresh tears sprung to Marie's eyes.

"Could you not spare even one hour to comfort me when you have caused me such distress? You used to find me desirable," she reminded him, pouting.

Philip weighed both the risk and the rewards of spending an hour with Marie. The Chevalier was known to be hot-tempered but, on the other hand, Marie was quite desirable and very willing too. With the demands that Monsieur was making on him, he rarely had the chance to get near a woman. Philip's carnal cravings could usually over-rule his commonsense and he sent the carriage on without him.

"One hour," he agreed, although he doubted he would need that long to satisfy either himself or Marie, and he was right.

"Do you still drink brandy?" she asked afterwards, as she lay in his arms. "Let me pour you some."

Philip had no wish to linger with her, but Marie was most persuasive and he relented.

It was good brandy and, as he drank it down, it seemed to warm him, unusually so if he had thought about it. Marie laid her head back on his shoulder and Philip relaxed as the warmth spread over him until his whole body was glowing.

He tried to listen to her conversation but her voice seemed to get farther and farther away. His head grew heavier until he closed his eyes and heard no more.

He was awakened by the feel of rough hands shaking him and he forced himself to awareness.

The angry face of the Chevalier Benoit was confronting him. "Explain yourself, my Lord," he demanded.

Philip knew that an explanation was likely to prove extremely difficult!

FOUR

Morgan listened impassively to Philip's account of the event.

"How much brandy did you say you drank?"

"One glass but, dammit, even if I'd supped the bottle I would have been aware of something. The bitch must have put a potion in it."

"Then you were fortunate. If she could give you a sleeping draught then she could just have easily have slipped some poison in your glass or cut your throat whilst you were sleeping."

"Why ever would she want to do that?"

"Revenge?" Morgan suggested.

"Well she will have that now, for I am forced to face her husband in a duel."

"Don't fight him," Morgan said. "Such a woman is not worth the risk of your life."

"I expect to win," Philip assured him.

"Even if you do and it becomes known that you have killed a man in a duel you may be thrown into prison."

"I agree that it is more than the jade deserves and yet, although I am resolved not to kill Benoit, I must answer his challenge," Philip said. "It has become an affair of honour."

"There is another reason why you should not fight." Morgan showed him a letter bearing the Earl of Shaftesbury's seal.

"He has been freed!" Philip guessed.

Shaftesbury was indeed free, although his stubbornness had caused him to hold out long after Buckingham and the others had been freed. Now he was most anxious for Philip's return.

"We could start for England right away," Morgan said.

Philip shook his head. "Would you have me called a coward? I shall meet Benoit tomorrow afternoon in the woods near St. Antoine, as arranged, and we will travel home the following day."

❧

Dusk was gathering as Philip and Morgan arrived at St. Antoine. They had borrowed two horses from Monsieur's stables and they tied them to a tree.

Benoit's coach was there and they saw the Chevalier, his sword moving to and fro in the dim light as he practised thrusts against imaginary foes. If he had intended the sight to be unnerving then he failed miserably.

Philip viewed him without the least concern for he was confident that he could beat him. He still felt quite incensed about the whole affair but he had more experience than to let his emotions interfere with his swordplay, for he knew that could be a fatal mistake. Indeed he was rather hoping that this might prove to be an extra advantage he had over Benoit, whose outrage had been plain the previous night when he had challenged Philip to the duel.

"Do you think you will be a match for this, Lord Devalle?" Benoit taunted him, making some more cuts through the air.

"More than a match, Benoit," Philip said. "I think the sooner we begin the better, for the light is fading fast and we shall soon need to hold flambeaux in order to see one another."

"Don't worry, my Lord, I shall have dispatched you long before it grows dark," Benoit said boastfully.

"Perhaps and perhaps not." Philip stripped to his shirt and breeches and faced the Frenchman unafraid, for he was strong and fit, and practised regularly with a sword.

Philip had never been a defensive fighter and his first riposte was designed to leave Benoit in no doubt of his intentions. Benoit was soon using all his energy parrying Philip's advances with no chance to launch a counter attack. He attempted a low lunge but Philip swiftly passed his blade under the Chevalier's and deflected the blow harmlessly upward. They disengaged briefly and Philip was pleased to see Benoit flushed from his exertions.

They came together again. Philip was taller than Benoit and more supple but he was not finding the Chevalier an easy man to fight. The lessons he had learned long ago from Signor D'Alessandro were deeply ingrained in him now and his sword became an extension of his body. His speed and strength soon gained him the upper hand and Benoit began to retaliate with more desperation than wisdom. Philip had waited for that and, seizing his opportunity, dropped low to the ground and then sprung up upon Benoit's left side. Benoit, caught off balance by the manoeuvre, spun around and fell, two gaping cuts in his sword arm. Philip, who was still unwilling to take his life, hesitated with his sword poised over the Chevalier's heart, expecting a submission.

It was then he saw a man appearing from the trees, his sword drawn.

He shouted for Morgan, but the Welshman was nowhere to be seen.

Philip's mind raced. All too clearly now he read the true situation. Benoit's attitude, now that he thought about it, had not been so much the passion of a jealous husband as the cockiness of one who knows he cannot lose. Too late he realised the whole situation had been engineered.

He cursed. It had been a trap and he had fallen into it. Worse than that, he had led Morgan into danger.

"Damn you, Benoit! For this you shall die." Philip plunged his blade straight through Benoit's heart.

Before he could retrieve it the other man was upon him.

Philip had no weapon now save his cunning and his speed and, although he was tiring fast, neither failed him.

He kicked his attacker's leg, causing him to stagger back and followed with two strong punches to his head. The swordsman lost his balance and went down. He tried to rise but Philip struck him again and stamped hard upon his hand, forcing him to release his sword.

Philip quickly seized it up but at the same moment he felt a fierce pain and an icy coldness in his left side. Then it felt as though his insides were being torn out of him.

As he collapsed to his knees he saw another sword, this one bloodied nearly to the hilt. His last realisation, as he ceased to be aware of anything, was that the blood upon it was his own.

Dubois wiped his sword blade. "Is he dead? he asked his accomplice, who was nursing his hand, his face swollen and one eye nearly closed.

"No, he still breathes, damn him."

"He is a hard man to kill, this Englishman," Dubois muttered.

"I'll finish him for you, with pleasure. I think the bastard broke my hand."

Dubois thought quickly. "No. One wound is enough if we are not to arouse suspicion and, anyway, he will die soon enough for he is losing a lot of blood. A few hours should do it by the looks of him and since that inept fool Benoit is dead, it will seem as though they killed each other when we produce Devalle's body. We will get the Chevalier home now and inform the authorities that Devalle escaped. Where's Benoit's driver?"

"He was knifed by Devalle's servant but I think I cracked his skull open."

Dubois managed to drag the bodies of Benoit and his driver onto the floor of the coach. His accomplice untied the two horses and sent them off and then looked down at Morgan, who lay senseless on the ground. "What about him?"

"Leave him. He's only a servant. Even if he does recover what can he do? Devalle, though, is another matter. Someone may discover him while he is still alive."

"You're going to take him with us?"

"We don't have to take him far. There is a place near to the Porte St. Antoine where a man may safely be left to die. A place where none come asking questions. Dubois smiled malevolently. "The Bastille!"

Philip recovered consciousness briefly and was aware of a searing pain in his side, the most terrible he had ever endured.

His hands had been bound and, from the sensation of movement, he guessed they were in a vehicle.

"So you are awake, my Lord," a chilling voice said, close by him. "So much the worse for you."

It was too dark for Philip to properly see the face of the man bending over him, but the voice jarred a chord in his memory. He tried in vain to grasp the name that was eluding him and as he lapsed back into unconsciousness he heard the man speak again.

"Not even Louis can save you now, Devalle!"

FIVE

☙

Morgan opened his eyes.

He moaned as he sat up, gingerly feeling a raw place at the back of his head. His hair was matted with blood.

The blood was still damp and he wiped his fingers on the grass, recalling where he was and what had happened to him.

He had spotted a movement amongst the trees whilst his master was fighting the duel and had suspected treachery.

Not wishing to distract him in the middle of what had become a fierce swordfight with the Chevalier Benoit, the Welshman had decided to investigate the matter for himself and had found an armed man lurking in the shadows.

Morgan's knife had dealt swiftly with that one but, too late, he had heard a movement behind him. Before he could turn he had felt a flash of pain that seemed to pierce his skull and then there was blackness.

He forced himself to his feet. It was dark but there was a moon and by its light he looked about him, dreading what he might see. There was nothing; no sign of his master or Benoit and no sign of the man he knew he had slain. It was uncanny, just as though a duel had never taken place there. Their horses were gone, but he saw hoof prints by the tree where he had tethered them, and he found the tracks of Benoit's coach. He found something else too, a dark patch upon the earth.

"Blood," he muttered grimly. "But whose?"

Morgan had been associated with Philip for long enough to know that he had a great many powerful enemies, and his heart was heavy with foreboding as he began the long trudge back to Philip's house. He was several times overcome with dizziness and had to stop to rest, but he arrived home in the early hours of the morning.

An armed guard was posted outside the door.

Morgan cursed in his native tongue. He desperately wanted to discover the reason for the guard's presence but he knew that the very fact of his being abroad at such an unseemly hour would excite suspicion, so he wearily turned away to find himself a place to hide until morning.

He found a dark doorway against which to crouch, wrapped in his cloak, but he dared not sleep for fear he should be discovered there. He was cold through to his bones and his head throbbed unmercifully as the hours ticked slowly by, but Morgan had the patience and endurance of the sturdy farming stock from whence he came.

When the first citizens of Paris moved about the streets upon their business Morgan left his hiding place and walked boldly along the street.

The house was still guarded and he deliberately walked almost past it and then slowed his pace and viewed the guard as though with idle curiosity.

"Ho, friend, what happened here?"

"The owner of this house is wanted by the law," the guard called back.

"What has he done?"

"He fought a duel and killed a man. Now, by order of the King, all of his possessions and this property are forfeit whilst he is a fugitive from justice."

A fugitive? Morgan did not think so. Whilst he was refusing to accept the possibility that his master might be dead, he thought it quite likely that he was a prisoner. But whose?

He considered quickly what he ought to do. There were only two people in Paris influential enough to aid his master in a situation as dire as this. One was Monsieur, but Morgan discounted him immediately. As well as being the brother of the King, Monsieur could never keep his counsel about the least thing and, besides, would probably be hysterical by now at the news of Philip's fate. The other person was the King's mistress, Madame de Montespan.

Athénais de Montespan spent several hours of every day beautifying herself in order to retain the adoration of the King, for she was clever enough to know that her wit alone, captivating though it was, would not hold him forever.

Very little was permitted to interrupt these essential moments of preparation for her day but, despite the early hour, she cleared the room of her attendants directly her page told her who was waiting to see her.

A moment later Morgan was ushered in, near dropping from exhaustion. He had risked a good deal by coming there, and Athénais was risking as much by receiving him, but the thoughts of both of them were only upon Philip.

"Morgan!" she cried. "Why are you not with your master?"

"I would be, my Lady, if I knew his whereabouts."

"Is it true that he has fled after being was discovered in bed with Marie Benoit and killing her husband in a duel?"

"I will tell you what I know to be true and you may deduce the rest."

Morgan quickly described everything that had occurred, from the time his master had left the Luxembourg to escort the Chevalier's wife home to the moment the Welshman had regained consciousness, alone in the woods.

Her pretty face was serious as she listened to him. "You say Marie Benoit drugged his wine so that he would be discovered in her bed?"

"I am convinced of it and that the duel was just a pretext to lure him to a killing ground."

"Surely Marie would not have been party to that. She was in love with him once."

"But he was not in love with her," he pointed out.

"Even so, it seems a harsh revenge to exact for his disinterest," Athénais said. "This is a bad business, Morgan, but why have you come to me?"

"I did not know who else to trust," he told her frankly. "My master always said you were a loyal friend to him."

"I am, indeed I am," Athénais assured him, "but what can I do?"

"Perhaps nothing, my Lady. I only wondered if you had any idea where he might have been taken. He may be wounded and in need of help."

Athénais shuddered. "There is one place where he might be. No, it is too dreadful to contemplate. Better he was dead than there."

"What place can be as foul as that?"

"A place where men are often hidden away to be forgotten and left to die, but let me tell you first that I know Marie Benoit well, for we are both clients of Catherine Monvoisin."

"The fortune teller?"

"She is much more than that. She brews up magic potions. Doubtless it was from her that Marie purchased Philip's sleeping draught, but La Voisin, as they call her, is also a priestess of sorts." Athénais lowered her voice to a whisper. "Some of her ceremonies must be performed with parts of corpses and she confided to me that she obtains dead bodies from a certain Monsieur Demeraud."

Morgan frowned. The pain in his head was making concentration difficult, but he could not see the connection between a priestess of the black arts and his master. "Who is this Demeraud?"

"A gaoler in the Bastille," Athénais explained, "and a very corrupt man. He hides prisoners where none will ever find them until it is too late. I fear that Philip may be in his hands."

"In the Bastille? How can that be when La Reynie has placed a guard upon his house, by order of the King, and will be searching the city for him?"

"The King knows nothing of it, I am certain, nor La Reynie."

Morgan could believe that the King was ignorant of the identity of every prisoner in the Bastille but not La Reynie, the Lieutenant of Police, and he said as much.

"I don't think you understand," she said pityingly. "If Philip is there you may depend he is no ordinary prisoner. He will be confined in a pit below ground."

"An oubliette?" Morgan stared at her. He had heard of these atrocities but he had never been quite sure if they existed, other than in the lurid tales of the Parisians. "Do you mean he will be left there to starve to death?"

"Most go mad before they die. I have seen their bodies, Morgan. They have staring eyes and nails ripped out where they have tried to claw their way to freedom." Athénais gasped suddenly, putting her hand up to her mouth. "So La Voisin's prophecy for Philip will have come true. She foretold that he would die in prison."

Morgan, like most Celts, was superstitious, but that did not mean he would blindly accept the hand of fate. "We must inform the King."

"No!" Athénais turned pale. "If you go to the King with such a tale you will destroy me."

Morgan looked at her, bemused. "Why?"

"Admit I know so much about the dealings of La Voisin?" Athénais cried. "I would deny it all and have you clapped in irons for your insolence, and that is no idle threat, I promise you."

Morgan did not doubt that for an instant, for a fire burned bright in her eyes, but he was worried nearly out of his mind by what she had told him and in no mood to heed her warning.

"Do what you please to me, my Lady, for my life is unimportant to me. I intend to save my master." He turned upon his heel but she ran to the door and was there ahead of him.

"No, Morgan! I want to save him too, but what I told you was in confidence. You must try to understand my difficulties," she pleaded. "Françoise Scarron, my children's governess, is trying to win the King from me. She makes trouble for me all the time and Louis takes her part against me, so I was forced to go to La Voisin. She helped me once before when I needed to drive Louise de La Vallière from the King's heart, but he must never know."

"You have used black magic on the King?" Morgan said in disgust.

"Oh, only the mildest of spells, nothing to harm him, but if he found out then I would be disgraced and Scarron would have won. I beg you, Morgan, not to do me so much hurt and, in return, I will help you any way I can."

Morgan sighed. "How can you help me other than by telling the King of my master's predicament?"

"With money. I understand Demeraud would sell his own grand-dam for the right price."

"Would he sell Lord Devalle's freedom?"

"Possibly. It would depend who wants him dead and whether Demeraud's greed will sufficiently inspire his valour. Whatever sum you need I'll gladly give you," Athénais said, for she was a woman of considerable means. All the proceeds of the Tobacco Tax came to her and many more benefits besides. "That is provided you agree to keep my part in this a secret."

Morgan agreed wearily and left by the back stairs, as he had come.

"You are a plucky little man," Athénais said after him. "No wonder Philip values you so."

The guard on duty at the Bastille gate grimaced when Morgan asked for Demeraud and pointed to the guardroom. "One of them will take you to him."

The other guards were more inquisitive. "What do you want with him?" one asked.

Morgan had already worked out an answer to that. "I have a letter for one of his prisoners."

"He'll not deliver it. You waste your time."

"What if I gave him money?"

"That's your choice, but he'll swindle you. His prisoners have no contact with the world. It is said that even King Louis does not know who he has down there." He laughed harshly and the rest joined in.

Morgan forced himself to laugh along with them. "Why should I care? My mistress can afford the price of sending a note to her lover."

The guard led him along some stone passages and then down some steps. The cold and darkness were oppressive this far into the prison, and the air was foul and damp. The further they went the more Morgan was filled with dread for his master's fate, but he took good care not to display his feelings as he confronted the coarse-featured and unshaven Demeraud.

The gaoler was a small man, shorter even than Morgan, though with the biggest pair of shoulders the Welshman had ever seen and calves so thick a man's two hands could not have spanned them.

"Well, where is your letter?" he asked Morgan after the guard had left them alone.

"I bring no letter," Morgan admitted. "I desire to ask a question of you, that is all."

"Questions are dangerous in here," Demeraud warned. "A man may lose his life as easily by asking them as by answering."

Morgan was undeterred. "Was a prisoner brought to you last night?"

"Perhaps," Demeraud said cagily.

"It would be much to your advantage if he is the one I seek."

"How much to my advantage?"

"Tell me first if he was an Englishman."

Demeraud shrugged his enormous shoulders. "He could have been English. He was in no condition to speak."

"But he is alive?" Morgan persisted.

"He may be. He was bleeding like a pig when they brought him in. What is your interest in this Englishman anyway?"

"He is my master."

"I should seek another. Someone important desires him dead, which is as good as saying he *is* dead," Demeraud said sagely.

"But you could save him if you wished?"

"His life is of no consequence to me, monsieur."

"Would it be of more consequence if I offered you, say, five hundred livres?" Morgan asked, controlling his anger with the utmost effort.

"He is becoming more interesting," Demeraud admitted, "but there are difficulties. Those who brought him here desired to have his body after he had died. How should I explain its disappearance?"

"You could say that La Voisin has stolen it," Morgan suggested, looking at him closely

Demeraud stiffened. "For a foreigner you know a great deal too much. Who told you to seek me out anyway?"

"Someone who also told me you like money."

The gaoler grunted. "How will you get that much?"

"I will get it, that is all you need to know," Morgan said firmly. "Do we have a bargain?"

"We do," Demeraud said, "but he's been down there several hours now and with an open wound. He's likely bled to death."

He beckoned Morgan to follow him. Down they went, down into the very bowels of the earth, it seemed to Morgan. They trod flight after flight of rough-hewn steps, which grew slippery as they reached the lower levels, where the damp cold seemed to wrap around them. With Demeraud's lantern as their only light, they turned into a narrow passageway at the end of which the gaoler unlocked a heavy iron door.

Inside the cave-like room the Welshman could see no-one.

"Well?" he asked Demeraud suspiciously, for he feared a trick. "Where is he?" He was well aware of the perilous position in which he had placed himself, for if his master was already dead then the gaoler would have no reason to let him go free, not when he knew so much about his affairs.

Demeraud stamped upon the dungeon floor. "We're on top of him."

Morgan glanced down to see a metal ring protruding from one of the stone slabs.

Demeraud tugged at the ring and the cover slowly lifted. As the lantern's light penetrated the darkness of the pit Morgan could see him, lying in a pool of filthy water. Philip's hands were still bound, as they had left him, and his clothes were soaked in his own blood.

He did not turn his head or make the slightest sound when Morgan leapt down into the pit beside him but he was breathing, laboured shallow breaths, and he was shivering, for the stinking water in which he lay was icy cold.

"He's alive," he said to Demeraud. "Help me get him out of here."

Demeraud looked down at him dubiously. "Do you still agree the price, even if he's turned mad?"

"Five hundred livres, mad or sane," Morgan promised impatiently, and together they lifted the motionless figure, made heavier by the saturated clothes he wore.

"He goes no further than this cell," Demeraud warned. "Not without the money."

Morgan bit back the futile words which sprang to his lips. His master needed medical attention and the only way that he could get it for him was to return as quickly as he could with five hundred livres.

He went back to Athénais, who listened tearfully as he told her of Philip's situation. "I will pay more than this," she assured him, giving him the money. "Whatever it takes to get him well and anything he needs to make him comfortable."

Demeraud took the bag of money and tipped it out, counting each coin before he would agree to the unconscious Philip being moved to a cell in the upper levels.

"Is there a surgeon who can tend to him?" Morgan said, laying him upon a hard, straw bed and stripping off his damp clothes to reveal a blood-caked gash. "This wound wants opening and cleaning out."

Demeraud looked doubtful. "I might be able to fetch a barber-surgeon for him. At a price."

"A barber-surgeon?" Morgan said disdainfully.

"It's the best you will get to come here. If you don't want one then you can tend your master for yourself. You choose."

"You'd better fetch the barber," Morgan muttered, for he had neither the equipment nor the knowledge to deal with such a wound, which was already exuding yellow matter.

The barber-surgeons of Paris were little more than hairdressers who had served a rudimentary apprenticeship in medicine, as opposed to the surgeon-barbers, who were trained at the College of Saint-Côme. No reputable surgeon would agree to operate except at the request of a physician, however, so Morgan accepted, reluctantly, that Demeraud was right.

Philip mercifully knew nothing of what followed. The barber cut clumsily into the seeping wound, making a jagged gash six inches long and then scraped out what pus he could with a curved knife. Afterwards he cleansed the wound with a noxious, oily substance and closed the cut unevenly with ugly stitches. Morgan watched him, sickened, and wondered what his master would say if he lived to see the awful scar he would always bear upon his side.

The barber next suggested bleeding to remove the poisons from Philip's system, but Morgan refused permission, for he reckoned the patient had lost enough blood already.

The man went cheerfully upon his way, having pocketed five livres for his labours and his silence. He was relieved immediately of a livre of that by the greedy Demeraud, who reminded the barber who had procured him such lucrative employment and what would certainly happen to him if he spoke about it to a living soul. This little piece of business done the gaoler visited his prisoner.

"Let's have a look at him." Demeraud reached out a grimy hand and roughly turned Philip's face toward him. "He's pretty now you've cleaned him up. Wait, I know him! It's Monsieur's friend, the soldier." Demeraud gave a hoot of glee. "Why, this is better than I'd hoped. It's going to cost you a fine few livres to keep this one alive, I warn you."

"And how much will it cost to buy his freedom?" Morgan said, with as much control as he could muster under the circumstances.

Demeraud shook his head. "That can't be bought, my friend, not for him, but he'll be comfortable, I will see to that, so long as there is money for his keep."

"And if there is not?"

"Then I'll drop him back into the pit, Demeraud said simply. "Perhaps you'd better hope he dies tonight, monsieur."

But Philip did not die.

Morgan sat beside his master hour after hour, changing his dressing and tending him devotedly but Philip was oblivious to him.

As though to escape the pain, his mind had slipped away into his past, and for the next few hours he relived erratically the miseries and pleasures of his twenty-eight years.

He wrestled and swam again with John Bone, he listened as Daniel Bennett told him of the wonders of the Court and he felt the stinging cuts of Henry's whip. He met Nell again on Strand Bridge, made love to Barbara and visited the Plague pest house. He half woke at this point and thought he still lay ill from the fever he had caught on that day. His eyes opened for a second and, seeing Morgan bending over him, he confused him with the Duke of Buckingham and murmured his name.

Demeraud, who had come to check on his prisoner's progress, heard him speak and pulled a face. "You see, he's mad. He thinks you are some lord."

"He is not mad but living in his memories," Morgan guessed, mopping his master's damp brow. "They may save him."

Philip passed on from the Plague to fight the Great Fire and then to France to ride victorious with his troops. He saw the horses' hooves thunder toward him as he lay, trapped and helpless, on the battlefield and this time it was Morgan's name he spoke as he recalled the Welshman pulling him free and saving his life.

For a long while after that Philip lay quiet and still. Visions of Jules Gaspard flitted through the confusion of his brain and, finally, he watched once more as his friend's coffin was lowered into the earth. The rest was all dull blackness.

When he next opened his eyes, Philip was aware only that he was in great pain. He did not remember what had happened to him, nor did he recognise his grim surroundings, but he did discern a figure slumped, exhausted across a table.

Even by the flickering light of the single candle he was unmistakable. A comforting, familiar presence in this nightmare world in which he had awakened.

"Morgan!"

✐

"Went wrong? How could it go wrong?" Louis de Quéroualle demanded of Dubois when he returned to London. "Your assassin failed to kill him at the Palais Royale but this plan was fool proof. I thought of it myself."

"You reckoned without Devalle's mettle, your Grace. He killed Benoit."

"Benoit was of no importance to me. I chose him because he was hot-headed enough to avenge his stupid wife's honour, but you were meant to ensure the outcome. You told me you had dealt him a mortal blow, such as he might have received in the duel, and that he would die in the Bastille. Did he die or did he not?"

"I don't know," Dubois admitted wretchedly. "His body was removed, I don't know how and nor does his gaoler, so he claims. He suspects it stolen for the purposes of practising the black arts by the woman known as La Voisin. She uses parts of bodies for her evil worship and she has her servants everywhere."

Louise cursed. "Yes, I know of La Voisin. Did you ask her whether she had taken him?"

Dubois shivered and crossed himself. "Not I, your Grace. She might have set the devil on me."

"But you do think he is dead?"

"Assuredly, your Grace. He could not have survived without help."

Despite the confidence of Dubois' prediction, Louise wanted to know for certain that Philip was dead.

Although she was King Charles' favourite mistress, matters were not going at all well for her lately. People shouted abuse at her in the streets and called her a Catholic whore. The London air was tense with hatred of the Papists and had been since Philip had organised anti-Catholic riots. There had been frequent similar demonstrations in the city streets since then and Louise held him totally to blame.

"Go back to Paris," she instructed Dubois. "If you should discover that he is still alive then you will kill him yourself, and I don't care how you do it."

"Yes, your Grace."

"And Dubois, one more thing." Louise smiled sweetly at him. "If you fail me a third time I shall seriously consider how essential you are to me."

Dubois swallowed. It did not take too much imagination to guess the fate of any who Louise deemed to be superfluous.

"Yes, your Grace."

SIX

Demeraud proudly uncovered a dish upon which lay some sardines cooked in wine. "I've brought you something to tempt your appetite, my Lord."

Philip, still fragile but able to move about with difficulty, treated him to a disarming smile. "You are very good to me, Demeraud. You give me everything but my freedom."

Demeraud *had* been good to him. He was being well rewarded by Morgan in Athénais' livres so that nothing was too much trouble for Philip's comfort and if Philip passed an hour in conversation with him he seemed to feel he had been doubly rewarded.

For Philip the arrangement was less satisfactory, for Demeraud was coarse and ignorant, he rarely washed and he had no manners whatsoever. Philip was as gracious towards him as he could bring himself to be, for in the gaoler's rough hands lay his fate as long as he remained inside that grim, grey fortress. Nonetheless, as the weeks slipped slowly by, he began to realise that Demeraud was never going to let him go.

"Don't I take good care of you?" Demeraud said. "Come, eat."

Philip picked at the food, more to please him than because of hunger. Although he knew he must restore his strength, he had little appetite, especially for fish. Paris was a long way from the sea and, even cooked so delicately, the sardines had an unpleasantly high flavour to one brought up on the fresh caught fish of the Sussex coast.

Why Demeraud?" he asked, as he had many times before. "Why do you keep me a prisoner when you know I have committed no crime?"

"Be reasonable, my Lord. If those who brought you here should discover that you live…," the gaoler made a cutting sign across his throat, "…farewell Demeraud."

"But I will protect you once I am free."

Demeraud laughed harshly. "You would not survive one day outside these walls."

"You are wrong," Philip insisted. "I have friends."

"You have no friends, my Lord, no friends in France, at least, and precious few in England I would guess."

"What would you know?" Philip said crossly.

"I know who brought you here and who he serves."

Philip also knew who had brought him to the Bastille, for the memory of the voice in the coach had come back to him.

"Monsieur is not afraid of Louis de Quéroualle," he said.

"Monsieur does what his brother tells him. It is always so. If his Majesty decided it then your fine Monsieur would sacrifice you like that," Demeraud snapped his fingers.

Philip feared he may be right. Monsieur might sulk or weep or throw a tantrum but he had obeyed Louis for so long it had become a habit.

"I don't believe the King even knows I'm here," he told Demeraud.

"Now that is where we differ, my Lord. I am certain that he does."

Morgan returned a little while later. The Welshman was allowed free access in and out of the prison and he slept in Philip's cell.

He had been visiting Athénais de Montespan, as he often did, but he had no good news to bring. She always gave him whatever money he needed to purchase clothes or other commodities for Philip but she still begged for his discretion and constantly warned him against attempting to make contact with anyone else. This day was no different. Philip remained a wanted man, the King was furious with him for flaunting the law and La Reynie had charged him in his absence with the murder of Benoit. He was safer where he was, she stressed. He must bide his time, be patient, let Louis' anger die a little.

"And in the meantime, I die a little each day that I am caged here like an animal, and all on account of the spite of an evil bitch." Philip's hatred of Louise de Quéroualle had grown beyond all reasonable bounds and Morgan's latest message of caution from Athénais only made him more infuriated. "To hell with patience! I have been a gambler all my life. Louis claims affection for me, or he did. Why should I not wager my life upon the King's regard? When he hears how I have been mistreated he will deal leniently with me I am certain."

Morgan's expression showed that he was not so certain. "What would you tell him, that King Charles' mistress had tried to have you killed because you refused to help Charles defeat Lord Shaftesbury?"

"But Louis supported Shaftesbury's endeavours. The proof of that was in the money which we carried across the channel."

"He did not support him openly," Morgan reminded him, "and only to help him oppose Lord Danby because he was responsible for bringing about the peace with Holland. If you send me with a message to King Louis you will be taking an extreme risk, in my opinion."

"And not only with my own life," Philip said despondently. "If you are right then there is no reason in the world why they should not kill you too, since you are my only contact outside this confounded place."

"I would take that chance if you decided on such a course," Morgan said staunchly.

"Yes, my friend, I know you would."

Morgan helped him to his feet. "It's time for your exercise."

Philip nodded resignedly. Movement was still very painful for him, but Morgan insisted that he walk five minutes of every daylight hour around the confines of his cell. This little exercise took most of Philip's strength and all his concentration, so he did not speak again until he stopped to rest, panting, against the cold stone wall.

"Once, Morgan, before any of this happened, I offered you the chance to leave my service and you refused."

"I would still refuse, my Lord."

Philip smiled. "I'm glad of that, for I'd not let you go now for a kingdom, but, loath as I am to lose your company in here, I have reluctantly decided that you can be of greater service to me elsewhere. Will you go to England for me, Morgan, and seek out the Duke of Buckingham?" Buckingham was the one man who Philip could always turn to for help and he could honestly think of no-one else who might be able to aid him now. "Athénais should give you the fare."

"I'll go, if you think it best, but I don't like to leave you alone and at the mercy of that foul Demeraud."

"I think I can cope with Demeraud, provided Athénais can find a way to send him money. It may be that Buckingham can think of some solution, but he must not tell Lord Shaftesbury where I am. He must never know the ease with which I let myself be taken, for it will avail me nothing to attain my freedom if, in doing so, I have lost the respect of the one man upon whom I can rely for my support. To him, and everyone else, he must say simply that I am in Languedoc visiting my mother's family."

"The Earl will be furious that you have ignored his order to return," Morgan warned him.

"Let him be furious. I would sooner he cut some more strips from my back for disobedience than that he dismissed me from his service as unworthy of his trust," Philip said. "In that man's hands lies my future, I do see that now."

"You are still determined to work for him again, after what has happened to you?"

"More determined, for his enemies are now my own. I have never run from danger and I shall not do so now." Philip let Morgan help him back into his chair. "I shall return to England just as soon as I am freed."

Morgan said nothing and Philip knew what was in the servant's mind. "If I am ever freed," added quietly. "How long will you wait for me? A year?"

"Much longer," Morgan assured him.

"No, a year is long enough. Take up residence in my apartment and remain there for one year, if you please. After that consider yourself discharged and seek another master. One with better prospects!"

"No matter what your circumstances, I am content to remain at your side," Morgan said doggedly, "even if it means I must pass my life inside this cell with you."

"And believe me, Morgan, when I say that I would be well content to have you here," Philip said truthfully. He had become quite dependent upon the Welshman, not only physically but mentally as well, and that was a dependence which would remain with him throughout his days. "It pains me very much to let you go but, selfish though I am, I would not wreck your life along with mine. Stay with me just one more month, if you would, and then I shall insist that you depart."

The month passed slowly and yet it seemed to Philip that the day for Morgan to leave still came too soon. Demeraud was no nearer to releasing him and Athénais, though generous with her money, still recommended caution.

Philip remained resolute in his decision to let him go, though he feared his own sanity might be leaving with him.

Buckingham listened in horror as Morgan told him what had happened.

"This is Shaftesbury's fault," he said angrily when the Welshman had done. "If it was not for his pigheadedness in declaring Charles' parliament illegal I would not have ended up in the Tower with him and your master would never have had to flee to France in the first place. Philip should not have got so deeply involved with the man."

Morgan had no argument with that. "Can you help him?"

"I'm not quite sure what I can do," the Duke admitted. "The plain fact is that this is not the time to be asking any favours of the King of France. Louis is still sulking over the marriage of Princess Mary to the Prince of Orange and he is not well disposed towards any Englishman, even me."

Morgan's heart sank. Buckingham had been his best hope. As well as having once been his master's patron, the Duke was one of the most high-ranking and influential men in England.

This did not earn him the esteem of the loyal Morgan, however. "So you will abandon him?" he said disgustedly.

"No, never," Buckingham assured him. "I love Philip like a son. I only meant that there is nothing I can do by way of interceding for him as things now stand. I do, however, have an agent in Paris by the name of Harrington and I will write to him today. He will have a better grasp of the situation there and he may be able to discover a way to aid your master."

Morgan had to be content with that but what neither he nor Buckingham could have suspected was that fortune had begun to take a wayward hand in his master's fate.

The Lieutenant of Police, La Reynie, received a visit from an earnest young lawyer, who had a most interesting tale to tell. It concerned a fortune teller, Mademoiselle Vigoreux, at whose house the lawyer had dined. More particularly, he spoke of a fellow-guest, Mademoiselle Bosse, who had boasted in her cups that she had nearly made her fortune selling poisons to the aristocracy.

La Reynie was a conscientious man, an angel to the destitute and homeless and a fierce campaigner to rid Paris of its vice and crime. Before he had been appointed to office folk had not dared to walk about Paris at night. Now lanterns hung above the streets, no ordinary citizens were allowed to carry arms and there were no safe quarters where law breakers might hide.

La Reynie's greatest problems were no longer the simple crimes carried out openly upon the street but the more covert offences; strange, convenient deaths that never could be proved to be the result of foul play, and with suspects too important to be tackled in the usual manner. Two years previously he had successfully prosecuted the Marquise de Brinvilliers for poisoning. He had been alarmed when she had hinted that the methods she used were common amongst society, although she had named no names.

All this made the lawyer's tale particularly important and La Reynie decided to have both Bosse and Vigoreux arrested. They confessed to everything and named all their associates.

Counted among these associates was Catherine Monvoisin.

The arrests of the fortune-tellers had not escaped the notice of Buckingham's agent, Harrington, nor had the fact that enquiries were being made into the affairs of Catherine Monvoisin, though these were of no significance to him until he received word from Buckingham. Harrington had assumed, along with the rest of Paris, that Philip had gone into hiding but, directly he had been apprised of the true situation, he acted swiftly and effectively.

La Reynie received an anonymous note bearing only six words, as it happened one for each month of Philip's imprisonment.

'Monvoisin - Demeraud, procurer of bodies, Bastille.'

La Reynie pounced.

The King wished to be informed of all developments and La Reynie attended upon him shortly after he had received the mysterious message.

"The gaoler, Demeraud, has confessed to everything, your Majesty, and I have personally carried out an investigation of the prison. It is, I fear, a nest of corruption, controlled by the most venal of men, but it seems this Demeraud is the worst of them. Here is a list of prisoners we have discovered of whom there is no record of admittance. God only knows how many others have died in there."

"Some things are better left alone," Louis said sternly, for it did not suit him to have too much lain bare concerning the Bastille. It had been a convenient place of disposal for many a troublesome courtier or politician, and Louis did not intend to change that.

"Nonetheless we have one prisoner who I am sure will be of special interest to you, unless your Majesty is already aware that he is resident in the Bastille."

By a device known as a lettre de cachet the King could hold anyone he pleased indefinitely without trial or sentence. "Who is he?" he asked La Reynie cautiously.

"Philip Devalle."

Louis looked at him in astonishment. He had not expected that. "How did Philip come to be in the Bastille?"

"He was taken there directly after his duel with Benoit, so Demeraud said, and in a bad state."

"By whose orders was he taken there?"

"Demeraud needed considerable persuasion to divulge that information, but it appears that it was Monsieur Dubois who entrusted him to Demeraud's care with orders that he was to be left to die untouched."

"Dubois you say?" Louis knew only too well whose servant he was. "Yet Lord Devalle did not die."

"No, your Majesty. It appears another personage bid higher for his life, but there the gaoler could not help even if he would.

Before he died under torture he revealed that Lord Devalle's servant was the only go-between, and he has since returned to England."

"What is Lord Devalle's state of health now?" Louis demanded of La Reynie.

"I have no idea. I have not seen him. I thought it wiser to wait until I knew what your Majesty was going to do about him."

"Do? Why set him free of course," Louis said without hesitation.

"But he has broken the law and killed a man by duelling," La Reynie reminded him. "You make a mockery of justice if you let him go free."

"On the contrary, if I do not let him go free then it could be argued that it was myself who had him placed there, and I can scarcely refute that without admitting my ignorance of affairs within my jurisdiction. That would never do. Besides, I like the man and he has served me well. I want him freed."

La Reynie bowed. "I will order his release immediately, your Majesty, but I wish to play no part in it, other than to confirm that he really is who Demeraud said he was."

"As you wish, but I would have him brought straight to me," Louis decided. "I must see for myself what they have done to him but tell him nothing. When he first glimpses me, I will be able to see what his feelings are for a king who has let him languish in prison for so long. It may be that he has turned against me."

"And if so?"

"If so then Philip Devalle would be a dangerous enemy," Louis said slowly. "Far too dangerous to remain at large."

La Reynie nodded, understanding perfectly, and went straight back to the Bastille.

"Have a carriage standing ready and send guards to fetch Lord Devalle," he told the Governor. "He is to be freed, by order of the King."

ॐ

Philip remained unaware of the arrests of the two women and of their relevance to himself. He still attended fastidiously to his toilet and attempted to exercise, as Morgan had made him do, but without his beloved servant his life was so intolerable that at times he wished that he could end it. His sole companion, after Morgan had left, was Demeraud, who had visited him several times a day, sometimes playing cards with him or telling him coarse jokes. Bored and lonely as he was, Philip found the gaoler's company no less wearisome than before. The brandy that Demeraud brought him did a great deal to compensate for his obnoxiousness, however. It dulled the pain that nagged at Philip constantly and lifted his mind, for a precious short while, from his troubles.

A month had passed and Philip, despairing that he had lost Morgan for nothing, grew near demented as each hopeless day followed another. Sinister changes were beginning inside him. He no longer desired his own death but was now utterly determined to survive his troubles. He had scores to settle and it was revenge which drove him through each dreary day of deprivation and discomfort. He forced himself to fight the pain, which seemed at times to grow worse rather than better and consoled himself with the thought of the opportunities he would have in Shaftesbury's service to repay Louise de Quéroualle for her treachery and the suffering he would cause her fellow Papists.

Once or twice Philip contemplated killing Demeraud and trying to escape but the prospect of so much physical effort was too daunting, He was still far from fit, and he had abandoned the idea, along with any hope of Buckingham's intervention.

He clicked his tongue irritably as his cell door was unlocked.

"And about time, Demeraud, you unfeeling animal. What do you mean by leaving me for so long with only this foul Paris bread to eat and one pathetic candle? Don't I pay you well enough?"

He stopped suddenly and blinked in surprise. Even by the poor light of his one candle he could see that it was not Demeraud who had entered but two uniformed guards.

"What is your name?" one of them asked.

"I am Lord Philip Devalle," he answered steadily, still reeling a little from the shock of seeing them, for in all the time he had been a prisoner he had seen none but Demeraud.

"Then you are to come with us."

Philip had no idea whether the arrival of the two men was going to prove to be a good thing for him or not, and his heart was pounding as he left his cell and walked along corridors and up steps until he emerged into the courtyard.

It had been a long while since he had been out in the open air and, although it was dark, the summer night seemed warm to him after the chill of his stone cell. A coach waited by the gates, its blinds pulled fully down, and he was bundled unceremoniously into it with one of the guards on either side of him. Before the door closed a third man materialised in the darkness of the courtyard and peered in, holding up a lantern.

"Yes, that's him."

Philip thought it was La Reynie's face he saw in the lantern light, but he could not be sure.

They set off at a fast pace but Philip had no notion of where they were going. He was calm now and almost resigned to his fate. The stealthy way he had been spirited from the Bastille did not bode well for him, he feared, and the silent presence of the two guards reinforced his worst suspicions.

The coach door was opened as soon as they stopped, as though they were expected, and the guards escorted him through a doorway and up a flight of steps.

After so many months of inactivity, the speed with which things were now happening was causing Philip's head to spin, and when another door opened in front of him he stared around quite blankly.

The guards had not accompanied him through that door, but there was a figure, dressed in a plain brown coat, at the other end of the room, facing away from him. As the man turned Philip recognised him and went down upon one knee.

It was King Louis.

Louis came toward him and, from his horrified expression, Philip guessed that he must bear little resemblance to the courtier who the King had shown around his gardens.

"Come, rise and greet me," Louis said gruffly, searching his face as though to read his thoughts, "or have they cut out your tongue in the Bastille?"

"I am still able to speak, your Majesty, although I fear I am not so able as I was in other respects," Philip said, getting up slowly and with difficulty.

"So I see." Louis was watching him with evident concern. "Do you suffer very much?"

"More some days than others," Philip said, for it seemed that, even when he felt well, an awkward action or sudden movement could cause a stabbing sensation in his side of such intensity that he would writhe in helpless agony. "It is with the greatest joy in all the world that I behold your Majesty again, although I know not how it came about."

"La Reynie is conducting an investigation. By good fortune one of the suspects was your gaoler. He was persuaded to submit a full confession and included in it a list of all his prisoners. Your name was amongst them but, until today, you must believe that I was unaware of your imprisonment. Neither do I know who perpetrated the deed. Your gaoler did not disclose that before he died."

The hard eyes above the prominent Bourbon nose defied Philip to disbelieve what he had said, but Philip had learned the way of the world a long, long while ago and he was not fooled.

He could believe that Louis knew nothing of his imprisonment but, having discovered it, it was inconceivable that he should not have also discovered it was Louise de Quéroualle who had been behind it. There were loyalties to be considered. After all Louise was Louis' own agent, placed in Whitehall to bend King Charles toward French policies. Philip guessed she would receive a private reprimand for her spitefulness, Marie Benoit would be permitted to retire into obscurity whilst Demeraud, the least guilty of the three, had been made the scapegoat.

Despite the injustice of it all, Philip did not care too much about the fate of the greedy gaoler but he greatly regretted the loss of six months of his life, and at such a cost to his health. He was not even sure what was going to happen to him now, for he had still committed a crime by breaking one of Louis most stringent laws.

He decided to throw himself upon Louis' mercy and confess to Benoit's murder.

Louis waved his hand to signify that the matter was not worthy to be pursued. "It is true that I was angry when I first heard of it, but I called off the search for you some time ago when I presumed you had managed to escape the country. Benoit's death I will accept as misadventure."

"Then I am free to go?" Philip said uncertainly.

"Completely free," Louis assured him, "but there is a question I would have you answer for me, before you go. Your gaoler could have let you die yet he did not because, he said, your servant paid him a considerable sum of money. I am curious as to where he got that money, since your property had been seized at the time, and even more curious as to how he found out where you were."

Philip managed a wan smile. "Morgan is a most resourceful man, your Majesty."

Louis nodded, as though that was the answer he had expected. "I will learn all in time, you must know that," he said. "Louvois and La Reynie have suggested that I appoint a special committee to deal with the investigation into these women who call themselves fortune-tellers. They perform foul, irreligious rituals, preparing all manner of disgusting substances and, it appears, their clients are amongst the most important people in the land. A disconcerting thought, do you not find it so?"

"Only if this committee does not find them out," Philip said blandly.

"Oh, it will. That is why I cannot leave this matter to the Parliament. There is scarcely a gentleman of breeding, or a lady come to that, who cannot claim some parliamentary relative, and they could hardly be expected to mete out justice upon their own kin."

Philip did not answer him. He would never betray Athénais but he guessed she would shortly be betrayed by her own past.

"What do you intend to do now?" Louis asked him.

Philip gave him a wry look. "I believe your Majesty would find me somewhat inadequate to fight against the Orangemen at present."

"I no longer fight the Orangeman," Louis said heavily. "You will not, of course, be aware of it but I am about to sign a treaty at Nijmegen pledging peace with Holland, though not before your country, and even your friend, the Duke of Monmouth, has fought for him against me."

Philip had not been aware of it and he expressed his condolences.

"The English are a tricky race," Louis said. "You, now, are half French and I would still like you to stay with me. You will be safe now, I will personally guarantee it."

It was a generous invitation but Philip knew what he had to do. "Your Majesty is gracious. I will be pleased to remain in France until I have regained a little of my strength but then I must return to England."

"To the Earl of Shaftesbury? See what enemies he makes for you?"

"I cannot spend my life hiding from my enemies, your Majesty. Besides, I believe I can trust Lord Shaftesbury to protect me."

Louis shrugged. "As you please. Perhaps Monsieur can change your mind. He has been worried to distraction over you. You ought to see him right away."

"I would like to go to my house first," Philip said, for did not feel up to dealing with Monsieur's tears and embraces just yet.

"Of course. You should be safe enough now, but have a care, for it is Friday, which is an unlucky day."

When Philip got back to his house he found that nothing had been disturbed, although his servants had been turned out. The place had an empty and forlorn feel and he decided he would visit Monsieur after all and arrange to stay with him at the Palais Royale until Morgan could rejoin him. Philip particularly craved the sight of Morgan and, besides, he knew he would need the Welshman's help if he was to regain sufficient strength for the journey home and all that awaited him in England.

He was exhausted, and still unable to quite take in all that had happened to him in the last few hours. He was in pain too, for he had walked much further than he was accustomed to lately, and he poured himself a large glass of brandy. As he did so he caught a glimpse of himself in a full-length mirror. There was no longer any pleasure in the sight. He had lost a great deal of weight and his face was deathly pale, with dark shadows beneath his blue eyes.

"A pox upon you, Quéroualle!"

He turned away in disgust and then froze, for he had heard a creak upon the stairs. Someone else was in the house.

"Perhaps you were right, Demeraud, when you predicted I would not survive one day outside the Bastille," he muttered. "Well, by God, I'll not go without a fight."

A sword hung on the wall behind him, the sword that he had taken into battle with him, and he took it down, but even that small amount of effort hurt him and Philip realised that he was incapable of using the weapon.

"Hell and damnation!" He backed against the wall, determined he would rise above the pain. He laid the sword down and, instead, unwound the linen band from around his neck, edging his way round the room as silently as he could until he was positioned behind the door.

The door opened a crack and then swung fully open. Philip recognised Dubois. He was holding a pistol.

Philip leapt at him, taking him totally by surprise. He managed to slip the linen band around the Dubois' throat and the pistol crashed down to the floor. He thrust his knee into the Frenchman's back and tightened the cloth around his neck until Dubois' tongue protruded from his mouth and he ceased to struggle.

Philip let him drop to the floor. He was panting from his exertions but he felt no pain now, only the sweet joy of revenge.

He downed the brandy he had poured and gave a wry smile as he looked down upon the man who had caused him so much suffering.

"Friday certainly turned out to be an unlucky day for you, Dubois!"

SEVEN

Philip raised his head and smiled at the welcome sight of the English coast, clearly visible in the brilliant August sunshine. "We're home, Morgan."

Morgan joined him and they stood together, leaning idly on the rail and inhaling the cool breeze that came from the cliffs, carrying with it the scent of sheep and thyme from the uplands.

Morgan glanced over to him. "This is a moment I feared you would never enjoy, my Lord."

"Nor would I, but for you," Philip said. "You have been a tyrant to me, mind!"

It was the truth. In the weeks since Philip's release from prison Morgan had bullied him unmercifully. Philip had learned to ride a horse again and to wield a sword, but he was neither as strong nor as fit as he once had been and he had often cursed his own inadequacies. Morgan had driven him on, encouraging him when he grew despondent and sometimes forcing him beyond the limits of his endurance. The sharp, stabbing pains in his side could still render him momentarily helpless but most of the time his discomfort was reduced to a nagging ache, which he had learned to tolerate.

The packet advanced quickly and first picturesque view of the port was somewhat marred as the details became clearer. The castle around which the town of Dover was built was badly decayed and so was the harbour, its fairway piled with shingle deposited in the rough weather.

The landing formalities were swiftly completed, for the

Customs Officers remembered Philip well, although he cut a very different figure now, for he was still thin and had taken to dressing in black, since he no longer wished to draw so much attention to himself.

Leaving their luggage to follow by wagon, Philip and Morgan set off across the downs on fast post horses. They covered the twelve miles to Canterbury in less than an hour and, although Philip's scar was causing him more nuisance than he cared to admit, he felt able to press on to the next relay. The following day they made for Gravesend to catch the wherry that would take them to London but, as usual, the harbour was blocked with trading vessels, from Newcastle colliers to the big merchant ships bound for the Mediterranean, and it was another day before they could commence the last stage of their journey.

For four hours the wherry drifted slowly up river to the capital, but Philip was not impatient. He had kept up a punishing pace for one who, only a short while ago, had barely been able to walk around his cell. As the boat rounded the bend at Limehouse and Philip saw the distinctive outline of the Tower and, beyond it, the great arched bridge, he could finally believe that he was home.

London afforded an impressive welcome to any traveller but Philip had good reason to consider himself most fortunate to be seeing it again.

"You have certainly taken your time, Philip Devalle." Shaftesbury sat back in his chair and regarded Philip with a frown.

"I have been in London barely a day, my Lord," Philip protested.

"That is not what I meant, as you well know," Shaftesbury snapped. "My message to you was sent months ago. Were you not at your house in Paris?"

"Not all of the time," Philip said carefully. "I went to visit with my mother's family in Languedoc."

"So I heard. I was not aware that the Pasquiers were so fond of you," the Earl said dryly. "More likely you have been in some sort of trouble. In future you will place our cause above all else. These are difficult times for us. When you endanger yourself, you endanger our whole party and, what is unforgivable, you endanger my plans. Now give me your assurance that you will not be distracted again from our purpose."

Philip was relieved. Knowing Shaftesbury's temper, he had expected worse. "My Lord, I hereby place my life at your disposal," he declared in a theatrical tone.

"Pretty words," the Earl muttered. "I hope you mean them. And what is all this?" He indicated Philip's plain black outfit. "Some new affectation?"

"I no longer choose to be a Gentleman of Fashion," Philip told him.

"I don't believe it. You have been too long a peacock to become a raven!" The Earl's sharp eyes scrutinised him closer. "You are a shadow of what you were when I last saw you, man. Are you ill or do you have the pox?"

"Neither," Philip said, somewhat irritably. "You will find me fit enough for your business. I presume you have some work for me to do?"

"You may depend I did not summon you back to enjoy the delights of Saint Bartholomew's Fair! Have you seen Monmouth yet?"

Philip had, for Monmouth would never have forgiven him if he had not called upon him the instant he was back in London. Besides, Philip had wanted to ascertain from the Duke the kind of reception he was likely to receive from Shaftesbury! "He says that many have pledged their support."

"I now need some undertaking upon which they can be employed," Shaftesbury said. "Make no mistake, Philip, this campaign must be planned as carefully as any you have fought in the field. London must be plunged into a state of blind hysteria that will undermine men's values and obliterate their consciences."

Philip raised an eyebrow. "And I am to be the perpetrator of this diabolical chaos?"

"You are more than equal to the task," Shaftesbury said. Just then a female voice sounded outside the door and he smiled. "It seems you are about to meet Theresa, who is the only other person I can trust."

"Your mistress?"

"You will find her quite devoted to me and loyal to our interests. I thought she might assist you."

Philip did not relish that prospect at all, but he had too much at stake to risk it upon such a minor issue. In any case he knew that Shaftesbury's amours were usually short-lived.

A second later Theresa entered, unannounced, and kissed the Earl affectionately. Philip noticed that she was small, like the Earl himself, and unfashionably slender, but the thing he noticed most about her was her hair, which was a vivid shade of auburn.

"Theresa, this is Lord Devalle," Shaftesbury told her.

Philip had tactfully looked away, but he turned back now as Shaftesbury introduced them.

Someone with more art might have been able to dissemble but Theresa made no effort to hide her feelings when she saw him. The eagerness left her face and she stared at him disbelievingly. "*You* are Lord Devalle?"

Philip had never before been greeted in that tone by a woman. It reminded him, more poignantly than anything else could have done, how much he must have altered. Theresa's slight had stung him like a stroke from Henry's whip. His smile died on his lips and he appraised her in a single, withering glance. "Do I detect a faint note of disappointment?"

Theresa blushed scarlet. "Why, no, my Lord," she assured him, but Philip knew otherwise.

"Theresa is attached to the Queen's household," Shaftesbury said, watching them both steadily. "By using her powers of observation as she goes about her duties she has made herself indispensable to me. You have my permission to engage her services in any capacity of which I approve and I am certain you will find her a useful ally."

Philip tossed his head. "I shall be better able to assess her worth when I have judged the value of the information she obtains."

"I don't know whether you will judge this to be of any value, my Lord, but it appears the King's life has been threatened," Theresa said, sounding piqued.

Shaftesbury leaned forward in his chair. "By whom?"

"I'm not quite certain," she confessed, "but a man named Kirkby waylaid his Majesty in Saint James' Park this afternoon and insisted he was in danger from an assassin's bullet."

"How do you know this?" the Earl said.

"The King confided it to me himself," she said smugly. "I try to walk in the park when he is there and I often managed to converse with him. I saw them talking together and I asked the King who he was and why he was muttering so alarmingly to himself as he walked away."

"Is Charles taking him seriously?" Shaftesbury said.

"I don't think so. He called Kirkby a crank to me and an over-zealous Protestant, which is intriguing, but I know he did agree to discuss the matter further with him."

"And how does he know this Kirkby?"

"Charles said Kirkby sometimes helped him in his laboratory, but I have found out since that he is a bankrupt merchant who now works as a tax gatherer for Lord Danby."

"Danby, eh?" The Earl looked interested at the mention of his old political rival. "We need to find out more. What a pity you cannot accompany Charles to Windsor tomorrow."

Theresa had only been at Court a short while and, although Shaftesbury had managed to procure her a minor place amongst the Queen's ladies, she was not sufficiently well established to be granted an invitation to accompany the King and Queen to Windsor Castle.

The look which Philip cast in her direction was not without a hint of triumph, even though he knew it was a little unworthy of him. "I shall be going to Windsor," he informed them. "The Duke of Monmouth gave me a personal invitation from the King."

"Why, that is excellent news," Shaftesbury said, "although I can't help but wonder at his motives."

"Perhaps he intends to make me another proposition, or it may be that he merely wants me to see his new fresco paintings! Whatever the reason, I thought I ought to go. Now if there is nothing else that you require of me I shall repair to Pall Mall where, I understand, Nell has arranged a small entertainment in honour of my homecoming."

"By all means. Theresa, go with him as far as Whitehall and see if you cannot discover the outcome of Kirkby's interview with the King."

Theresa looked dismayed, but she accompanied Philip to his carriage. She stared open-mouthed at the magnificent black and gold conveyance, and at Jonathon and Ned, so that Philip was sure he had impressed her in that, at least, if in nothing else!

Philip opened the door for her himself and she climbed in without a word and sat as far away from him as she could.

It was not yet dark as they left the Earl's house in Aldersgate Street and the Thames was still crowded with small craft, some sporting gay ribbons and streamers. Philip watched them, reminded of carefree Summer days so many years ago. Lost in his memories, he took little notice of Theresa but he was aware that she was sneaking furtive glances at him.

He turned toward her after a while. "When did you join us?"

His question seemed to take her by surprise. "My family live near Lord Shaftesbury's estate in Dorset."

"That was not what I asked."

Theresa's colour rose. "I came to Court in March, my Lord."

"And what have you achieved in that time, apart from finding your way into Shaftesbury's bed, of course?"

"I believe I am well thought of by the King," she said lamely.

"Really? I see I must not underestimate your capabilities!"

Philip was well aware that he was making her feel uncomfortable but he did not care, for she had hurt his feelings more than she could ever have guessed. He wondered what in the world Shaftesbury saw in her. Quite apart from the brightness of her hair, which he disliked, Theresa was no beauty to his mind. She had elfin-like features and slanting grey eyes and her figure was that of a child compared with the voluptuous Athénais.

He said nothing more to her until they arrived at Whitehall. Theresa swiftly reached out to open the door for herself, but he stayed her arm. No matter what his own feelings might be, Shaftesbury was evidently intending to entrust Theresa to his care and he knew he would have to look out for her if he did not wish to suffer the Earl's wrath on her account.

"Do you presume you would retain Charles' favour if your sympathies were discovered?" he said.

"I have nothing to fear, my Lord. I am not working against King Charles."

"He may not agree with you in that. Take care."

He made his tone one of command rather than concern and she nodded obediently.

"Off you go, then. I know you're in a hurry to escape me."

She took him at his word and leapt hastily out of the coach.

"So the great lover did not impress you then?"

Theresa's maid, Bet, had listened merrily, but without much sympathy, to the tale of her mortification. Bet was a pretty, spirited girl of eighteen, Theresa's own age, sharp-tongued but willing, if not always outwardly respectful.

"No, not at all. Oh, he was handsome enough, I suppose," Theresa allowed, "but so pale and plainly dressed, and not at all like a soldier. I thought he would be dashing and gallant, but I found him formidable."

"Are you still going to Mistress Gwynne's house with the rest of the Queen's ladies?" Bet picked up the dress she had laid out for the purpose.

"Indeed I am not," Theresa said decisively. "Let them all fuss over the man if they like. I have more important things to do."

She went directly to the King's chambers and spoke with the guard, who told her that Charles had visitors in the Red Room.

"Who are they?" she asked him.

"Mr. Kirkby is one, and it's the second time he's been here in as many hours," the guard confided. As to other, it is old Dr. Tonge, though why the King should wish to see him is beyond me. I know his brother, John, a captain in the Coldstreams, and even he says Israel Tonge is as mad as a May moon!"

Charles was beginning to think that as well when Israel Tonge produced a sheaf of papers, which were supposed to be proof that it was the Catholics who were plotting against his life. Tonge's evidence for this consisted of a testimony written by one who claimed to have held a position of trust amongst the Jesuits. A few men were mentioned by name, including the Queen's physician, Sir George Wakefield, who was apparently planning to poison him, and it was also alleged that Father Bedingfield, who was the confessor to Charles' brother, the Duke of York, had been sent by the Jesuits as a spy!

Charles decided to turn the matter over to Lord Danby. With any luck the whole thing would be quietly resolved before he even returned from Windsor.

He had just dismissed Kirkby and Tonge when Louise de Quéroualle appeared.

"What did they want?" she demanded.

Charles had no intention of telling either her or his brother about any accusations of a Catholic plot, otherwise he knew he would get no peace from the pair of them.

"Nothing important, Fubbs. Have you heard that Nell is giving a reception tonight?" he said, before she could press the point.

Louise sniffed disdainfully. "In honour of some actor, I suppose, or street-seller with whom she feels at home."

"No, in honour of Philip Devalle, as it happens, who, as you must have heard, is back from France having overcome, it would seem, every considerable obstacle that you set in his path."

"Devalle is of no consequence to me," Louise said airily. "I don't even know where he has been all these months."

"You certainly know that he spent some of them in the Bastille, because it was your agent who put him there."

"You knew?"

"Of course I knew. I do have some agents of my own." Charles told her pointedly.

"Yet you did nothing?"

"Why should I? He was less trouble to me where he was," Charles said. "Unfortunately, my cousin Louis is fond of him and had him freed directly he discovered his situation."

Charles decided not to tell her that is was through Buckingham's intervention that Louis discovered him. It did not do to give Louise too many people to hate!

"I never wanted him imprisoned in the first place," Louise said.

"I guessed that. You wanted him killed, but in such a way that no suspicions would be roused, and who, even amongst his closest friends, would be surprised to learn that Philip Devalle had died duelling over a woman?"

"It should have worked. I had reckoned without Dubois' incompetence and some blasted gaoler who would keep him alive to line his pockets."

"Well if it is any consolation you did partly succeed. I have heard that, from the look of him, Philip's health is on the decline."

"Hah! Then I shall see him fade away before my eyes. That will afford me exquisite satisfaction," Louise said contentedly.

"What a pity you are not on better terms with Nell." Charles gave her a wicked grin. "You might have seen him for yourself this evening."

For a moment Louise did look tempted, but her pride overcome her curiosity.

"I would not demean myself by associating with that woman," she said haughtily. "I never thought I would see the day when actresses could be appointed Ladies of your wife's Privy Chamber."

"No matter. You will see him soon enough, for I have invited him to Windsor. His recent misfortunes should have dulled his appetite for intrigue and it may be I can persuade him to turn against Shaftesbury now."

Lord Danby was a hard-headed northerner. After the first reading of Tonge's evidence he dismissed it as pure fabrication, but when he'd had more time to reflect upon it an entirely fresh aspect of the affair presented itself to him.

Despite the marriage he had arranged between the Princess Mary and the Prince of Orange, Danby was not really popular with his own party and he had many bitter enemies in the Opposition, Shaftesbury had recently defeated him in his efforts to maintain the armed forces and Danby was constantly criticised, regardless of the fact that, since he had been appointed Lord Treasurer, he had pulled the country through its financial difficulties. If he lacked Shaftesbury's wit and personal charm it was hardly his fault and yet, unfairly, even Charles displayed a greater respect for Shaftesbury's statesmanship.

Three years before, an attempt had been made to impeach him and Danby badly feared another might be successful. At the very least the publication of this so-called plot would serve to draw attention from himself, but there was quite another way that it might benefit his career. If the Protestants were called to unite in defence of their sovereign he would have won his argument justifying the need for a standing army!

Before he left to accompany the King to Windsor he contacted Israel Tonge and told him that if any more conclusive evidence could be found to substantiate his accusations he was to dispatch word of it immediately through Floyd, his messenger.

Philip travelled to Windsor with the Duke of Buckingham.

"But for you I might still be in the Bastille," he reminded the Duke gratefully as Buckingham's coach rattled over the dry Surrey roads.

"Think nothing of it, dear boy. I've got you out of scrapes before."

"This was a bit more than a scrape, George. Louise de Quéroualle was responsible and I will avenge myself on the bitch if it takes me my whole life."

"I don't think you should be too hasty," Buckingham said worriedly. "You could not produce the slightest proof that she was behind it and if you make rash accusations you will find yourself in a great deal of trouble."

"Accusations? I am not that stupid," Philip said. "My revenge will take quite another form. By the time I have helped Shaftesbury to poison the people's minds against the Catholics, folk will spit as they say the name of Quéroualle."

"Are you absolutely sure of what you're doing?" Buckingham said. "In my opinion Shaftesbury has already shown his hand too plain. He even demanded his own cook in the Tower because, he claimed, the Catholics were trying to poison him!"

"It was through you that I first began to work for the Earl," Philip pointed out. "You were the one who told me to make friends with him."

"I wish now that I had never done so," Buckingham said feelingly. "He is ambitious far beyond the dreams of other men, He will stop at nothing to gain the power he wants and he is too stubborn to heed the warnings Charles has given him."

"So are you for him still, or not?"

"I will help where I can," Buckingham promised, "for, as you know, I have no love for the Duke of York, but I'm damned if I shall let Shaftesbury lead me to the Tower again. I should have done what you did and fled the country."

"It might have been better if I hadn't, as matters turned out," Philip said ruefully. "I would have been safe from that bitch if I had been in the Tower with you."

"Just be careful of what you say to Charles about Quéroualle," Buckingham advised. "He loves her more than he has ever loved any woman."

"More fool him! Don't worry, George, I am the perfect courtier, remember? I know all the pretty words to say. You taught me!"

Buckingham smiled. "So I did! Well don't overdo it. He's not Louis, you know."

"Indeed he is not, more's the pity!"

"Lord Danby doesn't look too happy," Philip remarked to Monmouth, for the Lord Treasurer's face was grim. "I wonder what's upset him."

"Who knows? I did notice a messenger speaking with him just now," Monmouth recalled. "That might have something to do with it."

"It might. I will endeavour to discover what was in the message, when I have the chance. I'm sure Lord Shaftesbury would be interested to know."

"Do be careful, Philip," Monmouth begged him. "I don't want any more misfortunes to befall you."

"But every action that I take is in your interest," Philip said.

"I know that, but they are watching you now. And I'd not have you harmed for my sake."

"Many men will probably die for your sake before this is all over," Philip said softly.

"But not you," Monmouth insisted. "I would sooner sacrifice all my ambitions than risk you."

Philip looked at him despairingly. "My friend, you always were too sentimental!"

Charles swept into the room then, casting his eyes over his assembled guests. They came to rest on Philip.

"Lord Devalle! I feared you would decline to take advantage of my invitation."

Philip bowed, an action he could still perform with grace, if not with so much ease as before. "Your Majesty, after being deprived of your presence for so long I am only too delighted to have been afforded the pleasure of attending upon you once again."

Philip knew that the smooth words of a practised courtier had never made much impression on Charles, but the King smiled, as though pleased. "Give me your arm, my Lord, for I would walk with you."

Philip obliged and they passed out through the open doors onto the lawn, for it was a fine, mild evening.

"From the length of your stay in France I must deduce that the diversions of my cousin's Court are more pleasurable than those of mine," Charles began conversationally.

"Not at all. French and English women are pretty much the same, I have found. They delight our senses but, if we give them opportunity, they destroy us." Philip laughed to lighten his words but he still knew his meaning would be clear enough.

Charles glanced at him. "You are a cynic for your age, my Lord. Your years at Court must have done that to you, for you have been at Whitehall nearly as long as I have. I recall the day your father presented you to me, what were you then, fourteen?"

"Thirteen, you Majesty," Philip corrected him, wondering where this particular topic was leading.

"Indeed! Such a handsome youth and you looked at me with a boldness I had rarely seen in one so young. I should have had the wit to train you to me from the start but, instead, I let Buckingham take you and now I fancy it is too late to take you back. Or is it?"

"I outgrew the Duke's patronage long ago," Philip said evenly.

"But you have found another benefactor, one who has taught you more than Buckingham ever did. I will be direct with you, you are dependent upon the Earl of Shaftesbury, are you not?"

"Shaftesbury has been generous to me," Philip admitted guardedly.

"He has bought you, my Lord, and he chooses his merchandise with care. I have always known you were a clever man, though you try to conceal it with your affectations, and Shaftesbury knows that too. Are you clever enough, I wonder, to realise that one can serve one's King and not be seen to do so?"

Charles paused, as though waiting for an answer, but Philip said nothing. He already guessed at what was coming but he was intrigued to find out just what he was going to be offered this time to betray Shaftesbury.

"You do know what it is I want of you?" Charles said.

"Yes, I believe I do."

"I want you to continue to work for the Earl but pledge yourself to me and keep me informed of his plans."

"In other words, to relinquish my honour."

"There would be many advantages in such a sacrifice," Charles said. "Until the trap is sprung you would be practically immune from the law."

"And fittingly rewarded after Shaftesbury's head is laid upon the block?" Philip guessed.

"Men have been created earls for less."

"As you say, your Majesty, yet it has been my experience that a title is of very little practical value."

"Not even if it is accompanied by a sizeable portion of land and a sum liberal enough to properly signify your sovereign's gratitude?"

Philip thought Charles' offer was far better than the one which Louise de Quéroualle had made to him, of her body, but he still shook his head. "I fear my earldom must be purchased by some other means, your Majesty, for there is not a sum large enough in your kingdom to persuade me to what you ask."

The hard lines around Charles' mouth deepened. "It seems I was mistaken in thinking you a clever man. You are a fool, Philip Devalle. You might have saved your treacherous skin."

"I regret, Sire, that the terms of its salvation are unacceptable to me."

"Very well," Charles said presently, when he had completed another length of the lawn, still upon Philip's arm, as though his company was most agreeable to him. "Have it your way, but be warned. Should you once, my Lord, just once overstep the mark of prudence I shall ruin you."

"Then I had best endeavour to be prudent."

Charles rarely let his annoyance show. He held out his hand, which Philip dutifully kissed. "This refusal may cost you dear, Lord Devalle."

Philip sighed sadly as he watched Charles walk away, straight and dignified, every inch a monarch.

Such a pity he could not be trusted!

EIGHT

Philip was back in London before the week was out, and he had discovered the information Danby's messenger had brought him.

"Israel Tonge forged some treasonable letters, no doubt in an attempt to give some substance to all this," he told Shaftesbury. "The fool addressed them to Father Bedingfield, I suppose intending them to be intercepted by Lord Danby and used in evidence of his plotting against the King's life."

"So what went wrong?"

"What went wrong was that Bedingfield met the post boy first and received the letters himself! He showed them to the Duke of York who, in turn showed them to the King, though it has not been made public yet."

"So the game's afoot," Shaftesbury said gleefully. "How did you find out?"

"I have a friend in the Duchess of York's household."

"Henriette McClure," Shaftesbury guessed. "Is that woman still in love with you?"

"Naturally! She's still pursuing me too, since she has not yet found a titled husband to her liking."

"How very fortunate for our purposes! Do you happen to know where Tonge resides?"

"Yes, in the Barbican."

"You had better pay him a visit. If he is left to manage the affair much longer he will destroy this Popish Plot before we even have a chance to exploit it!"

"Why not send Theresa?" Philip suggested, for he didn't particularly relish dealing with religious fanatics. "She is anxious to be useful and Tonge might be less wary of a woman."

"Good idea! She can assure him of our sympathies and then promise him the support of an influential patron if he can put a valid case before the King's Council."

"Will he trust me?" Theresa wondered, when the Earl had told her what he wanted her to do.

"Probably not, but he must still see the sense of the advice you offer him, which will be to go to Justice Godfrey and swear a deposition of all he knows."

"Why Godfrey?"

Shaftesbury patted her cheek. "He once attempted to indict a friend of mine, the Earl of Pembroke, for murder. In return for that he is going to be awarded the dubious privilege of fame! Go to it, my pet, before the cautious Danby perceives what opportunity slides through his fumbling fingers and decides to take action for himself."

Theresa found the address Shaftesbury had given her in the Barbican but Tonge was already leaving the house when she arrived. He was a strange looking man, she thought, short and bent, with whiskers that seemed to sprout all over his face. She followed him at a discreet distance but it wasn't easy. He dodged between passers-by like a little imp, all the while mumbling loudly to himself, so that several people turned to stare.

She recalled the guard's description of him. "Mad as a May moon," she muttered. "I see why I was given this assignment. I'm sure the great Lord Devalle wouldn't want to waste his precious time dealing with the likes of mad old Doctor Tonge! "

Eventually he dived into a coffee house. Theresa was a little daunted, for she had never been in a coffee house. She paused for a moment to compose herself and then went in after him.

She spied Tonge straight away, in the company of another man, and shook her head in disbelief. This one was almost as conspicuous in his appearance as the man himself! About half Tonge's age, he had a thick bull neck of the same purple hue as his complexion, a chin so large that his mouth seemed to be in the very centre of his face and a large wart above one of his small, sunken eyes.

"This gets worse!" Her first instinct was to dodge out of there, but she knew she couldn't. Shaftesbury had given her a job to do and she had to prove to him that she was worthy of his trust.

The two men sat in a corner, their heads close together so that none should hear their conversation, and on the table between them were some papers. She had no idea who the second person might be but it occurred to her that she may have inadvertently stumbled across Tonge's mysterious witness.

She resolved to at least determine the nature of the documents they were discussing and, taking a deep breath, she crossed the room purposefully and seated herself at their table.

Abruptly the two men fell silent.

"Doctor Israel Tonge, I believe."

"Waal rarely!"

It was Tonge's companion who had spoken and Theresa stared at him in astonishment. He appeared to have a defect in his speech, for the sound he had just emitted might have been taken for the bray of a donkey.

"Way aye declaare," he continued. "This fain laayday requires reminding of her manners to distaarb two gentlemen engaayed in prayvat talk."

As her ears became more attuned to the high-pitched bleat Theresa realised that he was, indeed, speaking English but with such an excessively affected drawl that the words were distorted practically out of recognition.

It was a fashionable trait but even Lord Sunderland, the instigator of the fad, did not go to those extremes.

Theresa resisted the temptation to laugh and turned to him politely.

"Your pardon, sir, but I have business of a confidential nature to discuss with Doctor Tonge."

"I'll have you know that Doctor Tonge has no secrets from me," the stranger whined in his ridiculous accent, attempting to gather up the pages that were spread over the table.

Theresa was gratified for that piece of information, and more convinced than ever that he was Tonge's witness, particularly since she had managed to see what was written on the top sheet!

Shaftesbury listened closely as she related her encounter with Tonge and his companion. "You say his name is Oates?"

"Titus Oates, according to the documents, which he had called his Narrative. I am certain he is their witness."

"So Tonge really does have a witness," Shaftesbury said. "I hope he has trained him well. Would he impress the Council?"

Theresa pulled face. "He will not impress the King with his manner, but he does have a distinctive kind of speech, so he may be used to performing before an audience."

"An actor?"

Theresa shook her head. "Too ungainly."

"Might he perhaps be an orator upon a different kind of stage, say, a clergyman?"

Theresa thought back to the only clergyman that she remembered, John Highmore, the kindly village Rector at Wimborne St. Giles. "Oh no, my Lord, he could not be a clergyman. He seemed rather evil."

Shaftesbury smiled at that. "All men of God are not men of goodness, my innocent little sweetheart!"

They were in an upper room of the King's Head Tavern, and the Green Ribbon Club was holding a boisterous meeting below.

Shaftesbury was not yet ready to disclose his plans to them but he sent for Philip after Theresa had left and told him what she had discovered and that Tonge had agreed to visit Justice Godfrey and swear a deposition of all he knew.

"Shall we ever get the people to swallow such nonsense?" Philip wondered.

"The more nonsensical the better!" Shaftesbury reckoned. "If we can't bring them to swallow worse than this we shall never do any good with them."

"But what of the King? He may decide to take action against the accusers rather than the accused," Philip pointed out.

"Charles dare not lift a finger against us, in case it is rumoured that he, too, leans toward Rome."

"Maybe." Philip did not entirely share Shaftesbury's opinion of Charles' character and was beginning to have misgivings about the whole thing. "Why did you not use William Waller as the Justice? He is a member of the Green Ribbon Club whilst Godfrey has some Papist friends. He may warn them."

"Let him. It will do no good," the Earl said grimly. "I want you to visit this Titus Oates tomorrow. Frighten him a little and then buy him. With luck you can persuade him to discard Israel Tonge altogether, for he has played his part. Oates, I fancy, is a man with ambitions beyond any frail vision of heavenly justice! More likely a professional deceiver motivated by nothing nobler than greed. Theresa knows where he lives in Vauxhall, for his address was written on the papers she saw, in fact it might be a good idea if she went with you, since Oates already knows her."

Philip could think of only one thing which would make the prospect of frightening and buying Titus Oates any less appealing, and that was having to take Theresa with him to do it.

Theresa arrived at his apartments just before midday and Morgan showed her in. Philip thought she appeared to be a little nervous of the Welshman although, now that Philip considered it, Morgan did look quite formidable, especially with half his ear missing!

The first thing to catch her attention was the full-length portrait of himself in military uniform. Philip had arranged to have it shipped over from France and it dominated the room. She stared at it for quite a while and Philip wondered what was going on in her head, although, when he glanced at it and then at himself in a mirror, he thought he could guess.

He feared he had changed a great deal from those days when he had ridden off to war with Condé.

She turned to him but he concentrated on fixing a patch to his cheek, more to annoy her than because he wanted to look at his reflection.

He was not to know it but Theresa had taken more trouble than usual with her own appearance that day. Poor Bet had struggled with her hair for an hour before her mistress was satisfied, for Theresa had wanted to make a better impression on him, if only for Shaftesbury's sake.

Morgan brought him his sword and he buckled it around his waist. Theresa looked at it in admiration. "That is beautiful, my Lord."

"This?" Philip removed it from the scabbard and held it out to her. The hilt and guard were fashioned from gold and silver, wrought into a spiral of entwining leaves with emeralds, rubies and sapphires inlaid as flowers of a precious garland.

"It is exquisite," she said, turning the weapon over in her hands before she gave it back to him.

The sword had been a parting gift from Monsieur and Philip was about to tell her so, for he was very proud of it, but, as he twisted his body slightly to replace the sword in its scabbard, he was gripped by a pain sharp enough to take his breath away.

Theresa's face showed concern. "I heard rumours you had been wounded in a duel, my Lord. Do you suffer very much from your injury?"

Philip had been doing his very best to conceal his discomfort from Shaftesbury and the last thing he needed was for the Earl's mistress to report that she had seen him creased with pain.

"Is this a social visit?" he said coldly, when he had recovered. "I was under the impression that we had a job of work to do for Shaftesbury."

Her grey eyes opened wide and she looked angry. "I assure you, my Lord, that I would not be here now except at the absolute insistence of Lord Shaftesbury," she informed him and stalked out of the room.

Philip exchanged a look with Morgan, before putting on his black, plumed hat and following her. "Indeed you wouldn't, sweetheart!"

They crossed the river by the horse ferry, leaving Philip's coach in Lambeth and walking the rest of the way, for he did not want their arrival to be too obvious in case any others had begun to take an interest in Titus Oates.

It turned out to be a wise precaution. As they climbed the stairs to Oates' room Philip heard voices from within. Motioning Theresa to wait, he listened at the door.

"They are about to leave," he told her, when he had overheard some of their conversation.

The corridor was dimly lit and the three men who left the room a minute later passed by unaware of them pressed into an alcove.

"That was Tonge and Christopher Kirkby," Theresa whispered to Philip when they had gone, "but who was that with them?"

"That was Floyd. He works for Danby," Philip said, remembering him from Windsor. "What was he doing here, I wonder?" He rapped a loud tattoo upon Oates' door with his cane.

Oates opened up just enough to recognise Theresa and then attempted to shut the door. Philip kicked it ajar, flattening Oates, who was pushing against it with all his strength. They entered in time to see him pick himself up from the floor.

"Are your manners always this atrocious?" Philip said, looking around the dingy room distastefully. "I take it you are Titus Oates?"

Much of Oates bravado had faded when he saw Philip, nevertheless he obviously still felt bound to make his vexation plain.

"I am *Doctor* Titus Oates," he stressed, "but by what entitlement do you force entry into a gentleman's private lodgings and spoil his repose?"

Philip stared at him, horrified at the sound of his voice. He swung round on Theresa. "If this is a jest, young lady, you will find your humour ill-advised."

"I can't help the way he speaks," she protested.

"What's wrong with the way I speak?" Oates bleated, "and who are you to criticise me anyway?"

"I am Lord Philip Devalle."

Oates immediately began to apologise profusely for his impolite behaviour until Philip could stand it no longer.

"Enough, man," he cried. "Base grovelling is unbecoming from one who, a minute ago, tried to close the door on us."

"I was not to know that you were titled gentry," Oates said defensively. "You might have come to do me harm, for these are harsh days for an honest person, and I have few callers."

"I'm not surprised!"

Oates then begged them to accept some refreshment but, after running his finger across the filthy surface of the table, Philip declined for both of them.

"I'm here to put a proposition to you," he told Oates. "Firstly, where was Floyd taking Tonge and Kirkby?"

"To attend before the Council. Lord Danby sent word that the King is in a great hurry to have this matter sorted out following his return from Windsor."

"Indeed? That is excellent news," Philip said, "and it appears our visit is a timely one."

He came directly to the point, judging that Oates' mercenary mind would be incapable of grasping subtleties. Oates would receive a lump payment of £500 as soon as the Council was sufficiently convinced of his accusations to issue warrants of arrest and, after that, he would receive regular payments, dependent upon his successes. In addition he would have the protection of an influential patron but, in return, Oates must undertake to obey unquestioningly any command from his benefactors.

Oates readily accepted, for it did not take too much intelligence to reason that this offer, in addition to what he received from the state, would make him a rich man.

Philip then emphasised that these terms applied to Oates alone. His disassociation with the unpredictable and pious Tonge was the first condition of their arrangement. The second was that Oates found himself a fellow witness, for the testimony of two people was required in order to prosecute upon a charge of High Treason. Oates said that he knew of one who might be willing to assist him, provided he could be found in time and was not in prison.

The interview might have terminated then and there but Theresa, who had not contributed a word to the proceedings, spoke up. "Tell us something of your background, Titus Oates," she said.

Oates required no further bidding to talk of himself. Blissfully unaware of his own peculiarities, which Philip now saw included having one leg shorter than the other, he strutted around the room as he told them that he had been a curate, first in Sandhurst and then in Bobbing, before becoming a naval chaplain.

"Why would you leave a secure living to suffer the privations of navy life?" Theresa said.

"Several reasons. We sailed to Tangiers," he continued hastily, before she could ask what they were, "where I had the opportunity to hear many Catholic secrets and saw the path of duty fate had marked out for me." The high-pitched voice wavered with emotion and he put his hand to his heart. "I knew then that I must go amongst them, even at my own peril, and follow their doctrines in order to discover enough to destroy them. I became a Protestant chaplain in the house of the Papist Duke of Norfolk and there I learned that the Jesuits would gladly aid any convert to study for priesthood so I volunteered myself. I had no thought but to abuse their benevolence, of course, and I am proud to say that I confounded them utterly."

"Where did you study for the priesthood?" Philip said.

"In Spain, my Lord, at the college of Valladolid, and I later obtained a Doctor's degree from the University of Salamanca."

Philip thought that extremely unlikely, but he had heard enough. "That will suffice if you can relate as glibly before the Council."

Theresa agreed, with rather less enthusiasm, but Philip was anxious to be away from there. It had not escaped his notice that Oates was gawping at him in a way that made him feel most uncomfortable. It was one thing to be admired by the elegant and handsome Monsieur, quite another to be ogled by this repulsive, unwashed creature!

"Do not break with Tonge until after you have been called to the Council," he instructed Oates. "I will tell you when."

He made to leave but Oates stepped in his way. "Must you go so soon, my Lord? I have developed quite a taste for your company."

Philip brushed him aside, revolted by the sight and smell of him. "I have no taste for yours. Now let me by."

Oates reached out and fingered the velvet of Philip's black coat. "You would do well not to be so high and mighty with me, quality though you are." His face twisted into an odious leer. "It seems you have great need of me. Perhaps I may be even more valuable to Lord Danby."

Philip decided this was probably the time to carry out the other part of Shaftesbury's instructions. He smoothed down the cloth where it had been touched. "So you seek to impose your own conditions, do you?"

Without warning he struck Oates full in the face with the back of his hand. Clutching his jaw, Oates staggered back and Philip lashed out at him again, and with such force that he crashed to the ground, hitting his head on the table as he fell.

Theresa stared at him, a shocked expression on her face, but Philip ignored her. "You see, Oates, I can make you obey me with no reward whatsoever."

Oates nodded, dazed and quite incapable of speech.

"Be faithful and you shall have everything I promised, but be false and I shall kill you," Philip warned, shepherding Theresa through the door.

Outside the building even the stench of the dusty city street seemed preferable to the foul air and filth they had left behind them.

"I believe you actually enjoyed that," Theresa said, as they walked to the coach.

"Don't waste an ounce of sympathy on Oates," he advised her. "His sort is the scum of the earth."

"Is that why you attacked him?"

"No, but he was disrespectful," Philip said. He did not add that he was simply following Shaftesbury's orders, for he guessed Theresa would not wish to know about those.

"And can I expect the same treatment if I am disrespectful?"

Philip looked at her irritably. He had found the whole business of dealing with Titus Oates most disagreeable and he was certainly in no mood to have his methods criticised.

"I don't give a damn if you respect me or not so long as you obey me."

"What gall! I am not answerable to you," Theresa said.

"Indeed you are and whilst you work with me you will do as I say." Philip took her by the shoulders and turned her round to face him. "You may be Shaftesbury's pet at the moment but remember you play only a small part in his designs."

His eyes held hers and after a second or two Theresa ceased to struggle in his grip, as though the resistance had been drained from her.

"Why do you resent me so much?" she said quietly when he let her go.

Philip could not answer that. All she had done, if he was honest, was to unwittingly hurt his pride, but he could not bring himself to forgive her yet.

They did not speak again until they were back inside his coach.

"I would appreciate your returning me to Whitehall as quickly as possible," Theresa said stiffly.

"I am not going to Whitehall, I am going to the theatre," Philip said. He considered inviting her to join him as a peace offering, for he could see she was upset, but he decided against it. "When Jonathon and Ned have taken me to Drury Lane they will drive you to Whitehall or anywhere else you want to go."

"Do you mean I can drive where I like?" she asked him uncertainly.

"Of course."

Theresa looked delighted. "Say, to the 'Change, or Hyde Park?"

"Wherever you wish," Philip said, amused at how little it had taken to please her. "My carriage is at your disposal for the rest of the afternoon."

He alighted in Drury Lane and watched her settle back luxuriously into the black upholstery. Much as she seemed to dislike him, she evidently relished the prospect of being seen and envied as she travelled in a carriage all would recognise as his!

This was one female he really could not fathom, nor did he have the least desire to try.

"To the Royal Exchange," he heard her say to Ned. "And please drive as slowly as you can."

⁘

When Kirkby and Tonge returned a few hours later they found Oates unusually subdued, but they were preoccupied and did not pay him much attention.

"We were too late, the Council had already risen," Tonge told him. "We are to return in the morning but perhaps the delay is for the best, for we did see Lord Danby and he suggested a name for you to include in your statement. It was the Duchess of York's secretary, Edward Coleman, but whether he mentioned him out of malice to the man or through a desire to help us I could not be sure."

"Coleman? I should have thought of him before," Oates said. "He even visits gaols to convert prisoners. What did Danby say of him?"

"That such a meddlesome individual would be busy in a plot if any were afoot. He seemed to think we would find enough evidence on him alone to sway the Council."

"Then we must certainly include him," Oates said.

"Do you have any information regarding Coleman?" Kirkby asked him.

Oates hooted with derision. "What a precious fool you are, Kirkby."

Tonge motioned Oates to be quiet but the chemist had already guessed that he had been tricked into cooperating with them because of his access to the King and Danby.

"The man is a charlatan," he said to Tonge. "He has lied from the start, I see it all now. He will convince no-one. I, for one cannot even understand half he says. You do as you please but I shall continue no further with this tomfoolery."

"But does the end not justify the means?" Tonge said.

"I think not."

"Coward," Oates sneered, still bristling from Kirkby's slight about his voice.

"I am an honest man," Kirkby maintained. "I will play no part in a sham."

"But what if you are wrong and Oates does manage to persuade the Council?" Tonge said. "Once the arrests are made then papers can be seized and it is certain that somewhere amongst the letters of any Catholic there will be statements that can be interpreted as treasonable."

"And if he does not persuade them we can all be brought to trial as false witnesses," Kirkby reminded him. "I have no wish to feel the branding iron sear my flesh, have you?"

"But we are already in too deep to retreat," Tonge said. "We have nothing to lose by visiting Justice Godfrey again tomorrow."

Oates, who had already started adding Coleman's name to his Narrative, jutted out his great chin. "I agree."

Kirkby knew it mattered little what he thought or said. He felt the other two had used him disgracefully and that his part had already been played, but he accompanied them to Charing Cross early the next morning. They went to the wharf at the end of Hartshorn Lane, where Justice Godfrey lived and carried out his trade of wood-mongering.

Godfrey opened the door to them himself. He was still clad in his nightcap and gown, for it was not yet six o'clock, but the sight of them jolted him into awareness. He stared at the three in horror, as though he was confronting the figments of a bad dream.

"What do you want with me now?"

"Only a few more minutes of your time," Tonge said. "We want you to take Oates' oath upon another document."

"I won't do it." Their first visit had prayed heavily upon Godfrey's mind and it bothered him that he had not informed the King of their disclosures.

"Then we must go elsewhere, though your refusal may be misconstrued, especially since you have already witnessed part of the contents."

Godfrey looked unhappily at the papers in Tonge's hand and told his unwelcome visitors to be seated whilst he dressed. Fortunately he was not too long about it, for Oates, never slow to perceive an opportunity, had taken a fancy to a silver sweetmeat dish, which he was intending to conceal about his person when the others weren't looking. He scowled as Godfrey came back before he had a chance.

The Justice picked up the document, but he frowned when he read Coleman's name, for they were friends. "What is to be done with this accursed thing?" he asked, when he had taken Oates' oath.

"We intend to present it to the King's Council today," Oates told him. "They must be made aware of this poisonous growth which flourishes in our midst."

Godfrey looked shocked. "Surely you realise what panic will follow these disclosures. Innocent men will suffer."

"My concern is not with the innocent," Oates proclaimed piously, "but with traitors."

A few hours later the Council ordered the arrest of three of the men he had accused.

NINE

Shaftesbury was delighted.

"This Titus Oates has some merits as an orator, it appears," he told Philip, after Oates' appearance before the Council. "It appears the Councillors even became accustomed to his strange pronunciation after a while! At any rate they understood him well enough to give him warrants for the arrest of two Jesuits and a Benedictine. A good beginning."

"What of the King?" Philip said. "Surely Oates never managed to convince him."

"The King was not present. Apparently, his Majesty had more pressing business - with his racehorses at Newmarket," the Earl said disgustedly. "He placed the whole thing in Danby's hands and went off to enjoy himself. No matter, I've no doubt an urgent request for him to return is already on its way. That should annoy him."

"Was Edward Coleman mentioned in Oates accusations?" Philip said.

"Yes, why?"

"I have had Godfrey watched closely from the start of this and he paid a visit to Coleman's house shortly after Oates swore his deposition today. I warned you this might happen," Philip reminded him, although he knew the Earl would not care to recall such things.

"I think the time has come for you to deal with Justice Godfrey," Shaftesbury decided.

"Deal with him?" Philip said suspiciously.

"Yes. He must appear to have been murdered by the Papists as retribution for taking Oates' oath on the accusations against them. It should be a violent death, I feel, and his body discovered in some lonely place, but I will leave the matter entirely in your hands."

Philip was aghast. "You're surely not expecting me to murder him?"

"Why not? You were a soldier. You must have killed men before," Shaftesbury said.

The prospect was distasteful to Philip nonetheless. It was true that he had killed in battle and in self-defence, but never in cold blood and he certainly did not intend to murder a harmless old man, not even for Shaftesbury.

There was another thing to be considered too. If he had arranged for Godfrey to be watched then others could have done the same and, after Charles' plain warning to him at Windsor, he had no desire to be associated with the killing of a Justice of the Peace.

Morgan cursed Shaftesbury passionately, and in Welsh, when he heard what the Earl expected of his master now.

Philip waited patiently until he had finished, for he had found out that on the rare occasions Morgan displayed any emotion it was better to let him express it, which the servant usually did in his native tongue.

"I take you do not approve," he said, when Morgan had quietened down.

"He has no right to ask such a thing of you."

"On the contrary, he has every right I'm afraid," Philip said sadly. "We live comfortably, you and I, on Shaftesbury's money and, in exchange, I undertook to do whatever he asked. As King Charles so aptly put it, he has bought me, but it may be that I, in turn, can buy another. Go seek out Colonel Scott, if he's in town, and bring him here."

Scott looked happy to see him again. "I heard you were back in England but I thought you might have deserted me."

"On the contrary. I have a job for you."

"I am not much in favour with Lord Shaftesbury at the moment," Scott admitted. "He paid me for some information, which I fear was false."

"You're not likely to be in his favour if you sell him lies," Philip said, "but that is of no consequence since this is something you would be doing for me alone. I can pay you well, for I am comfortably situated."

"So I see." Scott looked enviously at Philip's elegant surroundings. "How do you manage it, my friend? The Earl heaps gifts upon you whilst I must scrounge a living where I can."

"I am a gentleman."

"And you are a rogue! A well-bred one, I will allow, but as devious as they come."

Scott was studying him as Philip poured them both a glass of brandy. They had last met just before Philip had gone to France but if Scott saw a difference in him since then he evidently decided, sensibly, to make no mention of it.

"Tell me about the Earl's new mistress," he urged instead. "Is she a tasty piece?"

"Theresa Fairfield? Not to my thinking, but then I like my women rounder and more compliant."

"You mean you haven't managed to seduce her yet?" Scott asked with a wink. "Don't tell me she's rejected the famous lover!"

"Nothing of the kind," Philip said crossly. "I have never found a woman I could not take if I had a mind."

`Scott laughed. "That has always been my boast also. Do you think I should try my luck with her?"

"Not if you value your life," Philip advised. "Shaftesbury seems to be more than usually fond of this one. I reckon he picked the flower whilst still in bud, for she is not like his usual whores."

"You've paid her some attention, then?" Scott teased, but Philip did not smile.

"I have very little choice. The jade is foisted upon me at every opportunity by the Earl. That is bad enough without my having to endure your impudent insinuations."

"Touchy!" The irrepressible Scott grinned, but he did not push the matter any further. "Now, how am I to earn your money?"

"I wish you to eliminate a political obstruction," Philip said.

"You mean murder?" Scott raised a bushy eyebrow. "I would have thought you capable of dealing with that yourself."

"Do you want the job or not?" Philip had no intention of discussing why he was prepared to pay good money out of his own pocket for Scott to perform the task Shaftesbury had given to him.

"Since you find me in a position of penury, as usual, how can I refuse you?" Scott said. "Who am I to, as you so delicately term it, eliminate?"

"Sir Edmund Berry Godfrey."

"The Justice?" Scott whistled through his teeth. "Who will benefit from his death?"

"Indirectly we all will. His sudden and mysterious disappearance will be blamed upon the Papists, which will lend credibility to a very insubstantial plot and may even raise our King from his apathy! Shaftesbury wants him discovered several days later, by which time the whole of London should be interested in him."

"Won't that mean the whole of London will be searching for him?" Scott said.

"Precisely. That is one reason I want no connection with it."

"What of me?"

Philip shrugged. "Your life comes cheaper than mine."

"Because you bear a title and I am only a poor colonel?"

"You are not even that," Philip said emphatically, "but I don't particularly care. All you need to do is to lure the man to you, kill him and then dispose of the body in the exact manner that I shall tell you. Could anything be simpler?"

"Not unless I was to take myself off to Newgate afterwards!"

"I shall provide for your escape to France," Philip assured him.

"Can I rely on that? Forgive my caution, but I have almost felt the rope around my neck once already and I fancy it might not slip off so easily a second time!"

"Would I take advantage of you?"

"Probably," Scott said. "If I have learned anything in my long and varied career it is to trust no-one cleverer than myself! How much will you pay me?"

"A hundred and fifty guineas, but you shall get nothing before the job is completed," Philip warned, "or you will likely drink it all away and be fit for nothing save wenching."

"You are growing nearly as hard with me as Shaftesbury," Scott complained.

"You will find much about me that has changed lately," Philip told him. "I am neither so tolerant nor as amiable as I was. I fail to see why that remark should amuse you, John Scott," he said heavily, seeing Scott's expression.

Scott's smile only broadened. "Maybe it's because I have never really thought of you as either of those things!"

Charles sat through the morning's session of Council without even troubling to remove his hat. Far from dominating the proceedings, as had been expected, he took no part in it at all; in fact, he did not even seem to be listening.

Those who knew him better were not so easily fooled. Danby, for one, was not deceived by his apparent boredom, for he had noticed that the King's eyes had never once left Oates as he paraded before the Council, dressed in the flowing black robes of a clergyman.

When they returned to their places around the table in the afternoon he still remained silent, even when Oates described how Sir George Wakeman, the Royal Physician, had accepted a bribe to poison him.

"Who else was present at this meeting?" Sir William Jones, the Attorney General asked him.

"Don Juan of Austria," Oates said.

No-one seemed inclined to argue with this, for the Councillors had become accustomed to the way Oates bandied around the names of those in high places. Sir William was about to pass on when a voice of quiet authority sounded across the chamber.

"What did he look like?"

Charles had finally spoken.

Oates sought quickly for a plausible answer, and then he recalled that Don Juan was a Spaniard, and all Spaniards were tall, lean and dark. "He was about your height, your Majesty, very thin and dark," he said brightly.

Charles laughed at that. "I know him well. He is short, fat and fair!"

Oates swallowed, aware that those around the table were nudging one another. "I could have made a mistake," he mumbled, "but surely his looks are of little consequence."

"Let us see if your memory of Père La Chaise is any better." Père La Chaise was King Louis' confessor. "You claim to have interviewed him also. Where did this meeting take place?" Charles demanded.

"At the Jesuit's house," Oates stammered, caught off balance again, "just by the Louvre."

"The Jesuits have no house within a mile of the Louvre."

Oates, expert at weighing an audience, glanced about him. Even though a few of the Councillors looked troubled, it was obvious that the majority were for him, including Danby, the most influential of them all. If the King did not choose to go with the tide, so much the worse for the King. Oates decided to make it clear, once and for all, that he defied any to oppose him.

"Your Majesty is, I am certain, too good a Protestant to know the whereabouts of Jesuit houses, just as your innocence and virtue prevent you from guessing the extent of Jesuit wickedness."

Charles had obviously heard enough. "For my part I call the fellow a lying knave," he muttered, none too quietly, and left the Council chamber.

"Danby chased after him. "What shall we do, your Majesty?"

"Whatever you please, only don't concern me with it. I am nauseated by the whole business. I cannot believe that this blatant merchant of deceit has duped you all, therefore I must presume you have sound reasons for humouring him."

"But are we to continue with the investigation?" Danby wanted to know.

"Act as you see fit. I am returning to Newmarket."

Danby went back into the chamber to find the rest of the Council still in discussion. Before long, virtually to a man, they had agreed their decision.

A messenger arrived at Shaftesbury's house in Aldersgate to say that Oates had left Whitehall accompanied by guards and equipped with warrants for the arrests of several Jesuit fathers and Edward Coleman.

Shaftesbury gleefully showed it to Theresa. "This affair is progressing splendidly, my darling."

Theresa could scarcely credit Oates' success. "But surely the King did not believe him."

"Of course he didn't. I never for a moment thought he would, but we have placed him in a devilish position," Shaftesbury said.

"If Charles opposes us it will appear that he is favouring his Catholic brother's interests."

"I suppose so." Theresa, although she did not realise it, was sharing Philip's uneasy feeling about the whole thing. Monmouth's Cause had seemed so fine and noble when she had first left her Dorset home to join Shaftesbury and she had been excited at the thought of helping him in his intrigues. Somehow this was not quite what she had expected.

The clouds were gathering and the afternoon light fading fast as she left Aldersgate to return to the palace. By the time her coach had reached Cheapside the first few drops of rain had become a steady downpour, lashing the windswept city, and before long the gutters, clogged with rubbish, were awash. The rainwater coursed down the centre of the street, swallowing rotting filth and human excrement as it went.

The pungent odour reached Theresa even through the closed carriage windows and she decided it was not a good evening to be abroad. She was convinced of this still further when her coach came to an abrupt halt. She tapped on the panel dividing her from the Earl's driver.

"Why have we stopped?"

The panel slid open and the driver's face appeared. "There is some kind of obstruction up ahead. I have been told to wait."

Theresa clicked her tongue impatiently. "Some cart overturned in the flood, I suppose. Can we not go another way?"

His answer, if he made any, was drowned out by the sound of horses' hooves and she saw that their delay had been occasioned by a party of soldiers turning into the road. They were riding upon either side of a coach, as though in escort.

"What stupidity," she fumed, for there was hardly width enough for even the two vehicles to pass in safety, but her indignation changed to curiosity as she noticed that there was a man walking a few paces in front of the guards.

He had no protection from the weather, not even a cloak, so that the rain streamed down his face and plastered his thin hair to his head. He wore priest's robes, which clung to him like soaking rags, and, as if he were not wet enough, the guards were driving him down the middle of the street, where he had no choice but to tread through the stinking torrent.

As the procession drew level the prisoner missed his footing upon the slippery cobbles and fell to his knees in the slime. She saw a small book that might have been a bible drop from his hands but as the priest reached for it he was forced to his feet and made to walk on.

Tears of pity sprang to Theresa's eyes. "Who is he?" she asked the driver.

"That's Father Jenison. They're taking him to Newgate prison, though he'll pass an uncomfortable night in those clothes, for they say the cells of Newgate are colder than the grave." He reined in the horses and took the coach as close into the side as he could, for the other one was practically upon them.

They passed so near that Theresa could see clearly into it, and she recoiled in horror. She recognised the occupant only too well.

It was Titus Oates, warmly wrapped and smirking at his victim's plight.

"Jenison is a Papist," Theresa reminded herself firmly, as she watched the carriage wheels crush the little book into the mire. "Poor devil."

When Oates returned to his poor rooms in Vauxhall that night he noticed that his lamp was already lit.

He stared at and sniffed the scented air suspiciously, then froze in terror as he heard a sound behind him. "Who is it?" he squeaked. "A Papist come to murder me?"

"If I was then you would be dead by now," Philip said as he stepped out of the shadows. "You really must try to be more alert or you will not last long in this game."

"In future I shall insist that a personal guard is present at all times, my Lord," Oates said, eyeing him warily. His face was still a little swollen from their last encounter.

"A wise precaution," Philip said. "From today you will have many enemies, but you have made friends too."

"Are you pleased with me, my Lord?"

"Yes, I suppose I am, though I act merely as a contact between yourself and the person who employs us both," Philip reminded him.

"Am I to know his name now?"

There was an evil smell in the room and about Oates' person as well. Before Philip answered he drew out a handkerchief doused with the same perfume that Monsieur used and waved it in front of his face, just as Monsieur often did, but Philip's action was not prompted, on this occasion, by affectation but necessity.

"Are you to be trusted, Titus Oates?" he wondered.

"Have I not proved so already, my Lord?"

"Hardly. You have acted so far purely out of greed and malice," Philip said, "but you have shown yourself to possess the cheek of the devil, and to be an adept liar to boot."

"So long as I have your approval, Lord Devalle."

"God forbid! I refuse to give you that. I am, however, of the opinion that you will serve our purpose excellently so you may as well know whose interests you advance besides your own. It is the Earl of Shaftesbury."

Oates looked delighted. "Am I to meet the Earl?"

"Eventually. For the present you will have to deal with him through myself.

Oates smiled, coming closer. "That will be no hardship, my Lord."

"Speak for yourself!" Philip pushed him away with the tip of his cane. It was evident that Oates had conceived some sort of passion for him and, whilst that might make him easier to control, it made his company even more repulsive to Philip. "Remember you act only in agreement with Shaftesbury and you will look to me for your orders and no other. Is that understood?"

"Perfectly, Lord Devalle," Oates simpered.

"And one more thing, no matter how much of a hero you may soon appear to the gullible people of this city, to me you are a servant, nothing more."

"A willing one, I swear it."

"I do hope so, for you should be warned that I tolerate disobedience no better than disrespect. Now to the main purpose of my visit, which concerns Edward Coleman."

Oates scowled. "Coleman fled before I arrived to arrest him. I think he was warned."

"I am sure he was, but it matters little. The fool surrendered himself to Sir Joseph Williamson an hour ago." Philip winced at the sound of Oates' gleeful squawk. "I presume he thought things would go better for him if he placed himself in custody, but they won't. You are to make quite sure of that."

"I will do whatever you say, my Lord." Oates seemed eager to demonstrate his obedience.

"Excellent! At that rate we shall get along quite famously, which is well since it appears we are to be spending a great deal of time together." Philip considered Oates' strange looks again and sighed at the thought of the company he had been reduced to keeping. "It is a pity you are so ugly, but you might make yourself more agreeable if you were to wash more regularly, and I suppose your parson's robes will be a bit of a novelty. We will not be meeting here again, I fancy."

"Thankfully not, Lord Devalle. Tomorrow I shift to my own apartments at Whitehall, by order of the Council, and I am to receive a pension of six hundred pounds a year and my own bodyguard."

"How swiftly your success has come, Titus Oates. Take care it does not desert you in as great a haste," Philip advised him as he left.

"Have no worry as to that, my Lord. Amongst those papers I lifted tonight must surely be a piece of cipher that can be interpreted as treason. They will all die horribly."

"What a very pleasant fellow you are, Titus!"

"Can I be blamed for wanting to exact revenge upon those who have wronged me?" Oates asked defensively.

"Not at all."

Philip had come to understand the motive of revenge only too well.

Justice Godfrey looked up listlessly as Scott was shown in to him, having given his name as John Newman. "My clerk tells me you have an urgent matter to discuss with me, Mr. Newman. Are you a tradesman?"

"Broadly speaking."

"My clerk usually deals with business matters."

"You misunderstand, Justice Godfrey," Scott said quietly. "I trade in sanctuary, not in wood."

Godfrey stiffened. "Who are you, sir, and what do you want with me?"

"I am a friend whose only desire is to help you."

"What leads you to suppose I am in need of help, Mr. Newman?"

"Come now, Justice, it will shortly be common knowledge that Edward Coleman is to stand trial for treason."

Godfrey swallowed. "I did hear he had been arrested but what has that to do with me? Although he is my friend I was never party to his affairs."

"Coleman burned a pile of correspondence just before his house was ransacked," Scott told him. "Don't you think it strange that he should do so - unless, of course, he had been warned to expect trouble?"

Godfrey made no reply, but only wiped his mouth nervously and stared at the ground.

"Before presenting his deposition to the Council," Scott continued, "Doctor Oates confided it to only a few people outside of his associates. One of them was you."

"You think it was I who warned him?" Godfrey said in a trembling voice.

"Several of more exalted standing than I believe you did," Scott said severely, "and they are not pleased with you."

"You tell me I have offended Coleman's condemners yet here is a letter I received this morning from his friends," Godfrey said, taking the letter out of his pocket and reading it aloud. "For the disservice you have done all Catholics you shall pay with your life."

"That is terrible," Scott said sympathetically, although he had actually written the letter himself and sent it to Godfrey by messenger that morning! "It seems you are caught between two fires."

"Indeed I am. Some blame me for not having done my duty and others for having done too much. How can you help, Mr. Newman?"

"I believe your wisest course of action would be to leave London altogether, as you did once before, after the Earl of Pembroke's trial."

Godfrey shuddered at the memory of that episode. "Might it not be construed as an admission of my guilt?"

"But you are not on trial, Justice. You only seek to escape a threat to your life. To flee may not be the most honourable course but should not prudence, on this occasion, take the place of valour?"

"If I did have a mind to leave how would it be managed in secret?" Godfrey asked him mournfully.

"I can arrange everything," Scott offered. "You could take refuge in Holland until the climate here is more favourable."

Godfrey looked at him suspiciously. "Why would you do this for me, Mr. Newman?"

"Not for nothing, I assure you." Scott had already decided that he may as well try to make a little extra money on top of what he was to receive from Philip. "Fifty pounds should see you safely there."

"But I have not that much money in the house."

"How much do you have?"

"No more than thirty."

Scott sighed. It had been worth a try. "Very well. I am not a greedy man. I will see to your departure for thirty pounds." He picked up a sweetmeat dish, prettily fashioned in silver with rosebuds for handles. "I'll take that too. I should be able to raise the remainder on it, but you must inform no-one of your intentions," he warned him, "not even your family or friends."

"Surely that will cause them unnecessary worry as to my whereabouts."

"They will have more cause to worry if your plans are discovered too soon," Scott said grimly. "When all is arranged I'll have a letter delivered to you and on it will be the place to meet me and the time. Make no preparations for a journey and, if any ask, tell them you are just going out for a walk."

TEN

Godfrey's mysterious disappearance caused more trouble than Philip had ever dreamed, for Shaftesbury's agents soon whipped up a frenzy of anti-Catholic feeling in the taverns and coffee houses all over the city.

It seemed that Scott had completed the first part of his task successfully but, even so, Philip was not pleased to receive a visit from him a few days later.

"What the devil are you doing here?"

"I wondered if you might, perhaps, allow me some trifling amount for this."

Philip looked disbelievingly at the sweetmeat dish that Scott drew from his pocket and held out to him.

"You want me to buy it from you?"

"It's a fine piece."

"Then sell it to a silver dealer."

"I would rather be cheated by you! Besides, if I am being watched and anyone suspects I am preparing to leave town it would be the finish of me."

"If you are being watched and you have led them here I shall finish you myself!" Philip looked at him suspiciously. "Did you steal it?"

"Certainly not. I took it as payment on a debt."

"From your appearance it would seem you collected a few other amounts owing to you," Philip said, for Scott was wearing a new coat, decorated with silver lace.

"I need more, and you said I would get no money from you until I finished the job."

"You are a damned nuisance. What do you want for this trinket?"

"It must be worth twenty pounds."

Philip snatched the dish from him. "I'll give you ten for it."

"When can I dispose of Godfrey's body?"

"The King is not due to return from Newmarket until Wednesday and Shaftesbury wants him here when the body is discovered so that he can see for himself how violently his people react to a Popish murder plot. I will give you your instructions then and you can deal with it that night."

Scott pulled a face. "I could wish it might have been earlier. The sooner I am away from my lodgings the better."

"Can't you spend a few days with that amorous widow you have taken advantage of for years?"

"Alas, the Widow Vane has finally suspected that I am only after her money! Could I hide out here?"

"Of course not!" Philip shuddered at the thought. "I am put at risk even by our meeting. The Earl of Pembroke lives near Leicester Fields and he has already agreed to provide a plain carriage for transport. He is eager to assist in any way he can and he might take you in if I asked him."

Philip fetched ten pounds from his strong box and gave it to Scott. "Use some of this to purchase yourself a good, strong horse to get you to the coast," he advised.

"But surely the authorities will be watching all the ports after the murder is discovered," Scott said.

"Just trust me!"

By the time Philip met with Scott on the Wednesday evening newsletters had carried the story across the length of the country, claiming the Justice to be the innocent victim of Papist revenge. Philip was as anxious as Scott to get the deed over, and doubly glad that it was not him who had to do it.

Scott looked relieved to see him. Since he could not risk been spotted by any who supposed him to be out of London, he had been forced to spend his time confined to the house with his host, the Earl of Pembroke, who he both disliked and feared.

"You can't imagine how pleased I am to see you, indeed to see anyone but that maniac Pembroke," he told Philip.

"He is somewhat strange," Philip admitted, "but he's served his purpose. Now listen carefully, for I have not much time. I have to attend a welcome home ball for the King at Whitehall in an hour, and you need not look so envious," he told Scott. "So far as I'm concerned it is simply an exhausting duty I could well do without."

"Not half as exhausting as lugging a corpse across London!"

"Quite." It had already occurred to Philip that, even had he been willing to kill for Shaftesbury, he would have been physically incapable of disposing of a body in his present condition. "That is one reason I am paying you this." He tossed Scott a bag containing his money. "I have decided that it might be better if we did not meet after tonight so I am paying you now and trusting you to follow my instructions. Count it later, blast you," he said irritably, as Scott looked into the bag." I can't linger here. You are to transport Godfrey to Dead Man's Wall. It's not far away and an appropriate place for him to be found, so Shaftesbury thought."

Scott looked dubious. "Not many pass that way in poor weather. It might be days before he is discovered."

"I have thought of that and made provision. You may be sure the area will be searched on Thursday, by which time, if you ride with all haste, you should be in Gravesend. Once there seek out the house of Mr. Cresswell. He is a Searcher at the port and he will clear whichever ship he has selected for your passage. You will be put ashore at Margate before the ship has made for open waters and from there you can ride post to Folkestone, where a fishing boat will be waiting to take you to Dieppe."

"Good plan! I should be able to confuse even the shrewdest investigator," Scott said approvingly.

"That is the idea. Cresswell should not ask you any questions, but if he does be close. He works for Shaftesbury and I would prefer it if none of this got back to the Earl. For the benefit of any others who may be curious, you have been left London for at least two weeks, and I have persuaded Sir Francis Rolle to swear that you have been his guest during that time."

Scott looked impressed. "You seem to have thought of everything."

"Naturally. I am not incompetent, you know! There is one more thing. When you arrive in France do you have any place to go?"

"I know the Paris streets."

"I'm sure you do," Philip said, "and the Paris whores! If I need you again I will make contact with you through the Café Procope, the coffee house near Saint Germain. I believe you will find its clientèle much to your liking!"

"You have only to call upon me anytime. There is nothing I would not do for you, and you may have my hand upon it." Scott said.

"A hand is as worthless as a word of honour from you, John Scott," Philip took the hand he offered, all the same. He rather liked Scott, but he was under no illusions about him. "It only remains for me to thank you for your services and, of course, to wish you good fortune."

"These are dangerous times for you as well," Scott reminded him, "although, with your luck, I dare say you will weather them."

"I dare say." Philip smiled faintly. "I had best go now, for I have to be seen about most prominently tonight if I am to avoid suspicion. Charles would dearly love to find some way to implicate me in this wretched affair."

He went straight to Whitehall, where the ballroom was decked out in splendour for the evening's entertainment, arranged in honour of the King's return from Newmarket.

Philip, leaning against one of the decorated pillars, saw Charles, deep in conversation with his brother. They seemed oblivious to the gaiety all around them and Philip would have given a guinea to hear what they were discussing so seriously.

He was not looking forward to the evening ahead. His side ached and he did not feel in the least like dancing. As he watched the other guests, dressed in bright colours, their silver lace catching the light of the hundreds of candles that burned in the chandeliers, he recalled a time when he, too, would have been a willing part of the spectacle but those days were long gone and he did not expect they would ever return.

He had a different reason for being there tonight and that was to render himself conspicuous. As he caught sight of his reflection in a mirror he could not help thinking that the black outfit he was wearing would make him more noticeable in this gaudy gathering than any other clothes he could have chosen.

Queen Catherine sat watching her husband wistfully. She still tried her best to please him and was dressed tonight quite outrageously. She had not even the wispiest piece of gauze across her shoulders and her tucker, instead of standing up on her bosom, was turned down to lie almost on her stays. Philip had always felt very sorry for her and he made a point of paying his respects as he usually did, for few bothered to do so.

Her ladies sat on stools around her feet and Philip recognised Theresa amongst their number, although she turned away as he walked by her to bow over the Queen's hand.

"We have missed you, my Lord Devalle. You attend too few social occasions at the palace," she scolded him.

"Alas, I fear I am not so welcome here as I once was," he said, wondering how much Charles had told her of his involvement with Shaftesbury. Probably nothing, he decided, for she seemed as grateful as ever for his attentions.

The Queen had lovely eyes, and they sparkled with pleasure as he raised her hand to his lips and treated her to one of his most winning smiles. "You will always be welcomed by me, Lord Devalle!"

As the night wore on Philip partnered a few, but mostly Henriette McClure, who took possession of him at every opportunity. Philip allowed her to do so on this occasion for, since the sole purpose of his appearance at the ball was to be seen there, it mattered little to him in whose company he passed the time.

He caught sight of Theresa, still sitting near the Queen, and thought how envious she looked of the dancers on the floor. It was unlikely that any of the young gallants would risk asking her to dance, since her name was linked with Shaftesbury's. She looked so small and wistful, perched on her little stool at the Queen's feet, that Philip suddenly felt rather ashamed of the way he had been treating her.

He decided the time had come to make amends and he went over to her.

Theresa eyed him distrustfully as he took her hand with a flourish and led her onto the dance floor.

There was a ripple of surprise. Obviously no-one had expected him to do that.

Theresa heard it too and glanced around. "Are you doing this in order to make a fool of me?" she asked suspiciously as the musicians struck up the first notes of the dance. "It would be just like you."

Philip could not believe his well-meaning gesture was being thrown back in his face. "Of all the ungracious jades!"

"Why are you dancing with me, then?" she asked when they came together in a figure.

"I mistakenly assumed you to have the manners of a lady," he said acidly.

"You talk of manners? I have known farmer's boys with better manners than you," she retorted, her colour rising.

"Then perhaps you should have stayed amongst them," he flashed back.

They separated then and did not come back together until the dance ended.

Philip made her a stiff bow. "Since you do not enjoy my company I shan't force you to endure it a moment longer."

"You would not leave me here?" Theresa looked mortified.

"You have gone out of your way to be unpleasant, so I consider my obligation to you is at an end."

"But people are watching us. Aren't you at least going to escort me from the dance floor?"

"Surely you would not expect an ill-mannered brute like me to comply with such fiddling points of etiquette," Philip mocked her.

By now they were the only dancers remaining on the floor and everyone, including the King, was staring at them. Rather than be made a laughing stock before the whole ballroom, Theresa obviously decided to swallow her pride.

"If I have been rude to you I am sorry but I implore you, my Lord, not to play such a mean trick."

Philip laughed. He had not truly intended to abandon her but still he waited an agonising second or two before taking her hand. He did not escort her back to her stool, for the Queen had already retired, but, instead, he led her through the open doors and out onto the terrace.

It has been raining and the autumn night was cool, the air fresh with the aroma of moist leaves. Theresa inhaled it deeply before turning to him, not defiantly, for once, but with tears in her eyes.

"I always seem to say the wrong things to you, don't I?"

Philip smiled at that. "Yes, you do. You really must learn to hide your feelings more."

"I don't know how to do that," she admitted. "I was brought up to be forthright and sincere."

"A countrified and out of fashion notion," he told her, "and one which will advance you nowhere here! You don't trouble to conceal your dislike of me, or your dismay when I annoy you. You must never let any reach your true self, Theresa, that way none can ever really hurt you. Try to remember that, it is good advice if you hope to remain at Court."

"I'll try to heed your advice, my Lord. Particularly if it will make us better friends," she added quietly.

Philip picked one of the roses still blooming on the bushes near them. He shook the moisture from its petals and then took out his handkerchief and wrapped the stem in the lace. "A peace offering," he said, tucking it into the top of her bodice.

Her face lit with pleasure and Philip thought she looked just like a little child. He wondered how this waif-like creature would ever survive amongst the hard, ambitious schemers of Whitehall.

"Are you happy at Court?" he asked her.

"Most of the time," she said slowly, "but surely even an accustomed courtier like you must want to escape occasionally."

Philip shrugged. "I have lived at Court for most of my life. It is really the only proper home I have ever known."

"But it is easier for you," Theresa said. "I am still new here and must be constantly on my guard lest I make enemies or break the rules, whilst you are accepted by everyone and may do exactly as you please."

"Don't you believe it, sweetheart! Everywhere I go the predators lie in wait for me. At the first mistake, the first sign of weakness, they will devour me."

"I'd never thought of it quite like that," Theresa confessed. "Do you enjoy such a perilous existence?"

"Let us say I thrive upon the challenge! I always take great care, mind, that people only see the side of me that I wish them to see."

"That's what I'm going to do from now on," she vowed.

"Good."

"And I don't really dislike you, my Lord," she said, a little shyly.

"In that case, if you have had your fill of music and gaiety, I'll escort you to your apartment," he offered, but even as he gave her his arm Henriette appeared on the terrace beside them.

"Why Philip Devalle, you should not be hiding yourself away out here," she said, giving Theresa a dirty look. "It is only right that the most handsome man present should be shared between every woman in the room."

Philip was not pleased to see her. He felt he had done his social duty for the evening and he was more than ready to leave. "I fear, my darling, there would be insufficient of me to oblige you all."

"But there is quite sufficient of you to oblige me, Philip." Henriette cast a contemptuous eye over Theresa. "I dare say you are ready for some entertaining company after the dull time you must have passed out here."

Philip saw Theresa quiver with indignation at this insult, but he frowned at her. It had the desired effect for, instead of giving way to her temper, she laughed unconcernedly.

"The night has suddenly grown a little chilly, I feel, my Lord. Perhaps we should leave now."

"Certainly." Philip blew a kiss to the irate Henriette as they turned to go. "Goodnight, my little vixen."

"You have made an enemy for me there, I fear," Theresa said as they walked down the many passages that led to her quarters. Whitehall resembled a rabbit warren in the complexity of its corridors, but Philip was well acquainted with them.

"Henriette is nothing compared to the enemies you'll make if you remain with Shaftesbury," he warned, as they stopped before the door of what Theresa grandly called her apartment, but which was every bit as cramped and draughty as those allotted to the courtiers at Versailles.

She invited him in and he accepted, in the spirit of their new amicability, and the first object to catch his eye was a painting of her. It was the kind of study that had become very fashionable amongst Court circles, depicting the subject as a character from history or the classics. The artist had represented Theresa as Boudicca, standing astride a chariot to which were harnessed two wild, white horses, with nostrils flaring. She was naked to the waist, with a brief leather tunic clasped at the side by a jewelled brooch and her hair streamed out behind her like a mane of fire.

Philip made a deliberate point of studying it, just as she had done when she saw his portrait, but he could not refrain from smiling. "Shaftesbury's idea?" he asked her.

"Yes." She looked embarrassed. "I was surprised to see you at the ball tonight, my Lord," she said, in an obvious attempt to change the subject.

"Don't tell me you've been missing me, Theresa?" he asked wickedly. "The truth is I desired to be seen tonight, and by as many people as possible."

"Tonight? Why tonight?" Theresa said. "Something is afoot, I know, but Shaftesbury will not tell me what it is. He reckons that, for my own safety, there are some things it is better I should not know."

"And he's right. It is better, both for your safety and," he touched her lightly on the forehead, "for your peace of mind."

"There is no need to be condescending," she said evenly, "after all we do both fight for the same thing."

"Do we?" His eyes sought out hers. "I wonder whether you even know what you are fighting for."

"Why, for Monmouth's Cause, to put your friend, the Protestant Duke, upon the throne."

"Because, in your opinion, he is entitled to be there?"

His question had evidently caught her off guard, for she seemed totally at a loss for an answer.

"As I thought! Such fine phrases as 'Monmouth's Cause' and 'the Protestant Duke' have no more meaning for you than the lessons you learned by rote as a child. Is it not the truth?" he persisted. "Come, girl, I am not trying to trap you, only ascertain whether your ideals are your own or those Shaftesbury has persuaded you to adopt."

"He has taught me sympathy for Monmouth," she admitted.

"Of course he has, and don't imagine his motives are as pure as yours," Philip said. "Shaftesbury knows perfectly well that Charles was never married to Monmouth's mother, and so do all the rest of us, including Monmouth, if we're honest."

"How can you speak so?" Theresa sounded really shocked. "The Earl searches constantly for proof of Monmouth's legitimacy."

"He pretends to, though only to inspire others with his enthusiasm," Philip said. "The Duke of York will never renounce his faith and, rather than allow a Catholic to become King, the people will accept any proof, however tenuous, of Monmouth's legitimacy, or so Shaftesbury thinks."

"And what do you think, my Lord?"

"Me? I am a gambler, sweetheart."

"Then you only follow Shaftesbury for your own advancement."

"Not at all," Philip corrected her. "His Majesty King Charles is both deceitful and a liar. I have never had an ounce of respect for him since he signed a secret treaty with the French promising to convert us all to Catholics in exchange for French aid. I have even less regard for his Papist brother and I shall do all in my power to thwart them both. Why do you work for Shaftesbury?"

"I love him," Theresa said simply.

"Do you?" Philip said in surprise. "That old whoremonger?"

"Why should you find that so extraordinary?"

"Because I never considered him to be a particularly lovable person," Philip confessed. "I seem to have judged you wrongly, sweetheart, for I thought you only an opportunist intent on improving her station in life. May I ask what he has promised you in return for your loyalty?"

"A place beside him always, that is all I want, though he did promise my father he would find a titled husband for me some day. Purely for the sake of appearances, you understand," she added hastily, as Philip smiled.

"Not in case he gives you a child, or tires of you?" Philip said cynically.

"That too, I suppose," she admitted, "but I guess you can understand now why I came to London to be with him. After all, you must have been in love yourself at some time."

"No," Philip said quietly, "I have not and I hope I never do. Only once in my life have I even grown really close to a friend, and that nearly destroyed me, but I wish you better luck."

A vision of Jules came into his mind and the pain he still felt at his loss came with it, but the striking of a clock broke into his thoughts.

"Midnight! I must go if Boudicca's reputation is not to be irretrievably damaged," he told her, glancing up at the portrait again.

"I have always thought that a foolish thing," Theresa said, blushing furiously. "Don't you?"

"On the contrary, I find its characterisation singularly appropriate." He winked at her. "Goodnight, Theresa. Doubtless events will throw us together again before too long."

Philip went straight home and sank gratefully into a chair with a glass of brandy. He had been on his feet for longer than usual and his scar was plaguing him, but it seemed he was not to be left in peace.

He groaned as the outside bell jangled. "Unless that is a woman eager for my tired and aching body you will please make my excuses, Morgan."

When Morgan returned his lips were twitching. "It is Miss McClure. I thought I should admit her, in view of what you just said."

"Thank you, Morgan," Philip said heavily. "I'm pleased this is amusing you! I know very well what I said but, irresistible as I am, I would hardly have expected her to call on me at this time of night."

"She might be spying for the Duke of York," Morgan suggested. "She is, after all, one of his wife's Maids of Honour."

Philip nodded thoughtfully. "That has occurred to me too. Well if York has sent her to keep an eye on me I had better let her do it, I suppose. It would suit me pretty well to have my whereabouts established on tonight of all nights and, after all, it seems a little churlish to turn away a female who has pursued me to my very door!"

Henriette flounced in, kissing him upon both cheeks. "I have forgiven you for the heartless way you treated me at the ball."

"So I see." Philip did not trouble to get up to greet her but only indicated the chair opposite him.

Henriette settled herself and hitched up her skirts a little to display her shapely legs, which were clad in green silk stockings.

"The Duke of York says that a woman's leg is not worth anything unless it is in a green stocking," she said, following his appreciative gaze. "What do you think?"

"I don't give a damn what colour your stockings are," Philip said. "What are you doing here, Henriette?"

"What the devil do you think I'm doing here?"

Philip laughed. "Do you care nothing for your reputation, sweetheart, visiting me at this hour?"

"Pah! The whole world knows that we are lovers."

"Of course they do, because you told them, but that's scarcely the same as being discovered in my bed," he pointed out.

"Don't you want to make love to me?" she asked him in a piqued tone. "I can't believe you are paying court to that skinny little creature with hair the colour of a copper kettle!"

"Why, Henriette, I do believe you're jealous!" Philip said, smiling. "That's very touching but, whether I want you or not, I hardly think it advisable for a lady seeking a titled husband to place herself in such a compromising situation."

"You could always marry me yourself," Henriette said. "If

you had my money you would no longer need to be dependent on the Earl of Shaftesbury."

"You mean I could be dependent on you instead?" Philip shook his head. "You may go far, my darling, but it will not be upon my name."

"I don't need you to advance me," Henriette said crossly. "I'll have you know the Duke of York has offered to teach me to ride."

"Perhaps you should try seducing him instead of me," Philip suggested. "He won't marry you, of course, but you may be able to wring a title from him and then you can dispense with the tiresome business of pursuing me!"

"But I like pursuing you, even though you do treat me badly." Henriette came over and refilled his glass. "You like it too, if you'd admit it."

In fact, Philip had often thought that, but for her bitchy nature, the sensual Henriette would make a perfect partner for him, certainly a better one than Marie de Bellecourt would ever have made, but he had no plans to marry anyone yet.

He was still not certain whether she had come of her own accord or whether York had sent her but he decided that it really did not matter either way. Henriette was lovely and she was willing, a combination Philip had never been able to resist.

"Well are you proposing to stay or not, my pet?" he asked her, finishing the drink she had poured him and getting to his feet. "The choice is yours but you had better make it soon, for I am getting drunker by the minute."

"You always were an ungracious bastard," Henriette told him genially as he unlaced her bodice.

ELEVEN

By one o'clock the streets were deserted. Scott was hitching a team to the carriage the Earl of Pembroke had provided when the Earl himself appeared.

"When you have collected the body, you are to bring it back here first," he instructed Scott.

Scott looked at him suspiciously. "Lord Devalle never mentioned any of that to me."

"Lord Devalle does not know of it, but I would have you do it all the same. I want to look upon the Justice."

"You want to *look* upon him?" Scott repeated incredulously. "Why?"

"It would give me pleasure. I shall not detain you long."

"Good God, man, the whole of London is being combed for him. As it is I shall be fortunate to escape apprehension. It is out of the question."

"Even considering the sanctuary you have been give these last few days?" Pembroke said sharply.

"Another mess Philip Devalle has got me into," Scott groaned. "Can you not look upon the body after it has been found? They will make a public spectacle of it if Lord Shaftesbury has his way."

"It will be meaningless then," Pembroke told him, rubbing his hands together, as though in anticipation of a treat. "I must be alone with him."

Scott had already reached the conclusion that his host was more than a little mad and he was not entirely sure how he would react if thwarted. Knowing that Pembroke had killed before, without good cause, he decided it might be wiser to humour him.

"Very well," he said heavily, "but only for a moment."

"What I have to do will not take longer than that," Pembroke promised.

Scott rolled his eyes in exasperation as he considered the inconvenience of keeping his word to Pembroke, but he had given it now and, with the resignation of one to whom the taking of risks is as much a part of every day as eating and sleeping, he dismissed it from his mind and continued with the task in hand.

The wheels clattered over the cobblestones as he turned into the road, seeming noisier than usual in the absence of any other sounds. Scott, dressed as a coachman and wearing a fair periwig, lest any recognised him, glanced nervously about but no shutters were opened.

There was no-one to be seen in the street when he reached the empty house where Justice Godfrey had so innocently gone to meet him. The manner of Godfrey's death had been left to him, indeed he had gathered that Philip wanted to know as little as possible about it, so Scott had resorted to the simple method of pushing him down a flight of cellar steps and finishing him with a knife's thrust to the heart. He could only hope that it was a violent enough end to satisfy Shaftesbury's purposes.

That had been the easy part, so far as Scott was concerned. He had been a villain all his life and had never been too particular as to how he earned his living but the prospect of disposing of a corpse, particularly this corpse, was not one he was relishing.

He took a large blanket with him to spread out on the cellar floor and rolled Godfrey's body onto it. Godfrey was a big man and no light weight to carry, especially since he had a sword buckled around him, so that Scott had a struggle to hoist him up the cellar steps. He dragged him from there to the road and pushed him onto the floor of the carriage. He had to prop him up in order to close the door but, in the darkness, he doubted any would suspect the carriage had an occupant.

He went back down into the cellar to check that no piece of evidence remained to connect the empty house with the murder and he picked up Godfrey's hat and wig, which had come off when he fell, and found the stick that he remembered the Justice had been carrying.

Pembroke was in the courtyard waiting for him when he returned and Scott jumped down, urging him to be swift. The Earl climbed in with Godfrey and Scott heard him talking in a low tone and fumbling in the confined space. When Pembroke withdrew he was smiling.

"Thank you, Colonel Scott. You have done me an immense service."

Convinced now beyond shadow of doubt that Pembroke was insane, Scott set off, eager to be away. He headed towards Dead Man's Wall, as instructed by Philip, but as he neared it his sharp senses told him something was amiss. He reined in the horses and looked around him.

On any other occasion Leicester Fields would be totally deserted during the hours of darkness and yet Scott fancied he heard voices, not very loud but sufficiently so to make them carry above the rustling of rabbits amongst the undergrowth.

He got down on his stomach and crawled along until he saw a reddish light that had been hidden from the roadway by a rise in the ground. From behind a hillock he spied four men sitting around a fire, drinking from a stone bottle which they passed between them. On the ground was sack and from it one of the men pulled out articles that glittered in the firelight. Scott saw silver candlesticks, silver cups and silver plates produced from the grubby sack as if it were a treasure chest.

"So, mine is not the only dirty work afoot tonight," Scott thought grimly, cursing his bad luck. He would have to find another place to dispose of Godfrey and, worse, he was in greater danger than ever if the thieves realised that he had discovered them.

Very stealthily he crept back the way he had come. As he approached the carriage the moon came out from behind a cloud and he noticed that part of the blanket had become trapped in the door. He opened it and frowned as a glint of metal caught his eye.

"What has that maniac, Pembroke, done?" He looked anxiously over his shoulder but he did not appear to have been followed so he decided to risk an examination of his passenger.

"My God!" Scott shook his head in disbelief. Godfrey sat exactly as he had put him, but from his breast protruded the Justice's own sword. It had been thrust through him with such force that six inches of it showed out of his back, and it had been this tip which had caught the light and attracted Scott's attention.

"This gets worse! Would that I could dump him here and have done with it," Scott muttered to himself, "but I dare not, for he would be sure to be discovered before I had got clean away."

Despite the nightmarish prospect of carting the much sought-after corpse through the streets, Scott was by no means beaten. He spread the blanket over again and then turned the horses and drove on, making as little noise as possible.

He had all along favoured Primrose Hill as an ideal spot, for Hampstead was a lonely area, and it was for there he now made. He arrived without mishap but, having learned caution from his previous experience, he stopped two fields away, deciding to continue the journey on foot.

If Godfrey had been difficult to handle before then he was far worse now. Scott managed to haul him out head first, but he landed in such a fashion that it appeared his neck was broken. Putting Godfrey's hat, wig and stick on the blanket with him, Scott half-carried, half-dragged the Justice across the muddy fields and over fences until, finally, he chose a ditch at the foot of the hill and laid his burden down.

It was not unlikely that the murder could have been committed at that secluded spot. To make it more convincing Scott positioned the body so that the point of the sword stuck in the ground, as if he had been impaled there.

"That should be a violent enough end, even for the Earl of Shaftesbury," he decided, fitting Godfrey's wig and hat in place. "Farewell, Justice. You have caused me more trouble than you will ever know." He took the stick and blanket with him and then, as an afterthought, removed Godfrey's gloves.

As he walked back across the fields he scattered the gloves and stick where they might easily be seen by any taking a walk upon the hill. He wondered what provisions Philip had made for the discovery of the body at Dead Man's Wall. Whatever they were there was little he could do about it, but he supposed Pembroke could contact Philip and inform him of the change of plan.

Pembroke, however, was in bed when he returned and Scott decided to leave without stopping to tell him anything. He had already delayed longer than he had intended and in a few hours it would be dawn.

"They will all find out soon enough," he reckoned as he gathered his things for his flight. It irked him that he would have to leave several bulkier items behind, including a new overcoat, of which he was rather proud, but he had a long, fast, ride ahead of him and he knew he must make his horse's burden as light as possible.

He had taken Philip's advice and purchased a large, strong bay, excellently suited to the hard travelling he must do if he was to reach Gravesend before any caught up with him.

Strapping a pair of pistols to his saddle, Scott set off upon the first stage of his journey to the coast.

It was Saturday afternoon before he reached Gravesend. The fair was there and the town was thronged with people, which suited Scott nicely for no-one would notice the arrival of another stranger. He wore his blonde wig all the same, in case any did.

A pretty young girl was calling her wares by the side of the road and Scott dismounted and took an apple from her tray.

She smiled at him. "Good day to you, sir. Are you come down for the fair?"

"Indeed I am, darling. Can you tell me where I might find some good refreshment nearby, for I am new to these parts?"

"If it's food and drink you want then John Skelton is your man. His house is just up ahead and he serves victuals while the fair is here."

"Then he will suit me fine." Scott grinned as the wind blew her cloak aside to reveal a bodice cut temptingly low, despite the raw weather. "What's your name, beauty?"

"Molly, sir."

Scott drew out a coin for payment for the fruit and wedged it between her breasts. She shrieked at the touch of the cold metal, but when she saw that it was silver she raised her eyes to him boldly. "If you have a mind I could show you the fair, sir, you being a stranger."

"A splendid notion, Molly! Call for me in an hour at Skelton's."

"Who should I ask for?"

"Godfrey," Scott said, using the first name that came into his head. "John Godfrey."

Skelton had no stable but a place was found for Scott's bay in the cowshed. He tended the lathered animal himself, for it had served him well, but, unbeknown to him, someone else had taken an interest in his mount.

The same person sat next to him at the table, where Scott tucked in ravenously to a plate of pork and sausages.

"Have you covered much distance today," the stranger asked him conversationally.

Scott looked up. "I? No, why do you ask?"

"I only thought that from the looks of your horse you might have ridden him hard."

"I raced him over yonder hill for a wager, that's all," Scott told him cautiously, "but he winds too soon and gets himself in a froth."

Fortunately, Molly flounced in then and put an end to the fellow's questioning.

Ah, there you are, Mr. Godfrey." She lowered her voice. "I only hope your hands are not as cold as your money!"

Scott's eyes twinkled. He was ready for a little pleasure after the strain of the last week. "I trust you will find both to your liking before the day is done!" He turned to the stranger. "Your pardon, sir. It seems my attentions have been claimed elsewhere."

They passed a merry afternoon, for Molly found plenty to delight her at the fair and Scott was ever generous to a pretty woman when he had the means. After he had bought her a shawl, a petticoat, some ribbons and more trinkets than she could hold in her two hands he stopped before a stall displaying gentleman's clothing, remembering he was without an overcoat. The previous day he had got very wet and he decided to buy one now he had the chance.

Molly wandered off to see what else she could find and he was about to make his purchase when the salesman looked up at him in surprise.

"Why, bless me if it is not Colonel Scott. What do you do down here, Colonel?"

Scott froze. "I believe you have made some mistake, fellow."

"But don't you know me, Colonel? I am down here for the fair too, but I work at the Leg, in Cannon Street, just opposite Mr. Payne's shop."

"You are confusing me with another," Scott said, cursing this unfortunate piece of luck. He went off in haste, leaving the salesman staring after him, dumbfounded.

"Did you know that gentleman?" asked a voice at the salesman's elbow. It was the same man who had questioned Scott at Skelton's.

"I thought I did, sir, indeed I would swear to it, but it seems he has a double."

"And might the one you know be named Godfrey?" asked the other, for he had heard Molly address Scott by that name.

"Not if he is the one I think. Wait though, who are you to be asking after him?"

"I am an official of the Clerk of the Passage. Tell me the name of he you took him for."

The salesman looked dubious. "To be fair I might have made an error, as he said, for this gentleman has light hair whilst he I know is dark."

"His name, booby, his name," the official said irritably, "or must I take you to my superiors?"

"He could be Colonel Scott from Cannon Street, in London. I beg you not to make me come with you," the salesman pleaded. "My master would beat me if I left my wares."

Before he had even finished speaking, the salesman saw he was alone.

"It has been an odd affair in all," Shaftesbury said, watching Philip closely. "Godfrey took an extraordinary amount of killing. It was revealed today that he a broken neck and a chest wound, and that a sword was thrust right through him."

Philip examined his cuffs meticulously, removing an imaginary speck of dust from the velvet. He had wondered how long it would be before the subject was broached. "I don't know how his neck came to be broken but you can thank your precious Pembroke for the bizarre embellishment of a sword thrust!"

"I guessed at that, though he would not admit it. He did, however tell me you engaged John Scott to do the deed I entrusted only to you." Shaftesbury brought his fist down hard upon the desk in front of him. "Dammit, Philip, how could you place trust in such a man? He is capable of neither loyalty nor honour."

"He is loyal to me," Philip told him, "and how much honour does a person need to murder an innocent old man in any case?"

"I vowed I'd never employ Scott again," Shaftesbury said, ignoring Philip's question. "He cheated me."

"So did I once," Philip reminded him.

"I have not forgotten that."

"And nor have I. You had me lashed for it, and that is not a thing one does forget, although it seems Scott's misdemeanours toward you went unpunished, which is hardly equable."

"Scott is a different case," Shaftesbury insisted. "He can go to the devil for all I care. You I have resolved to mould to my ways."

"Well so you have. I have become a veritable model of yourself, God help me, and, like you, I will not be told who I can and cannot place reliance upon," Philip said, angry that his judgement should be questioned. "Scott did exactly as I paid him to do, and that's an end to it."

"Perhaps and perhaps not. Samuel Pepys is following up an investigation of his own at the moment and it may well concern John Scott," Shaftesbury warned him. "Did you get him safely away?"

"Of course I did," Philip said huffily. "Do you imagine one who has attained the rank of Lieutenant-Colonel in the French army cannot organise a simple assassination?"

"In that case," Shaftesbury returned swiftly, "perhaps you can tell me, Lieutenant-Colonel Devalle, why it was that Godfrey was reported to be lying dead in Leicester Fields when his body was found in Hampstead?"

Philip would have dearly loved to discover the answer to that question himself!

"If you will excuse me, my Lord, I have some urgent matters to attend to," he said, preparing to beat a hasty retreat.

Shaftesbury smiled. "I thought you might have! Be wary, though, of Pepys. He is a persistent little man. By the way, I informed your dear friend Monmouth that you would be accompanying him to Justice Godfrey's funeral. From what I hear it is to be a splendid affair, fit for the departure of a royal. I would be surprised if there were not riots in the streets afterwards."

"I will personally make sure of it," Philip promised him.

Outside in the courtyard Philip had just mounted Ferrion when he heard his name called. He turned to see Theresa hastening toward him, her cheeks flushed and he hair awry, for it was a blustery October day.

Philip reined his horse and waited for her.

"I'm so glad to have caught you, my Lord. May I speak to you for a moment?"

Philip touched his plumed hat. "A votre service, mademoiselle."

Theresa smiled up at him. She seemed much more at ease in his company since the night of the ball. "I have been thinking a great deal about poor Justice Godfrey, my Lord. His murder worked out very well for us, did it not? Now the people will really have cause to hate the Papists."

"As you say," Philip agreed, in an even tone. "The Justice has done us a great service by dying!"

"My Lord...," Theresa hesitated as though unable to bring herself to voice her terrible suspicions. "Did Shaftesbury have anything to do with it?"

Philip searched her earnest face and saw the dreadful doubts written there.

"Of course not," he lied.

Theresa heaved a great sigh of relief. "Thank you, my Lord. You've no idea how much that's troubled me."

Philip leaned down and tucked a wayward auburn curl behind her ear. "Oh, I think, perhaps, I can guess."

Godfrey's funeral procession was a sight the citizens of London would not soon forget. Before the coffin walked seventy-two clergymen in black gowns and after it came a thousand followers, all in deep mourning, among them several Members of Parliament.

As the mournful bells tolled, the cortège moved slowly toward St. Martin's-in-the-Fields, Godfrey's old church, where the Rector, Doctor Lloyd, was to preach the sermon. Standing on either side of him were two bodyguards disguised as parsons, for the poor man feared he, too, might be struck down by Papists after delivering his sermon, the text of which was 'as a man falleth before the wicked, so fellest thou'.

No harm came to him, however, but throughout the day crowds gathered outside Westminster clamouring for action to be taken against the murderers and Shaftesbury decided this might be a good time to think about appointing a Committee, with himself at the head, to examine the plot against Godfrey.

"The first person I intend to examine is Pepys' clerk," Shaftesbury told Philip.

"You're going after Pepys?" Philip was surprised.

"Why not? All the time he is a suspect he can do us little harm with the investigations he himself has begun into the murder. He has become a mite too interested in your friend Scott, I fear. I am doing this chiefly to protect you, you know," Shaftesbury pointed out.

"I'm flattered."

"You are not without your faults, but you are still the most valuable instrument I possess! Sir Philip Howard's nephew, Captain Atkins, knows this clerk and he will swear that the man said Pepys had a grudge against Godfrey."

Philip also knew Captain Atkins. "He helped me to locate William Bedloe, the person Oates wants for his other witness," he told Shaftesbury. "He said that when he last heard of him Bedloe was in prison here in London, so I traced him through certain informed persons and discovered he was now in Bristol."

"So much trouble for one man?" Shaftesbury said. "Would not another have done who was not so difficult to find? The man is only required to lie, after all, and there must be a dozen you could pick out of the London streets in half an hour that would be prepared to do that."

Philip shook his head. "No. This Bedloe is the perfect one. He was once a letter carrier to Lord Belasyse. Who better to give evidence against Papists than one who has worked in a Catholic household, particularly the household of a Catholic already imprisoned in the Tower?"

Belasyse was one of three Catholic lords that Shaftesbury had caused to be arrested as being possibly implemented in the Plot.

"You may be right," the Earl said grudgingly. "Have you bought the man?"

"Yes, but he expressed a desire to make himself known to the state quite independently and travel down to London under guard, thereby claiming the five hundred pounds reward offered for information concerning Godfrey's murder!"

Pepys clerk, Samuel, did not appear to be intimidated by Shaftesbury's Committee, which was composed of the Duke of Buckingham, Lord Essex and Lord Halifax, Compton, who was the Bishop of London, the Marquis of Winchester and Sir Philip Howard, the uncle of the man upon whose evidence he had been arrested.

He refused to say one word against his master and the Committee decided to give him time for reflection whilst they discussed the case between themselves.

"You will not bully him as easily as you thought," Buckingham reckoned.

"And what would you suggest?" Shaftesbury asked him irritably.

"You could roll him down a hill in barrel of nails," Buckingham said brightly. "That is often most effective."

"But hardly subtle," Shaftesbury pointed out. "I would prefer to see if a spell in Newgate cannot lessen his loyalty."

When Samuel was brought back into the room Shaftesbury was more imperious.

"Samuel, I will be plain with you. Captain Atkins here has sworn a positive oath against you. We cannot answer Parliament by doing less than commit you to Newgate Prison. Are you certain there is nothing that you wish to tell us now that you have had more time to think? Nothing you have remembered?"

"There is one thing I have recalled," Samuel admitted.

"I thought there might be." Shaftesbury smiled knowingly at Buckingham. "What is it?"

"I recall now where I last saw Captain Atkins."

"It was not, then, several months ago, as you first claimed?"

"No, I was mistaken. It was scarcely a week ago, in fact, at a coffee house called Newman's in Gracechurch Street."

Buckingham and Shaftesbury exchanged glances. They both knew who used Newman's as a place to meet his contacts.

"He was talking to another gentleman," Samuel continued artlessly. "Lord Devalle. You must be acquainted with him, for he is very well known about town."

"You will not help yourself by attempting to involve those of higher standing than yourself," Buckingham warned him angrily.

"Take him to the cells," Shaftesbury ordered, and Samuel was led away.

When Philip called at Oates apartments the next morning he found Theresa already there, examining a small jointed stick which Oates had shown her.

"It's called a Protestant Flail," Oates said. "I bought it from a fellow in the street."

"Yes, I have heard of these." Philip took it from him and rapped it gently on her hand. "It is an ingenious device made by Stephen College, a rough and ready young man but one who might be useful. He has certainly lost no time in taking advantage of the hysteria. A nasty little weapon this, and one which will doubtless prove popular, since everyone feels compelled now to carry some kind of protection, even if they have no notion of how to use it!"

Theresa agreed. "The Earl says Lady Shaftesbury has taken to carrying a pistol inside her muff and he is advising all men to wear silk armour beneath their shirts."

"Perhaps they should wear it in their beds as well," Philip said, "since Sir Thomas Player, our city chamberlain, has been heard to complain that a man does not know if he might rise the next morning with his throat cut!"

Ever since Godfrey had been murdered, panic had gripped the city so tightly that good Protestants saw bloodthirsty devils everywhere in the guise of Catholics, waiting to leap out at them with pointed knives or batter them to death with clubs.

"I am doing my duty by ensuring that all I meet are kept constantly aware of the danger we are in." Oates showed them his cuff buttons, which were decorated with a sinister figure, rosary hanging at his belt, withdrawing a fearsome dagger from his cloak.

"Well I have this," Theresa showed them her fan, which was similarly painted.

"And I must confess to buying these." Philip laid a pack of playing cards upon the table. Each member of the suit of spades was adorned with a scene from what had become commonly known now as the Popish Plot against the King's life.

"Why, that is me," Oates squeaked delightedly, pointing to the three of spades.

"Before he grew a chin," Philip observed quietly to Theresa, for it did, indeed, depict him without that monstrous projection and even handsome!

"And here is Lord Shaftesbury," Theresa said, holding up a good likeness of the Earl confronting five Papists in chains, in one of his hands a bag of money and in the other a scourge. She copied his attitude and spoke the words written on it in an imitation of his tones. "Which will you choose?"

"They life and money all refuse…," Oates read from the bottom of the card.

"The fatal Pope they freely choose," finished a voice from the doorway. They all turned to see a handsome man in a black wig and military coat. "I have seen them too and also find them excellently entertaining."

"Bedloe!" Oates greeted him enthusiastically. "When did you arrive in town?"

"Only today. I had myself arrested, you know, and my brother James. That way we travelled here free of charge and made ourselves well known to the Secretaries of State. Forgive me, I forget myself. Have I the honour to be appearing before Lord Philip Devalle, the illustrious hero of the Rhine?"

"You have."

Even if Bedloe's moral code left much to be desired his manners, when he remembered them, were faultless. He bowed low and kissed Philip's hand, then turned to Theresa.

"And you, my Lady," he took a step back and viewed her with delight, "you are without doubt the most charming sight that has greeted these poor eyes in the last few months."

"You spent some of those months in prison, I believe," Theresa said, smiling wryly at the compliment as Bedloe kissed her hand too.

"Let us hope his brain works as rapidly as his tongue," Philip said.

Bedloe slapped Oates on the back with such force that he all but careered into Philip, to whom he had drawn possessively closer. "My friend shall answer for me there, eh, Titus? Do you recall how fine we fared in Spain?"

"You did well enough," Oates grumbled. "For myself I came out the loser by twenty pieces of eight and a book of great price."

"Titus! It was only ten pieces; you never in your life had twenty."

"Twenty," Oates repeated doggedly, "which you stole when I was out buying you food."

"Now that is typical of you, to sour the memory of our happy days together by recollecting the disappearance of such trifling items, which you must know I took only on a short loan."

"It was over a year ago."

"This conversation cuts me to the quick, for I truly reckoned a year to be short enough time to trust a friend. Still," Bedloe said, "if you have grown so mean, Titus, so petty, so small-minded that this will prove an obstacle to our friendship then I will repay you the value of everything I took."

"Go on then." Oates was all of those things.

"Ah! At this precise moment such a request would be embarrassing, for I confess I am, temporarily, without funds, but when I am grown fat and rich by assisting you in the witness stand then, dear Titus, you shall have it and doubled."

"Enough!" Philip stepped in between them. "Bedloe, do you always prattle so, and you, Titus, is this he you had me go to such trouble to seek out, on the understanding that he was your friend?"

"And so I am, my Lord," Bedloe hastened to assure him. "I see you value Oates highly, and you are right for, though many judge him by appearance to be dull and slow, I know him to have the cunning of a wolf, the courage of a lion, the deadly resolve of an eagle, the…"

"Yes, yes," Philip interrupted him, "we know well enough what he is, but what are you, master flatterer?"

"Why, a captain in the army, a plain military man."

"Yes, there seem to be quite a few of you around," Philip said cynically, guessing that Bedloe was no more a captain than Scott was a colonel! "And what brings you to us in such a poor state?"

"My Lord, I have suffered the most grievous run of bad luck that could ever befall a man."

"Similar to that which befell you at Valladolid?" Oates put in. "Before he took advantage of my hospitality he was under arrest," he told Philip. "He and his brother, who always travels as his manservant so that he might appear more of a gentleman."

"It was on account of a simple misunderstanding," Bedloe protested. "I was mistaken for Lord Gerard. It could happen to anyone."

"Particularly if they signed Lord Gerard's name to obtain money from a merchant!"

"They begin again! This is better than a play," Theresa laughed. "Your pardon, gentlemen, but the Queen expects me. It is my turn to read to her today and she already thinks I spend too much time away from my duties."

"You must not incur her suspicions," Philip said. "Go now, sweetheart. You too, Oates."

"Me?" Oates spluttered, red-faced with indignation. "Why?"

"Because I shall obviously get nowhere with Bedloe whilst the pair of you are bickering."

"May I remind your Lordship that these are my rooms?"

Philip prodded him with the tip of his silver-headed cane. "Out!"

Oates seemed about to argue further but he must have caught Philip's warning expression and thought better of it.

"Well as it happens I was just about to go out for an hour anyway," he conceded lamely, grasping Philip's hand and kissing it, as Bedloe had done.

When he had gone Philip turned to find Bedloe shaking with laughter.

"Dear Titus, he does not change. It is well that you are firm with him, my Lord."

"So glad my conduct meets with your approval," Philip said dryly.

"It certainly does, for I know Oates of old and the praise I gave him earlier was just a bluff. In fact, he has an obscenely evil mind and a streak in him so vicious it would shame a rat, and yet he has a great gift also. He can assume an attitude of such pious humility that respectable folk are persuaded to open up their homes and their purses to him. It is an outrageous dupe, but then," he finished charitably, "we all of us make our livings how we can."

"You are a familiar kind of person," Philip said. "It will not do for you confide our affairs."

"You will find me the very soul of discretion, my Lord," Bedloe promised.

"I had better. Now tell me what has happened to you so far."

"This morning I have seen the King, with both Secretaries of State, and I gave them a tale. Not having a chance to consult with you first I tried not to be too specific, but I can elaborate upon it tomorrow when I go before the House of Lords. "I claimed to have seen Justice Godfrey killed in Somerset House."

Philip nodded approvingly. "That will do. Who killed him?"

"Two Jesuits who are known to me, Le Faire and Walsh, aided by one of Lord Belasyse's gentlemen. I was offered two thousand guineas to remove the body which, of course, I refused, but I did see it carried out two days after the murder."

"And how was he killed?"

"He was stifled."

Philip groaned. "You could have chosen practically any method but that and been correct. Never mind, I'm sure you can talk your way out of it. One more thing, perhaps you could include another name amongst the murderers."

"Whoever you please, my Lord."

"Lord Shaftesbury is holding Mr. Pepys clerk in Newgate. His name is Samuel Atkins and you are to positively swear that he was there. It would suit me very nicely to have Pepys under suspicion for a while."

Bedloe tapped the side of his nose with his forefinger and winked. "I understand. By the by a strange-looking fellow accosted me as I went about these corridors searching for Titus. He said his name was Israel Tonge. What has he to do the Plot?"

"As little as I can contrive, or his brand of fiery Protestantism will be the ruination of us all," Philip said. "You, on the contrary, William Bedloe, seem to me to be an astute, unscrupulous adventurer. Your kind I have lately come to understand but, and I must be frank, there is one thing which bothers me about you. Can you truly work with Oates? Don't answer lightly, give it thought."

"There is no need, my Lord. You are concerned without good reason," Bedloe assured him. "Oates and I, for all our past differences, are both professional tricksters. That is why he wanted me; he knows I can be relied upon to play my part, particularly when there is as much at stake as in this game."

"This 'game' could cost me my head," Philip said severely. "You will play it by my rules entirely."

"My Lord, I am your humble servant. If I should ever give you cause to doubt my loyalty to you then you may strike me down for an ungrateful and unworthy wretch."

"That was what I had in mind," Philip said pleasantly. "One last piece of advice, Bedloe; claim no prior knowledge of Oates and the House of Lords will pay your disclosures twice the heed."

Bedloe took Philip's advice and when asked the next day if he knew Oates he flatly denied any acquaintance with him. He also included Samuel Atkins in his accusations.

The King still appeared to be treating the matter as lightly as he had before and remaining aloof from the panic which was gripping the rest of London. "Surely the man has received a new lesson in the last twenty-four hours," was his only comment during the proceedings.

Danby was disgruntled when he left the Council chamber. No matter what view Charles was taking, he could not forgive himself for allowing his old rival, Shaftesbury, to seize acclaim for the discovery of the Plot, acclaim which, but for his own hesitancy, would have been his. He was neither surprised nor very pleased to find Samuel Pepys awaiting him in his office.

"My Lord Treasurer, I have just heard that my clerk has now been accused of taking part in Godfrey's murder," Pepys said. "The price of his pardon will no doubt be to denounce me, which he has so far refused to do."

Danby nodded gravely. "This is a dreadful business, but I will be direct with you, Mr. Pepys, I cannot intervene for him."

"Cannot or will not, my Lord?"

Danby stiffened. "Mr. Pepys, I am not insensitive to the plight of your clerk, or unaware of the implications which proof of his guilt would place on you."

Pepys ignored that. "It is a sad reflection indeed of these jealous times in which we live that a man can be held on diabolical charges upon the word of such shabby scoundrels as this Bedloe and Captain Atkins, a man who I happen to know surrendered his ship to the Algerian corsairs in order to protect bullion he had no business to be carrying!"

"What would you have me do?" Danby said. "If the man has evidence it must be heard."

"I do not dispute that. It is the right of every man, unless he is a Catholic, to stand in a court of law and accuse who he chooses of any crime in the land. If, however, it transpires that those charges are false then should not the accused be allowed to go free without a slur upon his character?"

"Is it your contention, then, that your clerk will not be released, even if nothing can be proved against him? "

"And well you know it. Consider the members of this Committee that purports to examine Godfrey's murder. Who is there to uphold the rights of any belonging to me?" Pepys said. "Shaftesbury controls them all. He seems to have the entire country in his greedy grasp."

"Aye, the people love him just now," Danby said bitterly, "and while they love him he is strong, but the nation is fitful in its adulation, as I have reason to know. Shaftesbury is too wise to risk his popularity, even upon an issue of some consequence such as this."

"Some consequence indeed," Pepys agreed. "If he succeeds with my clerk he will have me and, since I serve the Duke of York, the Duke himself will be implicated, but who is there to stand against the Earl of Shaftesbury?"

"None that I can think of at this time," Danby said bluntly.

"So you go along with him?"

"For the present."

Pepys' puffy little eyes surveyed Danby with contempt. "A fine state we are in when all are mindful of their office and none of their duties. Well he shall find in me, at least, an adversary not afraid to cross him. I shall return his fire with fire. He thinks to use me against my master, York, but he forgets that there is one who, likewise, can be used against him. I speak of Philip Devalle."

"But Shaftesbury would move heaven and earth to protect Lord Devalle," Danby warned him.

"Then let us see him do it! I have carried out my own investigations into Justice Godfrey's murder and I have made some curious discoveries," Pepys said. "When Godfrey disappeared so mysteriously I had a watch put on the ports, so that any person acting suspiciously might be reported to me. One of my officials encountered a man called Colonel John Scott at Gravesend two days after the Justice's body was discovered. He stayed the night with Searcher Cresswell, but he must have guessed that we were watching him. He saddled his horse in the morning and rode into the hills and then the devious devil doubled back and must have got himself on board a ship."

"Do you know this Colonel Scott?"

"Only by reputation, for he once cheated my late cousin, the Earl of Sandwich, out of a considerable sum of money, but I tell you who does know him well, and that is Philip Devalle."

"That proves nothing," Danby said dismissively.

"There is more. Scott told the company at Cresswell's house that he had been staying with Sir Francis Rolle, but that I know to be a lie. Cresswell and Rolle are both known to Lord Devalle."

"This is dangerous talk," Danby said uneasily. "Devalle is a peer."

"So is Lord Belasyse, and Arundel and Powis, all of whom are now in the Tower," Pepys reminded him.

"But he is also one of Monmouth's closest friends. I entreat you to have a care, for these are deep waters into which you would plunge yourself."

"You advise caution when my clerk's life is at stake? No, I will have justice at any cost," Pepys said. "Shaftesbury is my enemy and yours too, or so I thought."

"You are too outspoken," Danby told him crossly. "Any who pit themselves against Lord Shaftesbury at the moment will be acclaimed traitors. The nation is in uproar over this Papist business."

"And likely to be whilst there are cellars searched for Papist arms and officers of Ordnance attending the Houses of Parliament with muskets," Pepys retorted. "Small wonder we mistake hedges for battle lines."

Danby gritted his teeth, knowing the last remark was meant as a slight to him. Word had recently come from Dorset of French landings sighted on the Isle of Purbeck and, as Lord-Lieutenant of the county, it was him who'd had the embarrassing task of reporting the imagined invasion!

"That story has been much exaggerated but, as for the rest, the gentlemen of the Committee of Examinations are doing their duty. Look, Mr. Pepys, I cannot ensure the safety of your clerk, and that's an end to it."

"But will you at least aid me in an investigation of Lord Devalle?"

"Never," Danby said firmly, "and my advice to you is to leave him well alone."

The Secretary of the Admiralty drew himself up to his full height, which was still less than that of the Lord Treasurer. "I thank you for your advice but, as always, my actions shall be dictated by my conscience. Good day to you, my Lord."

"And a good day to you," Danby muttered after him. "Pompous little man!"

TWELVE

❧

"Oates is in custody," Shaftesbury told Philip and Theresa.

Philip was not entirely surprised. "You underestimated the depth of King Charles' feelings for the Queen," he said. "I warned you this would happen."

"The Queen?" Theresa cried. "Surely you have not let Oates speak against her."

"He was only supposed to say that she gave money to the Jesuits to advance their cause," Philip explained.

"He said much more than that," Shaftesbury said. "First, he claimed to have overheard her tell some Jesuits in Somerset House that she would no longer suffer the King in her bed and then, as if that were not bad enough, he went on to say that he had seen a letter from George Wakeman in which she had consented to her husband's murder! I blame you for this," he said to Philip.

"Well of course you do!"

"You are supposed to have control of Oates."

"I can't go into the bloody Council chambers with him, can I?"

Theresa was looking from one to the other with an expression of horror. "How could you do this to the Queen, Lord Devalle. "She thinks you are wonderful."

"It wasn't my idea," Philip assured her.

"She is a Papist," Shaftesbury pointed out, "and cannot be exempted from suspicion if we wish to appear to do a thorough job. I don't understand it. Is Charles not anxious to be rid of her, barren as she is and unpopular?"

"If he intended to divorce her for her faults he would have done it five years ago, when you first proposed it," Philip said.

"I thought he waited for an opportunity to strengthen his own position whilst doing so. I have just offered him that opportunity."

"He will take nothing from you. Faith, you credit him with far too little guile. Why would he risk war with Portugal by divorcing his Portuguese wife when he already has an heir to his throne and ample provision for his bed? The problem now is what we are going to do about Oates."

"What are *you* going to do about Oates, you mean," Shaftesbury stressed. "He is your responsibility. You are answerable for him and I shall hold you to blame if anything befalls him or our Cause as a result of your mismanagement. Furthermore, I shall exact my retribution in the way that hurts you most – through your purse."

Theresa stared disbelievingly at him, as though she was seeing a side the Earl had never revealed to her before. Philip, on the other hand, had expected nothing less.

"What is to happen to Oates now?"

"After he had made his amazing revelations the King, apparently, demanded a description of the rooms where the Queen's alleged conversations took place. Oates' imagination ran riot, as usual, and now he is caught in a web of his own making, for Charles ordered that he be escorted to Somerset House tomorrow in order that he might point the rooms out."

"I'll need Theresa's help," Philip decided, for he had never been inside Somerset House, which was the Queen's palace.

"Then take her."

"No! I'll not help with this," Theresa vowed. "I refuse to do any harm to that poor woman. She has enough trials to bear."

Philip saw Shaftesbury's face darken with anger. He did not wait to hear any more but grabbed Theresa by the arm and took her with him.

When they reached his carriage, he pushed her inside and told Ned to start off immediately. "Be quiet now," he warned her.

Theresa shrank away from him but she was quiet.

"That's much better," he said when they were safely out of the Earl's earshot. "What a stupid little fool you are sometimes, Theresa."

"And you are a brute to ill-treat me so."

"Ill-treat you?" Philip exclaimed. "You should go down on your knees and thank me, girl. You just came as close as you could possibly come to being dispatched home to Dorset. Lord Shaftesbury will not tolerate your defiance."

"I had not thought of it quite that way," Theresa confessed, looking a little ashamed now of her outburst. "Can you not understand the way I feel, my Lord? The Queen has been so kind to me. I'm very fond of her."

"But you're *in love* with Shaftesbury," Philip reminded her, "or so you said. You are the daughter of a country squire, Theresa – no, don't bristle, hear me out. Without the Earl's influence and money, you would never have been able to come to Court in the first place. Now you have a chance to repay him for his generosity and I suggest you would be well-advised to take it. If you must know I don't like this any more than you do."

Theresa was shivering, and he recalled she had left her cloak behind at Shaftesbury's house. He removed his coat and tossed it to her. "Here, put this on. We can't have you dying of cold or Shaftesbury will deduct *you* from my allowance as well!"

Theresa smiled at that. "Thank you." She slipped the coat around her shoulders. "That smells nice," she said, inhaling the perfume on it. "I know what you say makes sense, my Lord, and I will help you if I can, but it still seems wrong."

"Right and wrong play very little part in our business, I'm afraid," Philip said heavily. "It is right that the Papist succession to the throne be thwarted, that is all you need to remember, and to do so we must rely upon such intrepid liars as Titus Oates, whose lust for glory has, on this occasion, got the better of his commonsense. He has to be seen to find those wretched rooms in which he claims to have heard these intrigues take place, and he won't do it without help. I have no idea how he described them but he has only been inside the place to beg in his humbler days, so he will never discover anywhere furtively enough situated that it could have been used for such purposes. You, on the contrary must know the building well."

"But how can I get to speak to him?" Theresa said.

"You can't. He will be closely guarded tonight, but I want you to be there when he tours Somerset House tomorrow. With luck you can find a way to point him in the direction of some secretive place, some private stair, anything that might convince them there was some essence of truth in his tale, even if the rooms do not fit with his description."

Her face fell. "What if they discover me?"

"Then it will be all up for you," Philip said frankly, "but if you do not do it then it will certainly be all up for Oates, and probably for Shaftesbury's plot as well."

"What about you?" she asked, snuggling deeper into his black velvet coat.

"Me?" Philip shrugged. "If things go badly for him Oates may decide to inform against me to save his own skin."

"Surely not! "Theresa stared at him aghast. "He wouldn't do such a base thing."

"You should not credit these rogues with any principles or honour, sweetheart," Philip said with a wry smile, "but don't help Oates for my sake; help him for the sake of the Duke of Monmouth, who is a good enough fellow at heart, and for your lover, who stands to benefit so greatly from the Duke's accession to the throne through all this."

Theresa nodded resignedly. "I will do whatever you say, my Lord."

"Good girl. Now, how shall we manage this? There will be guards swarming all over the place tomorrow and you will not be able to walk about for very long without incurring suspicion." He studied her and then smiled as an inspiration struck him. "I have it! With your figure you could easily pass for a boy!"

Theresa pulled a face at him. "Well we can't all be built like Henriette McClure!"

⌒∽⌒

Theresa knew well enough where her duty lay but it was with a heavy heart, nonetheless, that she arrived the following morning at Somerset House.

Being from the Queen's household, she had free access to the palace and she passed quite unnoticed, despite the extra precautions that were being taken in readiness for the morning's event.

Philip had procured her a page's outfit, which she had concealed in the basket of embroidery she carried on her arm, and the first thing she did was to retire into a closet to change. The clothes fitted her perfectly and a dark wig completed the transformation.

A soldier lounging on the stairs paid no attention to her but her chief fear of discovery was from the real pages. They would unmask her in an instant so she kept well clear of everyone. Or so she thought.

"What? Skulking here? Have you nothing with which to occupy yourself?"

Theresa caught her breath as she realised that the imperious voice with a faintly foreign accent was addressing her.

Looking up from the alcove where she had hidden herself she saw the quaint form of Countess Penalva, one of Queen Catherine's Portuguese ladies. It was not likely she would be recognised by her, for Theresa had as little as possible to do with that tight circle who, though they had been in England with the Queen for sixteen years, still clung doggedly to their own customs and old-fashioned clothes.

Theresa leapt to her feet with a suitably chastened expression. "I was resting."

"Your empty moments would be more profitably spent in prayer," the Countess said. "Remember that the devil has always some employment for idle hands."

Theresa thanked her for her advice, pleased to have been let off so lightly. She decided that if she was to keep out of trouble she had better appear to be busy, so she slipped down to the kitchen and demanded a jug of cordial for the Countess Penalva. Whilst it was being prepared she helped herself to an orange from a bowl and perched upon the edge of the long kitchen table, quite enjoying this part of her masquerade.

Now she had the perfect ruse and could go where she pleased, although she did not stray too far from the main entrance. At last she heard the sound of carriage wheels and secreted herself behind the drapes, where she could hear everything that passed.

The first voice Theresa recognised was that of Titus himself, for it was unmistakeable anywhere, and she peeped out to see him flanked by the Earl of Bridgewater and the Earl of Ossory. There was no way she could think of to make herself known to him without alerting the rest to her presence so she had kept her turquoise ring upon her finger. Shaftesbury had given her the ring and she always wore it, so she hoped that it would help Oates to recognise her, although she realised it would also increase her own danger.

Oates was not his usual cocky self. "Do not press so close, my Lords," he bleated. "You will fluster me."

Ossory regarded him severely. "Doctor Oates, let us waste no time. You have assured us that you can find these rooms in which you claim to have overheard her Majesty's words. Two large chambers with high ceilings, you said, both furnished all in red and with folding doors between."

Theresa grimaced. There were no such rooms in Somerset House. This was going to be even trickier than she'd feared.

Oates was protesting. "So I can, but you must allow me the chance to reacquaint myself with this place. It is three months since I was last here."

"Very well, we shall bear with you, only at least say in which direction we may start our search so that we can begin."

"Alas, I cannot rightly recall even that, but if we go this way then I shall soon know if I am right or wrong," Oates said, sounding desperate.

"That I must aid such a man," Theresa said bitterly to herself as she followed at a discreet distance.

"Do you think your rooms are to be found along this corridor?" Bridgewater said impatiently.

"No. I seem to think there was a staircase leading to them." Oates looked as though his spirits were sinking fast.

"A staircase, you say. There are many here. Which one?"

"How should I know until I have seen them all?" Oates said huffily.

They moved off again, with Theresa following, dodging into rooms whenever they stopped. She was still bearing a tray with the jug of cordial upon it in case any caught sight of her. Somerset House was a vast, rambling building and after a while Oates showed signs of wilting. Theresa had been able to think of no way to help him but she was struck suddenly by a notion so ingenious that she could have cried out for joy.

Ahead of them was flight of stairs, plain and unimposing, but beneath these stairs was a door, cunningly concealed behind a tapestry. Theresa had once been permitted to enter and had discovered that the door led to a secret little room which could be reached from other parts of the house by means of a maze of curious passageways. It was a room designed for lover's trysts, but it could equally well be used, she figured, for darker purposes.

It was true that the room did not fit Oates' description but, once inside, she trusted his loquacity to cope with the deficiencies. The problem was to ensure that he made the discovery.

"I believe," Bridgewater was saying, "that Doctor Oates makes fools of us."

"I beg your Lordships to have patience with me, for I feel we are near the place now."

"Nonsense, man! You were never in any secret rooms here. Why not admit it and have done with this?"

"Aye, that would be best," Ossory said. "Confess that you have wronged an innocent woman and throw yourself upon the mercy of their Majesties."

Theresa walked boldly past them, carrying her tray. As she drew level with the door she took a deep breath to prepare herself and then pretended to stumble. She dropped the tray and clutched at the tapestry, as though to break her fall, tugging it aside to reveal the door.

The men turned, startled by the noise, but still, it seemed Oates did not perceive his opportunity. In desperation Theresa held up her hand, showing him plainly the ring upon her finger.

His countenance was suddenly lit with a flash of insight. "The door," he cried, "there is the secret door, and near a staircase too, just as I said."

"Seize that blasted boy," Ossory ordered, and two guards rushed forward to obey but, as luck would have it, one slipped on the sticky liquid that Theresa had spilt on the floor. He crashed down, delaying the other sufficiently for Theresa to dart away.

Oates quickly took advantage of the confusion and hurried their Lordships toward the hidden door, his memory miraculously returned to him, and he succeeded in distracting the soldiers long enough for Theresa to escape.

She managed to reach the comparative safety of her closet and dressed quickly in her own clothes. She hid the pageboy's garb and wig inside a chest and then sat upon it and waited.

She remained there a long while, her heart racing as she

thought of what she had done. Shaftesbury would be pleased with her, she knew. Philip would be pleased too and, for some reason, his approval seemed to matter to her even more.

Although her mission had been successful she was still in danger of discovery but, when no more footsteps sounded outside and all voices had faded away, Theresa deemed it safe to emerge. With her basket, now containing only embroidery, on her arm she stepped out and began to walk briskly along the circular gallery. When she looked over the balcony she could see, four floors below, the main doors, and her freedom.

Alas her luck had finally deserted her. Ahead of her stood a guard.

"What is your business here?" he demanded.

Theresa swallowed nervously. "I am Theresa Fairfield, one of the Queen's ladies."

"And what is in that basket?"

"Only some sewing. What should it be?"

"I will be plain with you, Mistress Fairfield; we have been set to watch for an intruder."

"A criminal? Here?" Theresa feigned alarm. "Glory! Is nowhere safe for a poor girl?"

"It is a page we seek," the guard frowned and looked her up and down, "or, at least, someone who could pass for a page."

Theresa laughed. "You think I am your boy? That is a fine jest, sir."

"Is it not, though? Come closer, if you please, so that I might see if your pretty basket holds anything but sewing."

Theresa thrust it at him and tapped her foot, as if much vexed, whilst he sorted through it. "Well?" she asked when he had done. "Are you satisfied?"

"Perfectly. My apologies, I was mistaken," the guard admitted.

"May I go then?" Theresa asked him, her voice sounding steadier than she was feeling.

"Surely. I will escort you down myself."

"That will not be necessary," she said, but he waved aside her protests.

"I insist. Until this fellow-me-lad is caught we take no chances with the safety of the Queen's ladies."

He offered his arm and Theresa unthinkingly took it. Too late she realised what she had done and she tried to withdraw her hand, but it was too late. He had already spotted the Earl's ring on her finger.

"Not so fast, my lovely!" Gripping her wrist hard the guard called out triumphantly and a moment later Theresa was facing the furious Earl of Ossory.

"So it was you, Theresa Fairfield! Do you know what you did? You gave that blackguard Oates free license to accuse your royal mistress of a heinous crime against her husband."

This time Theresa could not run, indeed there would have been little point. She sighed wearily. "Did I do that, my Lord?"

"You know you did. This was found by the door you revealed to him." He held up a hairpin that must have fallen out from under her wig.

Theresa sniffed contemptuously. "That is your evidence against me, a pin, the like of which may be found in the hair of a hundred ladies of the Court?"

"I have no proof save this, but I saw the ring upon your finger and I know it was you who showed him that hidden door."

Theresa only smiled, though it was difficult for, truly, she felt more like crying.

Ossory must have taken it as a sign of her defiance. "You shall pay for this betrayal, young woman. I will see to it." he turned to the captain of the guard. "Captain, do your duty."

"Theresa Fairfield, I place you under arrest, in the name of the King."

Almost as bad as the shock of discovery was the awful indignity of being returned to Whitehall under escort.

Theresa had expected to be taken straight before the King but, instead, she was conducted to her own rooms and ordered to remain there. A guard was posted outside her door and, by order of the King, none were allowed to pass save for Bet, who took the whole thing in her stride.

"Shall you stay with me even though I am in disgrace?" Theresa asked her.

"I share in both your triumphs and defeats," Bet said staunchly.

"Triumphs" Theresa gave a bitter laugh. "There will be precious few of those, I fancy, after this. I am not at all sure what will happen to me but I imagine the very least will be that I lose my position at Court."

"The Earl will protect you, surely."

"Of course he will. You wait, he'll have us out of this mess in no time," Theresa said confidently.

But no help came and after a day had gone by Theresa began to fear that she really was alone. Bet, closely watched every time she sallied forth upon some errand, was unable to glean any information whatsoever and Theresa feared this lack of news to indicate the worst.

She did not know that Oates had been to the bar and persuaded the Commons to believe his tale. Nor could she know that every member of the Green Ribbon Club had risen to drink her health that same night.

The following morning a guard entered and instructed her to accompany him to the King's chamber.

"Well, Bet, this is it."

Bet embraced her and bade her to be strong. Theresa followed the guard with a firm step, but a quaking heart.

Charles did not look up as she was ushered in, nor for several minutes after, so that Theresa was left to stand fidgeting uneasily, her embarrassment mounting as he continued to ignore her.

She bore the humiliation with fortitude, though she could not but recall how, not so long ago, she had talked and laughed with him in St. James' Park with the other ladies. She accepted that those days of royal favour were forever behind her now and, when the grave, dark countenance finally confronted her, she was left in no doubt of it.

"So it has come to this, Theresa?" The jet-black eyes regarded her coldly. "Do I not hear you cry out for mercy? Are you not upon your knees, begging my forgiveness?"

"No, your Majesty," she answered in a small voice. "Your forgiveness I know I shall never have and I dare not hope for mercy."

"You are right upon the first count," Charles said, "but as for the second, we shall see."

This unexpected ray of hope lifted Theresa's spirits considerably, although he still looked stern.

"I know you now to be an associate of that undesirable element which seeks, by base lying, to poison the minds of the more susceptible members of my Court. They will not succeed, that I can promise, though they are led by one who, I have reason to know, is impatient of any power but his own and as proud as Lucifer besides. Lord Shaftesbury has crossed my path before and paid the penalty of his ambition, but he will not desist until he has brought about the ruination of himself and those who claim to aid the cause of my son. Philip Devalle and the rest may go to their damnation for all I care but I am saddened to see the Earl exert such influence over you, Theresa, for I had thought you above their treachery and deceit."

Theresa hung her head. There was really very little she could say.

Your friend, Oates, you will be jubilant to learn, has convinced the Commons that my wife is a traitor," Charles continued, "although she has never interfered in matters of state, as you must be aware. They voted for her removal from Whitehall but fortunately the House of Lords have not yet concurred, nor will they. Oates goes before them today with his scheming confederate

Bedloe, but I believe there are still some men left, even in these turbulent times, with a sense of decency and justice. Even so, Oates has done much damage and, thanks to your meddling, will not lose a particle of his prestige.

It is unthinkable for you to stay near one whose kindness you have so wickedly abused and therefore I strip you of your position and forbid you to ever hold another at my Court. You are to leave your room at the palace as soon as you can and you should consider yourself most fortunate that I have seen fit to be so lenient with you."

Theresa could hardly believe she was to suffer no other punishment but that. "Your Majesty is gracious," she said, relieved.

"You may be assured I do not choose to do this because I have any liking left for you," Charles assured her, "nor because I fear the Earl of Shaftesbury, but rather because if I were to punish you as you so richly deserve then some would exalt you as a Protestant martyr, and I will not have that. Now you may take yourself off and do as you please, for I wash my hands of you."

In the corridor outside, Theresa leaned against the wall, feeling numb and empty. From Charles explanation of his leniency she was certain that it had been a veiled suggestion from Shaftesbury which had ensured her release.

She very much wanted to see him but by the time she got to his house the Earl was already taking his seat in the House of Lords.

"I was pleased to see that Oates' effrontery did not desert him in time of crisis," Shaftesbury told Philip. "He strutted before the Lords on their benches, explaining that the reason he had not previously mentioned the Queen's conspiracy with Sir George Wakeman was that, at the time Wakeman was arrested, he himself had been so exceedingly weary from spending two nights priest-hunting in the service of the nation that he had plain forgot it!"

"And they accepted that?" Philip said.

"Oh yes, but the fools still refused to agree upon the Queen's dismissal. I protested, of course, but they are terrified of offending the King. Still, we did some good today, for I persuaded them to vote an address for the apprehension of every Papist in the land!"

"Impressive," Philip said, although he was beginning to wonder whether whole thing had not got out of hand. "So all ended well?"

"It did and it didn't. Be seated," Shaftesbury bade him, "for there is something I must discuss with you which concerns Theresa. She has lost her place at Court through this. I thought perhaps the time had come to find a husband for her."

"Who do you have in mind?"

"It must be someone who is devoted to our cause and who will not interfere with my relationship with her. He need not have money of his own, since I would continue to support her, but in order that she still has access to the Court it is desirable that he bears a title."

Philip stared at him as an awful suspicion entered his mind. "I trust you don't mean me."

"Who else?"

"No!" Philip leapt to his feet. "I will not do it and you cannot ask it of me."

"But I must. There is no-one else," Shaftesbury said simply.

"It is unreasonable," Philip protested.

"On the contrary, I consider it very reasonable in view of everything I have given you."

Philip was stunned at his audacity. "I declined to marry Marie de Bellecourt, even though to do so would have advanced me in the favour of the King of France, I have repeatedly rejected the advances of Henriette McClure, whose fortune would have made me independent of you, and now you want to wed me to the daughter of some country squire for your own convenience. It is unjust."

"You are making too much of it," Shaftesbury said dismissively. "You'll have to marry one day."

"When I do I would prefer my wife to be one of my own choosing."

"You mean love?" Shaftesbury scoffed. "How many marriages at Court are arranged with regard to sentiment? I have had three wives, and felt no love for any of them. The first I married for a house, the second for politics and the third for money. In any case I don't believe such a person as yourself is even capable of love."

"Then perhaps you do not know me as well as you think," Philip said quietly.

"I know you well enough," Shaftesbury said, "and I doubt you have ever cared a fig for anyone but yourself. You might as well choose a union that is going to bring you some benefit."

"That's all very well," Philip said, hurt at this harsh assessment of his nature, "and I can certainly see how this will benefit you, particularly if Theresa ever bears your child, but I fail to see how I will gain from it."

"You will gain from it by continuing to live outrageously upon my money," the Earl pointed out sourly. "As for a child, I would scarcely have thought that someone who has sired as many bastards as you in the bellies of other men's' wives could object to adopting one of mine."

"This is an insult to my family name," Philip insisted, for he knew he was more finely bred than Shaftesbury. "I come from a noble Norman line."

"You come from a noble line of madmen," Shaftesbury returned cruelly. "Your own brother abused you. Besides, I think it is a little late in your career to be concerned with family honour. You will do as I say, or I will cease to support you and you can go back into the army or take yourself off and wed Henriette McClure, if she'll still take you."

Philip knew he meant it. He also knew that he was no longer fit enough for the army and the prospect of belonging to Henriette did not even bear considering. "What does Theresa think of this?" he asked him sullenly.

"She doesn't know yet, but Theresa will have to do as she is told, unless she wishes to be returned to Dorset."

"You would do that to her? Your mistress?" Philip was disgusted. "She worships you."

"And I am fond of her but she will be of little use to me without free access to Whitehall. I blame all this on you, for she would have never had to take the risk she did if you had not let Oates get out of control. It is my opinion that since you caused this mess it is only right that you should rectify it."

Philip could think of no civil answer to make to that and he turned on his heel and left.

Morgan made no comment when he told him what Shaftesbury had said, although Philip was well aware that the Welshman's own opinion of the Earl could not fall any lower than it already was.

"What do you think I should do now?" Philip asked, turning to him for advice as he often did, for Philip had come to depend upon Morgan very much.

"I think," Morgan said slowly, "that you might as well agree to it. She may not come from as good a background as yourself but, from what I've seen of her, I reckon that you could do worse."

"By worse you mean Henriette," Philip guessed, for he knew how Morgan felt about her! "Very well," he sighed. "In my present state of health I cannot think of any other way to support myself at the moment except by working for Shaftesbury. I will marry his mistress, God help me."

∽

Theresa made a most unladylike whistling sound when Shaftesbury explained to her that every single Catholic could soon be arrested. She never ceased to marvel at the power he could wield.

"That is not all you achieved today, I think, my Lord. I know you intervened on my behalf."

"Perhaps I did," he patted her cheek, "but you did me a great service, and aided our cause. I am pleased with you but I shall never again allow you to attempt anything so dangerous to your liberty."

"I doubt I shall have the chance, now that I have lost my position at Court," Theresa said ruefully. "What do you intend to do with me?"

"I have conceived a practical solution to your problem," Shaftesbury told her. "How well are you agreeing with Philip these days?"

The question was so unexpected that she was momentarily taken aback. "Reasonably well, I suppose, though I am still a little nervous of him."

"But you don't dislike him, as you did in the beginning?" Shaftesbury persisted.

"No," she admitted. "He can be quite pleasant when he cares to be. Why do you ask?"

"Because, my dear, he is to be your salvation. I propose to give him to you."

"I don't quite understand, my Lord," Theresa said, fearing that she did, only too well.

"You are going to marry him. It is the perfect solution. Philip's name and rank will open doors for you that would have been firmly closed now that you are no longer attached to the palace. Your union with him will, quite simply, allow you to remain at Court."

"He won't agree to it," she gasped.

"He already has," the Earl informed her smugly, for Morgan had just delivered the news of Philip's change of heart.

"Not willingly?"

"Of course not. What would you expect? But I put it to him that I considered your disgrace to be his doing and that if he did not agree to wed you I would dismiss him from my service."

"He will hate me for this!"

"He may resent you, it is true," Shaftesbury allowed, "but the only thing that matters is that he will obey my order, and so will you," he added sternly, "unless you would prefer to return home to Dorset."

"No," Theresa wailed.

"Then all is settled. The ceremony will be carried out tomorrow in my private chapel."

Theresa left Shaftesbury's house sadder than she had arrived. "We are but cat's-paws, mere puppets to be manipulated and our lives moulded to the pattern of his choosing," she complained to Bet when she got back to Whitehall. "How easily he secures the both of us with his promises and his purse."

"At least it means that you can stay in London," practical Bet said, but even that seemed little comfort to Theresa at this moment.

She recalled wistfully the village weddings she had seen in Wimborne St. Giles. The shy bride and the laughing groom, aglow with love for one another, walking to the church with flower-garlanded maidens dancing around them. Then she thought of herself, to be married in a private chapel with none of her family there, and to a man who didn't even care for her.

To come to the bustling city had once been Theresa's dream, to become Shaftesbury's mistress her greatest desire and to be a titled lady her ambition. She had achieved it all now and she was finding the taste of success was nowhere near as sweet as she had supposed it to be.

⁂

Shaftesbury and Theresa were already in the chapel when Philip arrived with Morgan the following morning. The only other person present was Bet, who cast an interested eye over the Welshman.

Philip, having resigned himself to his fate, paid little heed to the ceremony. Directly it was ended Shaftesbury had a meeting at the House of Lords to attend and he left them together.

Philip motioned the two servants to leave.

"Well, Lady Devalle, it seems we are thrown together for life, whether we like it or not."

Theresa nodded. She seemed too disheartened even to speak.

"Life holds many disappointments, sweetheart," Philip told her gently, guessing at her thoughts.

Theresa's grey eyes filled with tears and Philip suddenly felt very sorry for her.

"Don't cry, Tess," he said softly. "I promise I will not be cruel to you." He tilted her face toward him and studied her elfin features as though seeing them for the first time which, in a way, he was. "Dear, God, you're scarce more than a baby!"

Theresa managed a smile at that as she dabbed her eyes. "I'm eighteen, my Lord, and you'll find I can be strong."

"Then be strong now," he advised her. "Dry your tears and leave this room with your head held high. Let Shaftesbury and the rest of the world think you are unconcerned by any of it, and I suggest we both try to make the best of a most unfortunate circumstance."

"I gain far more from this than you do, I realise that," she said.

"You gain only a title," Philip reminded her. "That I have found to be a very insubstantial thing. I am really not that good a catch, Theresa."

"I don't know much about you," she confessed.

"I am twenty-eight years old, without a penny to my name. I am a soldier by profession and inclination and, according to your beloved Shaftesbury, I care for no-one but myself! I drink more than is good for me, I am a gambler, and a womaniser and, as well, I am descended from a line of madmen! See what a parcel you have taken on, my dear?"

Theresa laughed a little shakily. "You are too modest, my Lord. Why, every woman at the Court desires you, as well you know."

"As a lover, sweetheart, not as a husband. Only you are to have that singular honour!"

He turned to go and Theresa took the arm he offered her. "I promise that I will interfere in your life as little as possible, my Lord."

"In that case," Philip decided, "you are going to make an absolutely perfect wife!"

THIRTEEN

Oates straightened his woolly periwig and gave his white collar a final twist before a mirror.

"Do you think I should wear a beauty patch?" he asked.

Philip was reclining upon a couch and recalling the days when he had watched the elegant Monsieur dress, not this strange freak of a man.

Oates coughed loudly. "A patch, I said."

"Mmm?" Philip returned from the Palais Royale to Oates' apartments at Whitehall. "What of it?"

"Do you think I should wear one?" Oates repeated.

"Titus, with a face as ugly as yours it hardly makes any difference."

"We cannot all be born with your advantages," Oates sniffed, regarding him with envy.

Philip had found that his constant unkindness toward Oates did not diminish the man's devotion to him one iota. "Cease preening yourself, you vain fellow. Your public awaits you."

"But the beauty patch…?"

"Would not be at all in keeping with your guise as a representative of the church," Philip said. "Has association with me taught you nothing of propriety and good taste?"

Oates concurred, as he generally did, and they left the palace to travel in Oates' coach to the Law Courts, where Edward Coleman was to be tried for Treason. From time to time Oates grinned broadly as he anticipated the outcome of the day's events.

Philip viewed his exhilaration with distaste. "You really are a callous bastard, Titus."

"Coleman will only get what he deserves."

"And you will enjoy every moment of his suffering."

"I admit it." Oates' small, sunken eyes seemed to recede even further into his head and the wart which grew upon one of his eyebrows twitched. "I hope he screams out for mercy, so that the entire nation may see how their Saviour humbles their enemies."

"My God, you're madder than Israel Tonge!"

"Then Bedloe must be judged by the same token," Oates said huffily.

Philip knew Oates was jealous of Bedloe, even though he needed him. "Not at all. He desires to convict Papists only to line his own pockets, but you want to grind your heel in their faces as well. I'll warrant you would accuse Coleman today even if there was no reward in it for you."

"Which only goes to prove I am a good Protestant."

"It proves something right enough," Philip said.

"And what of you?" Oates bleated, sensitive as ever to any criticism from him. "Why do you want Coleman convicted?"

"My dear Titus, you should know by now that any action which causes annoyance to the Duke of York has my fullest support, and I fancy that the execution of one who has laboured so diligently in his interest as Edward Coleman will annoy York mightily!"

They separated at the Courts, Oates to take his place as a key witness in the drama about to be enacted and Philip to join the throng of spectators who were eager to be present at this significant trial. He was met outside by Theresa, who had persuaded him to let her come.

Theresa had never been to a Court of Law before and seemed to be finding the whole thing exciting. Philip, who knew what was to follow, could not help but wonder if she would really enjoy the trial as much as she thought.

Westminster Hall consisted of one vast room. To their right Philip pointed out the Court of Common Pleas, where civil cases were decided and, in a corner, Chancery, where the Lord Chancellor, the 'keeper of the King's conscience' presided. Both of these courts were already in session, although they were divided from the communal space only by low partitions, which would have done nothing to keep out the noise.

A loud cheer went up from the vicinity of Common Pleas, momentarily drowning out all other sounds in the hall, and indicating that the verdict passed had been a popular one with onlookers.

The King's Bench, where cases of treason and murder were tried, was at the uppermost end, but there was barely space to walk about, so great was the press of people, and to reach it they had to force their way through the very thickest of the crush. The proximity of so many sweaty bodies was unpleasant and Theresa was choking on the foul air by the time Philip had led her through.

This end of the hall hummed with activity. There were several pedlars, such as might be found in the streets outside, calling out their wares above the din. Some sold pies, others oranges, whilst those suiting their trade to the locality offered ink, paper and pens. Philip stopped before one who carried around his neck a tray of sweetly scented herbs and, tossing him a coin, he took two bunches. He held one up to his nose and passed the other to Theresa, who swiftly followed his example.

They went on, encountering solicitors and clerks hurrying about their business, gaolers, who swaggered importantly, letting it be known who they were, and some men who stood alone or in pairs, doing nothing in particular and yet attracting attention by the very furtiveness of their attitudes.

"Who are they?" Theresa asked Philip.

He followed her glance. "They are strawmen."

"Whatever does that mean?"

"Why, that they are offering their services as witnesses to any prepared to pay highly enough for their perjured evidence."

"How on earth can you tell that?" she said.

Philip clicked his tongue. "Don't you know anything? Look at their shoes." He pointed out the wisp of straw each of them had tucked into their shoe buckles. "They are common Irish fellows mostly," he told her, "and unreliable."

The public seats surrounding the King's Bench were already nearly filled but they managed to find places close to the back, which suited Philip, who had no wish to advertise his presence. Seated with them were a good many students from the Inns of Court, waiting to take notes. An older man, who sat directly in front of Theresa, also had paper across his knees. She bent forward and squinted at the sheet but there was no writing on it, only squiggles and symbols.

She nudged Philip and pointed over the man's shoulder. "Why is he drawing those marks on his paper?"

"He is a pamphleteer, if you know what that is."

"Of course I do," she assured him grandly. "He writes down everything that takes place and then distributes his account for all to read, but he is just scribbling."

"That is shorthand," Philip explained patiently. "Hush now, they are coming in."

Theresa craned her neck to see the great men arrive, all carrying posies of herbs similar to their own. Philip pointed out Sir Francis Winnington, the Solicitor-General, and Sir William Jones, the Attorney-General.

"Can we count on 'bull-faced' Jones?" Theresa asked him. "Shaftesbury said he was sceptical of the plot."

"So he was at the beginning, but he has taken his lead from Danby, deciding that the folly of the many is preferable to the wisdom of the few. He now believes in its existence to such an extent that it is put about he has emptied his cellar of firewood in case the Papists use it to burn down his house!"

"Is there no man in office who is beyond corruption then?"

"I should very much doubt it, for none who are totally honest ever advance that far," Philip said cynically, for he had lately become convinced that this was true. "Here is Scroggs."

Lord Chief Justice Scroggs, a large, bold-looking man, made his entrance slowly and with fitting dignity. Behind him walked the Recorder, Sir George Jeffreys. The jury were ushered in and seated and, finally, Coleman himself was led in. He was quite composed, though very pale and thin after his sojourn in Newgate.

Jeffreys immediately began to read the indictment and the trial began.

"I call upon Dr. Titus Oates to give evidence for the Crown."

Oates entered, supremely confident. He bowed to their Worships before taking his place on the stand. Turning to face the courtroom, he rustled his silk gown and, in his drawling, high-pitched voice, commenced his evidence with all the enthusiasm of an Anabaptist preacher canting to his flock.

He told how he had first met with Coleman the previous November and had been asked to take a letter to Father Richard Ashbey, the Rector of St. Omer's College, where Oates had then been studying, He had opened the letter, for reasons he attributed to divine insight, and had found it to contain treason.

He paused for effect at this point, clasping his hands together and lifting his eyes to heaven in despair of such wickedness,

"What else is there against the accused?" Jones prompted. He appeared to have no taste for Oates dramatic style of oratory.

Oates glared at him. Whichever side the Attorney-General had lately taken, Oates was not likely to forget that it was Jones who had created the most difficulties for him in the Privy Council chamber.

Oates went on to relate other meetings with Coleman and other letters he had carried for him.

"Are all the letters to be produced as evidence?" Theresa asked Philip.

"No. The Prosecution has only a few which were discovered under Coleman's floorboards. Bedloe is to claim knowledge of those, although they are of no significance, even though they were in code and so ingeniously concealed.

"So what has he actually done?"

Philip shrugged. "He took bribe money from the French Ambassador, Barillon, that is all, but here is a man condemned by his pretentiousness. So eager was he to believe his own importance that he hoarded every piece of correspondence he received from France as though it were of national importance."

Coleman had good cause now to wish he had never done so as Oates continued to pile accusation upon accusation against him. He had not had any chance to obtain witnesses himself, nor any legal advice and when his turn came to cross examine Oates the only point he could raise was the fact that Oates, although he claimed to know him well, had been unable to identify him in the Council chambers. This availed him naught. Oates insisted it was the poor light and Coleman's periwig which had confused him.

When Oates stepped down Jeffreys called in Bedloe, who mounted the stand jauntily, clad in full military regalia. After the squat, limping figure of Oates the appearance of the debonair Bedloe must have made a pleasant change for the ladies amongst the spectators and he smiled at them. The jury also seemed to like him, for he had easy manners and an open countenance, but Philip knew that the gentlemen upon the Bench would not be duped by the practised charm of a trickster.

"They will not waste much time on him," he predicted, and he was right.

He had also been a letter carrier for Coleman, he explained, and he had carried many letters to Père La Chaise at the Louvre, most of which he had opened, he confessed brightly, and found they contained treason. He had also been given letters from France to deliver to Coleman and Father Harcourt, and confirmed the letters held in evidence in the courtroom were the same ones. The letters, those deemed the most ambiguous from Oates' haul, were then produced and read aloud to the jury.

Coleman had been persuaded to yield up his cipher to the Commons whilst he was in prison and he now stood with an impassive face as the Bench delved deeply into the hidden meanings of every phrase, giving each one a new and terrible interpretation.

"Several mentions are made in these letters of aid you have requested, Mr. Coleman. What means this aid?" Scroggs said severely. "Weapons?"

"No, my Lord," Coleman protested. "I have acted foolishly, I know that now, but I have never been a traitor. The assistance I received from my French friends took the form of money, which I passed on to others, though not for any such reasons as have been alleged here today."

Philip pulled Theresa closer. "I hear that Charles has offered him a pardon if he confesses. He'll not take it though. He would rather die than live out the rest of his time burdened with the weight of his falsehood. There is your incorruptible man, my pet. It is amongst the oppressed that you must seek him, not the oppressors!"

Coleman called Oates back to the witness stand. His one chance of proving his innocence was to pin Oates down as to the actual dates he was supposed to have met with him.

Oates did not like this at all and he did his best to be evasive, but Scroggs had to press him, for the sake of his own reputation as a justice. Eventually Oates admitted that one meeting had been in August.

Coleman looked delighted. He had been in Warwickshire for all of that month and, what was more, had a friend in court prepared to swear to the fact.

"Now there's a thing!" Philip smiled as he perceived the flustered faces of their Worships. "Who would have reckoned on him making a fight of it?"

"You don't sound unduly perturbed," Theresa said, as Coleman's witness gave his evidence.

"I'm not. Listen." All around them were beginning the first rumblings of dissent. "They fear they will be deprived of their spectacle."

Theresa looked a little frightened and Philip guessed that she had never before sensed the mighty power of what the Green Ribbon Club referred to as the 'Mobile Vulgus'.

This was not so of Scroggs, of course. When the crowd had quietened he put on his most sombre face. "We have listened to your witness, Mr. Coleman and I am bound to say that he seems earnest enough, but his words alone cannot clear you."

"But there are others I can call upon," Coleman cried.

"Then where are they?"

"They are not here, but I can find them if you give me more time."

"I'm sorry, Mr. Coleman. We can give you no more time."

"But these charges are false," Coleman insisted. "Allow me to prove Oates is a liar, for so he is."

"That must be for a jury to decide," Scroggs said.

"But I have never seen the man before today, save in the Council Chamber, and Bedloe not at all," Coleman said. "Why, they do not even swear to the same tale."

"That is enough," Scroggs interrupted him. "I will hear no more from you unless it is your confession."

Coleman hung his head as he heard these telling words. "Then I must throw myself upon your mercy, my Lord, for I will not confess to these heinous crimes of which I stand accused."

"We can leave now if you like, Tess," Philip offered. "Winnington will sum up for the Crown next, but there is no more evidence."

"I'm relieved it's over," Theresa admitted, "but shouldn't we wait for the verdict?"

Philip pointed to an ageing gentleman on the far side of the courtroom. "That's the Sheriff. It is he who impanels the Jury, and he has packed it today with Shaftesbury's own men. Does that answer your question, sweetheart?"

"Then this trial need never have been held at all?"

"It was a mere formality, especially as Lord Chief Justice Scroggs is too concerned with his own career to risk his popularity. If the people want blood," Philip said grimly, "he will give them blood."

Philip had been unwilling to relinquish his fashionable address, so Shaftesbury had bought a large house in King Street to accommodate him and Theresa.

They lived quite independently from one another and the arrangement suited him, for it meant they could both entertain who they pleased and keep their own hours.

They also seemed to have acquired an impressive number of staff, although he was not sure of exactly how many. The Earl had instructed Theresa to engage them as necessary, but she had promptly delegated the task to Bet, who had shown herself to be in her element at handling such matters. Philip found Theresa's maid quite formidable. Unlike his beloved Nanon, who had always been affectionate and considerate, Bet was opinionated and had a brisk manner about her that he was unaccustomed to experiencing from a servant.

Morgan, resigned to the female usurping of his domain, went quietly about his business as he always had and attempted, not altogether successfully, to keep out of Bet's way.

All in all, Philip found being married far less trouble than he had feared. Theresa had so far kept her promise and never interfered with his plans, indeed he hardly ever saw her, so he was surprised to find her waiting for him when he came home late on the night before Coleman's execution.

"I need to talk to you," she said, by way of explanation.

Philip was not in the mood to talk. His old injury hurt more in the cold weather, sometimes so much that he could barely walk about.

"Can't it wait until morning, Tess?" he pleaded.

"No, it can't. I'll never be able to sleep with this on my mind."

Looking closer at her, Philip saw she was plainly troubled by something. "What's happened?"

"Titus called for you whilst you were out."

"Did he upset you?" Philip said.

"On the contrary, I was glad of his coming. You see he recognised this on the hall table downstairs."

She held out a silver dish. Philip stared at it blankly for a moment, and then he remembered that it was the one he had bought from Scott.

"How could he have recognised it?"

"Because he had already taken a fancy to the wretched thing himself - at the home of Justice Godfrey."

Philip cursed under his breath as the full import of her words struck him. Scott had not only lied to him but put in his possession a damning piece of evidence that could connect him with the Justice.

He took the dish from her and tossed it onto the fire, and they both watched as it first turned black and then glowed brightly. A prod with the poker finally reduced it to a shapeless lump of molten metal.

That was not the end of the matter though, as he well knew.

"Did you murder Justice Godfrey, my Lord" Theresa asked him in a strained voice.

"Is that what you really think?"

"I don't know what to think anymore. It seems that the only things I see around me are deceit and evil. Even Coleman's trial was a sham."

"And you play no part in this deceit, I suppose?" Philip asked her testily. "You reap no benefits from our evil work? This self-righteous attitude comes well from you, who are supported by Shaftesbury just the same as me. It is a dirty business we are in, Theresa, but we are both in too deep now to escape and we have to see it through to the bitter end."

"Is that why you killed Godfrey?"

"I didn't kill him," Philip assured her. "Believe that, if nothing else, of me."

"Then how did you get the dish?

"Do you suppose I stole it from a man I had just murdered? I bought it, unwittingly, from a man who I employed to do the deed on Shaftesbury's behalf."

"You told me once that the murder was not Shaftesbury's doing."

"I lied to you," he confessed, "just as he has lied to you, but I think it is about time you knew the truth."

"What is his name, this man you say that you employed?" Theresa demanded.

"That you don't need to know," Philip said firmly, "but he is a person I should obviously have had more sense than to trust. If you don't wish to take my word for it then you had better ask your lover, who, it seems, can do no wrong in your eyes, though you can readily believe the basest things of me." Philip stood up wearily. He had been drinking for most of the night with Monmouth, for brandy was the only thing which seemed to dull his pain, and he was tired and cross and longing for his bed. "What did Titus want, by the way?"

"He came to see if you would accompany him to Coleman's execution tomorrow. I told him that I expected you would be taking Henriette."

"I would have taken you, but I scarcely thought you would have the stomach for it," Philip said, hearing an edge to her voice.

"I don't want to watch it," she informed him loftily, "but it makes me look a fool when you still go about with her."

"Hell and damnation!" Philip had had enough of this conversation. "How do you think it makes *me* look when I am cuckolded before all the world by your precious Shaftesbury? If it were not for him I would not be burdened with a wife at all! You do as you please, Theresa, and I shall please myself."

A crowd began to gather around Newgate prison. Whole families, infants strapped to their mother's hips, were waiting excitedly, passing the time by consuming food and ale.

Moving amongst them was Theresa, wearing a plain cloak, the hood of which was pulled up to partly hide her face.

"You'll see nothing there," said an assured voice behind her.

She spun round to see a skinny urchin in ragged trousers and a shirt with only one sleeve. His legs and bare feet were blue with cold. He jumped down from the wall where he was sitting. "You're small, like me, so you've got to be up front, on account of the hurdle."

"Hurdle?" Theresa repeated.

He snorted impatiently. "They'll be pulling him on a hurdle, so he'll be low down, see? You'd never hit him from here either."

She looked at him blankly and he sighed. "Haven't you got anything to throw?"

Theresa shook her head. "Have you?"

"'Course I have." He delved into his pockets and proudly produced two rocks, the size of his grubby fists. "You can have one if you like," he offered generously.

As he held it out Theresa saw that the little finger was missing from his left hand and she looked away quickly. "You keep them."

"Suit yourself, but it's good luck if you get him with it."

"Is it?"

The boy put his head to one side and looked at her. "I suppose you have been to an execution before?"

"Well…no," she admitted.

"I knew it! You'd best stick with me, then. I've seen dozens." He beckoned to her and, intrigued, she followed him. "Stay close to me," he ordered.

The next instant he dropped onto his hands and knees and snarled like a dog.

A fat woman in front of him squealed and got out of his way. "A mad dog! A mad dog!"

"Come on!"

Obediently Theresa pushed through to see other victims move aside until, in an amazingly short time, they were standing right beside the studded doors that were soon to open for Edward Coleman. The 'mad dog' had collected a couple of hefty kicks, one of which had opened a cut on his forehead, but otherwise he seemed none the worse for the experience.

"Now we'll see everything there is to see. Why do you hide behind that hood?"

"I may not want to be recognised," Theresa said mysteriously. "I have come here today to prove to someone that I have the stomach to watch an execution, but if it turns out that I haven't then I want no-one to know it."

He shrugged and reached under the arm of a pie seller, snatching the largest on the tray.

"Hey, you thieving little varlet!" The pie man caught him by the hair and lifted him almost off his feet, shaking him in order to make the pie drop from his hands.

Theresa paid for the pie in haste and her new friend devoured it noisily. She smiled as she imagined Philip's reaction to the sight! "What's your name?"

"Thomas."

"And how old are you, Thomas?"

"Twelve, I reckon. Nobody knows."

"You mother must know."

Thomas considered this. "Yes. I reckon she does."

"Then why don't you ask her?"

"I would if I knew where she was. She's long gone, but I know where my father is. He's in hell," he told her proudly.

"Thomas!"

"But it's true. There wasn't anywhere else for him after what he'd done," Thomas said.

"What did he do?" Theresa ventured, half afraid to ask.

"He was a murderer. The law didn't catch him though, he was too slippery. He hid out in Alsatia. That where all the worse one's go," he explained, seeing her puzzled expression. "Every kind of villain is there, even highwaymen, and the law never goes in after them. It's too risky. They each give up part of their gains for their protection and he, being stupid, got caught helping himself out of the coffers so they dealt with him in their own way. First they cut off both his hands and then they flogged him to death."

"Good God!"

"He didn't help him much! They do say, though, that he screamed so loud the devil heard him coming! I wonder if the Papist will scream."

Theresa swallowed. "Do they usually?"

"Some do, especially at the end. You might be sick when they pull out his guts, but I'll take care of you. I told you my name, what's yours?"

"It's Theresa."

"Are you somebody's maid, Theresa?"

"I am…," she hesitated and looked into his earnest little face, scratched and grimy but full of friendly concern, "…a maid," she finished.

"I thought so. Do you work in a big house?"

"Yes. The biggest in King Street."

"Sacre Bleu!"

Theresa stared at him in astonishment. "Wherever did you learn that?"

"From a harlot I know. She sleeps with French sailors. Look, the Papist comes out."

The mighty prison gates were, indeed, being opened and, as the excitement around them reached fever pitch, Theresa heard the terrified whinny of a horse. A second later it was led out, dragging behind it something which scraped and bumped over the cobbles.

"That's the hurdle," Thomas said.

Strapped to a tree trunk, powerless to move, Edward Coleman had no protection from the violence of the crowd, who surged forward, howling and hissing.

Lumps of wood, rotting vegetables and broken bottles were hurled from all sides, and those who could find nothing better to throw threw stinking mud or anything else they could pick up from the street.

Theresa glimpsed his face and felt her throat go dry. "Why don't they move him, poor devil?"

Soldiers took their places either side of the hurdle and those going in front of the animal cleared the way through the crush with pikes. A command was called and Coleman began his slow and frightening journey, though not before he was dripping with filth and smeared with the blood that started up from a score of cuts.

"How awful, to be exposed to this," she murmured.

"He's going to die soon anyway." With deadly precision Thomas aimed one of his rocks, grazing the defenceless Coleman on the temple.

"Stop that!" Angrily Theresa knocked the other one from his hand and turned about, seeking some avenue of escape. "I cannot watch this. It is monstrous." Panic stricken, she threw herself right into the mass, fighting with a strength she did not know she possessed.

"You'll be trampled," Thomas yelled, clinging to her. "There is no way out. We must go with them."

"No!" Theresa strained to see over the heads and raised arms. She let out a moan as she saw a familiar gold and black vehicle stopped a short distance away. The very last person she wished to see right now was Philip. "You are right, Thomas, there is no way out for me."

The crowd began to move as one, like a gigantic wave from the ocean, and, trapped within, they were carried forward whether they wanted to be or not.

Inside the carriage Philip tapped upon the panel behind him with his cane. "There's not much more to be seen here."

"Can we move on to Tyburn?" Henriette said, leaning out of the window to purchase an orange from a fruit seller's tray.

"Whatever you wish, my darling." Philip regarded her with a mocking expression. "I declare, Henriette, you are nearly as much of a ghoul as Oates!"

"It runs through the galleries that you have conceived quite an affection for that vile man," Henriette said, delicately peeling the fruit.

"Does it really? Then it must be true!"

"What a contrary mood you are in this morning," she said huffily. "It must be marriage that makes you so disagreeable. Is the squire's daughter not managing to please you?"

"Tess is not too much concerned with pleasing me, as well you know."

"You should have married me, Philip. We are very much alike and I believe you would have fallen in love with me, given time."

Philip shook his head. "Never. You amuse me, sweetheart, that is all. Besides, if you were Lady Devalle then York would never take you for his mistress, and who knows but that I might have need one day of a friend in that camp, though I am bound to say Coleman's high connections do not appear to have much assisted him." he indicated the gallows which had just come into view. Coleman was mounting the steps beside which the dreaded cauldron bubbled.

"Stop! Stop at once," Henriette cried frantically. "Your stupid blackamoor driver will go straight by and we shall miss it."

"Calm yourself," Philip said. "He already has his instructions, for I anticipated you, my little savage."

The coach did stop, in a position which afforded an excellent view. Upon the platform they saw Coleman, dazed and bloody, attempting to make his voice carry above the uproar.

Although he could hear nothing of what was said, it was obvious to Philip that, despite the ordeal he had already suffered and the prospect of what was to come, Coleman was not an abject repentant, cowering before the mob, nor was he using this final opportunity to beg for mercy. "How remarkably composed he is, damn his Papist soul."

"It would be more entertaining if he sobbed," Henriette reckoned.

"A pox upon his sobbing!" Philip muttered. "I would have had him confess. He is a stubborn fool."

Jack Ketch, the executioner, fastened the halter around Coleman's neck. After a brief exchange the signal was given and the outline of the writhing figure showed plain against the sky.

Henriette stroked her own white throat. "He had better cut Coleman down soon or he will be quite dead and we shall have no fun at all."

The impatient crowd bellowed as the twitching grew less and seemed to nearly cease altogether, but today Ketch was master of his trade. A minute before Coleman would have choked upon his last breath the rope was sliced and the almost lifeless body tumbled onto the board. Rough hands stripped off his clothes and held him down, although he could have not have resisted.

Henriette pressed herself hard against Philip, her hand instinctively travelling up the inside of his thigh as Ketch prepared to cut off Coleman's genitals. Her breathing grew faster and faster. "He saw the knife, I swear he opened his eyes and saw it, but he did not cry out. Why don't they make him cry out?"

Philip nearly cried out himself for she had grabbed him so tightly that he had to remove her hand!

"Behave yourself or I shall take you away," he warned her.

Ketch cut open Coleman's stomach and pulled out his bowels, holding the quivering, gory mess aloft for all to see before slinging it into the cauldron. The crowd cheered.

Henriette wrinkled her nose as a foul smell reached them from the pot. "How can you be so unmoved by it all?" She was flushed and breathless.

Philip was amused, and somewhat disgusted, to find that the cruel scene had actually aroused her.

Ketch brought down his axe and, with a single stroke, severed Coleman's head.

"There, Titus, your vengeance is complete." Philip tapped again upon the panel and the coach began to move off slowly through the crowds.

"But he is to be quartered yet," Henriette protested.

"I have decided that you have an unhealthy appetite, and that it ought to be discouraged," Philip said. "Now close the window, there's a good girl, and keep that stench out."

Henriette threw her orange peel out of the window and then closed it and drew down the blinds. She reached for him again, her breath hot and passionate in his ear, and this time Philip did not push her away. After all, there was a limit to his resistance!

✍

Thomas moved aside as orange peel landed on him and he blasphemed with a good deal more fluency than a boy of his age should have had.

"What was that?" Theresa asked as he picked a piece of peel off her cloak.

"A present from a lady! Do you feel better?"

"Yes, much, but what a dreadful thing to do, Thomas, to be sick here, in the street."

He grinned indulgently. "It was the first time you had seen an execution, after all."

"And it shall be the last. This day will trouble my conscience forever." Her gaze was drawn again towards the platform where Ketch's men cleared away the gruesome remains of his handiwork.

"Why should you be troubled by it?" Thomas sounded puzzled. "It wasn't your fault he died."

Theresa touched his dirt-streaked cheek. "Dear Thomas, for all your worldliness you are innocence itself."

Just then a shout went up, followed by the sounds of a scuffle.

"Quickly," Thomas cried. "They may riot."

Theresa feared he was right. The atmosphere about them was still tense and the slightest spark could set the pile alight. She clasped Thomas' hand and began to run, not caring which way she went so long as she put some distance between herself and the mob but, in her hurry, she lost hold of him and when she stopped her little friend was nowhere to be seen.

She sought desperately for him and called his name but she had no real hope of finding him. He had been so kind to her and she had wanted to thank him and give him the money to buy himself some shoes, but, regretfully, she abandoned the search and accepted she would never see Thomas again.

Theresa went on her way. She felt dispirited and her legs, unused lately to much walking, were so weary they could hardly support her. A coach drew level with her and she looked up warily but, having ascertained that it was not Philip's, she would have ignored it.

"Theresa, is that you?"

"Lord Lindsey!" she said, recognising him. "How thankful I am to see you."

In fact, Theresa would have been gladder to see almost anyone else. She had never been over fond of Lindsey but she had always been polite to him, for she knew he had served with Philip in France and that he was now a fervent member of the Green Ribbon Club.

"Were you alone amongst all the mêlée?" he asked her as she climbed in gratefully beside him.

"Why yes. I went to see the execution."

"The deuce! Were you sick?"

"Lord, no, I have seen dozens of the things," Theresa claimed airily.

"Forgive me, but I reckoned you less mettlesome. I confess I felt my stomach churn when they drew out his entrails and I saw he still breathed," Lindsey confessed. "It was though that hook was clawing inside my own gut."

"Yes, yes," she said hastily. "Can we drive on?"

When they arrived at the house Lindsey escorted her to the door. "Is Philip likely to be home?" he asked.

"I'm afraid not. You might see him later at the Club."

"Actually, Theresa, that was not the reason for my question."

Lindsey twirled the end of his moustache, looking at her intently, and Theresa realised that he had probably misinterpreted her look of pleasure at the sight of him!

"You are bold, my Lord," she reproved him.

"Pardon my frankness, but when I see an object that I want I pursue it."

At any other time, Theresa would have laughed at him and shut the door firmly in his face. She did not even find Lindsey particularly attractive, with his sandy-coloured hair and his moustache, which she suspected he had grown in an endeavour to conceal some of the freckles that marred the whiteness of his skin.

He had saved her from a long walk home, however, and she was grateful for that.

Also, at that moment, she was feeling sick and tired of Philip and even of Shaftesbury, for she knew they had both had a hand in Coleman's fate.

She recalled Philip's parting comment to her the previous night and decided she would take him at his word and do as she pleased.

After all, he probably wouldn't be home for hours.

FOURTEEN

In fact, Philip was already on his way home. He had satisfied Henriette in the coach so he had no reason to linger with her afterwards.

He was feeling a little guilty about the way he had spoken to Theresa and he resolved to see her and make friends directly he arrived. Her rooms were at the top of the house and he was about to climb the stairs, when Morgan appeared in haste and stood in front of him.

Philip stared at him in astonishment. "Whatever are you doing, man? Get out of my way."

The Welshman did not budge. "You cannot go up there, my Lord."

"Cannot?" Philip repeated. "This is my house."

"Not all of it," Morgan reminded him.

"Don't be so ridiculous! I often go up to see Theresa."

"I don't think she will be pleased to see you today."

"She was upset with me last night," Philip admitted, "but surely she will be over that by now."

Morgan stood his ground. "I don't think so."

"I promise I will go and make amends to her. There can't be anything wrong in that."

"I think it would not be wise just now," Morgan said carefully.

"You really are determined I shall not set foot upon these stairs, aren't you?" Philip put his head on one side and studied the Welshman. "I wonder why."

Morgan sighed. "Since you will have it I must tell you straight. She has a visitor."

"You mean Shaftesbury?" Philip guessed. "Why did you not say so at the start?"

"It is not the Earl," Morgan said quietly, "but it is a man."

That came as a shock to Philip. "A man, you say? And you allowed her to receive him?"

"There was little I could do. She is the mistress," Morgan pointed out, sounding aggrieved. "If anyone is to blame for this it is you."

"Oh, I might know it would be," Philip said. "How can this possibly be my fault?"

"Because you flaunt your mistress in her face."

"You're surely not suggesting I should be faithful to her?" Philip was vexed at the injustice of the accusation. "She doesn't even belong to me."

"Then why do you mind if she is entertaining another man?" Morgan asked craftily.

Philip could not honestly answer that, for he did not know. "I don't mind," he lied. "Why should I? It is Shaftesbury she is deceiving, after all, not me." He turned around to go back down to his own rooms. "If this is how she wants to behave then to hell with her." He cast another glance up the stairs. "Oh, what a silly little bitch!"

"You will not involve yourself in another dispute of honour, I hope," Morgan said sternly.

Philip raised his hands. "I swear it. If she wants to entertain a lover it is quite her business. I am curious, though, to know who it might be."

"Best you don't," the Welshman muttered as he left him.

Philip did not go directly downstairs. Instead he waited until Morgan's footsteps had died away and the house was silent. Even from where he stood he could distinctly hear a man speak.

"So, Richard Lindsey is the lady's fancy, is he?" Philip shook his head in disbelief. "Incredible!"

He waited where he was a little longer. He had no wish to eavesdrop, but the voices he could hear hardly seemed to be talking in the soft tones of lovers.

✍

Theresa had quickly regretted her impetuous invitation to Lord Lindsey. She had kept him at bay with every topic of conversation she could think of and, after an hour, it was evident that he had begun to grow impatient.

"I really think that you should go now," she suggested. "My husband might be home at any minute."

"When he does return he, no doubt, comes hot from Henriette McClure's bed," Lindsey snorted. "He is hardly fit to condemn anyone else for their faults. The man's an animal."

"I thought you were his friend!"

"I have never truly liked Philip," Lindsey admitted. "I had even thought I might replace him when he remained so long in France but for Shaftesbury there is, apparently, none to compare with him."

"He has served the Earl very well," she reminded him.

"By wet-nursing that repulsive creature, Oates? I am surprised the arrogant sod demeans himself, although," he added sneeringly, "for all I know Oates might appeal to him."

Theresa was beginning to feel a tiny bit cross. Whatever her private thoughts on Philip might be, she did not feel that an outsider was entitled to find fault with him. "What are you implying?"

"I would have thought it was obvious. Is he not a favourite of Monsieur? For all I know the great womaniser might be a filthy sodomite as well."

"Lord Lindsey! I will not tolerate the passing of such offensive remarks in my presence." Theresa sat down and turned her back on him, but he yanked her to her feet and pulled her roughly toward him.

"You are hurting me," she cried.

"Then cease your struggles and I will be gentler, you stupid jade."

Theresa only fought him all the harder. "Let me go!"

"Not until I have collected a fitting reward for my assistance."

"That you will not," she vowed, kicking him upon the shin, which made him partially loosen his grip, so that she was almost able to get free, but he pulled her back. "Does Philip help himself to Shaftesbury's whore, or do you fight him too? I can take you against your will, you know. It makes no difference to me."

Theresa cried out as, with one hand, he pinned both her arms behind her and pressed her against the wall.

Philip had heard enough.

He was up the stairs in seconds and burst through the door. He took in at a glance what was happening and fury welled up inside him. He crossed the room and grabbed Lindsey tightly by his cravat and threw him with his full force against the wall.

"Are you hurt?" he asked Theresa.

Theresa shook her head but she looked tearful.

"Fortunate for you, you bastard," Philip snarled at Lindsey, who was scrambling to his feet. "Get out of this house and, if you are wise, you will never again cause distress to my wife."

It was the first time Philip had referred to Theresa as his wife and he was surprised at how natural it sounded to him.

"Has Shaftesbury not taught you to be a contented cuckold?" Lindsey sneered.

Philip took a step toward him. "What did you say?"

"If you wish to fight me you are welcome to claim satisfaction in the normal way open to gentlemen," Lindsey said, backing away warily. "Not everyone is as adept as you at brawling, or perhaps you feel you are no longer equal to a duel."

"I am more than equal to any challenge you care to give me," Philip assured him quietly, although he was not entirely sure that he was, not any more.

"I would not want the world to say I took advantage of a man whose declining health gave me an unfair advantage," Lindsey said. "Is it the pox that saps your strength, Devalle? Picked up from one of your harlots, no doubt."

Philip sighed resignedly. If he was to keep his honour he no longer had any choice in the matter, regardless of the promise he had just made to Morgan. "Very well, Lindsey. You shall have your fight, if nothing else will rid us of you."

"At last!" Lindsey said triumphantly. "I have waited a long while for this day."

"I fancy you will wait more patiently for our next encounter."

"We shall see if you are so haughty when you entreat me to spare your life!"

Philip tossed his head disdainfully. "You always were a braggart, Lindsey. How soon would you have this settled?"

"As soon as you please. Tomorrow morning?"

"I would prefer to meet you in the afternoon, since I have some pressing matters to attend to in the morning," Philip said, recalling that he had a job to do for Shaftesbury.

"It would be advisable for you to attend to all your matters in the morning," Lindsey said, smirking, "since you may never have another opportunity to do so."

"Stop this madness, both of you!" Theresa, who had seemed dumbstruck during the exchanges between them, had found her voice. "I don't want you to fight."

"You should be quite ecstatic," Philip said. "I thought every lady at Court aspired to have at least one duel fought over her! Keep silent now, sweetheart, your part in this is over. The challenge has been made and answered. Morgan stands my second," he told Lindsey.

"What, your manservant?" Lindsey sniffed. "It is not usual."

"Nevertheless, I would have it so. He has attended me before on one of these occasions. I suggest Chelsea Fields at three o'clock."

"That will serve well enough. Until tomorrow, Devalle."

Lindsey departed, much elated.

"Bloody fool," Philip hissed after him, "and as for you, madam..." He turned to Theresa.

She drew back, as though fearful that his anger might be directed at her now they were alone.

"Come here," he said, more gently. "There is no need to be frightened of me."

She moved toward him uncertainly.

"Why Tess?"

Theresa swallowed. "I had no idea it would lead to this."

"I asked you why."

"I was only taking you at your word and doing what I pleased," she said feebly.

"I never thought you would take me quite so literally. And with Lindsey, of all people."

Theresa hung her head. "I'm truly sorry now, my Lord."

She looked such a picture of misery that he could not be cross with her. "Oh, Tess, what am I to do with you?"

"My Lord?"

"I merely wonder where the deuce is this intelligence with which Lord Shaftesbury credits you."

Theresa bit her lip. "I hadn't even considered what the Earl would say. He will be furious with me."

"The way I have arranged it he may never know, for Lindsey is unlikely to boast of his defeat."

"But what if he is the victor?"

Philip laughed at her frankness. "One of you more endearing qualities is the faith you have in me!"

"Don't jest," she begged. "I know of your reputation with a sword, but you should not be fighting him in your present condition."

"You left me little choice," he pointed out. "What if he had told the world that he was here at your invitation? How do you think the Earl would take to that?"

"I didn't give it any thought at the time," she confessed.

"Then I suggest you think about it now and learn a little wisdom for the future," Philip said.

"I will never do anything like this again," she vowed.

"Do it if you wish, but don't expect me always to be there to extricate you. And that's another thing; if you must take a lover behind the Earl's back could you not at least take one with whom you could agree? I only intervened because I heard voices raised in argument."

"But we were arguing over you," Theresa explained. "He said some dreadful things. He even called you a filthy sodomite!"

Philip groaned. "In heaven's name! Do you mean to tell me that is what has caused me all this trouble?"

"Don't you mind, then?"

"Not in the least. I presume he was referring to my friendship with Monsieur, and I can assure you that his friendship means more to me than the opinions of a jealous and petty-minded man like Richard Lindsey."

"I don't care. It was sufficient that he criticised you."

"Was it? Why? You do it," Philip reminded her.

"That's different. I'm your wife, I'm entitled. No-one else is."

Philip shook his head in despair. "Might I make one small request, wife? In view of today's outcome, should another person ever dare to speak against me in your presence will you please promise not to defend me?"

"No," Theresa said staunchly. "I could never promise that."

"Just as I feared." He tucked away a straggly strand of her hair which, as usual had escaped its pins. "I have to leave you now for

I am expected at the Club, which will no doubt be in a jubilant mood after the execution."

"I went to it," she admitted, in a small voice.

"With Lindsey?"

"No, he brought me home but I went all on my own. It was so horrible, my Lord. I wish I'd never gone."

Philip recalled Henriette's reaction to Coleman's suffering and thought how differently it had affected this sensitive little creature.

"You've certainly had a busy day! Why ever did you go? I knew you wouldn't like it."

"I thought to prove that you were wrong about me," Theresa admitted, "but I found out you were right, and now I don't believe I shall ever be able to get the memory out of my head."

Without really thinking what he was doing Philip kissed her lightly on the forehead. "There, it's all gone now."

She smiled at him. "Are you very angry with me?"

"I'm not angry with you at all," he reassured her, for it was the truth. The only emotion he had felt when he discovered her with Lindsey was a desire to protect her.

He would have to guard against that, he decided.

By the time Philip was able to return home from the King's Head, Theresa had retired to bed but she knocked upon his door early the following morning.

He was doing his hair, which was one feature of which he was still rather proud.

"Ah, good morning Lady Devalle." He peered at her reflection in his mirror. "Did you sleep well?"

"No," Theresa muttered crossly. "You might guess that I did not."

"I'm glad. You didn't deserve to rest last night! Since you are here, would you be so kind as to assist me? I am in a hurry today and Morgan has never really mastered this!"

Theresa sniffed the pot of perfumed oil. "It smells wonderful," she said, deftly brushing the oil on each curl, just as she had seen him do.

"It should. It is the same as Monsieur uses and very expensive!"

"Where are you going?" she said when she had finished and was clearing away the things, as naturally as though she'd always done it.

"I go to visit Secretary Williamson. Shaftesbury is attempting to discredit those who rumour that he plans to bring in a Commonwealth but, because Williamson is a friend of Samuel Pepys, he will allow his complaints to go no further than his office."

"But what does the Earl expect you to do about it?"

What Shaftesbury expected was for Philip to employ a veiled threat against the Secretary's life, but he thought it kinder not to ruin any more of Theresa's illusions concerning her lover.

"Don't fret, sweetheart, I will think of something," he said instead, "although, of course, it may well be my final action in this world," he teased her.

Theresa gave a little cry and impulsively threw her arms around him. "Don't say that! I am so very sorry."

He held her for a moment, surprised to feel her trembling. "Tess, I was only joking." Her eyes had filled with tears and he viewed her with alarm. "Don't tell me you are actually fond of Lindsey."

"Not at all. I'm crying for you." She clung tighter to him. "You might be killed."

"What?" Philip began to laugh, but he stopped when he perceived she really was in earnest. "Do you care what happens to me, then?"

"Of course I do." Her grey eyes raised up to his. Although still misted with tears, they were filled with sincerity.

Philip gently disengaged himself and turned away to put on his coat. "You are surely not thinking that I will die by Lindsey's hand?" He went back to the mirror and affixed a solitary heart-shaped patch to his cheek. "I trust the gods have reserved me for a more honourable dispatch than that!"

He winked at her over his shoulder as he left. "I may not live to what they term ripe old age but I assure you, sweetheart, I am not proposing to make a widow of you yet awhile!"

Philip arrived at Chelsea Fields at the stroke of the hour, riding Ferrion. He had come in great haste, for Shaftesbury had detained him. Lindsey was there already, with his manservant. So was Morgan and, to Philip's surprise, also Theresa, sitting on the steps of his coach.

He barely had a chance to catch his breath before throwing the reins to Morgan and removing his coat. That he handed to Theresa. "I am pleased you decided to watch me, Tess."

"I wouldn't miss this for the world," she told him.

"Then I shall try to be entertaining! Any words for your champion before he goes to meet his fate?" he asked her lightly.

"What can I say, my Lord, save that I admire you for your courage and for your selfless loyalty to Lord Shaftesbury."

"My what?"

"Isn't that the reason you are fighting Lindsey, to spare the Earl's feelings?"

Philip glanced at Morgan, whose expression was unreadable. "Of course it is, sweetheart!"

The wind had turned chilly. It whistled softly in the bare branches of the trees and caused the ruffles of their shirts to flutter slightly as they both took their positions. Philip noted with some pleasure that Lindsey did not look nearly so cocky now as he had the day before!

When they were both ready Morgan gave the word and a clash of blades jarred the silence of the wooded enclosure. Philip had not fought since the fateful duel in the woods near St. Antoine, or even had the opportunity to practise very much lately, but Signor D'Alessandro's lessons came back to him now, as they always did.

He soon had the feel of his opponent and fended off Lindsey's swift jabs with ease. Lindsey, though he might be fitter, was no strategist and reined futile blows against Philip's defence.

There were no assassins waiting to deal him a treacherous blow this time, but Philip knew his greatest enemy was likely to be his own health if the duel went on for too long.

Lindsey applied more determination to his thrusts, but in doing so he neglected his guard. Philip was quick to seize his opportunity and made a lightening lunge at his chest.

He had left himself so exposed that Philip's blade could have passed through him but, instead, Philip brought his weapon down, only scratching Lindsey's skin but cutting off one of the buttons of his shirt. Lindsey instinctively cried out, anticipating the feel of the sword's sharp tip, and Philip laughed, letting him know he had been tricked.

Flushed with fury, Lindsey redoubled his efforts.

Philip managed to cut the threads of another button almost immediately, leaving Lindsey's shirt gaping open, and all those watching, including Lindsey's own man, took no pains to hide their amusement.

Lindsey was by now incensed and Philip no longer jested with him. He knew he had pushed him to the limit and must expect a frenzied retaliation. This had always been when Philip was at his best. There were times when his sword became like a living part of him, making every movement seem instinctive and effortless.

Unfortunately, this was not one of those times.

Now that they fought in earnest Philip needed all his skill to hold Lindsey off. Several times the metal sliced the air dangerously close to his cheek and, although no harm was done, Philip knew he had lost his advantage, for the fast, feinting movements were giving him considerable discomfort.

He still succeeded in slashing Lindsey's left arm, but the effort hurt him badly.

Morgan called out 'first blood', but Lindsey signified that he wished to continue.

Desperation appeared to be lending Lindsey new strength. Philip had to turn sharply to block a thrust and the scar inside him felt as though it had ripped apart. He reeled back, feeling sick, and heard Theresa's cry of alarm.

He managed to keep his feet, although the effort caused him to bite his lip, but Lindsey, unaware of how badly he had hurt him, must have taken this to be another trick.

"We shall see how fine an actor you are when you are grovelling for mercy Devalle."

"To you?" Philip panted, swaying slightly. "Never!"

"For that insolence you shall do it on your knees."

Rashly, Lindsey aimed a vicious swipe at the back of Philip's legs but Philip, through no design of his own, staggered at what would have been the moment of impact. Lindsey overreached himself and lost his balance, crashing to the ground at Philip's feet.

Philip focused on him with difficulty, his blade hovering over Lindsey's chest. For a moment, with the dreadful pain tearing at his side, Philip was once more back in St. Antoine and the man lying at his mercy was Benoit.

"No, my Lord!" The sound of the Morgan's voice brought Philip to his senses. His hands were shaking as he lowered the sword. "Get up," he told Lindsey, whose eyes were wide with fright. "It is over."

Philip remained where he was, sustained by his will alone, until Lindsey and his servant had mounted their horses and were out of sight.

Then dizziness overcame him and the strength went from his limbs. Before Morgan and Theresa could get to him he had fainted.

༄

"How is he?" Theresa asked anxiously as Morgan came down from Philip's bedroom.

"He is still in pain," Morgan told her. "I am doing what I can for him."

"Have you sent for a physician?"

"No. He will not let me."

"Why ever not?" she cried.

"He has no faith in them. He swears their treatment killed a friend of his, although for myself I reckon Monsieur Gaspard would have died in any case."

"Was that the friend whose death caused your master such grief?" Theresa said, recalling Philip's words on the night of the ball.

Morgan looked at her uneasily, as though fearing he had already said too much, but he must have realised that her concern for him was real. "Gaspard's death was a great blow to my master," he said at length. "He has been very lonely since then."

"Lonely? Surely not," Theresa said. "There are always people fussing round him."

"Yet there are few who truly care about him."

"But you care, Morgan."

"He is my life," Morgan said simply.

Theresa had not forgotten Morgan's words to Philip at that awful moment when she had feared he was going to kill Lindsey. They had been spoken not as a plea but rather as a command, and Philip had obeyed them instantly. She wondered what strange bond existed between the pair.

"He does have Monmouth," she reminded him. "The Duke loves him like a brother."

"It is that friendship I most fear, for I am certain it will lead him to disaster," Morgan said grimly. "If I may speak plain, my Lady, in my opinion it was a sad day he ever fell into Lord Shaftesbury's clutches."

Theresa thought about some of the things Philip had been forced to do for Shaftesbury and she decided Morgan was probably right.

"Go down and see my maid, Bet," she told him. "She'll make up a physic for him. She knows a potion for every ache and ill and, though they may taste foul, they'll do him more good than his precious brandy."

❧

Philip was lying in bed, propped up on his pillows, with his eyes closed but he opened them as he heard Theresa tiptoe in.

"Well, well, if it isn't my troublesome little wife, who once swore she would not interfere with my life!"

"You can't reproach me more than I do myself."

Kneeling down beside his bed, Theresa buried her head in her arms and, to his dismay, began to sob.

Philip reached out and gently stroked her hair. "Do hush, Tess. I forget you take my words so much to heart. Come, dry your tears and sit on the bed beside me."

She did so, taking care not to hurt him. "Are you still in great pain, my Lord?"

"Not so great now," he lied.

"I'll make this up to you," she vowed. "I promise that from now on I will be the most obedient and dutiful wife a man ever had."

Philip groaned. "Make me no more promises, I beg you, sweetheart!" He took her hand, suddenly serious. "Actually, there is one thing you can promise me. Now that you are aware of the true state of my health I want you to keep it from Shaftesbury. If he asks what ails me you can tell him that I have caught a chill. Apart from Morgan, only Buckingham knows the full truth of what happened to me in France and you must let no-one but him in to see me for a while."

"What if Henriette calls?" Theresa asked him archly. "Do I let her visit you?"

"There would not be much point," Philip said, smiling at her tone. "There's only one thing she desires of me and I would be no good to her in this condition!"

Theresa smiled too, but she soon grew serious again. "How much longer can this go on, my Lord?" she asked him. "You should consult a physician."

"From what I have seen of the barbarous methods employed by men of medicine I have little to gain from that," Philip said. "Sometime I will show you what one of them did to me in France."

Theresa sighed. "I cannot make you see a doctor, since you have convinced yourself that it will be no use, but, though the Earl will never learn it from me, he must soon realise your true condition."

"Not, if I am lucky, until the end." Philip patted her hand, for she had made no attempt to withdraw it from his. "Don't look so sad. I am becoming resigned to my fate and I pray only that I live long enough to see those who did this to me defeated."

"Don't say that!" Theresa jumped up from the bed. "I'll not accept that nothing can be done for you. You're being stubborn."

Philip raised an eyebrow at that. "Stubborn, am I?"

"Yes. I won't believe you're going to die. I won't, I won't." Tears welled in Theresa's eyes again and, this time, she ran from the room.

Philip lay back on his pillows. The last few days had brought a change in his relationship with Theresa, and it was one he had not anticipated. His years at Court had accustomed him to the company of beautiful and sophisticated females and Theresa was neither of those things, but he did find her intriguing for she was unlike any woman he had ever met.

He was still pondering on that when Morgan entered a little later.

"Morgan, am I stubborn?"

"Yes, my Lord." Morgan put down the tray that he was carrying and Philip frowned when he saw the jug upon it.

"Whatever is that?"

"A physic. You will not enjoy it," Morgan warned as he poured a glass of the thick, dark liquid.

Philip stared at it in horror. "You are surely not suggesting I should drink that foul concoction?"

"Mistress Bet prepared it and you will drink it," Morgan said firmly.

"I'm damned if I will!"

Morgan held the mixture out to him. "Unless you drink it I shall take away your brandy."

Philip snatched the glass from him. "You are a tyrant, Morgan, I have always said so." He drained the glass and grimaced. "Dear God! What has she put in this?"

"Coral wort and gentian, I believe. It will heal your insides, so she says, and ease your pain."

"If I die now it will be from Bet's poisoning and your heartlessness," Philip grumbled.

Morgan gave him a long-suffering look and passed the brandy bottle over. "Yes, my Lord."

The duel left Philip in a delicate condition. It was a several days before he could even walk about and a full week before he felt fit enough to leave the house.

Determined that Shaftesbury should detect nothing wrong with him, he stood as steadily as he could whilst the Earl related what had happened that day at the trial of five Catholics accused of plotting against the King.

Oates and Bedloe, together, had managed to convict three of the men but the other two had been returned to Newgate because Bedloe had been unable to substantiate Oates evidence against them.

"It is his business to concoct some tale to support Oates in his accusations," Shaftesbury reminded him. "Bedloe is your responsibility and he has to be more positive in the giving of his evidence. As for that idiot brother of his! They put him on the stand today too and it is a wonder the pair of them were not arrested, and Oates with them! I wonder sometimes what I am paying you for."

"But the two priests are back in Newgate," Philip pointed out, aggrieved that once again he was getting the blame when things had gone wrong. "Gaol fever is rampant there, so I hear. They'll die in any case."

"That's not the point," Shaftesbury said. "They must be seen to die a traitor's death. The people press me and I have nothing to give them. You may tell Bedloe that I shall disown him unless he can come up with someone to convict of Godfrey's murder before the end of the year."

Bedloe looked gloomy when Philip relayed the Earl's message to him. "That only gives me two weeks, my Lord. What does he expect me to do? It's not my fault, surely, if he has been unable to get a confession from Pepys' clerk, or if the two Jesuits I accused have taken it into their heads to disappear. Am I supposed to conjure up more suspects out of the air?"

"You'll think of something," his brother, James, said loyally. "You always do. You are a genius."

"It is for sure you would be hard pressed to get by without me," the 'genius' muttered. "I've always had to think for the both of us," he complained to Philip, "and if I do not come up with something soon there is a likelihood that the promising career of

William Bedloe will end upon the gallows! Can't you help me, my Lord?"

"I'll see what I can do," Philip promised. He pointed to James. "And for God's sake keep him off the witness stand!"

His chance to help Bedloe did not come until two days before Christmas, when he received a message from a clerk at the Courts who he was paying to keep his eyes open for new developments.

"He says there is one who may suit your purpose waiting now in the lobby of the House of Commons, my Lord," Morgan told him.

In that case you had better find Bedloe and tell him to meet me in the lobby without delay," Philip decided.

He drew Bedloe aside as soon as he arrived. "In that room there sits a man awaiting examination," he explained. "Look at him well, so that you may remember him. His name is Miles Prance and he is a Catholic silversmith who makes ornaments for the Queen's chapel. He is here because a malicious lodger, who he threatened to evict, has sworn that he was absent from home at about the time Godfrey was killed. It should be simple enough for you to swear that you saw him at Somerset House on the night the Justice died."

"Aye, that's simple enough," Bedloe agreed, "but he'll deny it and there will only be my word against his."

Philip shook his head. "This time I intend to get a full confession, more, I'll have Prance naming his associates and joining us as a witness. If the two of you can swear to the same tale we can hang anyone we damn well please for Godfrey's murder."

Philip had good reason himself to want that particular matter resolved.

"What if he won't confess, my Lord?" Bedloe said.

"Leave that to me. Go straight to the 'Heaven' eating house, it is the nearest, and wait there," he told Bedloe.

"For you?"

"No, I am going to speak with Sir William Waller. I will arrange for this Prance to be brought there under escort. Directly you see him cry out that he was one of those who stood over Godfrey's body. Shaftesbury will do the rest."

"Then I am saved! A thousand thanks, my Lord."

"Your thanks are premature. Whether you are saved or not depends upon how convincing a liar you are," Philip reminded him.

"I am a perfect liar," Bedloe said proudly.

"Then, my friend, you are as good as delivered from your difficulties."

And so he was.

Philip went to see Shaftesbury on Christmas Eve and found him in excellent humour, for once.

"I understand the silversmith confessed to everything after you had him thrown into a hole in Newgate!" the Earl said.

"Yes, I thought he might," Philip said grimly. He had not forgotten his own experience in the Bastille, or that it was a Papist who had caused him to suffer it.

"He has even agreed to join us as a witness! I must find some way to repay you. There is surely some trifle that would amuse my fine peacock, who I doubt is any the less vain, for all he has discarded his brilliant feathers."

"Your approbation is recompense enough, my Lord." Philip still found it demeaning to be kept by Shaftesbury and rewarded as a master might reward a dutiful servant.

"Then at least you must agree to take better care of yourself." The Earl looked at him sharply, for Philip lately needed to use for support the silver-headed cane he had once carried for affectation.

"I am perfectly well," Philip lied. "Besides, there is so much yet to be done and," he added quietly, "so little time."

"But Monmouth has not yet even begun to gather his forces.

I shall appoint you his second-in-command," Shaftesbury said. "You shall travel the country with him, at his right hand, sharing his triumphs. You will recruit men from the farms and villages and they will flock to join you in their thousands. It will be a glorious campaign."

"A glorious campaign," Philip echoed, but with a trace of sadness, for he had finally begun to believe that he would never see the fruits of his endeavours.

"Your future is assured," Shaftesbury continued, although he could never have realised the irony of his words. "The people will idolise you, just as they will Monmouth. In all our history there will never have been a king of England so well loved by his subjects."

"And you will be the most powerful man in the land," Philip reminded him.

"When that day comes I will make you a general!"

Philip laughed, in spite of everything. When Shaftesbury was in a good mood it was hard not to get swept up in his enthusiasm.

"A toast," Shaftesbury said, pouring them both a drink from the brandy bottle on the table before him. "I predict that, by the last day of December, Charles Stuart will prorogue his Parliament. It is my belief it will not reassemble. He raised his glass. "To the coming year, and whatever it may bring."

Philip raised his own glass and attempted to sound more optimistic than he felt. "The coming year, and whatever it may bring."

FIFTEEN

The year began badly for Theresa. On a grey, gusty, afternoon, early in January, she received word that her mother had died.

Morgan, who had brought the letter up to her, stood by silently, guessing from her reaction at the nature of its contents. She passed the letter over for him to read.

"A fever, Morgan, that is all it says. I was not even aware that she was sick."

"I expect her illness was brief." Morgan's craggy face showed an honest sympathy which touched her heart.

"You would say that to comfort me, but are you not thinking, the same as I, that my father did not write sooner because he thought I would not bother to go home in any case?"

"You should not reproach yourself," Morgan said. "You are committed here and if you were not present to do your duty you would be no credit to those who place trust in you and, therefore, no credit to your family."

Theresa looked at him gratefully. "You make my motives sound so noble and yet I cannot help but wonder if I have grown selfish and thoughtless. Though there are times, I admit, when I question what we do, the truth is I have not once desired to go home."

As Theresa thought about the family she had not seen or considered for months she realised just how much she had grown apart from them.

"You are only eighteen years of age," Morgan pointed out. "It is natural that you should crave excitement."

"My husband says I am a child!"

That made him smile. "Let me fetch you some refreshment," he offered. "That will make you feel better."

Theresa derived a great deal of comfort from her food. "Bless you, Morgan, you understand me so well, but it is not your place to run around after me," she reminded him. "You have quite enough to do caring for your demanding master."

"He has not yet returned home, my Lady, and I would be pleased to attend to your needs," he assured her.

Though barely four o'clock, it was nearly dark. Theresa lit the candles and went over to the window. The wind lashed rain against the glass now and the rivulets of water gushed down like tears. It would be good to cry, she thought, resting her forehead on the cool pane, and yet she could not. She was genuinely sad but a little ashamed too for, mixed in with her sorrow, was a feeling of relief that, although she was the eldest daughter, now that she was married she would not be expected to live at home and run the house.

As she drew the curtains she looked down and saw that Philip was arriving home, water dripping from his cloak and hat. The door was opened and quickly shut as a gust of wind came in with him. It blew right up the stairs and under her own door, making the fire smoke.

Philip was cursing the weather and stamping his wet boots when Morgan appeared, carrying a plate of cold mutton pie for Theresa. Philip listened gravely to his news and decided to take the plate up to Theresa's room himself.

She was poking the logs in the hearth as he entered, trying in vain to persuade them to revive. "You are a treasure," she told him, without looking up as the door opened. "Before you go, could you do something with this wretched fire?"

"I'll consider it."

Theresa spun around, her hand to her mouth, as she saw that it was him who had entered instead of Morgan. He went over to the hearth and aimed a skilful kick at the logs with his mud splattered boot. Immediately the sulky flame flared into life.

"That's very good, my Lord, but I did not intend asking you to do it."

"So I gathered! Morgan has conveyed your sad news to me. You have my sympathy."

The tears that had eluded her before came now, and Philip pulled her gently toward him. "Cry on me, if it helps."

Theresa laid her head upon his chest and sobbed quietly for several minutes.

"It is a dreadful thing to lose your mother," he said softly, when she had calmed down a little. "I have no memory of mine, but I know I would have loved her and she would have loved me. Shall you go home for the funeral?"

Theresa sighed. "Yes, I must. I'll need to leave tomorrow to be there on time."

She sat down gloomily and picked at the pie he had brought her. Philip guessed that she was thinking about the long, lonely journey ahead of her, and Philip thought about it too. It would take her two full days to reach Dorset, perhaps more if the weather was against her. She looked so tiny and so vulnerable, and he knew he could not let her go alone.

"I had better come with you," he decided, although he did not relish the journey in midwinter either.

Theresa raised her head. "You mean to Dorset?" she asked uncertainly.

"If you wish it."

"Oh, yes. I would love you to come." Her relief was plain, but then her face fell. "The Earl would never let you leave London."

"On the contrary, whilst Parliament is prorogued there is little here for me to do at the moment. In any case he does not own me completely, no matter what you may think," Philip said. "It is decided then. Buckingham will lend us a coach and Morgan can take a message to the Earl. I will see to everything."

He turned to leave, but Theresa caught him by the arm. "Why are you doing this for me, my Lord?"

Philip wasn't even sure of that himself. "We start at first light," was all he said. "Be ready."

They were upon their way by seven o'clock the next morning. The persistent rains had left the Weymouth road awash with mud and, in some places, almost impassable. They were scarcely the twenty miles to Leatherhead before the coach became firmly lodged in the sticky mire, and they had to wait by the roadside in the freezing cold whilst Jonathon and Ned struggled to free it with poles.

The blackamoors strained and slipped in the mud, for they were more accustomed to managing Philip's ornate town vehicle than the heavy coach and four which he had borrowed from Buckingham, but at last they were on their way again.

Philip was not so much troubled by the cold as by the jolting of the coach and he winced as the wheels ran over a boulder.

"It is good of you to endure all this for me," Theresa said.

"Would you keep me in a glass case?" Philip asked her.

"No, but I am aware of how much more you are suffering since the duel. Shaftesbury has noticed it too, I fear. He said to me the other day that you had grown so thin and bloodless that he wondered if he had been driving you too hard."

"Shaftesbury would do better to worry over his own health," Philip said. "On Christmas Eve he was violently sick and coughed up blood, and I can hardly wonder at it. He drank sufficient to lay an average man upon his back."

"And you let him?"

"For heaven's sake! I am not his nursemaid. He knows perfectly well that brandy burns the abscess in his stomach.

Besides, he would no more heed me on that issue than he would concerning John Scott."

Shaftesbury felt that Scott would make a valuable witness against Samuel Pepys but Philip feared that bringing Scott back now would be playing right into Pepys' hands. Philip was not certain of how much reliance he could put upon Scott's loyalty if Pepys threatened to disclose some of the many dark secrets he might have unearthed about his past.

Philip knew that Theresa had heard mention of Scott but he guessed that Shaftesbury would not have told her too much about him so he said no more on the topic and, for the next few miles, they sat in silent contemplation of the Surrey hills.

At Guildford they stopped to rest the horses, choosing a small inn out of the town. Theresa devoured a plate of ripe game with turnips, washed down with a glass of red wine and followed by a plate of candied fruits, which she ate with her fingers.

Philip had no appetite and managed only a little cheese with the remainder of the bottle of wine.

"You really should take more than that," Theresa said, licking her sticky fingers. "The fare here is excellent."

"You appear to have done it justice for the pair of us!" He threw her a napkin. "Don't lick your fingers, please. Monsieur does that too and I cannot bear it."

She pulled a face at him but obediently used the napkin.

"That's better," he said approvingly. "I'll make a lady of you yet! Now, if you are replete, may I suggest that we continue our journey if we are to reach Winchester by nightfall?" he tossed a pile of coins upon the table and helped her to her feet.

The door was opened for them by a wench of about Theresa's age, who had been gazing at Philip from the moment he had entered. As he passed through she made a clumsy curtsey.

Philip smiled at her. "Thank you, sweetheart."

The girl looked about to swoon and clutched the doorframe for support.

"You certainly made an impression on her," Theresa said as the coach moved off again.

Philip shrugged. "Women usually find me attractive."

"I've noticed that! I wonder what my family will all make of you."

"All? How many are there?" Philip had not even thought to ask any questions about the Fairfield family.

"I have six brothers and sisters."

"Good God!" he stared at her aghast.

"I am the eldest, by two years, then there is Giles, he is quite a young man now, then Rosemary and Sophie, they are twins, then there's Anthony, named after Shaftesbury, Lucy and little Daniel. They are well-behaved," she added hastily. "The youngest are never permitted in company whilst the twins are so shy they speak only to each other and Giles, well Giles can be a bit difficult," she admitted, "but he is a good-looking boy and we were usually friends. I think you'll like him. Of course," she added hesitantly, "I realise they are not the sort of people you are accustomed to, but I hope it will not be too trying for you, my Lord."

"I dare say I can cope with them," he reassured her, amused by her concern. "After all they are now my family too, I suppose."

"Not much like your own, I'm afraid." Theresa sighed wistfully. "Oh, how I envy you your noble birth."

"You have no need to, surely, not now you are a titled lady."

"I may share your title but I am still a squire's daughter, for I can never share your heritage."

"And what is that worth?" Philip said. "I have a mad earl for a brother and my mother's family in France want nothing to do with me!"

"What do such things matter when your place in society is unquestioned?" Theresa said. "I would a hundred times rather be wed to a beggarly gentleman than to the richest of merchants."

"Then you have your desire, Lady Devalle, for in joining fortunes with me you have acquired one of the most finely bred and yet most impoverished peers of the realm," Philip reminded her.

"I was speaking generally," Theresa pointed out, blushing. "I know that I did not win your name fairly, for you would never have chosen me for yourself."

"Quite right." Philip watched her out of the corner of his eye and saw her expression of dismay. "I would have chosen Henriette McClure!"

Theresa burst out laughing as she realised he was joking. "No, you wouldn't!"

"No," Philip agreed, "I wouldn't, and nor would I have chosen you, though not for the reasons you seem to think. I care not, truly, if you are the daughter of a street trader or a duke. It is simply that, as things now stand, I would not have wished for the encumbrance of a wife at all. However, since I must have one, I suppose you will do as well as any!"

"Was that a compliment, my Lord?"

Philip was tempted to deny it, for he enjoyed teasing her, but she looked so delighted that he had not the heart. "Yes, it was," he said instead.

The weather and the light being against them, they made it only to Alton before breaking their journey for the night. Philip's side was aching badly and Theresa said she felt as though every bone in her body was bruised, but they both felt better when they had sat for a spell before a blazing log fire.

They were not left in peace, however, for the innkeeper saw few travellers since the weather had made the road so hazardous and he obviously welcomed the diversion. He seemed especially pleased to observe that they were people of quality and asked after all the latest news from London, so that it was late before they managed to get to bed and the morning arrived far too soon.

"There'll be snow before long," the innkeeper said sagely as he saw them off. He pointed to the heavy sky. "It's on its way, mark my words."

Theresa forced her fingers into her muff. "If he's right we could be stuck down in Dorset for weeks."

They settled themselves as comfortably as they could amongst the fur rugs and Theresa said she would try to sleep, as she was still very tired, but the lurching of the vehicle made sleep impossible for either of them.

At one point the rear wheels struck a rock and jerked the coach so violently that she was actually thrown from her seat to land on the floor at Philip's feet.

"I shall never be comfortable again," she complained, when he had helped her up. "I am stiff in every joint. The bits that don't hurt I can't feel at all." She blew upon her frozen fingers in a vain effort to restore their circulation.

"Rub them together," Philip suggested.

"And should I do the same with my feet?" she said huffily. "They are cold too."

Philip heaved a sigh and pushed her back further into her seat. She watched him open-mouthed as he grasped her right ankle and lifted her foot onto his knee. Next, he removed her shoe and stocking and rolled her skirt above her knee and then commenced to massage her toes and ankle to make the blood return. When he had replaced her shoe and stocking she promptly put her other foot upon his knee.

"Better?" he enquired when he had finished.

"Yes, much." She looked a little disappointed that he had stopped.

"Do I get some peace now?"

Theresa nodded, stretching like a contented cat. She snuggled down beneath her rugs and Philip smiled as he saw she was soon fast asleep.

∽

The coach turned into the drive just before dark. Squire Fairfield leapt to his feet and called his son.

"Giles, I hear carriage wheels. It must be Theresa. Bless the child, she has come home."

"In such a conveyance?" Giles was looking at Buckingham's coach, which was just visible as it rounded the last bend in the drive.

"Our girl is a titled lady now," his father reminded him as he went to call his other children out to see their sister.

"She is not alone," Giles said. "I can see another in the carriage with her."

"Probably a servant."

Giles did not rush out with the rest but hung back, for the vehicle had to pass by the window at which he stood, and when it did he saw clearly into it. First, he recognised his sister and then he let out his breath in a low whistle as he glimpsed her travelling companion.

"A servant? I think not!"

He looked down at his black mourning apparel with a pang of regret that it was not more stylish. Graceful in bearing and slender as a willow, Giles grew increasingly vain as he grew older. It irked him that he should not have better clothes to flatter his fine figure and that the opportunity to move in fashionable society was denied him.

Curiosity at length overcame his narcissism and he joined the welcoming party, though standing a little apart so that he would be better noticed. Theresa, who alighted by herself, went to him directly she had embraced her father.

"Why, Giles, how fine you look!" She took both his hands in hers. "I had forgotten that you were so handsome! May I still kiss you?"

Giles allowed it because he was pleased at her compliment.

"It is especially good to see you again," she whispered, "and just wait until you see the surprise I have brought!"

She hugged the twins and kissed the younger children, who were staring at their sister in all her finery as though she were a stranger. For a family reunion it was restrained, even considering the tragic circumstances of their meeting, and Theresa was more than ever aware of how she had grown apart from all but Giles.

She slipped one arm through his and one through her father's. "Now for my surprise. I have brought someone back with me."

"Your friends are always welcome here," Fairfield said.

"But he is not merely a friend, father. He is my husband."

"His lordship is in that coach?" Squire Fairfield paled. "Dear God, whatever can you be thinking to bring him here?"

"Father!" Theresa cried. "You are privileged to receive him."

"I know, child, but we cannot entertain him as befits his station, especially not at this sad time."

"For goodness sake! Are we such peasants that we must be ashamed to let him see us as we really are? Respect his rank by all means but, I beg you, keep your pride."

Giles, for his part, was not in the least put out. "I propose we invite him from the vehicle so that he may be at liberty to form his own opinion of us," he suggested, "To keep him waiting any longer would be plain discourteous."

"You are right, of course," Theresa said gratefully. "I shall fetch him without more ado." She turned to the children, who were still exclaiming at the sight of Jonathon and Ned, for they had never seen a blackamoor. "I trust you can all be relied upon to keep absolutely silent unless he speaks to you, which is unlikely."

Philip had waited patiently whilst all this went on.

"They have been informed of your presence," Theresa said when she returned to him, "though that is not to say that they are ready for you."

Philip descended from the coach slowly, partly because he felt that, after the obvious consternation his arrival was causing, he should probably make his entrance with fitting dignity, but mainly because he was stiff from sitting for so long.

The Squire bowed when Theresa introduced them. "We pleased and honoured to receive into our house a guest of your rank and reputation, my Lord, especially one who is so intimately acquainted with the Earl of Shaftesbury, who we proudly claim as our friend and benefactor."

Philip very much doubted that he was pleased at all. The younger children looked terrified of him, and he would not have known what to say to them anyway, but one person there caught his interest. Giles was, as Theresa had said, good-looking, with a fair skin and the same slightly slanting grey eyes as his sister. There the resemblance ended, for Giles' features were less angular than hers and his hair, which framed his face in soft waves, was of a much deeper shade of auburn.

Fairfield introduced them and Giles approached him, neither eagerly nor shyly but rather with a quiet self-assurance, and made him a most elegant bow, with that grace which cannot be attained but is inborn in those who have it.

Philip watched him with all the appreciation of an expert. He knew instinctively that he was meeting a kindred spirit.

Fairfield escorted them first to the chamber where Theresa's mother lay on a black-draped mourning bed. He left them alone and Philip remained by the door. Not having ever known the deceased woman, he felt he would be an intruder at such a personal moment, but he saw that Theresa was standing motionless in the middle of the room.

"Well get it over with," he said quietly. "You only have to do it once."

She turned to him, her eyes wild. "I can't."

"Don't be ridiculous! It's the living harm you not the dead."

"It isn't that, it's the bed. I saw it at my uncle's house when I was child and it terrified me even more than the sight of my dead aunt."

"You're frightened of the bed?" He went over to her and took her hand. It was trembling. "Hold on to me," he instructed her.

He took her to the bed and then held her hand firmly whilst she bent to kiss her mother's cheek.

"I trust you will not forget this act of gallantry the next time you are berating me for some fault or another," he said lightly as he led her from the room.

She managed a smile, despite her tears. "I never will, my Lord, I promise."

The funeral was to be held the following day and although it was not to be until seven o'clock in the evening, the preparations began at first light.

Several friends from the village were to go with the mourning procession from the house and, although the impending bad weather had dissuaded more distantly situated relatives from travelling, there were still a good many local members of the family to be catered for.

The household staff was small, consisting of only a cook, a slavey and three housemaids, but a footman had been borrowed for the day from one of the big houses in the village and also two ladies' maids to administer to the needs of the female guests.

Theresa summoned one of these to help her dress. She had never had a personal servant before she went to London but she had come to regard it as in keeping with her position. Alas, the village girl had not Bet's deftness. She fumbled with the awkward stays for so long that Theresa was quite frozen before they were on and fastened up her own bodice, deeming it quicker and less uncomfortable.

Her dress, mourning ring and gloves had been purchased in readiness for her by her father, but the plain black dress was far from being to Theresa's liking, for it neither fitted properly nor was comfortable. Her maid exclaimed over it nonetheless for, notwithstanding its faults in Theresa's eyes, the dress was made of satin and the girl stroked it longingly.

"You like this?" Theresa asked her.

"I think it is beautiful, my Lady."

Theresa wriggled inside the offending object. "Then it shall be yours after today, for it makes me look a positive fright."

The girl looked shocked. "I'd like it, my Lady, that I would, but shan't you stay in mourning for your dear departed?"

"I hadn't thought of that." Theresa peered at herself in the glass. "Well you shall have it anyway, for even I must wear black I cannot possibly wear this dreadful thing in London."

The black toilet set, kept for funerals, had been provided for Theresa's use but without Bet's assistance she managed very badly. The young village girl proved quite unequal to the task of coping with Theresa's long hair and, when she could tolerate being pulled about no longer, Theresa dismissed her and struggled with it herself. Eventually she got it to stay up, though the pins dug into her head and the black comb would not keep in place, but since she would be wearing a veil she supposed it would suffice.

Since Philip no longer wore anything but black he had no need to make any changes to his appearance. He was soon surrounded by quite a crowd of neighbours and relations, who could not have treated him with more deference had he been King Charles himself. Philip was content to hold court, with Giles hovering constantly at his side to make the introductions, whilst Theresa was busy

in the kitchen, supervising the preparation of the macaroons, biscuits and cold meats, which were to be served later with white wine and claret.

At six o'clock everyone assembled outside and dole-faced mutes were stood upon each of the ten steps down which the coffin was to be brought. Each person was then given a lighted taper and they followed the coffin down the drive.

As they turned into the road a sin-eater came forward out of the crowd that had gathered by the gate. While all watched he ate some bread over the corpse and drank a glass of ale. Squire Fairfield handed him a sixpence and he went on his way, having just taken upon himself all the sins of the dead person so that she might lie in peace.

The train of light snaked slowly through the village, to the accompaniment of chants from the poor of the neighbourhood, who joined on behind, carrying branches of rosemary and yew to represent the immortality of the soul.

Philip walked with Theresa and Giles, carrying a taper like the rest, but his thoughts were far away. Jules' funeral in Paris had been nothing like this traditional country affair but he could not help but be reminded of it all the same and he was relieved when at last the procession passed the village stocks and arrived at the church.

He found it difficult to concentrate upon the service and afterwards he walked to the graveside with Giles, who, he had noticed, seemed quite unmoved by any of it, unlike Theresa and the younger children. A strong wind whipped around them as the coffin was lowered into the earth, almost extinguishing the wax lights and, in the eerie, flickering half-darkness John Highmore, the Rector, intoned his solemn words above its howling.

Philip shivered, though not from the cold. The coffin he was seeing being lowered into the grave was not that of Theresa's mother but of Jules. As a handful of earth landed upon it he flinched and turned away, wishing that Morgan was there with him.

"Come away, my Lord." Almost on cue, Giles took his arm and led him to the black-curtained coach that waited to take them home.

Philip was grateful to him. Giles had somehow sensed what was going through his mind and had taken charge of the situation, exactly as Morgan would have done.

Theresa had one final duty to perform before she could join them in the coach. A horse and cart had drawn up at the church, laden with hampers of meat, bread and eggs, which she, Sophie and Rosemary distributed amongst the poor in payment for their mourning.

The drive home was a silent one. Squire Fairfield's grief was plainly etched upon his face and Philip thought Theresa looked exhausted. Giles, on the other hand, seemed so perfectly composed that Philip doubted whether he could be feeling anything at all.

For Theresa the day did not end after they arrived home. There were visitors to attend to and by the time she did manage to crawl into her bed she was so weary she could scarcely stand.

Tired as she was, she could not sleep. Her head was filled with the events of the day and, even with the fire made up high in her bedroom, she could not get warm. She got out of bed and went to sit on the hearth for a while, hoping the heat from the fire might make her drowsy, but it didn't and she started thinking about Philip. Giles had told her what had transpired in the churchyard and she was worried about him, for he had hardly spoken after their return and had retired to bed early.

She decided she would tiptoe down the corridor to his room to see if he was asleep.

Philip was not asleep. He was sitting at a table with his head in his hands. Beside him was a bottle of brandy that he had requested of Theresa's father and he had drunk a good half of it, trying to numb his brain, but his thoughts remained painfully clear.

He heard the door open quietly and glanced up. "Tess! What are you doing wandering about in the night?"

"I couldn't sleep."

"Nor I. Come in then, then, and sit beside the fire."

They sat for a few moments in companionable silence and he became aware that she was watching him intently, her expression one of genuine concern.

For the first time since Jules' death he felt the desire to talk about him. He told her everything, from their first meeting to the end, and she sat silent throughout.

"That is a tragic story," she said pityingly when he had done.

"The hardest thing to bear was seeing him die, day by day and hour by hour," he said. "Tortured by a damned physician and growing weaker as I watched him."

"Is that why you won't see a physician yourself?"

"Not entirely," he confessed. "I have suffered in their hands already. Would you care to see what a member of the medical profession did to me?"

Philip took off the dressing gown he was wearing and Theresa grimaced

when she saw the ugly mark on his side. He was about to cover himself again when she cried out in horror.

"What is it?" he asked her.

"The scars on your back!"

"Oh, I see." Philip never gave a thought to those anymore. "My brother used to beat me when I was a child and your lover had me flogged once."

"The Earl had you flogged?" she gasped.

Philip realised what he had unthinkingly said. "I should never have mentioned that."

"How could he treat you so?" She sounded stunned.

"You had best forget I told you," he advised her. "I ought not to be burdening you with my troubles tonight, sweetheart. I should be comforting you in your grief, not the other way about."

"I feel quite numb inside," Theresa admitted. "I am very tired, but this house is so cold I am sure I'll never sleep."

"I'm not surprised you're cold. You're wearing nothing but a shift!" Philip got into bed and pulled back the bedclothes. "Get in here with me for a while."

Theresa climbed in quickly and snuggled down next to him. "I am pleased you told me about Jules," she said. "I feel I understand you better now, but I cannot believe, from what you said of him, that he would want you to be sad."

"I'm sure you're right, but it is hard not to be sad when you are the one left alone."

"You are not alone, my Lord," she said quietly. "You have me and I would truly like to be your friend."

Philip was touched by that. He was accustomed to being around people who said a great many things they did not mean, but he knew that from Theresa the words were sincere.

"Sweetheart, that is worth a lot to me. And I really think," he added, smiling, "that since you are in my bed it would be quite in order for you to start to call me by my first name!"

"May I really? Thank you, Philip." She laid her head contentedly upon his shoulder.

Philip was aware of a quite unfamiliar sensation.

Ever since he had felt the stirrings of his manhood he had been easily aroused. It had begun the first time he had become aware of Nanon's nearness as she bathed him. In Barbara's expert hands he had known ecstasy and now the touch of any woman could excite him, whilst the mere feel of a female body pressed against his own stimulated desires he had never learned, or tried, to control.

As Theresa lay beside him, however, it seemed as though a pleasant warmth enveloped him and he felt a tingling, not from passion but from something he could not quite define. All he knew was that he was happy just to hold her in his arms.

The closest he had ever come to such feelings was with Nell. He had often wondered whether he had actually been in love with Nell all those years ago, but had been too young to know it.

His life had been just beginning then. There had been so much he had wanted to do, and love would have been inconvenient.

Now he feared it was too late for him to fall in love, for he was convinced he did not have much time left to live.

He felt a pang of regret as he watched Theresa, already sleeping peacefully, but Philip knew he must prevent her from becoming more attached to him than she already appeared to be.

Jules' slow death had nearly destroyed him and he wanted no-one, especially not this gentle little creature, to suffer in the same way over him.

Theresa soon began to miss the noisy city. It had never been her nature to be idle and the days spent talking with her father or dressing the twin's hair in the latest styles from Court soon became wearisome. She hadn't seen too much of Philip since the night of the funeral. He was spending most of his time with Giles, and there already seemed to be a familiarity between them which Theresa rather envied.

One crisp, bright afternoon she felt like getting out of the house so she and Giles saddled horses and rode to Ringwood.

They followed the meandering forest paths and crossed the sparkling streams which, swollen by rains, splashed swiftly over rocks and fallen branches. They dismounted by a rustic bridge and Theresa leaned over and looked into the swirling water.

"London seems a million miles away," she said softly, as though fearing to break a dryad's spell.

"Or two days upon the road," Giles said.

"You have no soul," she scolded him. "It has been good to have your company all the same. I shall miss you when we go."

"I might be going with you."

Theresa stared at him. It was the first she had heard of it.

"Why should I stifle here in the country whilst you enjoy the town?" Giles said, kicking a piece of loose bark from one of the supports of the bridge. "It isn't fair. I have already discussed the matter with your husband."

Much as she loved her brother, Theresa harboured no illusions about him. Giles had always been manipulative. Ever since they were small children it had infuriated her that he could get his way in everything. Giles never lost his temper when things went against him, as Theresa did, but his sweet disposition concealed an iron nature.

He had dominated their mother, whilst the younger children treated him with a respect they had never shown their big sister. Only their father did not defer to him, which she guessed was one reason Giles had determined upon leaving, for Giles needed to rule.

It was his way and would be throughout his life. Few would ever stand against him and none would ever get in the way of what he wanted.

A letter bearing Shaftesbury's seal had arrived for Philip on the London stage. He was reading it when Theresa returned from her ride.

"Parliament has been dissolved," he told her. "The country is at last free of Danby and his policies!"

"What happens now?" she wondered.

"Now there will be elections, sweetheart and, if we are lucky, the Whigs will be asked to form a government. The next few months will be exceedingly busy ones and Shaftesbury wants us to return to London without delay. We ought to leave tomorrow, for this weather may not hold."

"I can't say I'm sorry to be going. I'll tell my father." She hesitated at the door. "Giles says he wants to travel back with us."

"I know exactly what Giles wants," Philip said. "With Fairfield single-mindedness he seldom refrains from mentioning it a dozen times a day!"

As he had expected, she had not been gone many minutes before Giles came in and settled himself on the arm of Philip's chair.

"Theresa tells me you have received good news from London."

"Extremely good."

Giles toyed with the rings on Philip's fingers. "May I try them on?"

"Certainly." Philip slipped the jewelled rings from his hands and held them out to him.

"I shall be rich one day." Giles regarded his own slim hands, now adorned with the jewellery. "I shall own fine things like these."

"I don't doubt it."

Giles handed the rings back. "Have you always been ambitious?"

"Always. I was very like you," Philip said.

"Then you know what it is I want."

Philip had wondered how long it would be before the subject was broached again. "Yes, Giles, I know what you want, but I'm not sure I can help you."

"Why not?" the grey, uncompromising eyes rose to his. "Don't you like me?"

"You know very well that I do. You are a fascinating young man, and one who would be a credit to me, but I don't believe I can agree to be your patron."

"I understand." Giles looked hurt. "I shall not trouble you upon the matter any further, my Lord, for I would certainly not wish to inconvenience one who has so little regard for me." He got to his feet. "I will leave you now, for doubtless you have a great deal to do before your journey and I had better not take up any more of your valuable time."

"Giles, I recognise myself in all you do," Philip warned him. "Now you are employing the self-same tricks that I once used on Buckingham! That you wish to come to London I can understand, just as I can understand that my name and reputation would advance you."

244

"And is that the way you judge my motives?"

"Yes," Philip said frankly, "for they were mine when I first attached myself to Buckingham. I once used the Duke, just as once I used Monsieur. We are two of a kind, you and me. I knew that from the start."

"And you think I am using you? It's not true. I admire you," Giles said.

Philip regarded him cynically. "I am little to admire these days, I fear."

Giles shook his head. "I think you are magnificent. You'll not change my opinion of you – even if you don't want me beside you."

"It's not so much a case of what I want," Philip said. "Firstly, there is your father to consider. He may not approve of your going to Court. Mine didn't."

Giles dismissed that with a shrug. "Mine will not object to my leaving. I am quite a lot of trouble to him."

Philip could believe that. "But there are other things to consider. I have no money and it will take a great deal if I am to be as good a patron to you as Buckingham was to me, for I cost him plenty."

"But it will only be for a short while," Giles said, "for I intend to be a soldier soon, like you. Besides, the Earl of Shaftesbury can't refuse my sister anything. I'm sure she could persuade him to grant you an allowance for me."

"Even if she could I'd have so little time to spend with you," Philip said. "Shaftesbury is no easy master."

"I wouldn't mind. At least I'd be in London. You said yourself I was too elegant to spend my life amongst country clods."

"I don't remember saying that!"

"Well it's true in any case."

Philip looked at him. There was a determination in those delicate features and fire too. He sensed he had probably met his match.

He sighed. "You are a persistent little bastard, aren't you? Do as you please. I can't fight you anymore."

Giles smiled, for he had triumphed, as Philip guessed he generally did. "You won't regret it."

"I had damn well better not!"

SIXTEEN

Philip took his duties as a patron seriously. He insisted that Giles take lessons in dancing, music, singing and even philosophy, but he knew that the most pleasurable lessons of all for Giles were those spent receiving instruction in the art of fencing. Being slight of build and nimble, Giles showed promise of developing speed enough to satisfy even Philip.

He devoted what time he could to Giles and the pair became a well-known sight at coffee houses, at the theatre and at Court, where Giles quickly became a favourite with the ladies. Philip did not consider it any part of his obligation to pass judgement on his charge's morals, indeed he felt himself ill-qualified to do so!

He introduced him to Monmouth, who took to him right away, but Philip was careful not to involve him in any matter which concerned Shaftesbury and he refused to take him to the King's Head Tavern or any place where Party matters were discussed.

Philip saw very little of Theresa now. Sharing himself between two such demanding people as Giles and Shaftesbury, who had now replaced Danby as Charles' first minister, he had few hours to spend with her. That actually suited him rather well, for he feared they had grown closer than he had ever intended.

One afternoon when Theresa was alone with Giles she suggested that she teach him to play backgammon, the intricacies of which she had not long mastered herself. Giles accepted her invitation but they had scarcely begun when a great commotion sounded in the hall below.

Theresa rose from her seat. "Morgan has some trouble on his hands, I think."

"I am certain he can handle it. Sit down," Giles said.

She was about to do so when she heard her own name called. "It's me they want!"

"Are all your friends so rowdy?"

She ignored him. "I'm sure I know that voice. Wait here while I go down."

"What, and miss the fun? Not likely!"

Giles was quickly on his feet and they raced downstairs, just as they had when they were children.

Before they reached the bottom, they could see Morgan struggling with what appeared to be a frenzied demon clad in dirty rags. Bet was with him and the other servants stood around shouting encouragement.

"Theresa, help me!"

This time she was not in any doubt as to who it was.

"It's Thomas! Morgan, let him go at once."

In his surprise the Welshman loosened his grip and Thomas hooted in triumph.

"I knew you would remember me, Theresa."

Theresa blushed, recalling just how she had met this urchin from the streets, and that her stomach had revolted at the sight of Coleman's execution.

"Of course I remember you. What were you doing to him, Morgan? He was calling for me."

"Morgan was not to know you'd want to see him," Bet said protectively. "He speaks your name with such familiarity, and he asked me for the maid, so we little thought he really knew you."

"Ah!" Theresa saw now where the difficulty lay. "This is my fault, Thomas," she said gently. "I lied to you."

"But you do work here?"

"I am not a maid," she confessed.

"A housekeeper then, or perhaps a cook? It's all the same to me."

"No, Thomas, none of those. Oh dear, I don't know how to tell you this at all."

"I'll tell him," Giles said. "My sister is Lady Devalle, and the mistress here."

"Sacre Bleu! What trick is this?" Thomas made for the door.

"Don't go, I beg you." Theresa reached the door and blocked his path. He darted this way and that, like a frightened animal, but he could not get by.

"I plead with you to let me go. I will not bother you again."

"But why are you here?"

"I found out where you lived in case I ever needed help, but I want nothing from you now except my freedom."

Theresa stood aside straightaway. "You have it. I would never keep you here against your will. Now only tell me how I can help you?"

He shook his head. "No. All is different now. You are a lady."

"Nothing has changed." She took his hand. "We are still friends, Thomas, and you did me a great service, which I would very much like to repay. Are you in trouble?"

"You will shortly know in any case," Thomas said resignedly, "for I think I might have been followed here by the sergeant and his men."

"What have you done?" Theresa said.

"Why, nothing! They claim they saw me cut a lady's purse, but I am innocent, I swear it. I escaped them but they chased me and when I saw that I was near Lord Devalle's house I hoped that you might hide me. No matter, perhaps I can still outrun them."

Even as he spoke there came the rapping of the sergeant's stick upon the door. Thomas shrugged his thin shoulders philosophically.

"C'est la guerre! At least I've seen you once more before they lock me up."

Theresa gasped. "You will not go to prison, surely?"

"Not for long. They'll very likely hang me if there was more than twelve pence in the purse, or flog me if there wasn't."

"That is monstrous!"

The stick sounded again and this time a rasping voice accompanied it.

"Open up in the King's name!"

"They shall not take you, Thomas," she assured him. "I shall see to it that you have justice done. Morgan, Thomas has already proved himself a friend to me. We must help him."

"Whatever you say, my Lady," Morgan said, his face as expressionless as ever. "I'd better open the door to them, though, before they hammer it down."

The Welshman calmly faced the burly sergeant, who stepped, uninvited across the threshold.

"There he is! He'll not escape us now." The sergeant's two men would have entered with him had Morgan not stood his ground.

"What is the meaning of this intrusion?" Theresa demanded.

"Beg pardon, Lady Devalle, but we seek to apprehend this felon, who has taken refuge here."

"There must be some mistake." It was Morgan who had spoken, and all eyes turned to him. "This is my sister's child who, being orphaned, lives here with me."

Theresa looked at him with relief. Morgan had taken charge of the situation as capably as he always did.

The sergeant was less impressed. "Lives here? There must indeed be some mistake, for he is clearly nothing more than a ruffian of the streets, and we did see him take a lady's purse."

"Then your eyes have deceived you," Morgan said. "My nephew may be poorly dressed but he is not dishonest."

The sergeant turned to his men. "Is this the boy or not?" They both agreed it was. "There, now are you satisfied?"

"Not a bit of it." Theresa faced him fearlessly, shielding Thomas with her own slight frame. "I will not allow you to arrest this blameless boy."

"Unless you stand aside, my Lady, I regret I shall be forced to move you, at the risk of being disrespectful," the sergeant said.

"Lay a hand on Lady Devalle and those two apes of yours will have to carry you out of this house," Morgan said quietly.

"Do you threaten me?" The sergeant straightened to his full height and looked down at the stocky little Welshman.

Morgan did not waver. "That I do."

"So, you would obstruct an officer of the law in the performance of his duty? Then I shall arrest you with the boy. Seize him!"

The soldiers rushed inside and attempted to obey, but they were obviously unprepared for Morgan's strength and they were both spun round to land, dazed on the floor.

"Seize him, you incompetent fools," the irate sergeant roared.

They leapt on Morgan again and this time Bet joined the affray, kicking the sergeant as he was about to bring his stick down on Morgan's head.

"Stop that, or I shall arrest you with them, woman," he yelled.

Philip walked through the open front door at that moment and looked at the scene before him in disbelief.

"What the devil is going on here?"

"Philip, thank God you've come," Theresa cried. "Do something quickly. They're arresting Morgan, and it's all my fault."

"I might have guessed at that!" Philip turned to the officer. "What do you think you're doing?"

"This man is to accompany us and I beg your Lordship not to interfere."

"Interfere?" Philip glared at him. "The impudence! Unhand him this very instant or it will be the worse for you."

The sergeant swallowed. "I cannot, my Lord, for he obstructed me. My sworn and rightful duty now is to deliver him to Newgate prison."

Philip regarded him coldly. "Are you aware of who I am, sergeant?"

"All London knows you, Lord Devalle."

"And the man who you and your minions have so rudely seized is my personal servant, who has been these last six years in my employ. If you care to keep your position then release him now. I will myself answer for anything you claim he has done."

Morgan shook the men off disdainfully. "My Lord, permit me to explain."

"That will not be necessary, Morgan. I trust your judgement. Well, sergeant, explain yourself."

"We spotted this young ruffian lifting a purse."

The 'young ruffian' was hauled up by the collar and deposited at Philip's feet. In all the confusion he had not even noticed him before.

Theresa glanced at him pleadingly and he decided he had better play along. "Are you absolutely sure this was your thief?"

"Then it is true that you know him, my Lord?"

It was obvious from the sergeant's tone that he was disappointed.

Philip took his cue from that. "I don't doubt Morgan has explained him to you," he said.

"Aye. He said the boy was his nephew, but I don't believe it."

"What of my wife? She, I'm sure, substantiates his story," Philip said heavily.

"She does, but the fact remains that we have run this vagabond from nigh on Drury Lane."

"Then you have wasted your time and let the real culprit escape you," Philip said. "Why not search the boy? That ought to convince you."

They swooped down joyfully on Thomas and stripped his poor clothes off him, shaking out each article. They discovered nothing, just as Philip had expected. Accustomed to missing very little of what went on around him, he had been watching the boy closely.

Cursing them loudly, Thomas dressed himself again.

"So, were you right or wrong?" Philip said.

"I was wrong, my Lord," the sergeant admitted.

"Then be gone and do not show your miserable faces here again. Employ your lummoxes in rounding up some Papist scum if you would keep them busy."

Bet closed the door after them. All the other servants, save for her and Morgan, had disappeared about their duties directly Philip had returned and an awkward silence now descended upon the five people who remained to face him. It occurred to him, not for the first time, how much simpler life had been when there was just him and Morgan.

"Well?" he prompted.

"I suppose you are wondering exactly what this is about," Theresa began sheepishly.

"I will confess to experiencing a mild stab of curiosity as to why, directly my back is turned, my home should become a sanctuary for cutpurses!"

"Thomas is no thief."

"If that is what he told you he is not only a thief but a liar," Philip said. "Bet, come here please."

Bet came over to him, looking mystified.

"Unlace your bodice."

"My Lord!"

"Don't waste my time with girlish modesty." Without more ado he reached into the top of her dress himself and, to the obvious astonishment of all but Morgan, produced an embroidered purse. He tipped it out and three sovereigns rolled across the floor. "A novel way of increasing your ample charms, Bet!"

Bet flushed scarlet. "When did he do that?"

"Just before I suggested that the sergeant searched him."

Theresa giggled until her brother slapped her. "You are right, Giles, this is a serious matter. Thomas, you did take it after all."

"Well of course he did." Philip shook his head despairingly. "One glance at the fellow should tell you what he is."

"Oh, Thomas," she cried reproachfully, "how could you lie to me?"

"I thought you'd turn me over to them," he wailed.

"That would have been no more than you deserved, you wicked boy. You should count yourself extremely fortunate that Lord Devalle shielded you."

"I did nothing of the kind," Philip said. "I simply rescued Morgan from the consequences of his soft-heartedness."

"I saw him hide the purse too," Morgan admitted, "but I couldn't give the lad up. He has been scared enough by this, he need not hang for it."

"He's a cheeky little slubberdegullion!" Bet clipped Thomas round the ear, but not very hard.

Theresa sighed. "Our problem now is what to do with him."

"*Your* problem, sweetheart. I am finished with it." Philip waved his hand in a gesture of dismissal.

"You promised to take me to buy some silver lace this afternoon," Giles reminded him.

"Then let us go. I trust this tiresome matter will have been resolved by the time I return," he said to Theresa.

"How would it be if he stayed here with us?" she ventured. "Couldn't you train him to be a servant, Morgan?"

"He looks strong and he certainly has courage," Morgan said. "I reckon he would not be afraid of hard work if he had a fair master to whom he could be loyal."

"You see all that in him?" Philip said. "Morgan you are a marvel! So be it. He is in your care."

"Then he can stay?" Theresa cried.

"Aye, Tess, he can stay. It is not often Morgan forms a favourable opinion of anyone, but when he does I've found he's seldom wrong. Why, he even saw good in me!"

"But don't you want to know how he came to be here?" Theresa said.

"No," Philip said decisively. "I really think that I would rather not."

"Your Grace, you are a proper gent and no mistaking!"

The others all stared aghast as Thomas flung his arms around Philip and hugged him.

Philip looked down at the dirty little head which was pressed against his new black and silver brocade waistcoat. Then he looked at Theresa.

She was watching him with a horrified expression and, for once, seemed at a total loss for words.

His lips twitched but he fought back the desire to laugh. "Well, thank you, Thomas, but they have not yet made me a duke!"

✐

Philip was in the gallery of the court of King's Bench, watching as Pepys clerk, Samuel Atkins, was brought in.

He no longer stood accused of Godfrey's murder but of being an accessory to the act. Three other men had been named by Miles Prance, to replace the three that Bedloe had first accused, and who had fled. Philip had feared that Bedloe's original statement would not have been too easily forgotten, as he had been paid five hundred pounds for it, but the men were all found guilty. Titus had played a small part in that trial, just to lend some substantiality to the proceedings, but Miles Prance had done very well, after Philip had persuaded him that he would be a fool to refuse Shaftesbury's offer. Especially since the alternative was certain death.

Upon the other side of the courtroom Philip caught sight of Pepys, who glared at him in open hatred. Philip ignored him but, in truth, he was not looking forward to the trial. He had not agreed with involving Pepys' clerk in the first place and he now regarded him as a distinct embarrassment, for Pepys had assembled a number of witnesses to prove young Samuel's whereabouts at the time of Godfrey's murder.

The Prosecution's case hinged chiefly upon Bedloe. Philip thought he seemed quite flustered at the quantity of witnesses for the Defence and he did not look at all happy when his turn came to take his place upon the stand.

"Captain Bedloe," Lord Chief Justice Scroggs began, "you declared before the committee appointed to examine Justice Godfrey's murder that, at nine o'clock on the night of October fourteenth, you saw the defendant bending over the body of the Justice at Somerset House. Is that what you are prepared, under oath, to tell this court?"

"No, my Lord."

There was a shocked silence. No-one present had been prepared for Bedloe to recant. Except Philip.

Bedloe went on to explain that he could no longer be certain it was Samuel he had seen that night, despite what had told the committee, and that, now that he'd had a chance to think about it, the man had been older and, in any case, had been standing in the shadows.

"So, you will not swear it was he?" Scroggs asked.

"My Lord, I could not swear to take a man's life when I am uncertain."

"Would you swear that it was *not* he?" Attorney-General Jones said craftily.

This time Bedloe evidently thought he had better cooperate. "No, sir, I would not swear to the matter either way."

Samuel's witnesses for the Defence were far more positive, in fact they proved without a doubt that he was nowhere near Somerset House upon the night in question. The Prosecution's case was clearly lost.

Philip's reception from the members of the Green Ribbon Club was decidedly hostile that evening. They had become accustomed to triumphs, not defeats, and they clustered round him asking angrily how the acquittal had been allowed to happen. Philip was vexed and reminded them that, but for his labours, their Cause would not be nearly so far advanced.

Shaftesbury sat apart, neither excusing nor condemning him. When the clamour had abated, he beckoned him over and Philip resigned himself to receiving the sharp edge of the Earl's tongue as well. He was surprised to see him smile.

"Poor Philip! How they turn upon you. Such is the price you pay, I fear, to be my deputy."

"No reproaches from you, my Lord?"

"None. I see not quite what they expected of you. The trial was sooner than we anticipated and there was no time to even empanel the Jury. With his clerk released, however, we shall need to find another way to dispose of Samuel Pepys. The blasted man has been retained as Secretary of the Admiralty, even though those who sit upon the committee appointed for executing the office of Lord High Admiral are all our men. Such a thing is without precedent. It proves that Charles has no notion of how to manage the country's affairs."

Philip, on the contrary, thought it demonstrated a very high degree of political awareness. "He seeks to regain his popularity by giving the symbols of power to us, the people's favourites, whilst retaining his staunch and loyal followers," he said. "It seems that, whichever party is in charge, Pepys is to be permanently Secretary of the Admiralty."

"Not if I can help it," Shaftesbury said. "I have appointed a Parliamentary Committee to enquire into the miscarriages of the navy but, in the meantime, I still believe we should recall John Scott."

Philip groaned. "That again?"

"We have to break Samuel Pepys, or at least get him out of the way for a while. Scott is a mapmaker, is he not, and has spent some time in France? Who better to swear that Pepys was selling naval secrets to the French?"

"None better," Philip said reluctantly and, indeed, he could think of none save Scott who would be prepared to speak out at all against so powerful a person as Pepys, whatever the reward, "but he will still need someone to substantiate his story."

"You could do that," Shaftesbury suggested.

Philip stared at him. "You jest, of course."

"Indeed I do not. I am in deadly earnest," Shaftesbury said. "All you will have to do is go up before the House of Commons and concoct some story that agrees with Scott's. Is that so difficult?"

"You expect me to be a liar now, no better than Oates or Bedloe?" Philip was appalled at the prospect.

"It's only for this one time."

"But what if it is discovered that I give false evidence?"

Shaftesbury shrugged. "You are a peer. What can they do to you?"

"I don't particularly wish to find out."

"You will send for him and you will obey my orders," Shaftesbury said testily, "unless, of course, you have found a way of existing without my support for you and your protégé, whose needs I am now expected to provide for as well as your own."

"Very well," Philip said sourly, "but I still fear that what Pepys may reveal about Scott's character many turn the tables right about and likely land Scott in the dock. Of course, he may be persuaded by the threat of exposure to turn on me."

"Scott would not betray you, surely. He is your friend."

"There comes a point at which the most enduring friendships are put to the test. Do not overestimate my powers to draw men to me," Philip warned. "If faced with death there is scarcely a fellow who could resist temptation."

"What about you, Philip?" Shaftesbury said. "I cannot forget that Charles once offered you the chance to betray me."

"For God's sake! Have I not proved often enough that I am loyal to you?"

"Even so, I think I will take you with me when I next go to see the King," Shaftesbury said. "It will show him that I still own you, just in case he is considering asking you again!"

When Philip arrived home, there was a letter waiting for him from Charles Sackville. Philip had known him since Sackville had been Lord Buckhurst, the man who had once seduced Nell from the stage, but they had long since become amicable. Sackville, who was now the Earl of Dorset, had been appointed the Lord Lieutenant of Sussex, and it was in that capacity he was writing to him.

Philip's day had been a difficult one and his side was throbbing. He asked Morgan to read the letter out to him, whilst he sank gratefully into a chair with a recuperative measure of brandy. The spirit was the only thing which seemed to alleviate his pain and it took a larger quantity each day before he felt relief.

"My Lord, I write to tell you that your brother, Henry, has been placed in my custody after attacking and maiming a worker from your family estate. He is at present being held at Chichester and is a behaving in a manner which leads me to believe that his sanity has utterly left him. In view of our long acquaintance, I feel it incumbent upon me to offer you the opportunity to deal discreetly with this matter and I await your urgent instructions. Sackville."

"Hell and damnation!" This was all Philip felt he needed to make the day complete. "Why could Henry not have killed the man? Then they would have executed him and High Heatherton would be mine."

"That would have been better for you," Morgan agreed. "Shall you go down to Sussex?"

"For what purpose? Unless he's much altered, the merest sight of me will be sufficient to send him into a rage. Wait, though, Morgan." Philip smiled as he considered what he had said. "I see possibilities."

Morgan obviously saw them too. "You don't mean to have him proclaimed mad? My Lord, think of your family name."

"Now you sound like my father," Philip said. "For years he refused to put Henry into proper care and even on his deathbed he would not accept the truth. Henry, his eldest son, must have his title, his estate and all his fortune whilst I must struggle for a living how I can. I am not so sentimental, Morgan. Besides, Devalle insanity is no secret."

"Even so, my Lord, can you afford a scandal now?" Morgan said. "Some may accuse you of being touched with the same sickness."

"Perhaps I am." Only Morgan knew how many times Philip had questioned his own sanity. "I used to wonder whether I should not be stricken with the 'Devalle sickness' in my old age but that no longer troubles me, since I doubt now if I shall ever reach it. One thing I'm resolved to, though, is that I'll never die a pauper if I have it in my power to own Heatherton. I'll fight him in the Court of Common Pleas and I must surely win if I can show him to be mad. This time my precious brother has played right into my hands."

Delighted at the prospect, Philip poured himself another brandy and passed the bottle to Morgan. "Drink to my good fortune, Morgan."

"You haven't got it yet," the prudent Morgan reminded him. "What reply shall you send to this letter?"

"I shall tell Sackville that I thank him for his consideration in not dealing with my brother as a common criminal, and that I shall dispatch a doctor and attendants to Chichester straightaway with instructions to remove Lord Southwick from his care and commit him to Bedlam."

"Bedlam?" Morgan repeated disbelievingly, for some of the inmates of that accursed place were kept in cages. "He is an earl!"

"He is an animal," Philip said quietly. "I lived my childhood in the shadow of his cruelty. It is him I have to thank for the lash marks on my back and it is thanks to him that I received no proper education, since every tutor my father engaged was driven away by Henry's abuse and violence. For the first twelve years of my life I was allowed no friends outside of the estate and no contact with the world. Revenge will be delicious, have no doubt of that." He saw the Welshman's expression and sighed irritably, for Morgan's opinions were important to him. "You disapprove, I see."

"Whatever else he might be, he is still your brother. It is a question of blood, my Lord."

"I don't put too much store on that," Philip said frankly. "You are far dearer to me than my brother and if it was you in Chichester gaol then I would fetch you home and care for you myself, but I am damned if I can see what I owe him."

Philip meant that, every word, and Morgan was plainly touched by what he'd said.

"It might take you years to get High Heatherton through the courts," he pointed out.

"No matter. I doubt I shall have need of it for myself. I want it only as a legacy for Tess, for I doubt she's given the least thought as to what will happen to her when Shaftesbury discards her, as he's sure to do in time. Who knows whether she may have some of his bastards to bring up in my name by then, and I'd not see her destitute. She's not to know I said that, mind," he added warningly. "It would not do to let her know I care about her, for I fear she already grows too fond of me."

Morgan's eyes met his but the Welshman said nothing.

"I have tried to keep her distant, Morgan, truly I have, for her sake. Shaftesbury can give her so much more than I and in a year, perhaps less, she may be a widow. Would it be worth sacrificing so much for so short a life with me?"

"Why not let the choice be her own?" Morgan said.

Philip shook his head. "Tess will ever be ruled by her heart and there are some decisions best made for her. My way is by far the better one, I'm sure of it."

SEVENTEEN

_ɔ‿ɔ_

"I never married Lucy Walter." King Charles faced Shaftesbury and Philip defiantly. "Whatever it is you claim to believe, I did not marry her and I have not the least intention of saying that I did for your convenience."

The Earl looked cross. "It is not for our sakes you should be saying it, your Majesty, but for your son, Monmouth."

"Good God, man, it has never yet been proved that Monmouth even _is_ my son," Charles said. "I like to think he is for, although he is in some ways weak, he is a son any father would be proud to own, but, though he is the handsomest of all my children, I fear he resembles Robert Sidney far more than he does me."

"What kind of talk is that? Would your Majesty disown him?"

"Did I say so? No, my Lord, not even now that he has grown Colonel Sidney's wart upon his face! But he is a bastard, whether a royal one or not, and there is nothing on this earth can make him otherwise."

"Sire, you wrong the reputation of an innocent woman," Shaftesbury said.

Charles laughed. "Lucy was a woman of no particular virtue, as you know. She had a child by Arlington whilst I was a year in Scotland and, apart from him, it seems that half my Court had sampled her delights before myself! For all I know you might have had her too."

"Monmouth is no son of mine," Shaftesbury said indignantly. "I wasn't even there."

"No, you were a Parliamentarian by that time," Charles said evenly, "but let us not digress."

"Your Majesty forces me to employ less congenial measures," Shaftesbury warned.

"You refer to your Black Box? Produce it if you can. There are no articles of marriage in that or any other secret spot, since no marriage took place."

"I shall show otherwise."

"You are confident, Lord Shaftesbury. A little overconfident, perhaps."

"Should I not be, Sire, when I am certain of my facts?"

Charles dark eyes flashed, but he contrived to smile. "I believe it was Mr. Bacon who said that if a man begins with certainties then he will end with doubts."

"Your Majesty misjudges me if you think that I will waver in my purpose," Shaftesbury said.

"I know not what your purpose is entirely but let me tell you this – I would rather see my son, if so he is, hanged than sat upon the throne of England."

Philip, who had kept resolutely silent through this, was surprised at the vehemence of Charles' tone and he raised a cautionary eyebrow at Shaftesbury.

The Earl ignored him. "You have a duty to your people."

"You dare remind me of my duty?" Charles looked angry now. "Let me remind you, Lord Shaftesbury, and you, Lord Devalle, that by this time tomorrow my brother, the Duke of York, who is extremely dear to me, will be upon his way to Brussels, sent there by me to live in exile, and all on account of your persecution of his followers. No, I will not sign your blasted declaration, or any like it. I know my duty, gentlemen, and you shall find none firmer in its execution. That is my final word."

Charles and Shaftesbury glared at one another until Philip, realising an impasse had been reached, stepped in between them.

"My Lord, since his Majesty is adamant there seems little point in our remaining here."

"Lord Devalle is perceptive, on this occasion at least. I am prepared to give you no more time, since all discussion on this issue will be futile."

Philip touched Shaftesbury upon the arm. "I suggest, my Lord, that we withdraw."

Shaftesbury looked at him furiously but Philip was already bowing as he backed away. The Earl had no choice but to follow his example but he still could not bring himself to leave without a parting shot.

"The country shall soon learn the truth and that their sovereign would conceal it from them."

Philip cursed under his breath. He had feared that Shaftesbury would lose his temper, and he had.

Charles stiffened. "Shall they also learn the truth about their 'saviours', and the methods that you pious men resort to on their behalf? Shall they rejoice to learn that your agents at Stafford killed a man of eighty-four, who was flung down the stairs as they arrested him? I know far more about your exploits than you think, Lord Shaftesbury, and yours," he swung round on Philip, "you who stand silently at his side and who claim to be Monmouth's friend. I once reckoned you to be a man of honour. If there is still any of that virtue left in you, which I am inclined to doubt, then I ask you to dissuade my son from this madness. He trusts you, God help him." Charles turned back to Shaftesbury. "There is blood upon your hands, my Lord, and blood must pay for blood but, though I must suffer your iniquities upon the innocent, I see not why I must endure your impudence. I will write a declaration after all, Lord Shaftesbury, and in it I shall state quite clearly that I have married none save the Queen, and you may put that news about wherever you will. Good day, my Lords."

This time there was no doubting the finality of Charles' tone and no disputing their dismissal.

Directly they were back in Shaftesbury's office he fell upon Philip in a rage. "He works against us now. Why did you not support me in there?"

"What the devil could I have done?" Philip asked indignantly.

Shaftesbury had no reply to make to that and he lapsed into a brooding silence that lasted several minutes. Philip, still piqued at Charles' reference to his honour, did not feel like talking either, and it was the Earl who spoke first.

"He will admit to his son's legitimacy yet. I will make him do it."

"My Lord, you are a stubborn, stubborn man."

Philip got up to leave, but he was particularly uncomfortable that day and could scarcely straighten to his full height.

"What ails you?" Shaftesbury demanded.

"I have nothing but a slight touch of the ague."

"A slight touch of the ague?" Shaftesbury mimicked scornfully. "Then I had best purchase Pepys sweating chair for you! Do you think me blind or a fool? Damn it, Philip you are deteriorating before my eyes. You have not been yourself since you returned to England last August. It can't be the pox; left untreated that would have disfigured you by now. Oates has a private physician, Dr. Jones, to attend to his every bellyache. You are to consult him and if he cannot discover what is causing you to waste away then I'll have Locke examine you when he returns from France next month."

Philip knew that John Locke had very little regard for him and would be only too delighted to reveal any evidence of his incapacity. He decided Dr. Jones would be a better bet since he, at least, could possibly be bribed and he promised he would see him.

He went straight home but he was still not to get any peace.

"Master Giles asked to be informed directly you returned," Morgan told him, a little unwillingly.

Philip knew that Morgan had not taken to Giles. For his own part, Philip had many times blessed his decision to bring

Giles to London. Giles, when he wished to please, could be the most agreeable person in the world and Philip was finding real enjoyment in his company. Distancing himself, as he deliberately had, from Theresa, and having little energy or inclination lately to socialise, he had become quite reliant on him.

Giles presented himself as soon as Morgan had informed him of Philip's return.

"You promised to take me to the theatre this afternoon," were his first words. "We were supposed to be going to see Mr. Wycherley's new play, but you were home too late."

Philip sighed. He was feeling especially vulnerable after Charles' harsh words and he did not wish to be attacked. "I'm sorry, I had not forgotten but I had to go with Shaftesbury to see the King."

"It doesn't matter," Giles said magnanimously. "I have something more important to discuss with you."

"Not now, Giles," Philip pleaded.

Giles leaned over the back of Philip's chair and massaged the taut muscles of his neck and shoulders. "The Earl is working you too hard. I hate to see you like this."

Philip managed a smile. "But you like the money that it makes us!" Much as he enjoyed Giles' attentiveness he harboured no illusions about him.

"That was what I wanted to talk to you about." Giles poured him a brandy and set it beside his chair. "I might be less of a liability to you from now on."

Philip regarded him over the rim of his brandy glass. Giles seemed excited, and he wondered why. "Go on."

"Have you heard that the Duke of Monmouth is gathering recruits to fight against the Covenanters?"

Philip had heard. "Yes, what of it?"

"I thought I might ride with him."

The words stung Philip like the crack of Henry's whip. He needed Giles beside him at the moment, more than he would ever have let him know. "You want to join the army?"

"I always said that I would be a soldier one day," Giles reminded him.

"Even so, I little thought that you would want to go so soon."

"I shall miss you dreadfully," Giles said, "but surely you see how excellent an opportunity this is for me. Monmouth particularly asked if I would accompany him."

Philip considered the irony of that. Monmouth had asked Philip to go to war with him when Philip himself had been about Giles' age, and it had been the cause of a rift between Philip and Buckingham.

"It is out of the question," he said, feeling hurt that Giles would want to leave him after only a few months.

"I really don't see why. If it's a matter of the purchase of my commission then I'm sure Theresa can wring the money from Shaftesbury, if you can't give it to me."

"It's nothing to do with the money."

"What then?"

"I am responsible for you," Philip pointed out, "and, in my opinion, you are far too young to go to war."

"I do believe you're envious," Giles said. "You would choose to ride with Monmouth too, if you were fit enough."

"You can be very cruel for one so young," Philip said quietly. "When did you arrange this? Monmouth has never mentioned a word of it to me."

"I think he feared you would be cross with him for suggesting it. He said he would not take me if it would upset you."

"Why should it upset me?" Philip asked huffily. "I am only the person who has devoted every spare minute of his time to you since you prevailed upon me to bring you here."

Giles looked at him artfully. "Are you asking me not to leave you?"

Philip was not about to fall into that trap. He knew well enough that if he did so Giles would have ascendancy over him always, and then he would get no peace from his demands.

"No, dear God no, I shall never do that." Philip got to his feet angrily. Exhausted though he was, he did not feel he could stay in the house a moment longer. "Do as you please, Giles, I no longer care. Go and be damned!"

Philip stormed out, slamming the front door behind him.

∝

"I sometimes wonder if I am not a fool to place my trust in you, Philip Devalle." Shaftesbury glared at him. "It seems I can rely on you for nothing anymore."

"What is it now?" Philip wondered.

"Scott has been arrested for attempting to enter the country illegally. He was caught in a fishing boat, if you please, off the coast of Folkestone."

"Folkestone? What the devil was he doing there?" Philip said, bemused, for he had sent Scott very precise instructions for entering the country.

"You may well ask. Since you arranged his passage I can but assume you told him to land there."

"I most certainly did not."

"Then it would seem that you can no longer keep control of your minions."

"John Scott is not the easiest of men to manage," Philip pointed out.

"Your ability to wring obedience from such scum as Scott is your chief usefulness," Shaftesbury said unkindly. "If you allow him to defy your wishes in this way, if so he did, then I shall doubt your worth to me at all."

"What do you mean 'if so he did'?"

Shaftesbury placed his fingertips together and studied them carefully. "I would have thought my meaning would be abundantly clear. You are devious, Philip, that I know. You did not want Scott here; possibly you assumed that if he was stopped on entry I would wash my hands of him."

"Why should I take that trouble when I could simply have bribed him not to come?"

Shaftesbury shrugged. "Who can tell? I have never fathomed the workings of that trickster's brain you keep inside your pretty head. I have not forgotten that you crossed me once before. On that occasion I had you lashed, the next time you are dead. Need I say more?"

"No, you have said enough." Philip had stood leaning on his stick throughout the Earl's tirade and he looked longingly at a chair. "May I sit down?"

"Sit, lie or stand upon your head for all I care, so long as you attend to what I say," the Earl snapped. "Since I have no proof, this time, of your disobedience I shall not make your punishment too severe. The money which I gave you to send to Scott shall be deducted from your own allowance. Is that fair?"

"Whatever you say. I am in no position to argue with you," Philip said resignedly. "What is to be done?"

"I have an order from the Secretary of State for Scott's release. You will deliver it to Dover."

"Dover?" Philip said in dismay. The last thing he felt like was a long coach journey to Kent. "Could no-one else take it?"

"It is my wish that you should go."

"But a messenger could take that order," Philip protested.

"You will undo the harm that you have done. That way the lesson will be taught."

Philip shook his head. "I will not do it."

"Oh yes you will." Shaftesbury brought his fist down hard upon his desk. "You, Philip, will do exactly as I tell you, and you need not look so proud. You are in no position to defy me now."

"Because of Scott's arrest?"

"Because of this." The Earl picked up a sheet of paper. "By now I should imagine this delightful piece of literature has been circulated in all parts of London."

"What is it?"

"It is a pamphlet, as you can see, the work, no doubt of Roger L'Estrange, who hunts our presses down whilst publishing filth of his own. This little masterpiece he has entitled 'The Prince of Profanity', and I will read it to you."

'He points a jewelled finger, screams High Treason
And Innocents are quartered without Reason
Whilst Shaftesbury's Harlot jealous tears must smother
Because her Husband doth prefer her Brother!
A French Monsieur as well, mayhap, who knows
How many have plucked petals from this Faded Rose?
The Lion Devalle, haughtiest of his Race,
An ailing body and Apollo's face.
Scarce credit to his Noble Lineage
This worldly fraud upon a Pious Stage.
A Tarnished Flower rancid perfume gives.
Shall Good Men perish whilst this Sinner lives?'

Philip remained impassive throughout the reading. Scandal sheets were not uncommon and most people in the public eye found themselves to be targets at some time or another, including Buckingham and Shaftesbury himself. Philip was annoyed nonetheless, for this one involved his relationship with Giles, which was already a sore topic with him.

"I warned you that your friendship with Monsieur would be the ruin of your reputation," Shaftesbury reminded him, "and now you taint the names of all of us."

"You'll be telling me next that you believe I have seduced Theresa's brother," Philip said indignant that, instead of sympathy, he was receiving condemnation.

"What matters is not what I think but what the good citizens of London believe," Shaftesbury said. "Whether I decide to keep you with me any longer will depend on the way you conduct yourself from this day on, as well as how willing you are to obey my orders. You will start for Dover in the morning."

Philip was still fuming at the injustice of the situation when he arrived home. He did not feel like going in straight away, for the atmosphere between him and Giles had become strained since their argument a few days before and, instead, he went around to the courtyard entrance at the rear of the house, where the horses were stabled. As well as the matching pair of blacks, which Jonathon and Ned were unhitching from his carriage, there was the little Arab stallion, called Scarlet, which he had purchased for Giles, and his own beloved Ferrion. It was for his stall that Philip made.

"Quiet now, my beauty," he said gently. "It is only I."

Ferrion, recognising his voice, began to paw the ground.

"You think I come to ride you? Would that I could." Philip was no longer able to ride, for the exertion caused him too much pain. "I come only to talk to you, old friend, for I doubt there is anyone else who cares to listen."

The fiery Ferrion nuzzled him, as though he understood.

"We have seen so much together, you and me. The two of us have sailed the ocean, fought the wars, killed, loved and hunted, ridden through the snow and scorching heat. For what? To find myself smeared by scandal and afflicted by this blight that will soon cripple me completely." He buried his face in the horse's curling black mane. "Oh, Ferrion, what have they done to me?"

A rustling sound amongst the straw round Ferrion's feet made Philip start. "What have we here?" He drew his sword. "A rat?"

As the long, sharp blade glinted in the stable light someone gasped.

"A human rat? Come out and show yourself, you villain, for you cannot run from me in here. Thomas?" he said, as the intruder slowly appeared. "Is that you?"

"Yes, I'm afraid it is, my Lord." The boy scrambled up, shamefaced.

"How long have you been here?" Philip said.

"An hour or so."

"Impossible! This horse would trample you to pulp."

"Oh no, my Lord, he likes me, see?" So saying, Thomas reached up his hand and stroked the horse's nose. Ferrion stood as meekly as a lamb.

"That is incredible! I've never known him this friendly to anyone but me."

"I've always had a way with horses. I was a stable lad for a while, although I never did see a horse as fine as this, my Lord."

Philip hid a smile. "You are an expert, are you?"

"I like to think I am a reasonable judge of horseflesh."

Philip eyed him solemnly. "Then I am pleased that Ferrion meets with your approval!"

It was the first time he had spoken properly to Thomas since their original encounter. It had been decided by Theresa and Morgan that the boy should be trained as a manservant for Giles and Bet had presented him to Philip, scrubbed clean and wearing new clothes, with strict instructions, he gathered, not to speak unless first addressed.

Away from Bet it appeared the urchin had forgotten his lessons, and Philip decided he rather liked him!

"How would you like to ride my horse?"

"Ride him?" Thomas' eyes opened wide. "My Lord, are you in earnest?"

"If you think you could manage him then you may exercise him for me, since I am indisposed at present."

"I would like that very much, my Lord, but what of Master Giles? I am supposed to be his servant," Thomas reminded him.

"Master Giles is more than capable of seeing to himself, besides I doubt he will be with us too much longer," Philip said. "You may continue to wait upon him when he wishes it but I would reckon that a bright lad like you aspires to something higher than to be a spoilt young man's attendant. Now I would like to know what you are you doing out here."

"I'm hiding from Mistress Bet, my Lord," Thomas admitted. "Look at me. She'll jumble me around for sure."

Thomas emerged fully into the light, shaking off the straw, and revealed a ripped coat, muddy trousers and a blood-stained face.

Philip looked at him in astonishment. "You're in nearly as bad a state as when we took you in. Where are your shoes?"

"I lost them. I have still got my shirt, though," Thomas added brightly, delving into the pocket of his coat, "well, most of it."

"Have you been set upon?"

"You're very near the mark."

"How near?"

"It was me who set on them," Thomas confessed.

"I see." Philip prodded with his stick the crumpled piece of paper which had fallen out of Thomas' pocket when he had attempted to produce his shirt. Even in the dim light of the stable, he could recognise it as Roger L'Estrange's pamphlet. "I am sure you had your reasons."

"That I did, my Lord," Thomas said vehemently.

"And would you care to tell me what they were?"

"I'd rather not."

"Even if I presume you to be still a ruffian and rescind the offer I just made?"

Thomas' face fell. "Aye, even so, my Lord, though I would much regret it."

Philip smiled. "Morgan judged you well. I shall not penalise you, Thomas. You fought defending me, did you not?"

"I did, and I would fight for you again," Thomas said staunchly. "What is a bloodied nose compared with your good name?"

"Why should you care for my good name?"

"Because you are my master. I would do anything for you."

"So it would seem." Philip regarded him fondly. He felt particularly friendless at the moment and he was touched that Thomas had cared enough to defend him. "Don't you know you have picked a champion who will soon be trampled in the dust?"

"Not one of your condemners is fit to have you spit on them, my Lord," Thomas said. "You have plenty who will stand for you."

"Where? In Alsatia?"

"You could do worse," Thomas said. "They are rough people but their hearts are good and they look after their own."

"Then they should take to me," Philip said. "The most diabolical villains in London look to me as their friend and inspiration!"

"That's because you have the common touch."

"How dare you? I have no such thing!"

Thomas grinned. "I meant that the ordinary people like you. That is why the others fear you so much, my Lord, and why they seek to blacken your name."

"They would appear to have succeeded," Philip said heavily.

"Not at all. The people will be loyal to you and will cheer your carriage as they always have. They would sooner catch a glimpse of you than see a play."

"Then let us hope this drama does not reach its end too soon! I trust, Thomas, you will forget the words you overheard me speaking before you made your presence known. I would hate to have it put about that I was feeling sorry for myself."

"They are quite forgotten," Thomas assured him.

"Good. There is something else that you can do for me as well," Philip added. "I have to go away for a few days and I would be pleased if you could look out for Master Giles as best you can whilst I'm away. He is mentioned in that blasted pamphlet too and I am fearful he will get himself in trouble if any taunt him with it. Despite how he is treating me, I would be desperately sad if anything befell him. Come, now, let's go in. It grows too cold out here for me."

"But Mistress Bet…," Thomas began.

"You need not be afraid of Mistress Bet tonight. I shall protect you," Philip promised.

Thomas looked relieved. "She has a temper like the very devil, my Lord."

"Does she?" Philip picked a piece of straw out of the boy's hair. "Well so have I!"

At first light Philip was upon the road to Dover.

❧

The Commissioner of the Passage studied Scott with care. "The Earl of Shaftesbury has not yet ordered your release, we understand."

"He will." Scott was confident.

"It has been several days since you wrote to London, Colonel. How do you account for the delay?"

Scott couldn't, but he did not intend to let the Commissioner think he grew perturbed. "Lord Shaftesbury is a busy man. He will instruct you soon enough."

"But in the meantime, you are in custody and must submit to this examination."

Scott flashed him a disarming smile. "As you wish, but I assure you that you waste your time and mine."

"Be that as it may, you know why you have been brought here?" the Commissioner asked him.

"You have a warrant for my apprehension, so I was informed."

"A warrant issued last October, Colonel, when you left the country in a great deal of haste."

"I had been sent for by the Prince of Condé," Scott said glibly.

"For what purpose?"

"Are you not aware that I am famed throughout the world as a geographer?"

The Commissioner looked sceptical. "You were employed in that capacity by the Prince of Condé?"

"Certainly. These past few months I have been engaged in surveying lands in Picardy and Burgundy. The proof of this can be easily seen if you would fetch my trunks."

Scott's two trunks were brought in and opened. From the first he lifted out some maps of France, which he had fringed with blue silk.

"What is in the other trunk?"

"Only clothes."

"It would seem this mapmaking is a lucrative affair," the Commissioner said when he had seen contents of the second trunk.

"There are worse paid."

"Indeed there are. Come, now, Colonel, tell the truth. Why did you enter Folkestone in a fishing boat if, as you say, you were concealing nothing and why did you give the name of John Johnson when you were first arrested?"

"Those questions, I am not bound to answer, since the Earl of Shaftesbury will very shortly have me freed," Scott told him airily.

"He may and he may not."

At that moment the Commissioner's clerk entered. "A gentleman has just arrived bringing an order from Sir Henry Coventry, the Secretary of State, ordering Colonel Scott's release."

"Where is the order then?"

"He would not give it to me. He said that since he had been forced to inconvenience himself in such a fashion he will deal only with those responsible for the nuisance."

"He said what? Who is this person?"

"Lord Devalle, sir."

The Commissioner frowned. "He came with this himself? Then you had better ask Lord Devalle to enter, I suppose."

"Lord Devalle has already entered," Philip said, in an icy voice. "I grew tired of waiting whilst you talked amongst yourselves." He gave the Commissioner a contemptuous glance. "Release this man at once. Through your stupidity I have been called upon to make a most uncomfortable journey."

"We must see your order first, Lord Devalle."

"What impudence!"

"I mean no disrespect, my Lord, but I have to check whether the order is authentic."

Philip walked with dignity, if not with ease, to the Commissioner's table and tossed the order onto it. "Is this Colonel Scott?"

"Why yes, but are you not acquainted with him?"

"Not at all." Philip looked significantly at Scott, who caught his drift.

"I am honoured to have been rescued by so illustrious a person, my Lord," he said, bowing.

"I would not count upon it too much in the future." Philip offered him his hand, though without much graciousness.

"Will they let me go?" Scott whispered, out of earshot of the others.

"I expect so. Oh, you are a stupid bastard!"

The order, meanwhile, was being examined.

"Well, are you convinced?" Philip tapped his foot impatiently.

"The order seems to be quite genuine, my Lord."

"It is scarcely likely that I would have travelled down from London otherwise," Philip said tartly. "Is Scott free to go?"

"He is, my Lord."

"Then we will leave for London right away. That is if you have no objection," he added sarcastically.

"Whatever objections I may have are now superfluous, since they have been overruled, my Lord."

"Quite. No matter, you will doubtless soon discover some other innocent wayfarer you can threaten and delay. My coach is waiting, Colonel."

"I tell you, my friend, I was never gladder to see any man," Scott said when they were outside.

"Do not be familiar with me here, you fool," Philip hissed. "We are surrounded by Pepys' friends. Have I not taken risks enough for you already?"

"I feared the order would never come," Scott said, after the coach was safely on its way.

"I arrived with it as soon as I was able," Philip told him wearily. "I was three days upon the road."

"What? I could have walked as quick!"

"Perhaps you could, but I could not," Philip said bitterly. "A word of thanks would not be inappropriate, I think, for extricating you, yet again, from a predicament."

"Considering it was you who got me into this I would have said that you did no more than you ought," Scott joked.

Philip was not in any mood for levity. The journey had worn him out and he was in pain. "Do not address me like a servant," he snapped. "I would not need to be here at all if you had followed my instructions to the letter."

"You mean about my passage?" Scott looked sheepish. "It was ill luck that I was caught at Folkestone."

"You should never have been at Folkestone, and why did you make the crossing in a fishing boat?" Philip demanded. "What happened to the money I sent you for the passage and to bribe the captain of the boat you were meant to sail on, money, incidentally, that has been forfeited to me. Did you put it all upon your back?"

"I had some debts to settle, though I did buy some new clothes," Scott admitted, "but I will obey your every order from now on."

"It is not me you will be working for this time, Scott. It is Shaftesbury and, I tell you now, were it not for his insistence you would not be here at all, for it does not suit me too well to have you back."

"If you do not want me here I will return to France," Scott said. "I am your man, not Shaftesbury's, and I always will be."

"I do not require your fealty but your allegiance," Philip told him, a little softened by Scott's words. "As for your leaving, that would truly bring the Earl's wrath down upon me. No, you stay and do the best you can, since Pepys must already have learned that you are here."

The coach wheels bounced off a stone in the road and Philip dropped his cane, which he had been holding. As he bent down to retrieve it he was overcome with dizziness and had to press himself back in the seat to stop from keeling over.

Scott frowned. "Are you well?"

"Of course I'm well."

"You don't look it. You're an awful colour. Are you going to faint?"

"Don't be ridiculous!"

As Philip turned to look at him Scott's image shifted and he saw two of him.

Then there was blackness.

EIGHTEEN

❧

Giles was deep in thought as he left the house on his way to meet Monmouth. He had been thinking a great deal since the publication of the scandal sheet on Philip, for it had stirred emotions in him that he was not even aware he possessed.

Giles was self-centred and would to grow attached to very few people throughout his life but Philip was to be his greatest weakness. In spite of himself, Giles had come to care about him, even more than he cared about his own good name and ambitions.

It was all very inconvenient, but the fact remained that Giles no longer intended to go to war with Monmouth, and he was on his way to tell him so. He felt his place was at Philip's side just now and that if he left him it would look as though he was concerned by the insinuations. Philip had left for Dover before he'd had a chance to tell him of his change of heart but Giles resolved to do so directly he returned.

Despite the lateness of the hour he had no fear of being out alone although, as he was slight of build, he made a tempting target for a footpad. It was for that precise reason Philip had expressed a wish that he should never walk the streets at night unless accompanied by a servant.

Giles was so preoccupied he did not hear footsteps close behind him, or notice that a coach had drawn up alongside. He cried out as someone grabbed him, but a sack was swiftly thrown over his head and his arms were pinioned to his sides. His attackers bundled him into the coach and it started off immediately.

Giles was uncomfortable and considerably shaken by what was happening but he had not been hurt. When the vehicle stopped his captors removed the sack, which had been nearly choking him, and he was dragged out and pushed up several flights of stairs. In the corridor ahead a plain door, such as might be used by servants, was opened and then quickly closed behind him.

He appeared to be alone now and he looked about him. He was in a most magnificent apartment. The walls were hung with fine French tapestries, depicting Versailles and Saint Germain. Giles also noticed japanned cabinets, a massive clock and two great vases wrought of heavy silver. Above the chimney breast was an enormous portrait of the King.

"Well, Fairfield, have you guessed where you are?"

Giles spun round, startled, at the sound of the smooth voice with the affected drawl. The Earl of Sunderland had slipped silently through the door and was standing behind him.

Giles knew well enough who *he* worked for. "I was wondering whether I might be the guest, and I use the word loosely, of the Duchess of Portsmouth," he said evenly. "Now that I see you, Lord Sunderland, I am certain of it."

"My dear young sir, allow me to congratulate you on your self-possession. It would appear that Lord Devalle has trained you well, for some in your place would be quaking in their shoes."

"Why should I fear the Duchess, my Lord?" Giles said. "So far as I am aware I have done nothing to offend her, more the other way about."

"You are man of courage, Fairfield, but are you not a little curious as to why you have been brought here?"

"I will own up to that," Giles said.

"I understand you plan to leave Lord Devalle."

Giles had no intention of discussing his plans, or his change of heart, with Philip's enemies. "Is that the reason for my abduction?"

"Do not call it that – so vulgar. The Duchess means you well, I promise you."

"In that case why was I dragged here forcibly and not invited according to the normal manner of things?"

"I don't think she believed you would come."

"And she was right," Giles said, "but I fail to see why I should be of so much interest to her Grace."

Sunderland began to laugh and then stopped suddenly. "How very droll. I think he means it!"

"I am pleased to see that he has spirit." Louise de Quéroualle, the Duchess of Portsmouth, emerged from her bedroom, where she had evidently been listening to them. "I think you can leave us now, Lord Sunderland. You will not harm me, will you Giles?" She pouted prettily.

Giles was unmoved by that. "It is not my retribution you should fear, your Grace, but that of the Almighty."

"Why how you talk! I can't believe that it is Devalle who has taught you how to preach."

"I wouldn't be so sure of that," Sunderland said as he left the room. "He keeps close company with Titus Oates, who claims to be a minister of the church and has the impudence to imitate my speech to the point of ridicule."

"Lord Sunderland has not much liking for your patron, I'm afraid," Louise told Giles.

"And what of you, your Grace?"

"I loathe him," she said frankly. "Yes, I do, I positively loathe him. He has opposed me at every turn and done all he could to thwart me, though lately I believe it is I who inconvenience him. How fares his health?"

"I think he is a little better," Giles said wickedly.

"I know you're lying," Louise snapped. "Do not try to make a fool of me."

"Don't ask me foolish questions then," Giles returned swiftly. "You are well aware of how he is."

"You are impertinent!"

"I did not ask to be here," Giles pointed out, "and nor do I feel honoured by your none too gracious invitation."

"I apologise if my men were rough with you, Giles." Louise smiled at him in a winning way.

Giles was not so easily won. "They weren't half as rough as those you set upon Lord Devalle in France."

"Why should you care? You are leaving him, and who could blame you when he has dragged your name through the mud along with his own? You intend to join the army, I understand."

Giles regarded her. He had always been more of a listener than a talker and he saw advantage in listening now, for he guessed that if he told her he had changed his mind about going then he would never discover what she had wanted with him.

"I only want to be your friend, Giles," Louise said, when he did not speak. "I am offering to purchase your commission for you, and equip you better than the finest gentleman who ever went to war. Will you not ride as Lady Portsmouth's champion? Think, Giles, you would be quite independent of your sister and of Shaftesbury. I could buy you anything you wanted, a title too, for there is nothing that the King refuses me. How would you like to be an earl one day, say the Earl of Southwick?"

"But that is the Devalle's title," Giles said.

"Yes, I know. Philip fights his madman brother for it through the courts, I hear. He'll get it too, most likely, but on the day that Philip Devalle dies the title shall be mine, for he is the last of the line and I shall purchase it," she told him gleefully.

"Can you not be content with hounding him whilst he is alive?" Giles said, disgusted. "Must you debase his family name as well?"

"But the title could go to you, my pretty one." Louise stretched out her hand and touched his cheek.

Giles pulled away as though she had burned him. "I do not want it."

"Then some other title."

"Duchess," Giles said heavily, "though, doubtless, it amuses you to play this game with me, I tire of it. What is it you want?"

"I want Philip Devalle's head," Louise said simply. "I want him publicly disgraced. I want him executed."

"For what crime?"

"For his part in Justice Godfrey's murder."

Giles had heard a good deal of talk about that murder since he came to London. No-one, in his presence at least, had blamed Philip for it, but Giles had already come to the conclusion that there were some aspects of Philip's life about which he would prefer to remain in ignorance. "Have you proof that he was involved?"

"No, but with your help I can wring a confession from him." She took a small, brown bottle out of her bureau drawer and held it up to Giles. "I've heard that he consumes great quantities of brandy to relieve his pain. All you have to do is tip the contents of this vial into his glass."

Giles removed the cork and sniffed the contents with distaste. "What is it? Poison?"

"No, a secret potion distilled for me in France by La Voisin, before she was arrested. The effect of it is twofold, it will cramp his stomach and it will cause his mind to wander. He will be in greater agony than he has ever known and be convinced that he is dying. You can then prevail upon him to unburden his soul before he leaves this world and, in his delirium, he should confess to everything. I will have a witness concealed within earshot and before Philip Devalle recovers from the effects of my elixir he will be imprisoned in the Tower."

Giles had never seen such malevolence in any face as he saw now in hers. Louise's eyes grew small, her nostrils flared and her lips were drawn back to show her teeth, which she bared like fangs. He shuddered to think how much she must hate Philip to come up with such a desperate plan as this.

"Well?" she demanded. "What do you think?"

"I think it is diabolical," he said.

"We must take care, though, that Shaftesbury never learns of my part in this," Louise stressed. "I do not want him for an enemy. He might be useful to me one day."

The prospect of Shaftesbury being used by Louise de Quéroualle was almost more than Giles could bear straight-faced. "Even King Charles cannot use Shaftesbury," he reminded her.

"The King does not present him with an opportunity such as the one I intend to offer him."

"What can you offer Lord Shaftesbury?"

"My son, Charles Lennox," Louise said. "He is seven years old and I believe it time that he was fitted to assume the role of sovereign when his father, King Charles, dies."

Giles had not expected that. "You are proposing to make your son king?"

"Does he not have as much right to the throne as the bastard Duke of Monmouth, who Shaftesbury seeks to put there?" Louise said. "With Devalle out of the way and Monmouth's Cause in ruins, as it is sure to be when one of the Duke's closest friends is denounced as a murderer, the Earl of Shaftesbury will welcome my alliance. With my son he will have another chance to gain the power he craves. Well? Will you help me?"

"Not for anything!" Giles said decidedly.

Louise's smile faded. "There is no danger to yourself, I promise you. If you but slip the potion into his drink then I will do the rest. A small act, surely, for such great rewards and, after all, he will soon be dead in any case."

"Then let him die with dignity."

"Giles, you should know that no-one makes a fool of me." A warning note had crept into Louise's voice.

She was a ruthless woman, of that Giles had no need to be reminded, but fear was an emotion which touched him as rarely as did any other. Giles' courage was not the courage of the bold and reckless, but rather the cold kind which is possessed by the dispassionate. He viewed her calmly. "You are wasting your time, your Grace. I shall not help you bring down my brother-in-law, and that's an end to it."

"So be it." Louise fairly spat with rage. "You will regret this, Fairfield."

Giles had a feeling she may be right, but it made no difference to his resolution.

Her guards still stood outside the door through which he had entered. Louise opened it and called them in. "Seize him."

Once again Giles found himself manhandled. While they held him firmly Louise hit him across the face with such force that he tasted blood inside his mouth.

"I want him killed."

"You cannot kill him, your Grace." Sunderland had entered with the guards. "If Lord Devalle does not search for him then his sister will, and I need hardly remind you of whose mistress she is."

Louise looked at Giles furiously. "He'll pay for refusing me."

"What price your vengeance, Lady Portsmouth?" Sunderland said. "Best to forget he ever came here. Let him go, he is no danger to you."

"He might speak of what he heard me say."

"Who would take notice of him? Devalle? He cannot hurt your Grace with scandal."

"But the people already hate me."

"Do you not think they will hate Devalle too, after the literature you have circulated about the town?"

"So it was you who did that?" Giles struggled to be free of his captors. "You had that filth written about him, you evil bitch."

"See how he speaks to me?" Louise shouted at Sunderland. "I don't care what you say. He shall be punished for his insolence."

Sunderland shrugged. "Very well. I wash my hands of it."

"Take him by the back stairs to my carriage and convey him to the Heath at Hampstead," she commanded her guards. "There you are to tie him to a tree and empty out his pockets, so that any who find him will presume him to have been attacked by robbers. After that I want him beaten till he bleeds and left there, bound and gagged." She cackled gleefully. "It will be morning before he is found and with any luck he will be dead, though who could say it was by Lady Portsmouth's hand?"

"I can't agree with this," Sunderland said.

"You have already washed your hands of it," Louise reminded him.

Giles was bustled down the back stairs, a handkerchief fastened across his mouth to keep him quiet. Once outside he was hastily deposited in the coach and they set off at a brisk trot for the outskirts of the city.

Giles found it difficult to breathe through the gag but there was little he could do about it, since the guards had tied his hands, and he feared there was far worse discomfort to come.

When they stopped he saw they were in a dark, secluded spot. Giles knew he was in real danger now, but he resigned himself to his fate with a coolness that surprised him. If he was going to die then he resolved to do it bravely and the chief regret in his mind as they dragged him out was that he would never have the chance to be reconciled with Philip.

A figure leapt down from the back of the carriage, as stealthy as a shadow. There was no sound as bare feet touched the grass.

The guards untied Giles' hands and pushed him to the ground. From out of the corner of his eye he saw someone who was holding up a stone. It was Thomas.

Giles' hand closed around a large stone also.

Thomas hurled his missile and caught the nearest guard so square upon the head that he dropped down, stunned.

Swift as lightning, Giles grasped the other guard's foot and brought him down. He clubbed him hard with the stone but the driver, meanwhile had drawn a pistol. Before he could fire it, Thomas leapt upon his back. The pistol dropped from his hand and, as Thomas dived out of the way, Giles grabbed the weapon and fired. The driver did not move again.

Giles tore the gag from his mouth. "You saved my life! How in heaven's name did you get here?"

"I was riding on the box," Thomas said. "Lord Devalle feared that you would get yourself in trouble with so much on your mind and he charged me to watch over you. I saw you set upon but there was not much I could do about that, so I followed the carriage and waited until they brought you out again."

"I can't thank you enough, Thomas."

Thomas grinned. "Maybe you will find the opportunity to do the same for me one day. It is good to be in credit for a favour."

Giles offered his hand, which Thomas took. From that moment a friendship was forged between them which would grow in strength over the years. It was a friendship which transcended differences in birth and upbringing, and it was one which would benefit them both many, many times throughout their eventful lives.

Giles prodded the driver with his foot. "I think this one's dead. I've never killed a man before."

"They would have just as quickly done for you," Thomas reminded him. "It was scum like this who worked that dirty deal upon Lord Devalle in France." He got into the driver's seat and took up the reins. "Now I think we should get out of here before the other two come around."

"In the Duchess' coach?"

"Why not? After all the inconvenience she's caused us the very least her Grace can do is offer us transportation back to the city!"

"Can you drive it?" Giles asked, as he climbed up beside him.

"I expect so."

Giles smiled. "I can see you're going to make a very useful friend, Thomas!"

⁊

By the time Giles and Thomas arrived home Philip had returned from Dover, after a harrowing journey, and had gone straight to bed, exhausted.

He was standing by the window when Giles came to see him the following morning and, from the concern which showed in his visitor's face, he realised that he must be looking as bad as he felt!

Without a word Giles came to him and clasped him in a brief embrace.

Philip was surprised, for Giles was not normally an affectionate person. "What's this? Pity?" he asked him, a little stiffly, for that was the last thing he wanted. "Not contrition, surely, not from you."

Giles nodded. "I am truly sorry, for I know my words hurt you and I do most earnestly desire you to forgive me."

Now Philip really *was* surprised. He had not expected that at all. "You're forgiven," he said. He noticed then, for the first time, that Giles' lip was swollen and that he had a bruise upon his cheek. "What happened to you?"

Giles told him everything and Philip listened, horrified. "Dear God! They might have killed you but for Thomas, and all on account of me. I should have guessed the bitch would try a trick or two behind my back." He was silent for a moment, considering all that Giles had said. "Do you want me to tell you about Godfrey?" he asked him at length.

"No," Giles said decidedly. "It would make no difference to the way I feel about you whether you killed him or not. I never realised quite how much you meant to me until I read that scandal sheet."

"Your name has been tainted by it too, I fear," Philip said wryly.

"I don't give a damn about that. There is nothing could persuade me to part from you after this."

Philip could tell that he meant it, but he knew, with regret, that he could not allow Giles to remain with him. Not now.

"Giles listen," he said quietly, "for there is something I must say to you and it will not be easy for me. You must have heard by now that I was taken ill upon the journey back from Dover."

"You should never have had to go to Dover," Giles cried passionately.

"I know, but it was Shaftesbury's way of punishing me and there is little I can do to defy him at the moment. My indisposition has left me somewhat weakened and, though you are very dear to me, I feel I am no longer fit enough to fulfil my duties as your patron."

"That is unimportant to me now," Giles began, but Philip stopped him.

"No Giles, you want more from life than to be tending to an invalid, which is what I fear I shall soon become. I think the army is a better choice for you after all."

"But I don't wish to go now," Giles protested. "Are you sending me away?"

"I'm afraid I must, and not only on account of my worsening health," Philip said. "I had already decided on this when I learned that the bastards had besmirched your name along with mine and now, after this business last night, I am convinced it is the best course."

"I will be much more cautious in the future," Giles promised.

"Even so, you are no match for her. Witness what she did to me."

"She tried to kill you and you are still alive," Giles reminded him. "You won that hand, not lost it."

"It was a hollow victory and my winnings were merely a little time. She shall not destroy your life as she did mine," Philip vowed. "I am much too fond of you to allow you to be hurt and, if you have affection for me, you will do exactly as I say. Monmouth is a fine commander and he will take care of you for my sake. Why, in many ways the army will be good for you. My only fear is that a soldier's life will change you so much I shall scarcely recognise you when you return to me!"

Philip tried to speak lightly, but Giles looked sad.

"I shan't see you again, shall I?" he said wretchedly.

"Perhaps." Philip looked away. For once he could not meet Giles' intense gaze. "And perhaps not."

Shaftesbury fixed his piercing eyes upon Scott. "Your arrest at Dover was not a very auspicious start, Scott."

"I trust I shall redeem myself at Pepys' hearing, my Lord."

"I trust you will as well," Shaftesbury said sourly. "You have already been paid generously for your part in the proceedings and the only person ever to have cheated me and lived is Philip Devalle. I had him thrashed because I liked him. I am not particularly fond of you."

"Speaking of Lord Devalle," Scott said, "is there no-one else who we can call upon to verify my story?"

"No, there is not," Shaftesbury told him tetchily. "No-one else will do. Philip is known to have been in France at the time in question and, besides, he is a person of sufficient rank and importance to be taken note of by the Commons. Why, is he unwilling to appear?"

"No, not at all," Scott hastened to reassure him. The fact was that Scott doubted whether Philip would be even capable of making an appearance. "I merely wondered whether it is wise to use him in case anything goes wrong and it reflects adversely upon yourself, my Lord."

"Nothing will go wrong," Shaftesbury said. "Pepys can't harm me and I shall always protect Philip, provided he obeys me without question, which is something I hope he has finally learned to do."

Scott could say no more on the subject but, once outside the Earl's door, he shook his head at Theresa, who was waiting for him. "I did my best but, well or ill, Philip will have to play his part."

Theresa had been fully prepared to dislike the notorious Colonel Scott but, on meeting him, she had found it quite impossible. For one thing his genuine concern for Philip's state when they had arrived back had warmed her heart and, for another, Scott was charming to all women, whether old or young, ugly or beautiful. Theresa knew of his reputation but, even so, it was difficult not to be captivated by his rakish good looks or flattered by his attentiveness and she had to remind herself sometimes that Scott was nothing but a trickster who preyed upon rich and gullible women!

"Shaftesbury is going to kill him at this rate," she said.

"You love your husband, don't you?"

The question took Theresa by surprise. She had never admitted that to anyone, not even to herself, and she was definitely not about to do so now to John Scott, who would almost certainly tell Philip. "I love Shaftesbury," she insisted, not too convincingly, for the truth was that she loved him a great deal less than she had when she first came to London.

Scott grinned. "Of course you do!"

Theresa accompanied Philip to the lobby of the House of Commons. The Bedloe brothers and Oates were there ahead of them, and in great form, shouting salutations to their friends and insults to their enemies.

Philip watched them benignly. Since his pain had become more intense, Morgan no longer frowned disapprovingly when he demanded brandy before he was even dressed in the morning.

He might have been drinking but he was not too mellowed to notice Theresa talking closely with Scott, who arrived shortly after them, and he summoned her back with a peremptory gesture.

She went obediently to his side and he took her arm.

"This is a significant moment, sweetheart," he confided, before he and Scott were called to take their places. "From today your husband is no better than the scum you see before you." he indicated Oates, the Bedloes and Scott, who had joined in the noisy exchanges with the crowds.

"That's not true," Theresa said. "You are a man of honour, no matter what Lord Shaftesbury makes you do, and I am always proud to be your wife."

Philip looked into her grey eyes, so very like her brother's in colour yet so very different in expression. "I don't deserve you," he said huskily. "You and Morgan must be the only people in the world who still believe in me."

"Do you not believe in yourself?" she asked him quietly.

Philip considered the question. "No, Tess," he decided. "Not anymore."

Inside the House Sir William Harbord, who was conducting the proceedings, rose and turned toward Samuel Pepys and Sir Anthony Deane, Pepys fellow Member of Parliament for Harwich, who was accused with him of treason. "I am indeed much saddened by the duty I must now perform," Harbord said. "The former Secretary of the Admiralty, Mr. Samuel Pepys, is, I believe from my investigations, guilty of piracy, popery and treachery."

Pepys, pressed by the Admiralty on the one side and Shaftesbury's committee on the other, had been forced to resign as Secretary, a position everyone knew Harbord coveted for himself, but Pepys faced the Commons defiantly as Harbord read out the charges against him.

The first was that, during the Dutch War, he had fraudulently procured a sloop called 'The Hunter' for Sir Anthony Deane and

Pepys' brother-in-law, Balty St. Michel, and that he had furnished her, out of government stores, as a privateer. In this capacity 'The Hunter' had seized as a prize a London ship called 'The Catherine'.

The next charge was that he had filled the navy with the Duke of York's own Catholic nominees and kept a Jesuit named Morelli in his household.

Lastly, and worst of all, as Harbord stressed, was that four years ago Deane had taken to France a number of confidential maps of English coasts and harbours, together with other naval secrets, which Pepys had sold to the King of France for vast rewards.

"I am most sorrowful to say this about a man with whom I once did live in terms of friendship," Harbord ended piously.

Scott was called first to the bar.

"Now will you tell us, Colonel Scott, exactly what you saw take place four years ago at the house of the late Monsieur Pellissary in France?"

"I will, sir, for it is my duty." Scott bowed to those present.

The Members looked impressed with this dark stranger, elegant in his dress and manners, and they listened hard as he explained that he had been on his way to visit Monsieur Pellissary when he saw him, through a window, being handed a package by Sir Anthony.

"I knew it was my duty, as a loyal and devoted Englishman, to discover the contents of that packet," Scott told his audience, "so when I next saw Monsieur Pellissary I questioned him outright. I fear that is my nature, gentlemen, I am a most straightforward, honest person."

"And did Monsieur Pellissary divulge the contents to you?" Harbord asked.

"Certainly he did, he even showed the papers to me, and I saw that each one bore the signature of Samuel Pepys. Being myself a maker of maps and charts I saw straightway that the information they contained was of such importance that if it should get into the possession of the King of France it would enable him at any time to burn the English fleet as it lay in harbour."

Scott, who was a master of his art, paused for just sufficient time for this choice morsel to whet the appetite of his listeners and then he made a sweeping gesture toward Pepys. "This man hoped to sell the papers to King Louis for the sum of forty thousand pounds."

There was a gasp of horror in the House.

"This is indeed a serious thing," Harbord said, "for if all happened as you say then Mr. Pepys must be regarded as a traitor. Have you anyone to substantiate your story, Colonel Scott?"

"Lord Philip Devalle, as it happens, accompanied me to Pellissary's house that day and saw what took place through the window," Scott claimed, with an apprehensive look at Philip.

"Is Lord Devalle present?"

Philip heaved himself to his feet and, leaning upon his silver-headed cane, he walked with slow and unsteady steps up to the bar.

Harbord frowned when he saw him. "Are you indisposed, my Lord?"

"For God's sake, Harbord," Philip hissed, "get on with what I have to do and don't keep me standing here whilst you ask damn fool questions."

Harbord coloured. "I see you are yourself, my Lord."

"Well who were you expecting? Monmouth? Mine is the most substantial name that you will find to reinforce you."

"Lord Devalle," Harbord began hastily, "Colonel Scott has stated that on the day he saw Monsieur Pellissary take a package from Sir Anthony Deane you were, in fact, beside him."

"I was not beside Deane."

"I did not mean that."

"Be precise then."

"Yes, my Lord," Harbord said between gritted teeth. "Where were you at that time?"

"I was beside Scott."

"And you saw this transaction take place?"

"Why, just the same as he did."

Deane stood up. "But Lord Devalle claimed at Dover that he did not even know Colonel Scott."

Philip was ready for that. "Alas, with all this talk of a Popish Plot we good Protestants go often in fear of our lives and must resort to subterfuge when surrounded by the agents of those who may prove to be enemies of our country."

"Quite so," Harbord said. "You have heard it, gentlemen, the word of one well known to you and a respected member of the Country Party."

Philip sat down again and Harbord next called to the bar John James, who had once been Pepys' butler until he had been dismissed after being caught in bed with the housekeeper by Morelli, Pepys' musician. He testified that Morelli was certainly a Papist and that he never left the house without he carried with him a dagger and a pistol.

"Is this Morelli associated with the Popish Plot?" Harbord asked. "Lord Devalle, can you tell us?"

"I mentioned Morelli to Dr. Oates, who knew of him and assured me he was deeply implicated in the Plot," Philip said dutifully.

"In that event surely this charge against Mr. Pepys is as serious as that made against those Papist lords imprisoned in the Tower."

All agreed it was.

Pepys stood. "It is misfortune that I am charged with all these ills at once and by surprise," he said. "I will not complain but I am bound to say that it is strange no word was spoken to me in Committee. As a member of the Commons and an Englishman I should have been acquainted with the charges before I came here."

"You are acquainted with them now," Harbord pointed out, unsympathetically. "How do you answer?"

Pepys answered strongly. He had never been concerned, directly or indirectly, with 'The Hunter' he insisted, and the House was at liberty to peruse his books and see he told the truth. As to the matter of Morelli, whilst Pepys could not deny that the musician was a Catholic he was one of such mildness that he had once fallen under the suspicion of the Inquisition, and had resided in Pepys' house solely to provide entertainment for the household. The most serious charge, that of treason, he denied absolutely.

"What of Colonel Scott's testimony?" Harbord asked. "How do you answer that?"

"All I know of Colonel Scott is that six months ago I attempted to have him arrested, following the murder of Justice Godfrey," Pepys said. "I subsequently presented papers to this House which showed him to be a felon."

Philip groaned to himself. Just as he had feared Pepys' intended to attack Scott.

However loud cries of protest were already being heard from all over the House and Harbord evidently knew how to take advantage of that.

"I should warn you, Mr. Pepys, that you do a grave injustice to an honest man," he said severely. "The Colonel is a fine gentleman, a close friend of the great De Witt and once commanded eight regiments in Holland. Do you decry such an able military person?"

Pepys jutted out his chin. "I do, and any who would give false evidence in order to give credence to his lies."

The House fell silent and Philip was aware that all eyes had turned to him.

"Was that rather rash remark intended for me?" he said, his voice sounding clear in the stillness.

Pepys clenched his fists. "It was, my Lord."

"You are aware, I'm certain, that it is counted an offence to speak derogatively of a peer?"

"You have no need to remind me of your rank, Lord Devalle, or of the way that you abuse those privileges it buys you," Pepys said hotly. "I suspect it was your wicked influence which decided the Committee to take these steps against me in the first place."

Nothing could have been further from the truth!

"The Committee's decision was arrived at after due discussion and consideration of the facts at their disposal," Philip said, "which is to say by the fair and proper means."

"My Lord, if you in all your life did anything by the fair and proper means I should be a lot surprised."

"This goes too far!" Philip, got to his feet, struck by the injustice of his situation. He had never wanted to appear here today in the first place and now he was being attacked. "May I remind you that it is not I who stand accused, Pepys?"

"Not today, perhaps, but your turn will arrive, Lord Devalle. You have a lot to answer for."

"Not half as much as you. I am a Protestant."

"Your father was a Protestant," Pepys said, "he whose name you bear and cheapen by using it to ennoble sordid causes, and your mother was a Huguenot, of that I am aware. Even so, it would seem that you are attracted to the company of French Catholics, or do you deny your relationships with the Duc D'Orleans and Jules Gaspard?"

Philip reeled from that blow. He had grown accustomed to insinuations about Monsieur but no-one had ever dared to taunt him about Jules. Even to hear Jules' name upon Pepys' lips was detestable to him. Jules belonged to another time and another Philip. His memory was the one sacred thing remaining in Philip's life, and to have that memory laid bare before the House during these sordid proceedings was more than he could endure.

He saw the Members craning their necks eagerly as he approached the bar. He had no clear idea of what he was going to do; he only knew that he wanted to silence the obnoxious man who had degraded, by his jibe, the gentlest and bravest person Philip had ever known.

The demons were in his head now and he seized Pepys around the throat and shook him with a strength born of fury.

There was a commotion in the House. Philip felt himself being pulled back and then saw that Harbord had positioned himself between him and Pepys.

"Whatever do you think you're doing, you maniac?"

"That pompous little wretch insulted me."

"Control yourself. This House is not the place to seek out personal vengeance," Harbord reminded him.

Philip shook off those who held him. "Very well, I am composed now."

"Thank God for that," Pepys muttered. His hands were trembling as he tried to replace his wig, which had fallen off. "I shall excuse your gross behaviour since it is obvious to everyone that you are foully drunk."

"I move," Harbord said quickly, before it all broke out afresh, "that Samuel Pepys and Sir Anthony Deane be taken into the custody of the Sergeant at Arms until the matter of their treachery can be examined further."

NINETEEN

❧

"What the devil did you think you were doing?" Shaftesbury said angrily. "You made a laughing stock of me by your behaviour in the House of Commons. You were so drunk that Pepys perceived it and you grew so violent and abusive Harbord says he had to have you restrained."

"Harbord exaggerates," Philip said.

"You attacked Pepys. Don't deny it."

"He insulted me."

"He mentioned that Jules Gaspard was a Catholic, and so he was," Shaftesbury reminded him. "Pepys merely demonstrated that you took a Catholic into your home, which was saying no more than we said of him with his Papist musician. I'm sorry, Philip, this time you have gone too far. You shall not win me round as you have so many times before. There is already the matter of the scandal sheet and now this. I will be frank with you; you are no longer beneficial to the Cause."

Philip looked at him blankly. "No longer beneficial?"

"You, of all people, should have been above reproach. You were my figurehead; I wanted you to ride alongside Monmouth, proud and strong. You are poison to me now."

"Monmouth would not agree with you," Philip said, stunned by this attack.

"The Duke of Monmouth may still take you if he pleases, but you shall not join him in my name," Shaftesbury said. "You are back to what you used to be before I took you in hand. You always were undisciplined, Philip, and you have only to look in a mirror to see what drinking and immoral living have done to you."

"I'll not deny the drinking, but as for the rest, that is unjust," Philip said hotly.

"Then how do you explain the things they say of you?"

"I must attribute them to spiteful people who seek to put me down and, finding no facts dangerous enough to use against me, must resort to malicious fiction but, since you will not believe me, all I can do is promise to be more of a credit to you in the future," Philip said with a sigh.

"It is too late for promises," Shaftesbury told him. "You had your final chance."

"Oh, come, desist! I know that you are angry with me and I am sorry if my actions embarrassed you."

"Philip, this time I do not pretend. Please try to understand that what I must do pains me as much as it will distress you. I see that I must put it bluntly. You are of no further use to me."

Philip flinched as though he had been struck. "No further use?" he repeated disbelievingly.

"That is what I said. Our association is at an end."

Philip stared at him, stunned. "What about Oates?"

"You are to have no more contact with him. From today he is answerable to Lord Lindsey."

"Lindsey?" Philip cried incredulously. "Oates detests him."

"I am in no doubt of that since witnessing his dudgeon here this afternoon. If it is any comfort, I will tell you that Oates demonstrated his own feelings so strongly I had to threaten that, unless he was cooperative, I would have Bedloe take his place."

"Lindsey is to have Bedloe too?"

"Yes, and Prance. Scott has always been your man and he will no doubt do as he pleases but you are to have nothing more to do with any of *my* witnesses. Their names are no longer to be linked with yours."

Philip felt numb. "So this is how it ends," he said tonelessly.

"It is not a decision I have arrived at lightly," Shaftesbury insisted. "You have served me well and I know I shall never find your like. I will continue to support you until you can find other means and alternative accommodation, for I would prefer you to no longer reside in the same house as Theresa. I hope you will not offend me by refusing to accept my money and regard as paltry charity what is a gesture of extreme appreciation for all you have done for me."

"A pension?" Philip gave a wry smile. "You will not have to pay it long."

"You won't bear me any ill will for this, I trust," Shaftesbury said, sounding a little uneasy.

At any other time Philip might have found it amusing that the man in whose service he had been forced to do such base things was now plainly afraid of him. He regarded the Earl with disdain.

"You have made me many things, you bastard, but I am not yet quite a savage!"

Once inside his carriage Philip drew down all the blinds and told Jonathon and Ned to make good speed back to King Street.

His thoughts were in turmoil. Since his imprisonment in the Bastille his only purpose had been to destroy the lives of those who had destroyed his. All he had done since then had been toward this end and now it seemed that he had sacrificed his honour for nothing. Revenge was sometimes the only thing that had driven him through one painful day after another. If he was to be cheated of it now there was no reason to continue, no point in suffering through the last few weeks of his life just to give his enemies the satisfaction of witnessing his decline.

Suddenly his mind cleared. He was calm and he was resolute. And he knew exactly what he would do.

Before he went into the house Philip took all the money out of his pockets and handed it to Jonathon and Ned. "You have served me well," he told them, "and I thank you."

The two Negroes rolled their eyes at the sight of the gold sovereigns he had given them and he was aware that they watched him curiously as he made his way up to the house.

"Morgan!" he called loudly as he entered, but Bet appeared instead.

"Morgan is not here, my Lord."

"That is a pity." Philip would have liked to have seen him one more time.

Bet was watching him with concern as he wearily climbed the stairs. "Are you feeling worse, my Lord?"

"I am tired, Bet, so very, very tired."

"Let me help you to your room."

Before he could refuse she took his arm and together they slowly climbed the stairs.

He smiled at her as they neared the top. "You take good care of me, Mistress Bet. I am grateful to you."

"We must take care of you, my Lord, for where would any of us be without you?"

"Far better off, I'm certain."

"I'll hear none of that," she told him crisply. "Sit down and I will fetch your brandy."

"Not tonight, Bet, for I need a clear head. Now listen to me, please, and pay heed to what I say. It will save my having to write it all down, and I don't believe I am up to that just now." As he spoke Philip removed the five jewelled rings from his fingers and laid them on the table before him. "These are to be given to Giles when he returns from the wars." He next slipped Jules' silver bracelet off his wrist. "This I want to go to Morgan. I know that he will treasure it for what it meant to me, and he is to have all of Jules' other possessions to dispose of as he wishes. This," he removed the diamond pin from his black lapel, "is yours."

Bet gasped. "My Lord, I can't take that."

"I wish you would." He pinned it onto her dress himself. "I would like Thomas to have Ferrion. My Paris house and everything else that I possess goes to your mistress." Philip could not bear to think about Theresa, for he knew if he did he would never have the resolve to carry out what he planned.

Bet frowned. "Are you going away, my Lord?"

Philip nodded. "Yes, I am going soon, for I hate farewells."

"Has this something to do with Lord Shaftesbury?"

"It has indeed."

"I knew it," Bet cried passionately. "I tell you this, my Lord, if I could meet that Shaftesbury face to face now I would give him a piece of my mind, earl or not!"

"I never knew you thought so highly of me," Philip teased her gently, for Bet's brusque manner rarely changed, whether she was speaking to the skivvy or the master of the house, and he had more than once received the sharp edge of her tongue.

"Oh, you can be difficult at times," she allowed, "but, as Morgan says, men of your kind are rare and must be considered differently from ordinary people."

"Is that what he says? Bless him! Shall you marry Morgan?" It had not escaped Philip's notice that Bet was keen on the Welshman, though Morgan was typically reticent about it.

"If he ever asks me."

"Tell him it is my wish that he marries you. Poor Morgan," Philip added sadly. "He will be lost without me. Take good care of him, and of your mistress."

"We will miss you, all of us," Bet said tearfully.

"But not for long." He patted her upon the cheek. "You must not weaken, Bet. You are the most hard-headed of all my household and it is you I am relying upon to hold the rest together."

When Bet had gone Philip went over to a rosewood escritoire and took a small pistol from one of the drawers. On reflection he decided it was probably just as well that Morgan was not there, for he would never have had the opportunity to do what he had determined to do. "Forgive me, my old friend," he murmured. "You must try to see that it is for the best."

He was loading the pistol when the door burst open and he laid the weapon quickly on the table.

Theresa entered, still in her cape and hat. "I've just come from Shaftesbury."

"With a message?" Philip asked, with the faintest trace of hope.

Theresa had none to offer him. "I'm afraid not. He refuses to change his mind. That is the reason I have parted from him."

Philip looked at her aghast. "You have what?"

"I want no more to do with anyone who treats his most loyal follower so callously."

"You did not tell him so, I trust."

"Most certainly I did."

Philip had not bargained on that. "You silly girl. What have you done? Run back and beg him to forgive you."

"I shall do no such thing. Lord Shaftesbury and I are finished," Theresa said. "I have nothing left to say to the man. Bet tells me you are going away."

"I am, and what will become of you when I am gone?" Philip said.

"You surely did not think that I would let you leave for France with none to care for you."

"I'm not going to France. Should I not cut a pitiable figure in Paris?"

"Then let us go to some place where no-one knows us," she suggested.

"And there wait for me to die? No, Tess, it is better just as I have planned it." Even as he spoke Philip clutched his side as the pain gripped him again. She would have gone to him but he put up his hand to warn her off. "I want no sympathy, from you or anyone."

"Do not deny me the right to feel compassion for my husband, please," she said.

Philip closed his eyes and sighed. In his present frame of mind this was far more than he could take. "Tess, stop it, I beg you."

"No, I have been silent for too long. I love you, Philip." Theresa smiled, as if a heavy load was lifted from her and all had been resolved by simply saying it. "I love you."

Philip thought it was probably the first time anyone had said those words to him and truly meant them.

"Don't be silly," he said, in a gentler tone. "You cannot love me, not as I am now. I should soon lose my looks and be completely crippled up with pain."

"To me you will always be handsome."

"Tess, why are you doing this?" Philip asked her in exasperation. "You must return to Shaftesbury. It is with him that you belong."

"I want to go with you," she said stubbornly.

"Well you can't. Where I am going I go alone."

Theresa frowned and he saw that she had sensed a hidden meaning in his words. "What exactly have you planned?"

"You'll learn soon enough." Philip hated himself for this, but he knew he must be resolute. He cared about Theresa far too much to want her grieving over him. "For now it must suffice for you to know that we shall never meet again after today."

"You are leaving me forever?" she cried. "Doesn't the fact that I love you make a difference?"

Philip hesitated, but only for a moment. "Not the slightest bit."

Theresa's cheeks reddened. "Then I trust you will be gentlemanly enough to forget what I just said."

"Your words will be forgotten very quickly, on that you may depend," Philip said. "Come and say goodbye to me, sweetheart."

She went to him and he held her elfin face in both hands, taking in every detail of her, from her trembling lips to her grey eyes, moist from the tears he had caused her to shed.

Philip had felt the desire to kiss her on many occasions and this time he did not have sufficient strength to fight it.

As his lips devoured hers Philip felt tears pricking his own eyelids, and a passion deeper than he had ever felt before took hold of him.

The love which he had waited all his life to find had come too late.

He forced himself back to reality and pushed her roughly from him, still panting from the intensity of his emotions.

Theresa looked a little faint. She had evidently not expected him to kiss her, and certainly not like that. "You do care for me, don't you?" she ventured. "Just a bit?"

Philip shook his head and turned away from her. "No, Tess, I do not care for you. I care for no-one but myself, I thought you knew that. Leave me now, please. I wish to be alone."

Theresa ran blindly from Philip's room and down the stairs, passing Morgan in her haste. As she reached the bottom step a sudden thought flashed through her head, a thought so dreadful that she stopped stock still and clutched the balustrade. "Morgan," she cried, "he has a gun. He's going to kill himself!"

Morgan reacted with amazing speed. Before Theresa could even collect her thoughts, he was already up the stairs and through the door.

Philip had just picked up the pistol for the second time and he spun round, startled, as Morgan charged in on him.

"Give me the pistol, my Lord."

"No." Philip backed away from him.

"Give me the pistol," Morgan repeated.

Philip shook his head. "This time you cannot save me, Morgan."

"I will not let you destroy yourself," Morgan warned him.

"I am already destroyed," Philip said quietly "It is over for me, Morgan, can't you see that?"

"You shall not die with dishonour." Morgan advanced upon him determinedly. "Do as I say and lay the weapon down."

Philip had allowed the Welshman to control him for so long that part of him still wavered and he might have obeyed, but a stab of pain reminded him how little his life meant to him anymore.

Morgan had backed him toward the open doorway. He lunged at Philip suddenly and brought him crashing down upon the landing.

Philip was hurting, although he managed to hold him off and they rolled over as Morgan wrestled him for the pistol, but Philip was not as strong as he once had been. Morgan wrenched it from his grasp and hurled it away.

Philip leapt up with a cry of rage. Pain and frustration had driven him beyond the limits of his reason. He attacked Morgan viciously, reining blow after blow down upon him until the Welshman, fighting now for his life, lowered his head and butted Philip hard in his side.

Philip howled in agony and grasped him by the shoulders and then threw him with all his might against the wall.

Morgan hit his head and slid to the floor, dazed.

Philip no longer knew what he did. The demons were in his head and his only urge was destroy himself and any who stood in his way. He picked up a bronze ewer that stood upon the landing and held it over the Welshman's head.

"Philip, no!"

Theresa's voice cut through the darkness in his mind like a knife cutting through a black curtain. He looked down at Morgan, horrified at what he had been about to do.

He took a step back, but the ewer was heavy. Philip lost his balance and staggered onto the ornate wooden balustrade that went around the landing.

It was not strong enough to bear his weight. He fell through it and hurtled down to the flagstone floor below.

∽

John Locke, Shaftesbury's agent and personal physician, viewed his patron curiously. "Why does Lord Devalle mean so much to you? I have never understood it."

"Philip has served me very well," Shaftesbury said simply. "Because of him a bonfire burns this very night outside the King's Head Tavern celebrating Pepys's committal to the Tower. Philip was my lieutenant. He has performed discreetly tasks I could not have entrusted to any other."

"Yet you dismissed him. Was that wise?" Locke said.

"I had little option. He was becoming a political embarrassment."

"You don't think that he perhaps knows too much about you?"

"What is your point?" Shaftesbury said tartly.

"I would have thought that to be obvious, my Lord. I am simply wondering how desirable it is for Philip Devalle to live."

"It is medicine you are required to practise now and not philosophy," the Earl said. "Can you save the man or not?"

"I am a competent surgeon, Lord Shaftesbury, as you know. Allowing for the risk of shock or poisoning of the blood, I feel safe in saying that I could do exactly as you wish with him."

Their eyes met and Shaftesbury knew what Locke was inferring.

"I would not want his death upon my conscience."

Locke shrugged. "Then all I can say is that I hope you do not curse me for my expertise in years to come. Although," he added craftily, "I would need his wife's permission before I operated on him."

"So the decision would not be in my hands," Shaftesbury said slowly, grasping his meaning.

309

"Precisely so, my Lord. Your conscience would be clear, whatever happens."

It had cut Shaftesbury to the quick that Theresa had chosen Philip over him, particularly after all the Earl had done for her. It seemed to him an apt revenge that, if she spurned him, she would be signing Philip's death warrant.

"I shall talk to Theresa before I make up my mind," he told Locke. "She may have come to her senses and decided to stay with me now."

"I doubt it," Locke said frankly. "Philip Devalle has always had a rare power over women."

Theresa looked up anxiously as Shaftesbury and Locke came upstairs to see her. Despite the fierceness of their argument only that afternoon, the Earl had come unhesitatingly to her aid with no trace of resentment, yet Theresa felt uneasy.

She had told him nothing more than that Philip had been drinking and had fallen through the railing, for only a trusted few would ever learn the truth.

"Will Philip die?" she asked them in a shaky voice.

Locke glanced at Shaftesbury. "Not necessarily, Lady Devalle. By a miracle he survived the fall with no more than a few broken ribs but, whilst examining your husband, I made an odd discovery. He has a piece of bone lodged in his side. I'd say a sword tip must have chipped a rib and broken it off inside him."

"Would that have caused him pain?"

"Considerable pain. It has been embedded there some time, from the looks of the duelling scar, probably infecting and lacerating the tissue all around it. He must have been in agony at times."

Theresa avoided Shaftesbury's sharp eyes. "He was. He thought he was dying."

"And so he is unless I can remove it."

"An operation?" Theresa stared at him in horror.

"You speak the word as though it was the rack I was suggesting," Locke said. "It may save his life. I can bind his broken ribs but the real damage is inside him."

"An operation," Theresa repeated. "Even to speak the dreaded word made her feel sick inside. To her it signified only untold suffering with almost certain death at the end of it. "What if you fail?"

"He'll die. There is a risk, of course there is, but people do sometimes recover from these things you know."

"Not very often. The decision must be his."

"No, my Lady, it is yours to make," Locke stressed. "His mind is confused, for he is slipping in and out of consciousness. He would never understand."

"Then wait till it is clearer. Are you so anxious to carve him up?"

"It would be best to do it now, whilst he is in this state," Locke said. "He might be saved a great deal of the pain."

Shaftesbury, who had stood by silently all this while, came forward now. "Leave us alone for a moment, Locke."

Theresa did not really like Locke, yet she would infinitely have preferred for him to stay. Now that she and Shaftesbury were alone, an awkward silence descended upon them.

"Well, Theresa, do you really love him?" he asked at length.

"Yes, my Lord," she said, in a quiet voice.

"Enough to sacrifice your chances of happiness?"

Theresa did not reply.

"You surely don't believe you could be happy with Philip?" he said. "Come, use your head, girl. If he lives, which is unlikely, he will regain his strength and his looks, and you can never hope to hold him then. No woman ever has. He will use you and discard you as he has so many women foolish enough to fall in love with him."

"I am his wife," she reminded him.

"Only because I made you his wife," he said scornfully. "Besides, what difference do you think that will make to him? Do you imagine that a marriage bond I forced on him will persuade him to be faithful to you? You'll always have to share him."

Theresa was in no mood to discuss Philip's possible failings as a husband. "What is it you want, my Lord?" she said wearily.

"I want your promise that you will leave him and come back to me. Only give me that and all the harsh words that have come between us shall, for my part, be forgotten and we shall be just how we were before you let him come between us."

Theresa looked at the man who she had adored for as long as she could remember. Shaftesbury was clever, powerful and rich; she would be a fool indeed, she knew, to discard him for Philip, who had nothing to offer her, not even love.

She did not hesitate.

"My Lord, I regret I cannot do as you would wish. Despite my best endeavours, I have grown to love the man you gave me for a husband, even knowing all his faults."

"So be it," Shaftesbury said coldly. "I shall not mention it again. Your future, whether Philip lives or dies, is in your hands now. What do I tell Locke?"

"How do you rate his chances with this operation?"

"Slender, but without it, none."

"Then I really have no choice, do I? Are you still willing to let Locke perform the surgery?"

Shaftesbury smiled strangely, although Theresa did not see, for he was already walking away from her. "Locke has my full permission to do whatever is necessary."

After Shaftesbury had gone Theresa went down to Philip's room. He lay upon his bed with his eyes closed and was aware of nothing as Morgan held a cup up to his lips, forcing him to drink.

"It is rosewater, liquorice and white of egg," he told her, by way of explanation. "Bet made it up to ease his pain when they cut him."

"Forgive me, Morgan, for the suffering I am causing him." She studied Philip's peaceful countenance. He looked already dead and her stomach churned within her. She recalled the day when he had stood beside her when she had paid her last homage to her mother. Irrationally, she wondered who would help her if it was Philip who was laid out upon a mourning bed.

She bent and quickly kissed the lips that once had taunted her with cruel words, all of which she could forgive now. "Good luck, my love."

"I'll stay with him whilst Locke does what he has to do," Morgan said.

"Shall I stay too?"

"No, indeed not. It will not be pleasant," Morgan warned her. "He would never want you to witness it."

Theresa was really quite relieved. "I'll pray for him."

"Do so. He will need all our prayers tonight."

Outside Philip's door preparations had already begun. Locke, in his shirt sleeves and with an apron covering him, was laying out some implements upon a tray. The sight of the probes and the razor-sharp blades made her feel a little odd and she hurried past.

She sat down on the stairs, for she had not strength to go any further and she felt the need to be close by.

Locke went into Philip's room and closed the door, so there was nothing left to do but sit and wait. The minutes ticked slowly by on the great clock in the hall below and Theresa was joined by Bet and Thomas, who sat down on either side of her.

The stillness was suddenly broken by a shriek of pain that seemed to pierce the walls and fill the house with sound. Theresa jumped up, shaking, and Bet took hold of her as, for the second time, the awful sound assailed their ears.

When it faded they could hear an urgent hammering on the outside door.

"Who can that be at this, of all times?" Bet muttered crossly. "Whoever it is they are not inclined to wait."

"Open quickly," a voice called. "It is Buckingham!"

He ran in directly Bet opened the door. "Theresa, where is Locke? We have to stop him."

Theresa stared at Buckingham stupidly. "Stop him? Why?"

"He must not be allowed to operate. He's going to kill Philip."

Theresa gave a little cry. "It's too late!"

Another animal screech from Philip's room confirmed that she spoke the truth.

"My God!" The Duke made for the stairs, with Theresa close behind him.

"Wait!" Bet cried. "You can't burst in on Locke like that. If his knife should slip now he will blame the both of you. Morgan must be warned."

Thomas was already up the stairs and standing by Philip's door. Without a word he slipped quietly into the room.

"I pray we are in time," Theresa said weakly. "If not then I have murdered him, for it was I who gave permission for this damned operation."

"You were tricked. You must not blame yourself," Buckingham insisted. "How could you have known what both of those fiends were planning?"

"Both? Oh no!" Theresa shook her head. "Please tell me this was not Shaftesbury's doing."

Buckingham put a comforting arm around her. "Theresa, it is well you know your enemies just now."

She laid her head upon his shoulder, all the spirit sapped from her. "I truly think that, outside of this house, I do not have a friend left but for you, your Grace. I shall be ever grateful to you."

"There is another you should thank, the more, perhaps, since it was he who warned me of Shaftesbury's intent – Lord Lindsey."

Theresa was confused. "Why would Lindsey warn you? He hates Philip."

"Like me he grows disillusioned with the Earl. This incident has caused the final rift between Shaftesbury and I," Buckingham said. "I have no particle of respect left for him now, for to treat Philip in this way, after he has served him so faithfully, is plain despicable."

Theresa sat down on the stairs again with Bet, whilst the Duke paced up and down worriedly until, at last, Philip's door opened.

Locke emerged, his face a grim, grey mask. The operation had been a difficult one and his state of mind could not have been helped by having Morgan's knife levelled at his ear throughout the greater part of it.

"Well, Lady Devalle," he said, wiping his blood-stained hands upon a towel, "your husband lives."

TWENTY

Monsieur picked his way delicately through the site where excavations had begun upon the new pond that Le Nôtre had designed on the extreme north side of the gardens. Versailles was progressing rapidly now. It had become Louis' absolute passion and work was going on everywhere in the house and gardens.

Louis waved to him as he approached. "What do you think of my Pond of Neptune?" he demanded.

Monsieur looked at the huge semi-circular shape being dug out by an army of workmen and nodded obligingly. He would appreciate it well enough when it was finished but he had not his brother's vision. "I need to talk to you."

It was difficult to talk to Louis in private, for he was constantly busy or surrounded by people and his only free time was spent reviewing his construction works.

"It must be important to bring you out here," Louis said.

"It is. We have to speak concerning Philip. How is he? Have you heard? I'm so worried about him."

"I received word from Ambassador Barillon this morning," Louis told him. "I understand he is recovering well."

"But what will happen to him now?" Monsieur said.

It was that thought which was worrying Louis too, although for rather different reasons. He had not been sorry to learn that Philip had severed relations with the Earl of Shaftesbury, for he had come to realise that, under Shaftesbury's influence, Philip had become a sinister force. It had not escaped his notice either that there were several prominent Englishmen, the Duke of

Buckingham amongst them, who had begun to extol the virtues of Louis' old enemy, the Prince of Orange, and Philip was close to Buckingham.

Louis had been content enough to let Philip support the cause of Monmouth, a cause Louis dismissed as futile and no threat to him at all, but to allow Philip to join forces with the Orangeman was unthinkable. Louis did not want Philip for an enemy.

"He is penniless," Monsieur continued. "I hear he is even being forced to sell some of his clothes and jewellery." To Monsieur this was the ultimate sacrifice!

"And what would you have me do about it?" Louis said. "Send him money? I hardly think our cousin Charles would appreciate that after Philip has been such a trial to him."

"I think we should have him home," Monsieur said decidedly. So far as he was concerned France was Philip's true home and always would be.

Actually, nothing would have suited Louis better than to have Philip out of temptation's way and employed upon some useful undertaking, such as fighting, once again, for France's glory. Even so, Louis knew he could not ask him to come back. Monsieur, though, was a different matter.

"Why don't you write to him?" he suggested, without taking his eyes off the Pond of Neptune.

"May I?"

"But of course. He is your friend. You could say, if you like, that if he returned I might be persuaded to find him employment again as a Lieutenant-Colonel in my army."

Monsieur clapped his hands in glee. "Do you think he will come?"

"Oh, he'll come," Louis predicted, walking toward Le Nôtre, who was approaching the brothers, carrying his plans. "Philip is a devious man, brave, stubborn and occasionally misguided, but one thing I have never considered him to be is stupid!"

∽

"Shall I do your hair now?" Theresa took Philip's silver hairbrush and the pot of perfumed oil over to him.

Since Philip's operation she had waited on him tirelessly. One of the duties she seemed to like best of all was attending to his blonde curls, which had grown very long during his convalescence.

Philip enjoyed this too; in fact, he enjoyed everything she did for him. No reference had been made by either of them to their conversation just before his accident. It was almost as though both had agreed to delay the matter until the proper time arrived.

Philip had, indeed, had a great many things to think about since the moment when he had properly regained consciousness and realised that he was no longer a dying man.

He smiled at Theresa as she performed her task.

"You have become quite expert at this," he said. "Shall you always do it for me, even when I'm better?"

"I might, if you are nice to me," she said pertly, "but I fear you have become quite spoiled, what with Morgan, Bet and Thomas fussing over you, as well as me."

"I know." He stretched luxuriously. "And I love it."

"Love it you may, but Doctor Jones says your ribs are almost mended and your wound is healing well." Oates had loaned him his own physician for as long as Philip needed him. "I think you should be doing more for yourself now."

"Don't tell me you are going to become a tyrant to me, like Morgan!" he teased her, and she pulled a face at him.

Thankfully Philip remembered very little of the operation, and even less of his fight with Morgan before it. The demons had left his head and he was himself again, and as obedient to the Welshman's will as he had been before. As soon as he was able to stand up Morgan had made him walk around his room, exactly as he had before in the less congenial surroundings of his Bastille cell, and on fine days made him exercise in the garden. It had been painful at the start but the knowledge that, this time, he would make a full recovery had driven him on.

When Theresa had finished his hair, she went into his dressing room and came out carrying one of his plain black coats, which was all she had ever seen him wear.

"Not that," he decided. "One of the others. You choose. I believe that it is time this 'raven' became a 'peacock' once again!"

Theresa delightedly delved amongst his many colourful clothes and chose a brocade coat in a deep shade of rose pink. "I'd love to see you in this."

"Then so you shall," Philip promised. "Stay here and help me."

It was not a command so much as a request for, in truth, Philip could hardly bear her out of his sight any more. Now that he was allowing himself to notice her it seemed that he discovered new and appealing things about Theresa every day; the way she would bite upon her bottom lip when she was concentrating fiercely, her habit of blowing a strand of hair aside if it fell across her face and the ready flush that came to her cheeks if she looked up and saw him watching her. Those and a score of other little quirks that were all her own had begun to fascinate him.

When he was dressed and had put on the coat, Theresa clapped her hands.

"You look splendid!"

"Why thank you, Tess." He made her a little bow, for movement was growing easier again.

As he preened himself before a mirror he caught sight of Theresa's reflection. She was watching him with a strange, almost wistful expression.

Before he could ask her what was the matter, the outside door bell sounded and she ran down to answer it. Theresa had to do a great many things for herself lately. The household staff had all left, for they had been in the pay of Shaftesbury and Philip had no money to spare for servants' wages.

Bet and Morgan now ran the house between them, with the help of Thomas, who could turn his hand to anything. Jonathon and Ned had chosen to stay as well, even though Buckingham had offered to employ them.

It was Buckingham who was calling. He had done so regularly since the accident but today he had important news.

"The King has prorogued Parliament," he told them.

"The mighty Whig Parliament has fallen?" Philip said. It scarcely seemed possible. He had always thought of Shaftesbury as invincible.

Buckingham was viewing him with satisfaction. "You look fitter every day, and I am pleased to see you've learned to dress again." He turned to Theresa. "What do you think of your handsome husband now?"

"I scarcely know him," she said, with a trace of sadness in her voice as she left them alone together.

"She loves you, Philip," Buckingham said.

"I know she does."

"And do you love her?"

Philip hesitated, but only for a second. "Yes, George, I rather think I do."

Buckingham laughed. "So, the great lover has finally lost his heart, and to his own wife! Have you told her?"

Philip shook his head.

"Why ever not?" Buckingham said. "They do like to be told, you know!"

"It's easier for you, who fall in love a dozen times a year," Philip said. "And you are a man of property. Only consider my position. I am no nearer to gaining Heatherton. I have no money and, now, no means of earning it. This very house we live in belongs to Shaftesbury. What have I to offer her? John Scott could give her more, for Christ's sake. At least he has a profession, even if it is chicanery!"

"All Theresa wants is you," Buckingham said.

"I am not enough."

Buckingham smiled at that. "You are being too modest, Philip, and that is a thing I never thought I would be saying to you. You are a prize fought over by the women of two Courts! Of course you are enough, man. Theresa knows exactly what you are and what you have to offer her. The time has come for you to clutch at happiness and not to question it."

Philip groaned. "You are as impractical as ever. What do we live on, after I have sold what little I possess?"

"You live as you have always lived, dear boy, upon your wits," Buckingham told him, "and, now that you have raised the subject, I have just the proposition on which you can employ them."

"Not one of your disastrous business ventures," Philip pleaded, for over the years the Duke had persistently tried to persuade him into those.

"Not this time. What I have to offer you is a future safe from harm. An opportunity bringing with it, ultimately, greater rewards than Shaftesbury, for all his ambitions, could ever have bestowed upon you. Interested?"

"I love you dearly, George, but in all the years I've known you I have never seen you turn your hand to anything with success." Philip said.

"Well this time, my cynical friend, you will have to eat your words," Buckingham predicted. "Firstly, tell me, how do you feel about Prince William?"

"The Orangeman? I thought him a formidable enemy when I was defending Woerden from his charging force," Philip said. "Why do you ask?"

"I wonder whether you could ever regard him as a friend."

"What exactly are you up to now?" Philip said suspiciously.

"I have joined with Savile in favouring him for the succession."

"Since William is married to York's daughter he will surely gain the throne on York's death in any case, should the Duke of York ever become king," Philip pointed out.

"Some of us are not prepared to wait that long," Buckingham said quietly.

"I see." This was a lot to take in. "And what of Monmouth?" Philip wondered.

"Philip, his own father calls him a blockhead! What is he but a puppet controlled by an avaricious master?"

"He is my friend," Philip said simply. "Shaftesbury can go to blazes now, for all I care, but Monmouth is a different matter. I can't betray him. That much honour still remains in me."

"I expected you to feel this way, but won't you even give it a thought?" Buckingham said. "Prince William is a Protestant and a military man. Dutch or not, I believe he would govern well, without any scheming politician guiding him."

"Then follow him if your heart is set upon it but, I pray you, do not try to include me in your plans. I am under no illusions as to Monmouth's suitability to rule but I don't believe I could ever work against his interests, not even to avenge myself on Shaftesbury."

"That is a pity, for there is something that you do not know," Buckingham said. "In his correspondence with Savile, Prince William particularly mentioned wanting you to join him."

"Now you go too far," Philip protested. "Why should the Dutchman want me?"

"Perhaps he, too, remembers Woerden," Buckingham said. "At any rate he said you were a man who he would sooner have as his friend than his enemy. Have you any notion of how much import it would have if you, of all people, took up the Orange Cause?"

"Yes, I have. I would bring it instantly into disrepute," Philip said ruefully. "In case you have forgotten, there has been a pamphlet circulated portraying me as a sodomite and I was so drunk in the House of Commons that I might have killed Pepys if Harbord had not acted quickly. I hardly consider myself a very desirable ally."

"Well that's where you are quite wrong, dear boy," Buckingham assured him. "The pamphlet has been accredited to evil Papists trying to smear your glorious name. On account of that, and thanks to Titus Oates' powers of oratory on your behalf, an effigy of Louise de Quéroualle was last night hanged upon the steps of the new cathedral! The incident at the House has been entirely blamed on Samuel Pepys and lost him what little support he ever had from the people for his effrontery in insulting a good Protestant, and for no better reason than that he had given evidence against him."

Philip laughed. "Are you are telling me I have now become the people's hero?"

"Scoff if you like, but I'll wager you will have Lord Shaftesbury entreating you to return to him before too long."

"Now why should he do that?" Philip said, amused at the thought of Shaftesbury entreating with anyone, least of all him. "A short while ago I was poison to him, or so he said."

"Let us just say he has had time to reflect since then."

"On what, for goodness sake?"

"On how much he needs you."

"He should have thought of that before," Philip said. "Anyway, he has Lindsey now."

"Lindsey has already left him."

"I don't believe it," Philip cried. "That man has bitched and clawed to usurp my place ever since I returned from France. He has it now, with all that it entails."

"He had not the stomach for it. He has joined with us."

"Another one? Poor Monmouth. Shall you take them all?"

"There is only one I really want, and that is you," Buckingham said. "Promise me you will at least consider it."

"Oh, very well. I will consider it," Philip promised, though without much enthusiasm. "I'll consider anything at the moment."

"Even Shaftesbury?" Buckingham said.

"No. I'll not consider Shaftesbury."

"He'll try anything to get you back, you know, especially now that he has lost his Parliament," Buckingham warned.

"Dammit, George, he tried to kill me," Philip pointed out.

"Even so, I know how persuasive Shaftesbury can be and I fear he may entice you again."

"Not this time," Philip assured him.

Monsieur's letter could not have been more welcome. Philip was aware, once again, of just how fortunate he was to have him for a friend. He had actually favoured returning to France all along but he had been unsure of how he would be received in France now. Louis' invitation, for Philip recognised the letter for exactly what it was, altered everything and he was no longer in any doubt as to what he should do.

"All you need to worry about now is whether you and I can survive the rigours of the French army again," he said to Morgan.

"What if the mistress does not want to go to France?"

That thought had not even occurred to Philip. "Of course she'll want to go."

"I'm not so sure. She knows no-one in Paris."

"There are several other Englishwomen living there already," Philip reminded him. "Barbara for one."

"Very welcome she will make your wife feel, I'm sure!"

"That might have been a bad example," Philip allowed. "Elizabeth de Grammont, then. She has always lectured me to settle down and marry. She will take care of her. Besides, Theresa will soon make friends of her own."

"She doesn't even speak the language," Morgan pointed out.

"Then she can learn it. You did. Anyway, I'll be with her until we go to war."

"Monsieur will take possession of you the instant you arrive in Paris," Morgan predicted.

Philip knew that he was right in that. "I'll see if Monsieur can persuade his wife to take her as one of her ladies," he said. "Madame despises me but I fancy she will quite take to Theresa. That might solve the problem."

"I don't think it will."

Philip sighed in exasperation. "What do you suggest then?"

Morgan's expression was unreadable, as usual. "It's not my place to give you advice, my Lord."

"It might be a little late in our relationship for you to assume the role of the respectful servant," Philip said heavily. "Come, out with it. What would you have me do?"

"Tell her how you feel about her," Morgan said unhesitatingly.

"She must already know."

"I don't think she does. You need to actually say the words."

"That's very fine advice coming from you," Philip said, recalling what Bet had said about Morgan. "You'll be saying next that I have to tell *you* how much you mean to me before you agree to come! Trust me, Morgan, everything will be fine."

Philip heard from Shaftesbury that same day.

It was Scott who brought him the message. "Shall you go?" he asked.

"Why not? I want to hear him beg me to return to him."

"You wouldn't work for him again, surely. Not after what he tried to do."

"Did I say so? No, Scott, I have other plans." Philip showed him Monsieur's letter.

"So Louis wants you back, does he?" Scott guessed, when he saw Monsieur's signature.

"The King of France always was an excellent judge of men!"

"I might be leaving too," Scott said. "You know that Pepys applied for his discharge under his own writ of Habeas Corpus?"

"The Act that Shaftesbury himself brought in? What cheek!"

"It's not funny," Scott grumbled. "He claimed that no cause has been assigned for his and Deane's commitment in the Speaker's Warrant and he reckoned that they should be freed, since the House that had them put in custody is now prorogued. He failed, of course, but who knows what he will try next? Frankly, without you, I no longer feel I want to work for Shaftesbury. Oates and Bedloe feel the same, especially after Wakeman's acquittal."

George Wakeman, the Queen's physician, had been found not guilty of treason, the first of the Plot's victims to leave the courts a free man and to place the testimony of Oates and Bedloe in question.

"I'm flattered you feel that way, but the three of you were lying rogues before you ever met me," Philip reminded him.

"Be that as it may, speaking for myself I always felt that your presence lent us an air of..." Scott searched for the right word, "...probity," he decided upon.

"Well thank you, Scott. That comes very well from the bastard who once sold me a silver dish that might have connected me with a murder," Philip said, "but if you consider that my association with you has elevated you three scoundrels just imagine what it must have done to me! I have finished with it all and I pray that I am never again called upon to earn my living in such a way."

"It's all very well for you," Scott said. "You have a choice."

It was the truth. For the first time in a long while Philip had a choice, and it was a choice between the Earl, the Orangeman and the King of France.

Philip made sure he was looking his most impressive best when he called at Shaftesbury's house later that day. He still carried his silver-topped cane, though only for affectation again now, and he was wearing his favourite blue velvet coat, edged with silver lace.

"You look well," the Earl told him. "My surgeon did a good job on you."

Philip raised an eyebrow. The circumstances being what they were, only Shaftesbury would attempt to take the credit for his condition! "Perhaps you should convey my thanks to Locke," he said, with a touch of sarcasm.

The Earl chose to ignore it. "I have missed you, Philip."

"Yes, I'm sure you have!"

"Why are you surprised? You and I have always had a good relationship."

"If you discount the fact that you once had me beaten senseless in the street and flogged in your presence until I bled." Philip returned swiftly, "not to mention the fact that I now have good reason to suppose you tried to have me killed."

Shaftesbury dismissed all that with a gesture. "Well if you're going to bear grudges then you are useless to me."

"You told me that two months ago," Philip reminded him, "and there's another thing; when I would have sold my very soul to remain with you I recall that you dismissed me from your service."

"I was wrong," Shaftesbury said. "That is why I asked you here today, to suggest we put it all behind us and continue as we were."

Philip shook his head in wonderment. "How much am I expected to forgive, for God's sake?"

"I always had the greatest affection for you," Shaftesbury said.

"You treated me abominably."

"I apologise."

"You really must be desperate." Philip had never heard Shaftesbury apologise to anyone.

"I am," Shaftesbury admitted. "You must have heard that Wakeman was acquitted?"

"There was no way you could have won that one, you know," Philip said. "The verdict was decided by the King before it even went to court. The rumours have it that Scroggs was bribed to sum up for the defence."

"He's lost his popularity at any rate. Before he left to go on circuit my Brisk Boys threw a half-hanged dog into his carriage with him," Shaftesbury said gleefully. "Wakeman has fled overseas because he has been threatened with a second prosecution and now your blasted witnesses have lost their nerve. Lindsey can't control them."

"I could have told you that," Philip said. "Anyway, I hear from Buckingham that Lindsey's left you too."

"Did Buckingham tell you why?"

"I understand that, like Buckingham, he has begun to favour Prince William for the succession."

Shaftesbury looked at him sharply. "You are still intimate with Buckingham. You would not join with him against me?"

Philip made no answer to that; indeed, he saw no reason why he should.

"So, we have the truth," Shaftesbury said angrily. "I don't know how you have the gall to stand there and admit it. You once pledged to aid Monmouth and yet you would desert him for the Dutchman. Where's your loyalty?"

Philip took a pinch of snuff, inhaling it elegantly, with the affectation that he knew Shaftesbury detested. "I thought loyalty was not too much in vogue this season!"

"Don't be flippant!" Shaftesbury snapped. "Philip Devalle, if you do this I will ruin you, I swear it."

Philip eyed him coolly. "You cannot touch me, Shaftesbury. I shall not join with Buckingham or with you either. I'm my own man now."

"And how do you think to live?" Shaftesbury demanded. "I am only too well aware of how much you cost to keep, what with your clothes, your gambling debts and the thousand other of your extravagancies. Just how do you propose to maintain yourself and Theresa?"

"I shall keep us on a Lieutenant-Colonel's pay," Philip told him. "I have received an offer from Louis to return to the French army. You're too late, Shaftesbury, my decision is already made. I am going to France."

"Stay and I will use my influence to have High Heatherton transferred to you before the year is out," Shaftesbury promised.

"I am going to France," Philip repeated. "As for Heatherton, I'll take my chances with the courts."

"It may take longer than you think," Shaftesbury warned. "And what of Giles?"

"Giles has Monmouth to befriend him now. Besides, if he is old enough to serve his King then he is old enough to fend for himself at Court," Philip said. "I don't believe that Quéroualle will attempt to hurt him again, especially if I make it plain that I have severed connections with him. It is my guess he will do very well here."

"I'll watch over him, if you like," Shaftesbury said.

"I doubt he will let you. He has little regard for you," Philip said frankly.

Shaftesbury shrugged "I have never found him as intelligent as his sister, although Theresa was fool enough to fall for you." The Earl shook his head sadly. "Perhaps it was I who was the fool to imagine she would be able to resist you. I miss her."

"Your tricks won't work on me," Philip warned. "You are trying to win my sympathy because you've lost the game you started."

"I will not say I started the game, although I took advantage of it, but it is over now," Shaftesbury said.

"You will shortly find another," Philip predicted. "You do still have Monmouth after all." He tipped his hat to the Earl. "Now, if you will excuse me I have much to do before I leave England."

"You are determined on this?"

"Quite determined."

"You'll come back to me one day," Shaftesbury said.

If experience had taught Philip anything at all it was that life was a series of constantly shifting patterns and he had come to know the world too well to ever close the door upon an opportunity, lest he should one day have need of it. "Perhaps," he said, "but in my own time and on my own terms."

Shaftesbury nodded and Philip knew he had told him what he had most wanted to hear. "I'll keep you informed of how affairs stand here," the Earl offered.

"If you wish."

As he drove home Philip thought about how much he had changed since he had come back to England just over a year ago. He had been a sick man then, bitter and vowing vengeance on his enemies. Now he was looking forward to what the future might hold as he returned to France to start a new life, with Theresa by his side.

England had changed too, during that year.

A commotion in the street ahead showed that Shaftesbury's Wapping 'Brisk Boys' were at work, stirring up the citizens of London, as they had been doing ever since Wakeman's acquittal.

Philip smiled as he listened to the apprentice boys, singing their now familiar chant.

"Our juries and judge have shamed the plot
Have traitors freed to prove it not,
But England shall stand when they go to pot.
Which nobody can deny."

TWENTY-ONE

⁂

When Philip got back he saw that Thomas was in the stables, lovingly grooming Ferrion, as he did every day.

"Are you looking forward to seeing Paris, Thomas?"

"Yes, my Lord," Thomas said excitedly, "but I don't care where we live so long as I can stay with you."

"I would no more think of leaving you behind than I would Ferrion," Philip assured him. He had grown fond of Thomas and guessed that, being a true creature of the city streets, he would soon be as much at home in Paris as he was in London. "Is your mistress at home?"

"No, my Lord. She went out for a walk."

There was nothing particularly unusual in that. They were close to St. James' Park and Theresa often went there. He gave it no more thought but went indoors, where Bet was busy filling crates with the items they were taking with them and Morgan was taking down Philip's portrait, painted of himself in his uniform. It was good to know he would soon be wearing it again when it had once seemed so unlikely that he ever would.

He recalled watching Theresa as she first looked up at the portrait. He smiled at the memory and marvelled at how his feelings for her had altered since then. He resolved to take the advice of Buckingham and Morgan and tell her how much she meant to him.

When he heard Theresa return he was looking at the empty trunk Morgan had given him for his things. The Welshman would normally have filled it for him but he was too busy with other jobs and Philip, having never packed his own trunk in his life, was wondering how to begin.

He was pleased when she came straight up to see him.

"Have you come to help me pack my trunk, sweetheart?" he said, without looking at her. "You must have packing to do for yourself before we go to France."

Theresa did not answer him and he turned around. Her face was flushed and she looked nervous, very like her brother had looked when he had come to tell Philip he was planning to leave him.

Philip had a sudden, awful feeling of misgiving. "What is it, Tess?"

"I'm not coming with you," she said quietly.

"I see." Philip kept his voice calm, but her words had stunned him. "What do you intend to do, go back to Shaftesbury?"

"No, I'm going home to Dorset."

"What?" He could hardly believe what he was hearing. "Why would you do that? You'll suffocate back in the country."

"That is all you know. I'm sick of London and this life we lead here," she said passionately.

"So am I, which is the very reason I am leaving."

"But there is more. I'm sick of justices who mock the law and of witnesses who twist the truth. I'm sick of greedy politicians and of scheming courtiers. Can't you understand that?"

Philip was beginning to understand only too well and to appreciate the irony of his situation. After a lifetime of philandering he had finally found a woman he truly wanted, only to find that, apparently, she did not want him. "And you're sick of me," he guessed.

Theresa hung her head. "No, not of you, but you belong with them and I do not. We're different kinds of people, Philip, worlds apart. If I go to France with you then I must live in your world. You don't need me there."

"Need you? Hell, of course I need you! Anyway, you are my wife."

"Only because I was foisted on you to avoid my own disgrace. You should never have had to marry me and there is no reason I can see why you should feel under any obligation to me now. I am nothing but a burden to you and you will manage far better without me."

"And that is why you intend to leave me?" Philip said in amazement. "Tess, you are well aware I cannot offer you a fortune, not just yet at any rate, but Heatherton may be mine one day. Until that time we have my house in Paris and I give you my assurance that I will provide for you as best I can. I ask only that you come with me and help me build my life again. You told me once that you loved me," he reminded her, "or were those words intended only for a dying man to hear?"

"By no means. I still love you, Philip, and I always will, but you have changed."

"Towards you?"

"Not towards me," she admitted, "but since you have recovered I see you as you used to be before I met you."

"Go on," he prompted as she paused.

"There have been so many beautiful and famous women in your life, Philip."

"So that's it? My reputation? Surely you won't hold that against me, just because I had a few affairs," he protested.

"A few affairs? Philip, your exploits are a legend! You even bedded King Charles' mistress!"

"What has that to do with it? Those women were in my past." Philip could not see where the problem lay. "You, I hope, will be my future, and you can have me all the time for just as long as ever you may want."

"But you are still who you are and they will still pursue you at Versailles, the same as they do at Whitehall," Theresa said. "As Shaftesbury says, I'll always have to share you."

"Damn Shaftesbury!" Philip understood, now that he knew who had put the doubts into Theresa's mind. He took her in his arms. "I cannot pledge that I will be a perfect husband, Tess, but I will try my hardest to make you happy and I will always be your friend. If you can find it in your heart to love me for what I am, rather than for what I am not, then I will do my utmost not to disappoint you."

"But you're not in love with me," she said flatly.

"Of course I am, you silly girl!"

Theresa's face lit like the sun. "You've never said so."

Philip knew he was going to have to say it now if he was not to let this precious chance of happiness slip away from him.

"Tess, I love you and I want you with me always. My heart and happiness lie in your hands. If you leave me now you will destroy me."

He kissed her and he felt just as he had on that fateful night when his life seemed to be at an end. He wanted to breathe in her breath, to taste her skin, to feel her press against him, but he wanted more. He wanted to understand her fears and think her thoughts; to touch not just her responsive body but the very essence of her being.

To be a part of her.

Theresa clung to him as though she would never let him go and he knew he had finally found the right words to say, those that came from his heart. Philip had enjoyed a lifetime of adventure, yet it had been, at times, a shallow and a lonely one. Theresa, he knew, was the one person who could give his existence point and purpose.

"So are you coming to France with me or not?" he asked her lightly, when she finally released him.

She burst out laughing. "I had better come, if only to protect you from all those amorous Frenchwomen! I suppose you want me to pack your trunk for you now?"

She was standing next to his bed and he pushed her gently so that she fell back onto it. Her eyes were sparkling as she looked up at him expectantly and Philip wanted her more than he had ever wanted any woman in his life.

"Later, sweetheart!"

ALSO BY THE AUTHOR